凱信企管

**用對的方法充實自己，
讓人生變得更美好！**

凱信企管

用對的方法充實自己，
讓人生變得更美好！

凱信企管

用對的方法充實自己，
讓人生變得更美好！

凱信企管

用對的方法充實自己，
讓人生變得更美好！

精準

7000 單字 滿分版

中級進階篇
Level 3 & Level 4

2201～4200單字

使用說明

7000 單字以六大學習元素—「完美六邊型緊扣式學習架構」,精準記單字,不論是學測、多益、全民英檢中級都能輕鬆過關,英語力大躍進。

收錄單字完整多義,學習滴水不漏

記住拼字的同時,單字的多重意思及不同詞性收錄詳盡,不論怎麼考都不怕,精準答題不誤用,滿分必備因素一次掌握。

cast [kæst]

動 用力擲、選角
名 投、演員班底
同 throw 投、擲

英英解釋,協助更精準理解單字

中文直譯常常無法精準地翻譯英文單字的字義。全書每一單字用英英解釋再次完整說明字義,用字能更準確,也能加強單字的深刻記憶。

英英 feeling certain about something

3

生活例句營造感官情境，強化單字記憶

善用感官讓單字自然記憶。利用例句營造情境，完美地理解單字並加深記憶，除能跟上出題方向，同時也能自然地提升生活口語能力。

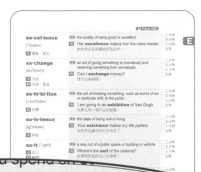

例 The **expense** of this trip is unaffordable.
這趟旅程的費用超過我可以負擔的。

4

特別設計：「熟悉度評量表」，掌握學習成效

單字到底是記得三分熟、七分熟，還是滾瓜爛熟，用評量表檢測最準確。除了促進自我學習動力，還能在考試前，快速針對不熟悉的單字加強複習。

5

單字／例句音檔全收錄，學習隨時都可以

全書單字／例句音檔 MP3 收錄，QR Code 隨手一掃，藉由頻繁地用聲音刷腦記憶，刺激聽覺，單字一定記得住。

全書音檔雲端連結

因各家手機系統不同，若無法直接掃描，仍可以至以下電腦雲端連結下載收聽。
(https://tinyurl.com/bdf3t8x8)

PREFACE
前言

　　你還再用「死背」的方式來背英文單字？！腦容量真的很有限，若用老方法來記單字，可能會讓你越背越忘，進入單字煉獄的痛苦輪迴中！

　　每回聽到學生們談到記單字的痛苦經驗，都忍不住替他們覺得辛苦！但英文單字又是考試拿分最重要的關鍵，不背又不行，到底該怎麼辦呢？

　　其實市面上 7000 單字的學習輔助教材已經相當多了，「如何選擇最好、最適合的」也常是學習者們最頭痛的問題；這亦是我們在一開始撰寫這本 7000 單字時，不斷在思量的。如何能有別與市面上的 7000 單字書，我們著實想了很久，於是決定讓台灣有許多教學經驗的 Michael 老師和從小在美國唸書的 Tong 老師聯手撰寫，**結合對台灣考情的了解與在地生活英語的應用**，讓 7000 單字的選字、例句的編寫，不僅能精準的符合 108 年新課綱注重英文與生活結合，徹底地讓學習者有效記憶單字，更能明確地理解單字及片語如何應用在句子裡，還能同步實際在日常裡發揮口說功能，齊步提升英語力，跨大步朝大考滿分邁進。

　　《精準 7000 單字滿分版》，我們特別著重三大部分：

　　一、收錄單字完整多義及不同詞性

　　單字的多重意思及不同詞性收錄詳盡，不論考題怎麼變化都不怕！答題能更精準，口說不誤用，單字一次學好學滿。

　　二、用感官情境法學單字

　　帶你用五感去感受單字。搭配生活例句及英英解釋，在腦海裡營造視覺畫面、創造英文環境，助你強化單字記憶；再利用音檔，刺激聽覺，考試沒問題，溝通也 OK。

　　三、單字評量表掌握學習成效

　　單字是三分熟、五分熟還是滾瓜爛熟，用評量檢測最準確！每一個單字特別設計「評量表」，除了掌握學習效果，亦能在考試前，快速複習拿高分。

　　期待這一本《精準 7000 單字滿分版：中級進階 Level 3&Level 4》，能有效並無痛的幫助大家往記憶 4200 單字邁進，不論是學測、多益、全民英檢中級都能輕鬆過關，亦能全面提升英語能力。

CONTENTS

目錄

Level 3

中級進階
英文能力

邁向
3200單字

Aa

a·board [ə`bord]

副／介 在船（飛機、火車）上

英英 get on or into the vehicle, such as a ship, plane or a train

例 Who was the first passenger going **aboard**?
誰是第一個上船的人？

☐ 三分熟 ☐ 五分熟 ☐ 七分熟 ☐ 全熟

---

ac·cept·a·ble
[ək`sɛptəbl̩]

形 可接受的

英英 able to be accepted; capable of being accepted

例 Is she an **acceptable** spouse?
她是可接受的伴侶嗎？

☐ 三分熟 ☐ 五分熟 ☐ 七分熟 ☐ 全熟

---

ac·ci·dent
[`æksədənt]

名 事故、偶發事件
同 casualty 事故

英英 an unfortunate or awful incident that happens, which is unexpected and unintentional

例 Many people died in the **accident**.
許多人死於這場事故。

☐ 三分熟 ☐ 五分熟 ☐ 七分熟 ☐ 全熟

---

ac·count [ə`kaʊnt]

名 帳目、記錄
動 視為、負責

英英 a description of an issue or event; to regard as

例 She **accounts** herself elite.
她視自己為菁英。

☐ 三分熟 ☐ 五分熟 ☐ 七分熟 ☐ 全熟

---

ac·cu·rate
[`ækjərɪt]

形 正確的、準確的
同 correct 正確的

英英 exact or correct in all details; be able to be successful in reaching the target which is set

例 Please give me an **accurate** number.
請給我一個正確的數字。

☐ 三分熟 ☐ 五分熟 ☐ 七分熟 ☐ 全熟

---

ache [ek]

名／動 疼痛
同 pain 疼痛

英英 a continuous pain

例 My tooth **aches**.
我牙痛。

☐ 三分熟 ☐ 五分熟 ☐ 七分熟 ☐ 全熟

---

a·chieve·(ment)
[ə`tʃiv(mənt)]

動 實現、完成
名 成績、成就

英英 to accomplish something with effort, skill, or courage

例 I believe I can **achieve** the unachievable.
我相信自己可以實現那些無法實現的。

☐ 三分熟 ☐ 五分熟 ☐ 七分熟 ☐ 全熟

A

ac·tiv·i·ty

[æk'tɪvətɪ]

名 活動、活躍

英英 things are happening or being achieved or people are moving and acting around

例 We learned a lot from the **activity**.
我們從這活動中學到很多。

□ 三分熟
□ 五分熟
□ 七分熟
□ 全熟

---

ac·tu·al ['æktʃʊəl]

形 實際的、真實的

英英 real or current; existing in fact

例 What's the **actual** reason for us to break up?
我們真正分手的理由是什麼？

□ 三分熟
□ 五分熟
□ 七分熟
□ 全熟

---

ad·di·tion·al

[ə'dɪʃənḷ]

形 額外的、附加的
同 extra 額外的

英英 not contained in the main; added, extra, or supplementary

例 It is the **additional** request.
這是附加的要求。

□ 三分熟
□ 五分熟
□ 七分熟
□ 全熟

---

ad·mire [əd'maɪr]

動 欽佩、讚賞

英英 regard with respect or applause; look at with satisfactions; to give compliments to

例 I **admire** my English teacher.
我欽佩我的英文老師。

□ 三分熟
□ 五分熟
□ 七分熟
□ 全熟

---

ad·mit [əd'mɪt]

動 容許……進入、承認
反 forbid 禁止

英英 confess to be true or to be actual

例 She never **admits** her mistakes.
她從不承認自己的錯誤。

□ 三分熟
□ 五分熟
□ 七分熟
□ 全熟

---

adopt [ə'dɑpt]

動 收養

英英 to legally take other child and raise up as one's own

例 The couple **adopted** the poor boy.
這對夫妻收養了這個可憐的小男孩。

□ 三分熟
□ 五分熟
□ 七分熟
□ 全熟

---

ad·vanced

[əd'vænst]

形 在前面的、先進的
同 forward 前面的

英英 far on in improving something; moving something toward

例 The **advanced** English learners in the elementary school can write an essay.
學習領先的英文學習者，在國小就可以寫出一篇作文了。

□ 三分熟
□ 五分熟
□ 七分熟
□ 全熟

---

ad·van·tage

[əd'væntɪdʒ]

名 利益、優勢、好處
同 benefit 利益

英英 a condition that puts someone in a favourable position; to give someone a chance to be successful

例 What's the **advantage** for me to help you?
我幫你有什麼好處？

□ 三分熟
□ 五分熟
□ 七分熟
□ 全熟

🎧 **Track 003**

ad·ven·ture

[əd'vɛntʃɚ]

名 冒險

英英 an unusual, exciting, and daring experience, probably with danger

例 Tell me about the **adventure**.
告訴我有關這趟冒險。

☐ 三分熟
☐ 五分熟
☐ 七分熟
☐ 全熟

---

ad·ver·tise(ment)/ ad ['ædvɚ'taɪz(mənt)]/[æd]

動 登廣告
名 廣告、宣傳

英英 present or describe a product or event in some particular medium in order to promote sales

例 I don't want to see the **ads** on the newpapers.
我不喜歡看報紙上的廣告。

☐ 三分熟
☐ 五分熟
☐ 七分熟
☐ 全熟

---

ad·vice [əd'vaɪs]

名 忠告
片 give an advice
給……忠告

英英 recommendations which are offered with regard to future action

例 Her **advice** helps me a lot.
她給我很多有用的忠告。

☐ 三分熟
☐ 五分熟
☐ 七分熟
☐ 全熟

---

ad·vise [əd'vaɪz]

動 勸告

英英 recommend a course of action; to give someone advice

例 What did he **advise** you?
他勸告你什麼？

☐ 三分熟
☐ 五分熟
☐ 七分熟
☐ 全熟

---

ad·vi·ser/ ad·vi·sor

[əd'vaɪzɚ]

名 顧問

英英 someone whose job is to give advice about a subject or an issue

例 We need an **advisor** for our trip to Australia.
我們需要一名顧問負責我們澳洲的行程。

☐ 三分熟
☐ 五分熟
☐ 七分熟
☐ 全熟

---

af·fect [ə'fɛkt]

動 影響
同 influence 影響

英英 to make a difference to something or someone; have an effect on something or someone

例 The typhoon **affects** the traffic a lot.
颱風影響了交通。

☐ 三分熟
☐ 五分熟
☐ 七分熟
☐ 全熟

---

af·ford [ə'ford]

動 給予、供給、能負擔

英英 have sufficient or enough money, time for someone or something

例 I can't **afford** the cost of the car.
我無法負擔這輛車的花費。

☐ 三分熟
☐ 五分熟
☐ 七分熟
☐ 全熟

---

af·ter·ward(s)

['æftɚwəd(z)]

副 以後

英英 later; in the future time

例 I won't see her **afterwards**.
以後我不會看到她了。

☐ 三分熟
☐ 五分熟
☐ 七分熟
☐ 全熟

A

ag·ri·cul·ture

[ˋæɡrɪˌkʌltʃɚ]

名 農業、農藝、農學

英英 the practice of farming, including the rearing of crops and animals

例 China has been a country of **agriculture**.
中國一直以來都是農業大國。

□三分熟
□五分熟
□七分熟
□全熟

air-con·di·tion·er

[ˋɛrkənˌdɪʃənɚ]

名 空調、冷氣機

英英 a system for controlling the humidity and temperature, used to keep cool in a building or vehicle

例 Taiwanese can't live without **air-conditioners** in the summer.
一到了夏天，臺灣人沒有冷氣就活不下去了。

□三分熟
□五分熟
□七分熟
□全熟

al·ley [ˋælɪ]

名 巷、小徑

英英 a narrow passageway or path between or behind buildings

例 You can find the best restaurants of the area in the **alley**.
你可以在這條巷子中找到當地最好的餐廳。

□三分熟
□五分熟
□七分熟
□全熟

a·maze·(ment)

[əˋmez(mənt)]

動 使……吃驚
名 吃驚

英英 surprise and astonish

例 It **amazed** me that he was actually younger than me.
他居然比我還年輕，真是太讓我震驚了。

□三分熟
□五分熟
□七分熟
□全熟

am·bas·sa·dor

[æmˋbæsədɚ]

名 大使、使節
同 diplomat 外交官

英英 a diplomat officially sent by a nation to represent it in a foreign country

例 The **ambassador's** family is threatened.
這位大使的家人受到威脅。

□三分熟
□五分熟
□七分熟
□全熟

am·bi·tion

[æmˋbɪʃən]

名 雄心壯志、志向

英英 a mighty desire to do something or to achieve something

例 His **ambition** made him succeed and fail.
他的野心讓他成功也讓他失敗。

□三分熟
□五分熟
□七分熟
□全熟

an·gel [ˋendʒəl]

名 天使

英英 a spiritual which is believed to act as a messenger of God; to describe someone who is kind and pure

例 I felt she's an **angel** of my life.
我覺得她就像是我生命中的天使一樣。

□三分熟
□五分熟
□七分熟
□全熟

Track 005

an·gle [ˋæŋg!]

名 角度、立場

英英 the space between two lines or surfaces at or close to one point where they meet

例 Try to look at the picture from another **angle**.
試著用另外一個角度看這張畫。

□ 三分熟
□ 五分熟
□ 七分熟
□ 全熟

---

an·nounce·(ment)

[əˋnaʊns(mənt)]

動 宣告、公布、通知
名 宣佈、宣告
同 declare 宣布

英英 to declare something in public; be a sign of

例 The winner of the game is going to be **announced** soon.
即將公布的是這場遊戲的贏家。

□ 三分熟
□ 五分熟
□ 七分熟
□ 全熟

---

a·part [əˋpɑrt]

副 分散地、遠離地
反 together 一起地

英英 separated by a distance in space

例 Though they grew **apart**, they are close to each other.
雖然他們是在不同地方長大的，他們彼此還是很親近。

□ 三分熟
□ 五分熟
□ 七分熟
□ 全熟

---

ap·par·ent

[əˋpærənt]

形 明顯的、外表的
同 obvious 明顯的

英英 obviously or clearly seen; easy to be noticed or understood

例 It was apparent that there was no way out.
這裡很明顯的沒有路可以出去。

□ 三分熟
□ 五分熟
□ 七分熟
□ 全熟

---

ap·peal [əˋpil]

名 吸引力、懇求
動 引起……的興趣

英英 make a serious or heartfelt request; to ask someone for something with sincerity

例 Could you hear people's **appeal**?
你可以聽到人民的懇求嗎？

□ 三分熟
□ 五分熟
□ 七分熟
□ 全熟

---

ap·pre·ci·ate

[əˋpriʃˌʌet]

動 欣賞、鑑賞、感激

英英 recognize the value or significance of

例 I **appreciate** your help.
我感激你的幫忙。

□ 三分熟
□ 五分熟
□ 七分熟
□ 全熟

---

ap·proach

[əˋprotʃ]

動 接近

英英 come near from far in distance or time

例 The train is **approaching**.
火車正在進站。

□ 三分熟
□ 五分熟
□ 七分熟
□ 全熟

---

ap·prove [əˋpruv]

動 批准、認可

英英 to believe that someone or something is fine or acceptable

例 Did your supervisor **approve** your suggestion?
你的上司批准你的提議了嗎？

□ 三分熟
□ 五分熟
□ 七分熟
□ 全熟

A

a·quar·i·um

[əˋkwɛrɪəm]

名 水族館

> 英英 a water-filled glass tank for keeping fish or other water animals
>
> 例 My father brought me to the **aquarium** very often.
> 我爸爸以前常帶我去水族館。

☐ 三分熟
☐ 五分熟
☐ 七分熟
☐ 全熟

a·rith·me·tic

[əˋrɪθmətɪk]

名 算術
形 算術的

> 英英 caculate number, such as adding or multiplying
>
> 例 I am terrible at **arithmetic**.
> 我算術很糟糕。

☐ 三分熟
☐ 五分熟
☐ 七分熟
☐ 全熟

ar·riv·al [əˋraɪvl]

名 到達
片 arrival hall 入境大廳

> 英英 the action or process of arriving
>
> 例 Why do many people gather in the **arrival** hall?
> 為什麼那麼多人聚集在入境大廳？

☐ 三分熟
☐ 五分熟
☐ 七分熟
☐ 全熟

ash [æʃ]

名 灰燼、灰

> 英英 the soft, gray powder remaining after something has been burned
>
> 例 She burned his love letters into **ashes**.
> 她把他的情書燒成灰燼。

☐ 三分熟
☐ 五分熟
☐ 七分熟
☐ 全熟

a·side [əˋsaɪd]

副 在旁邊

> 英英 to keep in one side or out of the way
>
> 例 He put my portfolio **aside**.
> 他把我的資料夾放在旁邊。

☐ 三分熟
☐ 五分熟
☐ 七分熟
☐ 全熟

as·sist [əˋsɪst]

動 說明、援助
同 help 說明

> 英英 an action of helping someone on something
>
> 例 He wants me to **assist** him.
> 他要我援助他。

☐ 三分熟
☐ 五分熟
☐ 七分熟
☐ 全熟

ath·lete [ˋæθlit]

名 運動員

> 英英 a person who is good at sports
>
> 例 He is one of the greatest **athletes** in the world.
> 他是世界上最偉大的運動員之一。

☐ 三分熟
☐ 五分熟
☐ 七分熟
☐ 全熟

at·tempt [əˋtɛmpt]

動／名 嘗試、企圖
片 attempt to 企圖

> 英英 to achieve or complete something with efforts
>
> 例 I didn't **attempt** to hurt you.
> 我並不是企圖要傷害你的。

☐ 三分熟
☐ 五分熟
☐ 七分熟
☐ 全熟

🎧 **Track 007**

at·ti·tude

[ˈætəˌtjud]

名 態度、心態、看法

英英 a settled way of thinking or feeling something; the point of view on something

例 Your **attitude** decides your attitude.
你的態度決定你的高度。

☐ 三分熟
☐ 五分熟
☐ 七分熟
☐ 全熟

at·tract [əˈtrækt]

動 吸引

英英 drawing attention by offering something interesting or entertaining

例 Her elegance **attracts** him.
她的優雅吸引了他。

☐ 三分熟
☐ 五分熟
☐ 七分熟
☐ 全熟

at·trac·tive

[əˈtræktɪv]

形 吸引人的、動人的

英英 pleasing or appealing

例 The story is so **attractive** that many people listen to it again and again.
這故事很吸引人，所以人們聽了一次又一次。

☐ 三分熟
☐ 五分熟
☐ 七分熟
☐ 全熟

au·di·ence

[ˈɔdɪəns]

名 聽眾
同 spectator 觀眾

英英 spectators or listeners at an event or a performance

例 The **audience** will be touched by your story.
你的聽眾會被你的故事所感動。

☐ 三分熟
☐ 五分熟
☐ 七分熟
☐ 全熟

au·thor [ˈɔθɚ]

名 作家、作者
同 writer 作者

英英 a writer of a book, an article or a special column

例 I'd love to meet the **author** of this book.
我想要見這本書的作者。

☐ 三分熟
☐ 五分熟
☐ 七分熟
☐ 全熟

au·to·mat·ic

[ˌɔtəˈmætɪk]

形 自動的

英英 operating by itself with little human control

例 This machine is **automatic**.
這臺機器是自動的。

☐ 三分熟
☐ 五分熟
☐ 七分熟
☐ 全熟

au·to·mo·bile/

au·to [ˈɔtəməˌbil]/

[ˈɔto]

名 汽車
同 car 汽車

英英 a motor car

例 **Automobiles** were too expensive for most people at this age.
在這年代，汽車對於一般人來說都太貴了。

☐ 三分熟
☐ 五分熟
☐ 七分熟
☐ 全熟

a·vail·a·ble

[əˈveləbḷ]

形 可利用的、可取得的

英英 able to be used or got easily; not occupied or busy

例 When will this computer be **available**?
這臺電腦何時才可以用呢？

☐ 三分熟
☐ 五分熟
☐ 七分熟
☐ 全熟

A

av·e·nue [ˈævəˈnju]

名 大道、大街

英英 a broad road in a town or city

例 I want to visit the Fifth **Avenue**.
我想要拜訪第五大道。

□三分熟
□五分熟
□七分熟
□全熟

---

av·er·age

[ˈævərɪdʒ]

名 平均數

英英 caculated by adding several amounts together and then dividing the total by the number of amounts

例 The **average** amount of the salary in this country is very high.
這國家的平均薪資很高。

□三分熟
□五分熟
□七分熟
□全熟

---

a·wake [əˈwek]

動 喚醒、提醒

英英 to make someone wake up or wake someone up

例 When will you **awake** tomorrow?
你明天幾點起床？

□三分熟
□五分熟
□七分熟
□全熟

---

a·wak·en

[əˈwekən]

動 使……覺悟

英英 to make someone realize something

例 Her ambition was **awakened**.
她的野心覺醒了。

□三分熟
□五分熟
□七分熟
□全熟

---

a·ward [əˈwɔrd]

名 獎品、獎賞
動 授與、頒獎

英英 a prize or reward

例 The **award** of the competition is attractive.
這比賽的獎品很誘人。

□三分熟
□五分熟
□七分熟
□全熟

---

a·ware [əˈwɛr]

形 注意到的、覺察的

英英 having knowledge about a situation or fact

例 Are you **aware** that the lions are around you?
你注意到獅子在你附近嗎？

□三分熟
□五分熟
□七分熟
□全熟

---

aw·ful [ˈɔful]

形 可怕的、嚇人的
同 horrible 可怕的

英英 very scary or frightening

例 This moive is awful.
這部電影很嚇人。

□三分熟
□五分熟
□七分熟
□全熟

---

ax/axe [æks]

名 斧
動 劈、砍

英英 a heavy-bladed tool with a wooden handle, used for chopping wood or trees

例 He brought an **ax** to chop the wood.
他帶著斧頭要砍木頭。

□三分熟
□五分熟
□七分熟
□全熟

Bb

Track 009

---

back·ground
[ˋbækˏɡraʊnd]

名 背景

英英 part of a scene that forms a setting for an event; a person's education, family or experience

例 To understand the novel, the historical **background** of jazz music is important.
要了解這本小說，爵士樂的歷史背景很重要。

☐ 三分熟
☐ 五分熟
☐ 七分熟
☐ 全熟

---

ba·con [ˋbekən]

名 培根、燻肉
片 bring home the bacon
養家餬口

英英 salted or smoked meat from the back or sides of a pig

例 Let's buy some **bacon** to make a hamburger.
我們買一點培根做漢堡吧。

☐ 三分熟
☐ 五分熟
☐ 七分熟
☐ 全熟

---

bac·te·ri·a
[bækˋtɪrɪə]

名 細菌

英英 small living things with cell walls but lack an organized nucleus,which can cause disease

例 Wash your hands before meals. Your hands are full of **bacteria**.
飯前要洗手，你的手上充滿了細菌。

☐ 三分熟
☐ 五分熟
☐ 七分熟
☐ 全熟

---

bad·ly [ˋbædlɪ]

副 非常地、惡劣地

英英 very seriously, unpleasantly

例 He treated her **badly** so she left him.
他對她很壞，所以她離開了。

☐ 三分熟
☐ 五分熟
☐ 七分熟
☐ 全熟

---

bad·min·ton
[ˋbædmɪntən]

名 羽毛球

英英 a game with rackets in which a shuttlecock is hit back and forth by two people

例 Could you teach me how to play **badminton**?
你可以教我如何打羽毛球嗎？

☐ 三分熟
☐ 五分熟
☐ 七分熟
☐ 全熟

---

bag·gage
[ˋbæɡɪdʒ]

名 行李
同 lugguge 行李

英英 personal belongings which you take with you while travelling

例 May I put my **baggage** here?
我可以將我的行李放在這裡嗎？

☐ 三分熟
☐ 五分熟
☐ 七分熟
☐ 全熟

---

bait [bet]

名 誘餌
動 誘惑

英英 food put on a hook or in a trap for catching fish or other animals

例 The worms are for **bait**.
這些蟲是釣魚的餌。

☐ 三分熟
☐ 五分熟
☐ 七分熟
☐ 全熟

ba·lance [ˈbæləns]

名 平衡
動 使平衡
片 balance sheet
　　收支平衡表

英英 an even distribution of weight coming stability

例 I tried to **balance** the time I spend on my study and my part-time job.
我試圖平衡我讀書跟打工的時間。

☐ 三分熟
☐ 五分熟
☐ 七分熟
☐ 全熟

B

---

ban·dage
[ˈbændɪdʒ]

名 繃帶

英英 a strip of material which is used to tie up a wound or to protect an injury

例 He was hurt so seriously in the accident that his body was covered by a **bandage**.
他在那場意外中嚴重受傷，所以他全身包覆著繃帶。

☐ 三分熟
☐ 五分熟
☐ 七分熟
☐ 全熟

---

bang [bæŋ]

動 重擊、雷擊
名 碰撞聲

英英 a sudden loud noise or a painful blow

例 The **bang** scared the children.
那一聲巨響嚇到小孩子了。

☐ 三分熟
☐ 五分熟
☐ 七分熟
☐ 全熟

---

bare [bɛr]

形 暴露的、僅有的
同 naked 暴露的

英英 not covered by anything and shows its surface

例 The girl's feet are **bare** so I gave her some shoes.
那女孩的腳暴露在外，所以我給了她一些鞋子。

☐ 三分熟
☐ 五分熟
☐ 七分熟
☐ 全熟

---

bare·ly [ˈbɛrlɪ]

副 簡直沒有、幾乎不能

英英 without the appropriate or usual covering or contents; without possibilities

例 I could **barely** believe that I won the lottery.
我很難相信我中了樂透。

☐ 三分熟
☐ 五分熟
☐ 七分熟
☐ 全熟

---

barn [bɑrn]

名 穀倉

英英 a large farm building which is built for storage or housing livestock

例 The emperor was happy that the **barn** was full.
皇帝很開心穀倉是滿的。

☐ 三分熟
☐ 五分熟
☐ 七分熟
☐ 全熟

---

bar·rel [ˈbærəl]

名 大桶

英英 a large cylindrical container which is used for storing wine or other liquids

例 The **barrel** is for the wine.
這桶子是裝紅酒的。

☐ 三分熟
☐ 五分熟
☐ 七分熟
☐ 全熟

---

bay [be]

名 海灣

英英 a broad curved inlet of the sea

例 I am going to the **bay** to see the sunset.
我去海灣看日落。

☐ 三分熟
☐ 五分熟
☐ 七分熟
☐ 全熟

🎧 Track 011

beam [bin]
動 放射、發光
片 off beam 離題

英英 a ray or a line of light shinning from something
例 The **beam** made me unable to open my eyes.
這道光讓我無法張開眼睛。

☐ 三分熟 ☐ 五分熟 ☐ 七分熟 ☐ 全熟

beast [bist]
名 野獸
片 beauty and the beast 美女與野獸

英英 a wild animal, especially a large or dangerous mammal
例 There are **beasts** in the forest.
森林裡面有野獸。

☐ 三分熟 ☐ 五分熟 ☐ 七分熟 ☐ 全熟

beg·gar [ˋbɛgɚ]
名 乞丐

英英 a poor person who lives by begging for food or money
例 I threw some coins into the **beggar's** bowl.
我丟一些零錢到那乞丐的碗裡。

☐ 三分熟 ☐ 五分熟 ☐ 七分熟 ☐ 全熟

be·have [bɪˋhev]
動 行動、舉止
同 act 行動

英英 manner; act in a specified way
例 I feel he **behaves** weirdly today.
我覺得他今天舉止很奇怪。

☐ 三分熟 ☐ 五分熟 ☐ 七分熟 ☐ 全熟

be·ing [ˋbiɪŋ]
名 生命、存在
片 human being 人類

英英 existence; the essence of a person
例 Human **beings** need to change to avoid the global warming.
人類需要改變以避免全球暖化。

☐ 三分熟 ☐ 五分熟 ☐ 七分熟 ☐ 全熟

bel·ly/stom·ach/tum·my [ˋstʌmək]/[ˋtʌmɪ]/[ˋbɛlɪ]
名 腹、胃

英英 the front part of the human body below the ribs, between the chest and the legs
例 I drank too much, and I felt my **belly** was full of water.
我今天喝太多了，以至於我覺得我的肚子都是水。

☐ 三分熟 ☐ 五分熟 ☐ 七分熟 ☐ 全熟

be·neath [bɪˋniθ]
介 在……下

英英 extending or directly underneath; below or under
例 The house is **beneath** the tree.
這間房子在這棵樹下。

☐ 三分熟 ☐ 五分熟 ☐ 七分熟 ☐ 全熟

ben·e·fit [ˋbɛnəfɪt]
名 益處、利益
同 advantage 利益

英英 advantage or profit; a payment made by the state to someone entitled to receive it
例 What's the **benefit** for me to do so?
我做這件事的利益是什麼？

☐ 三分熟 ☐ 五分熟 ☐ 七分熟 ☐ 全熟

B

ber·ry [ˋbɛrɪ]

名 漿果、莓

英英 a small round roundish juicy fruit without a stone, which is growing on particular trees

例 I bought some **berries** to make the jam.
我買了些莓果來做果醬。

□ 三分熟
□ 五分熟
□ 七分熟
□ 全熟

---

bi·ble [ˋbaɪbḷ]

名 聖經

英英 the holy book of the Christian religion, consisting of the Old and New Testaments

例 They swear with their hands on the **bible**.
他們的手放在聖經上發誓。

□ 三分熟
□ 五分熟
□ 七分熟
□ 全熟

---

bil·lion [ˋbɪljən]

名 十億、無數

英英 the number equivalent to a thousand million, 1,000,000,000

例 There are **billions** of people suffering from poverty.
有數十億的人生活在貧困之中。

□ 三分熟
□ 五分熟
□ 七分熟
□ 全熟

---

bin·go [ˋbɪŋgo]

名 賓果遊戲
片 bingo wings 蝴蝶袖

英英 a game in which players take turns to call the numbers on printed cards, the winner being the first to mark off all their numbers

例 I play **bingo** with my kids.
我跟我的孩子們玩賓果遊戲。

□ 三分熟
□ 五分熟
□ 七分熟
□ 全熟

---

bis·cuit [ˋbɪskɪt]

名 餅乾、小甜麵包

英英 a small, flat, crisp cake, which usually tastes dry and sweet

例 We baked some **biscuits** this afternoon.
今天午後我們烤了一些餅乾。

□ 三分熟
□ 五分熟
□ 七分熟
□ 全熟

---

blame [blem]

動 責備
同 accuse 提告

英英 to criticize someone for his / her fault or wrong or something bad happened

例 My mother always **blames** me for wasting money.
我媽總是責備我亂花錢。

□ 三分熟
□ 五分熟
□ 七分熟
□ 全熟

---

blan·ket [ˋblæŋkɪt]

名 氈、毛毯

英英 a large piece of woollen material which is usually used as a covering for warmth on the bed

例 She asked for a **blanket** on the plane.
她在飛機上要了一條毛毯。

□ 三分熟
□ 五分熟
□ 七分熟
□ 全熟

---

bleed [blid]

動 流血、放血

英英 to lose blood

例 My arm's **bleeding**!
我的手臂在流血！

□ 三分熟
□ 五分熟
□ 七分熟
□ 全熟

🎧 **Track 013**

bless [blɛs]

動 祝福

片 God bless you.
上帝祝福你。

英英 to ask for God's help for someone or something, or to make someone holy

例 The baby was **blessed** by everyone.
這嬰兒受到所有人的祝福。

☐ 三分熟
☐ 五分熟
☐ 七分熟
☐ 全熟

---

blouse [blaʊs]

名 短衫

英英 a woman's or girl's shirt

例 The woman in the **blouse** is my advisor.
穿著短衫的女人是我的指導教授。

☐ 三分熟
☐ 五分熟
☐ 七分熟
☐ 全熟

---

bold [bold]

形 大膽的

同 brave 勇敢的

英英 confident and not fearing danger

例 The boy is **bold**.
這男孩很大膽。

☐ 三分熟
☐ 五分熟
☐ 七分熟
☐ 全熟

---

boot [bʊt]

名 長靴

英英 an item of footwear covering the whole foot and ankle, and sometimes the lower part of leg

例 I bought **boots** for the coming winter.
因為冬天即將來臨，我買了長靴。

☐ 三分熟
☐ 五分熟
☐ 七分熟
☐ 全熟

---

bor·der [ˈbɔrdɚ]

名 邊

同 edge 邊

英英 the line between two countries or other areas,which divides a country from another

例 The **border** of the country is dangerous.
這國家的邊界很危險。

☐ 三分熟
☐ 五分熟
☐ 七分熟
☐ 全熟

---

bore [bor]

動 鑽孔

名 孔、無聊的人

同 drill 鑽孔

英英 to make a hole on something

例 The villagers are **boring** a well.
村民正在鑿井。

☐ 三分熟
☐ 五分熟
☐ 七分熟
☐ 全熟

---

brake [brek]

名／動 煞車

英英 a device for slowing or stopping a moving vehicle; to slow down or stop the car suddenly

例 It's dangerous to **brake** in a sudden.
突然煞車很危險。

☐ 三分熟
☐ 五分熟
☐ 七分熟
☐ 全熟

---

brass [bræs]

名 黃銅、銅器

英英 a bright yellow alloy of copper and zinc

例 The earrings are made of **brass**.
這副耳環是黃銅做的。

☐ 三分熟
☐ 五分熟
☐ 七分熟
☐ 全熟

---

brav·er·y [ˈbrevərɪ]

名 大膽、勇敢

同 courage 勇氣

英英 when someone is brave and courageous; actions that are brave

例 We admire her **bravery**.
我們欽佩她的勇敢。

☐ 三分熟
☐ 五分熟
☐ 七分熟
☐ 全熟

B

breast [brɛst]
名 胸膛、胸部

英英 people's chest
例 She has a beautiful tattoo on her **breasts**.
她胸部上有漂亮的刺青。

☐ 三分熟 ☐ 五分熟 ☐ 七分熟 ☐ 全熟

breath [brɛθ]
名 呼吸、氣息

英英 the air that goes into and out of your lungs to keep you alive
例 The scenery took my **breath** away.
這美景讓我屏息了。

☐ 三分熟 ☐ 五分熟 ☐ 七分熟 ☐ 全熟

breathe [brið]
動 呼吸、生存

英英 to move air into and out of the lungs to keep alive
例 Is the patient **breathing**?
那病人還在呼吸嗎？

☐ 三分熟 ☐ 五分熟 ☐ 七分熟 ☐ 全熟

breeze [briz]
名 微風
動 微風輕吹、輕鬆通過

英英 a light and gentle wind
例 Your smile is like a **breeze** in the summer.
你的微笑就像夏天的微風。

☐ 三分熟 ☐ 五分熟 ☐ 七分熟 ☐ 全熟

bride [braɪd]
名 新娘

英英 a woman on her wedding day or just before getting married
例 I want you to be my **bride**!
我要你當我的新娘。

☐ 三分熟 ☐ 五分熟 ☐ 七分熟 ☐ 全熟

bril·liant [ˈbrɪljənt]
形 有才氣的、出色的

英英 very talented; outstanding
例 The student is not merely **brilliant** but also hard-working.
那學生不只是有才氣，還很認真。

☐ 三分熟 ☐ 五分熟 ☐ 七分熟 ☐ 全熟

brook [brʊk]
名 川、小河、溪流

英英 a small stream or river
例 We used to swim in the **brook**.
我們以前都在這條小河游泳。

☐ 三分熟 ☐ 五分熟 ☐ 七分熟 ☐ 全熟

broom [brum]
名 掃帚、長柄刷

英英 a long-handled brush used for sweeping or cleaning
例 I used a **broom** to sweep the floor.
我用掃帚掃地。

☐ 三分熟 ☐ 五分熟 ☐ 七分熟 ☐ 全熟

brow(s) [braʊ(z)]
名 眉毛

英英 a person's eyebrow
例 "Are you sure?" the teacher said with her **brows** raising.
「你確定嗎？」這名老師邊說，邊挑眉。

☐ 三分熟 ☐ 五分熟 ☐ 七分熟 ☐ 全熟

🎧 **Track 015**

bub·ble [ˋbʌbl̩]

名 泡沫、氣泡
片 bubble tea 泡沫紅茶

英英 a ball of air in the thin sphere of liquid

例 The fish made lots of **bubbles**.
這些魚吐出很多的泡泡。

☐ 三分熟
☐ 五分熟
☐ 七分熟
☐ 全熟

buck·et/pail
[ˋbʌkɪt]/[pel]

名 水桶、提桶

英英 a container with a handle and an open top, which is used to carry liquids

例 The bucket is filled with **wine**.
這桶子裡裝滿了紅酒。

☐ 三分熟
☐ 五分熟
☐ 七分熟
☐ 全熟

bud [bʌd]

名 芽
動 萌芽
同 flourish 茂盛

英英 a knob-like growth on a plant which develops into a leaf or flower

例 I feel so happy to see the **buds** in spring.
我在春天看到新芽都會感到很開心。

☐ 三分熟
☐ 五分熟
☐ 七分熟
☐ 全熟

budg·et [ˋbʌdʒɪt]

名 預算

英英 a plan to show how much money an organization will need to spend and will earn

例 The **budget** of this department is obviously not enough.
這部門的預算明顯不夠。

☐ 三分熟
☐ 五分熟
☐ 七分熟
☐ 全熟

buf·fa·lo [ˋbʌfl̩o]

名 水牛、野牛

英英 a heavily built wild ox with long curved horns

例 I have never seen any **bufflalo** since I moved to the city.
自從我搬到城市後，再也沒看過水牛了。

☐ 三分熟
☐ 五分熟
☐ 七分熟
☐ 全熟

buf·fet [ˋbəfət]

名 自助餐

英英 a meal consisting of different types of dishes from which people serve themselves

例 We are full because we ate a lot in the **buffet** this morning.
我們很飽，因為我們在早餐的自助餐吃很多。

☐ 三分熟
☐ 五分熟
☐ 七分熟
☐ 全熟

bulb [bʌlb]

名 電燈泡

英英 a light bulb

例 My father changed the **bulb** in my room.
我爸爸換了我房間的電燈泡。

☐ 三分熟
☐ 五分熟
☐ 七分熟
☐ 全熟

bull [bʊl]

名 公牛

英英 a male cow, or the male of particular animals

例 Do you consider the **bull** fierce?
你認為公牛很兇猛嗎？

☐ 三分熟
☐ 五分熟
☐ 七分熟
☐ 全熟

B

bul·let [ˈbʊlɪt]

名 子彈、彈頭

英英 a small, metal projectile fired from a small firearm

例 The investigators regard the **bullet** as an important evidence.
調查員認為子彈頭是很重要的證據。

☐ 三分熟 ☐ 五分熟 ☐ 七分熟 ☐ 全熟

---

bump [bʌmp]

動 碰、撞
片 bump into 碰見

英英 to hit something or someone with force

例 I **bumped** into my teacher this morning.
我今天早上碰到我的老師。

☐ 三分熟 ☐ 五分熟 ☐ 七分熟 ☐ 全熟

---

bunch [bʌntʃ]

名 束、串、捆

英英 a number of things growing or fastened together or in a close group

例 I gave her a **bunch** of roses on Valentine's Day.
我在情人節那天送了她一束玫瑰花。

☐ 三分熟 ☐ 五分熟 ☐ 七分熟 ☐ 全熟

---

bur·den [ˈbɝdṇ]

名 負荷、負擔

英英 a heavy load; the hardship you are facing, worry

例 Some people don't want to have a baby because they think it as a **burden**.
有些人不想要有小孩，因為他們覺得這是種負擔。

☐ 三分熟 ☐ 五分熟 ☐ 七分熟 ☐ 全熟

---

bur·glar [ˈbɝglɚ]

名 夜盜、竊賊

英英 a person who enters buildings and commits burglary

例 The **burglar** broke into my house.
那竊賊闖入我家。

☐ 三分熟 ☐ 五分熟 ☐ 七分熟 ☐ 全熟

---

bur·y [ˈbɛrɪ]

動 埋

英英 put or hide something underground

例 With the energy of love, she can **bury** her painful memory of her childhood.
有愛的能量，她能夠埋藏她童年痛苦的回憶。

☐ 三分熟 ☐ 五分熟 ☐ 七分熟 ☐ 全熟

---

bush [bʊʃ]

名 灌木叢
片 beat around the bush 拐彎抹角

英英 a plant with branches growing directly from the ground

例 The robber hid in the **bush**.
那強盜犯藏身在灌木叢中。

☐ 三分熟 ☐ 五分熟 ☐ 七分熟 ☐ 全熟

---

buzz [bʌz]

名 作嗡嗡聲

英英 make a noise sound; make a low, continuous humming sound

例 I couldn't sleep because of the mosquitos' **buzz**.
蚊子嗡嗡叫讓我整晚睡不著覺。

☐ 三分熟 ☐ 五分熟 ☐ 七分熟 ☐ 全熟

Cc

🎧 **Track 017**

cabin [ˋkæbɪn]

名 小屋、茅屋

英英 a small private room or house made of wood

例 We are going to stay in the **cabin** on the weekend.
我們週末要待在小屋中。

☐ 三分熟
☐ 五分熟
☐ 七分熟
☐ 全熟

---

cam·pus

[ˋkæmpəs]

名 校區、校園

英英 the land and buildings of a university or college

例 There are some dogs in the **campus**.
這校園內有幾隻狗。

☐ 三分熟
☐ 五分熟
☐ 七分熟
☐ 全熟

---

cane [ken]

名 手杖、棒

英英 a long wooden stick which is used by old, ill or blind people to help them walk

例 The old man with a **cane** is smiling.
那拿著手杖的老人正在微笑著。

☐ 三分熟
☐ 五分熟
☐ 七分熟
☐ 全熟

---

ca·noe [kəˋnu]

名 獨木舟
動 划獨木舟

英英 a narrow boat with pointed ends and move with a paddle

例 Do you want to try to row the **canoe**?
你想要試著划獨木舟嗎？

☐ 三分熟
☐ 五分熟
☐ 七分熟
☐ 全熟

---

can·yon [ˋkænjən]

名 峽谷
同 valley 山谷

英英 a deep gorge, usually with a river flowing through it

例 Have you ever seen such a magnificent **canyon**?
你曾看過這麼壯觀的峽谷嗎？

☐ 三分熟
☐ 五分熟
☐ 七分熟
☐ 全熟

---

ca·pa·ble [ˋkepəbl̩]

形 有能力的
同 able 有能力的
片 be capable of 有能力

英英 having the ability to do something

例 The group is **capable** of doing the project.
這個團隊有能力完成這計畫。

☐ 三分熟
☐ 五分熟
☐ 七分熟
☐ 全熟

---

cap·i·tal [ˋkæpətl̩]

名 首都、資本
形 主要的

英英 the most important city in a country, usually its seat of government center or political area

例 What's the **capital** of Australia?
澳洲的首都是哪裡？

☐ 三分熟
☐ 五分熟
☐ 七分熟
☐ 全熟

---

cap·ture [ˋkæptʃɚ]

動 捉住、吸引
名 擄獲、戰利品

英英 to grab something or attract something; control something or someone by force

例 The photographer **captured** the moment of the light.
攝影師捉住了這一剎那的光線。

☐ 三分熟
☐ 五分熟
☐ 七分熟
☐ 全熟

car·pen·ter

[ˈkɑrpəntɚ]

名 木匠

英英 a person who makes or repairing wooden objects or structures

例 The **carpenter** made the table.
這木匠做了這桌子。

□ 三分熟
□ 五分熟
□ 七分熟
□ 全熟

C

---

car·riage

[ˈkærɪdʒ]

名 車輛、車、馬車

英英 a four-wheeled passenger vehicle, which is pulled by two or more horses in the past

例 The duke is in the **carriage**.
那伯爵在馬車上。

□ 三分熟
□ 五分熟
□ 七分熟
□ 全熟

---

cast [kæst]

動 用力擲、選角
名 投、演員班底
同 throw 投、擲

英英 to throw forcefully; to choose someone to play a role in a play or film

例 I **cast** the stone into the lake.
我用力把石頭擲到湖中。

□ 三分熟
□ 五分熟
□ 七分熟
□ 全熟

---

ca·su·al [ˈkæʒʊəl]

形 偶然的、臨時的

英英 just occasional or temporary

例 He broke his leg, so he looked for a **casual** passerby to help him.
他腳斷了，所以他正在等一個碰巧路過的人幫他。

□ 三分熟
□ 五分熟
□ 七分熟
□ 全熟

---

cat·er·pil·lar

[ˈkætɚpɪlɚ]

名 毛毛蟲

英英 the larva of a butterfly or moth, which is small and long with many legs

例 All the butterflies used to be **caterpillars**.
所有的蝴蝶都曾經是毛毛蟲。

□ 三分熟
□ 五分熟
□ 七分熟
□ 全熟

---

cat·tle [ˈkætl]

名 小牛

英英 large farm animals with horns and cloven hoofs, kept for their meat or milk; cows and oxen

例 The **cattles** are protected.
這些小牛都是受到保護的。

□ 三分熟
□ 五分熟
□ 七分熟
□ 全熟

---

cel·e·brate

[ˈsɛləˌbret]

動 慶祝、慶賀

英英 mark a special enjoyable activities for a particular important occation

例 Let's **celebrate**!
我們來慶祝吧！

□ 三分熟
□ 五分熟
□ 七分熟
□ 全熟

---

cen·ti·me·ter

[ˈsɛntəˌmitɚ]

名 公分、釐米

英英 a unit of length equal to one hundred of a meter

例 The length of the table is 100 **centimeters**.
這桌子的長度是一百公分。

□ 三分熟
□ 五分熟
□ 七分熟
□ 全熟

🎧 Track 019

ce·ram·ic

[sə'ræmɪk]

形 陶瓷的
名 陶瓷品

英英 made of clay that is permanently hardened and shaped by heat

例 The bowl is **ceramic**.
這個碗是陶瓷的。

☐ 三分熟
☐ 五分熟
☐ 七分熟
☐ 全熟

---

chain [tʃen]

名 鏈子
動 鏈住

英英 a connected series of metal links, which are for fastening or pulling

例 The monster is tied by the **chain**.
這怪獸被鏈子綁住了。

☐ 三分熟
☐ 五分熟
☐ 七分熟
☐ 全熟

---

chal·lenge

['tʃælɪndʒ]

名 挑戰
動 向……挑戰

英英 something needs great or special effort to complete

例 Dare you **challenge** the man?
你敢挑戰這男人嗎？

☐ 三分熟
☐ 五分熟
☐ 七分熟
☐ 全熟

---

cham·pi·on

['tʃæmpɪən]

名 冠軍
同 victor 勝利者

英英 a person who has beaten other competitors to win a sporting contest or other competition

例 Are you the **champion**?
你是冠軍嗎？

☐ 三分熟
☐ 五分熟
☐ 七分熟
☐ 全熟

---

change·a·ble

['tʃendʒəbl̩]

形 可變的

英英 able to be changed or modified

例 Is the manager's decision **changeable**?
這經理的決定是可以改變的嗎？

☐ 三分熟
☐ 五分熟
☐ 七分熟
☐ 全熟

---

chan·nel ['tʃænl̩]

名 通道、頻道
動 傳輸

英英 a television station; a path for water to flow along; to direct into a particular course

例 It's not the **channel** I am looking for.
這不是我在看的頻道。

☐ 三分熟
☐ 五分熟
☐ 七分熟
☐ 全熟

---

chap·ter ['tʃæptɚ]

名 章、章節

英英 a main separation of a book to divided each text

例 What can you learn from the **chapter**?
你可以從這個章節中得知什麼呢？

☐ 三分熟
☐ 五分熟
☐ 七分熟
☐ 全熟

---

charm [tʃɑrm]

名 魅力、護身符
片 charm offensive
魅力攻勢

英英 the quality of attracting or fascinating others

例 The shortest **charm** is the name of someone.
最短的護身符（魅力）就是某人的名字。

☐ 三分熟
☐ 五分熟
☐ 七分熟
☐ 全熟

C

chat [tʃæt]
動 聊天、閒談

英英 talk to someone in an informal way or without any particular subjects
例 I am **chatting** with my girlfriend.
我正在跟我女朋友聊天。

☐三分熟 ☐五分熟 ☐七分熟 ☐全熟

---

cheek [tʃik]
名 臉頰

英英 either side of the face below the eye and between your mouth and ear
例 She kissed me on my **cheek**.
她在我臉上親了一下。

☐三分熟 ☐五分熟 ☐七分熟 ☐全熟

---

cheer [tʃɪr]
名 歡呼
動 喝采、振奮
片 cheer up 振作起來

英英 shout for approal or in praise or encouragement
例 **Cheer** up, my dear.
親愛的，振作點。

☐三分熟 ☐五分熟 ☐七分熟 ☐全熟

---

cheer·ful [ˈtʃɪrfəl]
形 愉快的、興高采烈的

英英 happy, optimistic and pleasant
例 The good news made them **cheerful**.
這好消息讓他們興高采烈。

☐三分熟 ☐五分熟 ☐七分熟 ☐全熟

---

cheese [tʃiz]
名 乾酪、乳酪

英英 a food made from the pressed curds of milk, which is either firm or soft and semi-liquid
例 I need a **cheese** burger.
我要一個起司堡。

☐三分熟 ☐五分熟 ☐七分熟 ☐全熟

---

cher·ry [ˈtʃɛrɪ]
名 櫻桃、櫻木

英英 the small, round soft red or dark red stone fruit with a hard seed in the middle
例 I want to decorate the cake with some **cherries**.
我要用櫻桃裝飾這個蛋糕。

☐三分熟 ☐五分熟 ☐七分熟 ☐全熟

---

chest [tʃɛst]
名 胸、箱子
同 box 箱子

英英 the front surface of a person's or animal's body between the neck and the stomach
例 We can learn his disease by **chest** x-ray.
我們可以從胸腔 X 光知道他的病情。

☐三分熟 ☐五分熟 ☐七分熟 ☐全熟

---

chew [tʃu]
動 咀嚼

英英 to bite the food in the mouth to make it softer and easier to swallow
例 I am **chewing** the pearls in bubble milk tea.
我在咬珍珠奶茶的珍珠。

☐三分熟 ☐五分熟 ☐七分熟 ☐全熟

child·hood

[ˈtʃaɪldˏhʊd]

名 童年、幼年時代

英英 the period of time of being a child

例 The trauma in his **childhood** made his lack of confidence.
童年的創傷讓他缺乏自信。

☐ 三分熟
☐ 五分熟
☐ 七分熟
☐ 全熟

---

chill [tʃɪl]

動 使變冷
名 寒冷

英英 to make cold; to become a feverish cold

例 The air-con **chilled** the room.
冷氣機讓房間冷卻下來了。

☐ 三分熟
☐ 五分熟
☐ 七分熟
☐ 全熟

---

chill·y [ˈtʃɪlɪ]

形 寒冷的

英英 unpleasantly and unfriendly cold

例 It is **chilly** in Taipei in April.
臺北的四月還是很冷。

☐ 三分熟
☐ 五分熟
☐ 七分熟
☐ 全熟

---

chim·ney [ˈtʃɪmnɪ]

名 煙囪

英英 a vertical pipe which allow smoke from stove escape to the outside of the building

例 The little boy is cleaning the **chimney** for his family.
那個小男孩在掃他家的煙囪。

☐ 三分熟
☐ 五分熟
☐ 七分熟
☐ 全熟

---

chip [tʃɪp]

名 碎片
動 切
片 potato chips 洋芋片

英英 a small, thin piece broken off because of cutting or breaking a hard material

例 Let's eat fish and **chips** in London.
我們在倫敦吃點魚和薯條吧！

☐ 三分熟
☐ 五分熟
☐ 七分熟
☐ 全熟

---

choke [tʃok]

動 使窒息

英英 something is blocking your throat and making you stop breathing

例 I was **choked** by the smoke.
這煙快要讓我窒息了。

☐ 三分熟
☐ 五分熟
☐ 七分熟
☐ 全熟

---

chop [tʃɑp]

動 砍、劈

英英 cut with an axe or knife

例 I **chopped** the wood.
我劈開木頭。

☐ 三分熟
☐ 五分熟
☐ 七分熟
☐ 全熟

---

cig·a·rette

[ˏsɪgəˈrɛt]

名 香菸
同 smoke 香菸

英英 pieces tobacco rolled in a small paper tube for smoking

例 How many **cigarettes** can I bring?
我可以帶多少香菸？

☐ 三分熟
☐ 五分熟
☐ 七分熟
☐ 全熟

C

cir·cus [ˋsɝkəs]

名 馬戲團

英英 a travelling company of acrobats, trained animals, and clowns, which usually give the performance in a large tent

例 The training in the **circus** is cruel for animals.
馬戲團的訓練對動物來說是很殘忍的。

☐ 三分熟
☐ 五分熟
☐ 七分熟
☐ 全熟

civ·il [ˋsɪvḷ]

形 國家的、公民的
片 civil right 公民權

英英 relating to ordinary citizens

例 Education is part of our **civil** rights.
教育是我們國家的公民權之一。

☐ 三分熟
☐ 五分熟
☐ 七分熟
☐ 全熟

clas·si·cal
[ˋklæsɪkḷ]

形 古典的

英英 music, art or culture relating to ancient Greek or Latin literature

例 I prefer **classical** music.
我偏好古典的音樂。

☐ 三分熟
☐ 五分熟
☐ 七分熟
☐ 全熟

click [klɪk]

名 滴答聲

英英 a short, sharp sound as of two hard objects coming smartly into contact

例 The **click** is annoying at night.
半夜時鐘的滴答聲很惱人。

☐ 三分熟
☐ 五分熟
☐ 七分熟
☐ 全熟

cli·ent [ˋklaɪənt]

名 委託人、客戶
同 customer 客戶

英英 a person or a customer receiving the services of a professional person or organization

例 Most of our **clients** are satisfied with our service.
大部分的客戶都很滿意我們的服務。

☐ 三分熟
☐ 五分熟
☐ 七分熟
☐ 全熟

clin·ic [ˋklɪnɪk]

名 診所

英英 a place, often a part of hospital, to where specialized medical treatment or advice is provided

例 I went to the **clinic** because I was sick.
因為我生病了，所以我去診所。

☐ 三分熟
☐ 五分熟
☐ 七分熟
☐ 全熟

clip [klɪp]

名 夾子、紙夾、修剪

英英 a flexible or metal device for fastening an object or objects together or in place

例 I use **clips** to fix the paper.
我用夾子固定紙。

☐ 三分熟
☐ 五分熟
☐ 七分熟
☐ 全熟

clue [klu]

名 線索

英英 a fact or a sign that helps to clarify a mystery, solve a problem or give answers to questions

例 Do you have any **clue**?
你有任何線索嗎？

☐ 三分熟
☐ 五分熟
☐ 七分熟
☐ 全熟

🎧 **Track 023**

cock·tail [ˈkɑkˌtel]
名 雞尾酒

英英 an alcoholic drink, which is consisting of a spirit mixed with other drinks, such as fruit juice

例 I come to the bar for this **cocktail**.
我來酒吧就是為了這一杯雞尾酒。

☐ 三分熟
☐ 五分熟
☐ 七分熟
☐ 全熟

---

co·co·nut [ˈkokəˌnət]
名 椰子

英英 the large brown seed of a tropical palm, containing hard white meat which can be eaten and a white liquid

例 Thailand is famous for fruits, such as **coconuts**.
泰國以椰子等水果聞名。

☐ 三分熟
☐ 五分熟
☐ 七分熟
☐ 全熟

---

col·lar [ˈkɑlɚ]
名 衣領

英英 a band of clothing around the neck, usually sewn on and made of different material

例 There is a stain on the **collar**.
領口上有污漬。

☐ 三分熟
☐ 五分熟
☐ 七分熟
☐ 全熟

---

col·le·ction [kəˈlɛkʃən]
名 聚集、收集
同 analects 選集

英英 the action of collecting; a group of objects with same type that are collected by one person

例 The stamps are my **collection**.
郵票是我的收集品。

☐ 三分熟
☐ 五分熟
☐ 七分熟
☐ 全熟

---

col·lege [ˈkɑlɪdʒ]
名 學院、大學

英英 an educational place providing higher education after the age of sixteen or specialized training

例 She's my classmate in **college**.
她是我大學同學。

☐ 三分熟
☐ 五分熟
☐ 七分熟
☐ 全熟

---

col·o·ny [ˈkɑlənɪ]
名 殖民者、殖民地

英英 a country or area under the control and occupied by a more powerful country

例 Singapore used to be the **colony** of British and Japan.
新加坡曾經是英國跟日本的殖民地。

☐ 三分熟
☐ 五分熟
☐ 七分熟
☐ 全熟

---

col·umn [ˈkɑləm]
名 圓柱、專欄、欄

英英 a special piece of writing in a newspaper or magazine which is always written by the same person and with a particular subject

例 He's a writer for the **column**.
他是專欄作家。

☐ 三分熟
☐ 五分熟
☐ 七分熟
☐ 全熟

com·bine

[kəm`baɪn]

動 聯合、結合
同 join 連結

英英 to join or mix together; arrange some things into a group

例 I **combine** these two issues in my paper.
在我的論文中結合了這兩個議題。

☐ 三分熟
☐ 五分熟
☐ 七分熟
☐ 全熟

C

---

com·fort [`kʌmfət]

名 舒適
動 安慰
片 comfort food
安慰／開心食品

英英 a pleasant feeling of physical ease and freedom from pain or constraint

例 My mother **comforted** me.
我媽媽安慰我。

☐ 三分熟
☐ 五分熟
☐ 七分熟
☐ 全熟

---

com·ma [`kɑmə]

名 逗號

英英 a punctuation mark (,) indicating a pause between parts of a sentence or separating the single thing in a list

例 You put the **comma** in the wrong place.
你把逗號放錯地方了。

☐ 三分熟
☐ 五分熟
☐ 七分熟
☐ 全熟

---

com·mand

[kə`mænd]

動 命令、指揮
名 命令、指令

英英 give an authoritative order usually one given by a soldier

例 I **command** you to stand up.
我命令你站起來。

☐ 三分熟
☐ 五分熟
☐ 七分熟
☐ 全熟

---

com·mer·cial

[kə`mɝʃəl]

形 商業的
名 商業廣告
同 business 商業

英英 making or intended to make a profit by buying and selling products

例 This resource is not for **commercial** use.
這資源不允許商業用途。

☐ 三分熟
☐ 五分熟
☐ 七分熟
☐ 全熟

---

com·mit·tee

[kə`mɪtɪ]

名 委員會、會議

英英 a group of people appointed for representing a larger organization

例 The **committee** approved the thesis.
口試委員都同意這篇論文了。

☐ 三分熟
☐ 五分熟
☐ 七分熟
☐ 全熟

---

com·mu·ni·cate

[kə`mjunəˌket]

動 溝通、交流

英英 share or exchange information or ideas with others

例 Due to the lack of **communication**, their relationship is getting worse.
因為缺乏溝通，他們的感情越來越差了。

☐ 三分熟
☐ 五分熟
☐ 七分熟
☐ 全熟

🎧 **Track 025**

com·par·i·son

[kəmˋpærəsn̩]

名 對照、比較
同 contrast 對照

英英 the action or an instance of comparing; two people or more are compared
例 These two pictures are **comparison**.
這兩張照片是對比。

☐ 三分熟
☐ 五分熟
☐ 七分熟
☐ 全熟

---

com·pete

[kəmˋpit]

動 競爭

英英 try to gain or win something by defeating over others
例 These two classes are **competing**.
這兩個班級正在競爭。

☐ 三分熟
☐ 五分熟
☐ 七分熟
☐ 全熟

---

com·plaint

[kəmˋplent]

名 抱怨、訴苦

英英 an act of complaining about something
例 Her **complaint** about the goods is valued by the manager.
她的抱怨受到經理的重視。

☐ 三分熟
☐ 五分熟
☐ 七分熟
☐ 全熟

---

com·plex

[ˋkɑmplɛks]

形 複雜的、合成的
名 複合物、綜合設施

英英 complicated and difficult to understand; consisting of many different and connected parts
例 The problem is more **complex** than you think.
這問題比你想像的複雜。

☐ 三分熟
☐ 五分熟
☐ 七分熟
☐ 全熟

---

con·cern [kənˋsɝn]

動 關心、涉及

英英 to relate to; be relevant to; to get involved
例 He doesn't **concern** about you!
他一點都不關心你。

☐ 三分熟
☐ 五分熟
☐ 七分熟
☐ 全熟

---

con·cert [ˋkɑnsɝt]

名 音樂會、演奏會

英英 a musical performance given in public
例 I went to the **concert** last night.
我昨天聽了場音樂會。

☐ 三分熟
☐ 五分熟
☐ 七分熟
☐ 全熟

---

con·clude

[kənˋklud]

動 締結、結束、得到結論
同 end 結束

英英 to jump into end or conclusion
例 The teacher **concluded** our discussion briefly.
老師簡短的總結我們的討論。

☐ 三分熟
☐ 五分熟
☐ 七分熟
☐ 全熟

---

con·clu·sion

[kənˋkluʒən]

名 結論、終了
片 in conclusion 總之

英英 the summing-up of a text or an issue
例 In **conclusion**, we need to start our work now.
總之，我們需要趕快開始動工了。

☐ 三分熟
☐ 五分熟
☐ 七分熟
☐ 全熟

C

con·di·tion
[kənˋdɪʃən]

名 條件、情況
動 以……為條件

英英 the particular state that something or someone is in

例 The health **condition** is terrible in this area.
這裡的健康條件很差。

☐ 三分熟
☐ 五分熟
☐ 七分熟
☐ 全熟

cone [kon]

名 圓錐

英英 an object which is with a flat, round or oval base and a top which becomes narrower until it forms a point

例 I need to eat an ice cream with a **cone**.
我要有圓錐餅乾的冰淇淋。

☐ 三分熟
☐ 五分熟
☐ 七分熟
☐ 全熟

con·fi·dent
[ˋkɑnfədənt]

形 有信心的
同 certain 有把握的

英英 feeling certain about something

例 You are too **confident** about your plan.
你對你的計劃太有信心了。

☐ 三分熟
☐ 五分熟
☐ 七分熟
☐ 全熟

con·fuse [kənˋfjuz]

動 使迷惑

英英 make something hard to understand, not understandable

例 I am **confused** by your explanation.
你的解釋讓我迷惑了。

☐ 三分熟
☐ 五分熟
☐ 七分熟
☐ 全熟

con·nect [kəˋnɛkt]

動 連接、連結
同 link 連接

英英 bring together as a link; to link with something else

例 The theory is **connected** to another.
這理論跟其他的有連結。

☐ 三分熟
☐ 五分熟
☐ 七分熟
☐ 全熟

con·nec·tion
[kəˋnɛkʃən]

名 連接、連結

英英 the state of being related to someone or something else

例 The **connection** between mothers and children is strong.
母親跟子女的連結是很強烈的。

☐ 三分熟
☐ 五分熟
☐ 七分熟
☐ 全熟

con·scious
[ˋkɑnʃəs]

形 意識到的
同 aware 意識到的
片 be conscious of
意識到

英英 a link or relationship; the action of connecting

例 She is **conscious** of the problem between them.
她意識到他們之間的問題。

☐ 三分熟
☐ 五分熟
☐ 七分熟
☐ 全熟

🎧 Track 027

---

con·sid·er·a·ble

[kən`sɪdərəbl]

形 應考慮的、相當多的

英英 be aware of or to notice that a particular thing or person exists or is present

例 Her boyfriend is **considerable**.
她男朋友考慮很多。

☐ 三分熟
☐ 五分熟
☐ 七分熟
☐ 全熟

---

con·sid·er·a·tion

[kən`sɪdə`reʃən]

名 考慮

英英 significant or notable

例 Have you ever **considered** your parents when you made such a decision?
當你做這樣的決定時是否有考慮過你父母？

☐ 三分熟
☐ 五分熟
☐ 七分熟
☐ 全熟

---

con·stant

[`kɑnstənt]

形 不變的、不斷的

英英 make something hard to understand, not understandable

例 The institution provides **constant** help for the poor families.
這機構不間斷的提供協助給弱勢家庭。

☐ 三分熟
☐ 五分熟
☐ 七分熟
☐ 全熟

---

con·ti·nent

[`kɑntənənt]

名 大陸、陸地

英英 any of the world's main continuous expanses of land on the Earth's surface, surrounded by sea

例 The territory of Russia covers two **continents**.
俄國的領土範圍涵蓋兩個大陸。

☐ 三分熟
☐ 五分熟
☐ 七分熟
☐ 全熟

---

con·tract

[`kɑntrækt]/[kən`trækt]

名 契約、合約
動 訂契約
同 pact 契約
片 make a contract
簽合約

英英 a legal written or spoken agreement intended to be enforceable by law; to establish by formal agreement

例 Our company will make a **contract** with yours.
我們公司會跟你們公司簽合約。

☐ 三分熟
☐ 五分熟
☐ 七分熟
☐ 全熟

---

couch [kautʃ]

名 長沙發、睡椅

英英 a sofa for several people to sit on

例 He slept on the **couch** last night.
他昨晚在沙發上睡著了。

☐ 三分熟
☐ 五分熟
☐ 七分熟
☐ 全熟

---

count·a·ble

[kauntəbl]

形 可數的

英英 a countable noun can be made plural and can be used with "a" or "an"

例 Is it a **countable** noun?
這是可數名詞嗎？

☐ 三分熟
☐ 五分熟
☐ 七分熟
☐ 全熟

---

cow·ard [`kauəd]

名 懦夫、膽子小的人

英英 a person who is lack of courage

例 The boy is called **coward**.
這男孩被叫是膽小鬼。

☐ 三分熟
☐ 五分熟
☐ 七分熟
☐ 全熟

C

---

cra·dle [ˋkredḷ]

名 搖籃
動 放在搖籃裡

英英 a baby's bed or cot, especially one that swings from side to side; to place in a cradle

例 The baby sleeps in the **cradle**.
這嬰兒在搖籃中睡著了。

□ 三分熟
□ 五分熟
□ 七分熟
□ 全熟

---

crash [kræʃ]

名 撞擊
動 摔下、撞毀
片 car crash 車禍

英英 an accident that damanges an obstacle or another vehicle

例 There was a car **crash**.
這裡發生一場車禍。

□ 三分熟
□ 五分熟
□ 七分熟
□ 全熟

---

crawl [krɔl]

動 爬

英英 move slowly forward with the body stretched out along the ground

例 There is a snake **crawling** on the floor.
這裡有一條蛇在地板上爬。

□ 三分熟
□ 五分熟
□ 七分熟
□ 全熟

---

cre·a·tive
[krɪˋetɪv]

形 有創造力的
同 imaginative 有創造力的

英英 involving the use of the imagination or original and usual ideas in order to produce something

例 The students in Taiwan are **creative**.
臺灣的學生很有創造力。

□ 三分熟
□ 五分熟
□ 七分熟
□ 全熟

---

cre·a·tor [krɪˋetɚ]

名 創造者、創作家

英英 a person who creates something special

例 The **creator** of the robot found it problematic now.
這機器人的創造者現在發現它有很多問題。

□ 三分熟
□ 五分熟
□ 七分熟
□ 全熟

---

crea·ture [ˋkritʃɚ]

名 生物、動物

英英 a living thing, such as plants or animals in particular

例 All **creatures** are equal.
所有生物都是一樣的。

□ 三分熟
□ 五分熟
□ 七分熟
□ 全熟

---

cred·it [ˋkrɛdɪt]

名 信用、信託
動 相信、信賴
同 faith 信任
片 to one's credit
　　承認某人的功勞

英英 the facility of being able to receive goods or services before payment, based on the trust that payment will be made in the future

例 I will pay by **credit** card.
我要用信用卡支付。

□ 三分熟
□ 五分熟
□ 七分熟
□ 全熟

---

creep [krip]

動 爬、戰慄

英英 move slowly and carefully, especially in order to avoid being noticed

例 The cockroach **creeps** on my desk.
這蟑螂在我桌上爬。

□ 三分熟
□ 五分熟
□ 七分熟
□ 全熟

---

crew [kru]

名 夥伴們、全體船員

英英 a group of people who work and operate on a ship, boat, aircraft, or train, or give the service on a plant

例 Our **crew** will help you with that.
我們的夥伴會協助你。

☐ 三分熟
☐ 五分熟
☐ 七分熟
☐ 全熟

---

crick·et [ˈkrɪkɪt]

名 蟋蟀

英英 a brown or black insect related to the grasshoppers but with shorter legs, which makes short loud noises

例 I found a **cricket** on the leaf.
我在葉子上找到蟋蟀。

☐ 三分熟
☐ 五分熟
☐ 七分熟
☐ 全熟

---

crim·i·nal

[ˈkrɪmənl̩]

形 犯罪的
名 罪犯

英英 guilty of; a person who committs a crime

例 The motivation of the **criminal** makes him forgivable.
這罪犯的犯案動機讓他變得情由可原了。

☐ 三分熟
☐ 五分熟
☐ 七分熟
☐ 全熟

---

crisp/crisp·y

[krɪsp]/[ˈkrɪspɪ]

形 脆的、清楚的

英英 descirbe the weather is cool or fresh or describe sound or view is very clear

例 The cookies are **crispy**.
餅乾很脆。

☐ 三分熟
☐ 五分熟
☐ 七分熟
☐ 全熟

---

crown [kraʊn]

名 王冠
動 加冕、酬報
同 reward 酬報

英英 a circular decoration for the head, usually made of gold and jewels, and worn by a king or queen at official ceremonies

例 Have you ever seen the **crown** of our country?
你有沒有看過我們國家的王冠？

☐ 三分熟
☐ 五分熟
☐ 七分熟
☐ 全熟

---

crun·chy [ˈkrʌntʃɪ]

名 鬆脆的、易裂的

英英 describe food that is firm and making a crunching noise when bitten or crushed

例 The dessert is **crunchy**.
這種甜點是鬆脆的。

☐ 三分熟
☐ 五分熟
☐ 七分熟
☐ 全熟

---

crutch [krʌtʃ]

名 支架、拐杖

英英 a long stick with a crosspiece at the top usually used for supporting a lame person

例 My grandfather needs a **crutch**.
我爺爺需要一支拐杖。

☐ 三分熟
☐ 五分熟
☐ 七分熟
☐ 全熟

---

cul·tu·ral

[ˈkʌltʃərəl]

形 文化的

英英 relating to the culture or beilef of a society; relating to the arts, music or intellectual achievements

例 Gender unequality can be a **cultural** issue.
性別不平等可以說是一種文化的議題。

☐ 三分熟
☐ 五分熟
☐ 七分熟
☐ 全熟

D

cup·board

[ˈkʌbəd]

名 食櫥、餐具櫥

英英 a piece of furniture or small recess with a door or doors and usually shelves, used for storage

例 I got the cup from the **cupboard**.
我從廚櫃拿出一個杯子。

☐ 三分熟
☐ 五分熟
☐ 七分熟
☐ 全熟

cur·rent [ˈkɜnt]

形 流通的、目前的
名 電流、水流
同 present 目前的

英英 not fixed; flowing freely;, happening or being used or done now

例 This project is not proper for **current** situation.
這計劃不適合現在的情況。

☐ 三分熟
☐ 五分熟
☐ 七分熟
☐ 全熟

cy·cle [ˈsaɪkl̩]

名 週期、循環
動 循環、騎腳踏車

英英 a series of events that are regularly repeated in the same or particular order

例 I ride a **cycle** to school every day.
我每天騎腳踏車上學。

☐ 三分熟
☐ 五分熟
☐ 七分熟
☐ 全熟

Dd

dair·y [ˈdɛrɪ]

名 酪農場
形 酪農的、牛奶製的

英英 a place on the farm for the processing and distribution of milk and milk products

例 **Dairy** is important for western diet.
乳製品對西方飲食來説是很重要的。

☐ 三分熟
☐ 五分熟
☐ 七分熟
☐ 全熟

dam [dæm]

名 水壩
動 堵住、阻塞

英英 a barrier constructed across a river to collect water, in order to form a reservoir and provide water for an area; to confine the water of

例 The water in the **dam** must be clean.
水壩中的水一定要是清澈的。

☐ 三分熟
☐ 五分熟
☐ 七分熟
☐ 全熟

dare [dɛr]

動 敢、挑戰
同 brave 勇敢的面對

英英 have the courage to do something difficult

例 **Dare** you tell him the truth?
你敢跟他説實話嗎？

☐ 三分熟
☐ 五分熟
☐ 七分熟
☐ 全熟

darl·ing [ˈdɑrlɪŋ]

名 親愛的人
形 可愛的
同 lovely 可愛的

英英 a person who is adored or loved

例 My **darling**, go to bed now.
親愛的，現在該上床睡覺了。

☐ 三分熟
☐ 五分熟
☐ 七分熟
☐ 全熟

dash [dæʃ]

動 碰撞、投擲

英英 to move, run or travel in a great hurry

例 I **dashed** a die.
我擲骰子。

☐ 三分熟
☐ 五分熟
☐ 七分熟
☐ 全熟

deaf·en [ˈdɛfən]

動 使耳聾

英英 cause to become deaf and unable to hear the other sounds near you

例 The music is so loud that it **deafens** me!
音樂太大聲讓我都要聾了！

□ 三分熟
□ 五分熟
□ 七分熟
□ 全熟

---

deal·er [ˈdilɚ]

名 商人
同 merchant 商人

英英 a person who purchases and sells goods

例 The **dealer** might deceive you.
這商人可能騙了你。

□ 三分熟
□ 五分熟
□ 七分熟
□ 全熟

---

dec·ade [ˈdɛked]

名 十年、十個一組

英英 a period of ten years

例 I have known him for a **decade**.
我認識他十年了。

□ 三分熟
□ 五分熟
□ 七分熟
□ 全熟

---

deck [dɛk]

名 甲板

英英 a floor of a ship for walking on, especially the upper level

例 The sailor stands on the **deck**.
這船員站在甲板上。

□ 三分熟
□ 五分熟
□ 七分熟
□ 全熟

---

deed [did]

名 行為、行動

英英 an action or behaviour that is performed intentionally

例 His **deed** is not forgivable.
他的行為是不可原諒的。

□ 三分熟
□ 五分熟
□ 七分熟
□ 全熟

---

deep·en [ˈdipən]

動 加深、變深

英英 make something deeper; become deep

例 The problem **deepens** their misunderstanding.
這問題加深他們的誤會。

□ 三分熟
□ 五分熟
□ 七分熟
□ 全熟

---

de·fine [dɪˈfaɪn]

動 下定義

英英 give the meaning or definition of a word or phrase

例 It depends on how you **define** a hero.
這取決於你如何定義英雄。

□ 三分熟
□ 五分熟
□ 七分熟
□ 全熟

---

def·i·ni·tion
[ˌdɛfəˈnɪʃən]

名 定義

英英 a statement of the exact meaning of a word or phrase

例 Your **definition** on this term is not clear.
你對這專有名詞的定義不夠明確。

□ 三分熟
□ 五分熟
□ 七分熟
□ 全熟

---

de·liv·er·y
[dɪˈlɪvərɪ]

名 傳送、傳遞
同 distribution
分配、分發

英英 the action of delivering or transferring something, especially letters or goods

例 I want to check the **delivery** of my goods.
我要確認我的商品的輸送。

□ 三分熟
□ 五分熟
□ 七分熟
□ 全熟

D

---

de·moc·ra·cy

[dəˋmɑkrəsɪ]

名 民主制度

英英 a form of government is based on the belief in freedom, in which the people have a voice in the exercise of power

例 The **democracy** of this country needs some improvement.
這國家的民主制度尚須努力。

---

de·moc·ra·tic

[ˌdɛməˋkrætɪk]

形 民主的

英英 relating to or based on democracy

例 Is it a **democratic** country?
這是民主國家嗎？

---

de·pos·it [dɪˋpɑzɪt]

名 押金、存款
動 存入、放入

英英 a sum of money or something valuable put in a bank or other account

例 You need to pay the **deposit**.
你需要付押金。

---

de·scrip·tion

[dɪˋskrɪpʃən]

名 敘述、說明
同 portrait 描寫

英英 the process of describing something

例 Your **description** is clear enough.
你的描述很清楚。

---

de·sign·er

[dɪˋzaɪnɚ]

名 設計師

英英 a person who designs things or goods

例 The dress is made by one of the best **designers**.
這件洋裝是最好的設計師做的。

---

de·sir·a·ble

[dɪˋzaɪrəbl]

形 值得嚮往的、稱心如意的

英英 very attractive, useful, or necessary

例 The gift is **desirable**.
這禮物很讓人渴望。

---

de·stroy [dɪˋstrɔɪ]

動 損毀、毀壞
反 create 創造

英英 to damage or attack something very badly that cannot be used

例 The city was **destroyed** by an earthquake.
這座城市在一場地震中摧毀了。

---

de·tail [ˋditel]

名 細節、條款

英英 small individual items or facts collectively

例 Please tell me the **details** of the activity.
請告訴我這活動的細節。

🎧 **Track 033**

---

de·ter·mine

[dɪ`tɝmɪn]

動 決定
同 decide 決定

英英 to decide to do something very firmly

例 You efforts **determine** if you will succeed.
你的努力決定你會不會成功。

☐ 三分熟
☐ 五分熟
☐ 七分熟
☐ 全熟

---

dev·il [`dɛvl]

名 魔鬼、惡魔

英英 an evil spirit; an evil being

例 You used to be like an angel, but now **devil**.
你曾經像個天使，但現在是惡魔。

☐ 三分熟
☐ 五分熟
☐ 七分熟
☐ 全熟

---

di·a·logue

[`daɪə͵lɔg]

名 對話
同 conversation 對話

英英 talks between two or more people as a feature of a book, play, or film

例 In their **dialogue**, they show great affection to each other.
從他們的對話中，可以看出來他們對彼此很有興趣。

☐ 三分熟
☐ 五分熟
☐ 七分熟
☐ 全熟

---

diet [`daɪət]

名 飲食
動 節食
片 on a diet 節食

英英 the kinds of food or drink that a person, animal, or community habitually eats or drinks; prescribed course of food taken to lose weight

例 Salad is common in American **diet**.
沙拉在美式的飲食很常見。

☐ 三分熟
☐ 五分熟
☐ 七分熟
☐ 全熟

---

dil·i·gent

[`dɪlədʒənt]

形 勤勉的、勤奮的

英英 careful and conscientious in a task or work on something with a lot of effort

例 The **diligent** boy finally won the champion.
那勤奮的男孩最終得到了冠軍。

☐ 三分熟
☐ 五分熟
☐ 七分熟
☐ 全熟

---

dim [dɪm]

形 微暗的
動 變模糊

英英 not very brightly or clearly, with a little dark

例 The child doesn't want to go into the **dim** room.
那孩子不願意走進去那微暗的房間。

☐ 三分熟
☐ 五分熟
☐ 七分熟
☐ 全熟

---

dime [daɪm]

名 一角的硬幣

英英 a ten-cent coin

例 I gave the beggar a **dime**.
我給了那乞丐一角硬幣。

☐ 三分熟
☐ 五分熟
☐ 七分熟
☐ 全熟

---

dine [daɪn]

動 款待、用膳

英英 eat dinner or the main meal of the day

例 We will **dine** in the dinning room.
我們在餐廳用膳。

☐ 三分熟
☐ 五分熟
☐ 七分熟
☐ 全熟

D

dip [dɪp]

動 浸、沾
名 浸泡、（價格）下跌

英英 to sink, drop, or slope downward; to put something into a liquid

例 The clothes are **dipped** in the water.
衣物都浸到水裡面。

□ 三分熟
□ 五分熟
□ 七分熟
□ 全熟

dirt [dɜt]

名 泥土、塵埃
片 dirt road 泥土路

英英 a substance that causes uncleanliness, such as dust or soil

例 The book is covered with **dirt**.
這本書被塵埃覆蓋住了。

□ 三分熟
□ 五分熟
□ 七分熟
□ 全熟

dis·ap·point

[ˌdɪsəˈpɔɪnt]

動 使失望

英英 fail to fulfill the hopes or wishes on something or someone

例 His achievement never **disappoints** his parents.
他的成就從不會讓他父母失望。

□ 三分熟
□ 五分熟
□ 七分熟
□ 全熟

dis·ap·point·ment

[ˌdɪsəˈpɔɪntmənt]

名 令人失望的舉止

英英 the feeling of being disappointed

例 I saw **disappointment** in her eyes.
我從她的眼中看到失望。

□ 三分熟
□ 五分熟
□ 七分熟
□ 全熟

**disco/
dis·co·theque**

[ˈdɪsko]/[ˌdɪskəˈtɛk]

名 迪斯可、酒吧、小舞廳

英英 a club or party at which people dance to pop or modren recorded music

例 Would you like to go to the **disco** tonight?
你今天想要去迪斯可嗎？

□ 三分熟
□ 五分熟
□ 七分熟
□ 全熟

dis·count

[ˈdɪskaʊnt]

名 折扣
動 減價

英英 a deduction from the usual price of something

例 May I have a **discount**?
可以給我打折嗎？

□ 三分熟
□ 五分熟
□ 七分熟
□ 全熟

dis·cov·er·y

[dɪˈskʌvərɪ]

名 發現

英英 the action or process of discovering or finding out

例 The **discovery** of this planet influenced science a lot.
發現這顆行星對科學的影響很大。

□ 三分熟
□ 五分熟
□ 七分熟
□ 全熟

dis·ease [dɪˈziz]

名 疾病、病症

英英 the action or process of discovering or finding out

例 Is the **disease** curable?
這疾病是可以治癒的嗎？

□ 三分熟
□ 五分熟
□ 七分熟
□ 全熟

Track 035

disk/disc [dɪsk]

名 唱片、碟片、圓盤狀的東西

英英 a flat, round object; an information storage device for a computer

例 The **disk** goes with the book.
這張光碟片附在書後。

- 三分熟
- 五分熟
- 七分熟
- 全熟

---

dis·like [dɪsˈlaɪk]

動 討厭、不喜歡
名 反感

英英 to feel distaste on something or someone

例 The girl **dislikes** her mother.
這小女孩不喜歡她媽媽。

- 三分熟
- 五分熟
- 七分熟
- 全熟

---

ditch [dɪtʃ]

名 排水溝、水道
動 挖溝、拋棄
同 trench 溝、溝渠

英英 a long narrow channel dug to hold or carry water; to make a trench

例 The bike fell into the **ditch**.
這腳踏車掉入水溝裡了。

- 三分熟
- 五分熟
- 七分熟
- 全熟

---

dive [daɪv]

動 跳水
名 垂直降落
片 go diving 潛水

英英 jump into a deeper level in water; to swim down under water using breathing equipment

例 We went to Kenting to go **diving**.
我們去墾丁潛水。

- 三分熟
- 五分熟
- 七分熟
- 全熟

---

dock [dɑk]

名 船塢、碼頭
動 裁減、停泊
同 anchor 停泊

英英 an enclosed area of water in a port for putting goods onto or repair of ships; to arrive at a pier

例 Jack met Rose on the **dock**.
傑克是在碼頭遇見蘿絲的。

- 三分熟
- 五分熟
- 七分熟
- 全熟

---

dodge [dɑdʒ]

動 閃開、躲開
同 avoid 躲開

英英 avoid by a sudden quick movement or avoid being hit by something suddenly moves toward quickly

例 I don't like to play **dodge** ball.
我不喜歡玩躲避球。

- 三分熟
- 五分熟
- 七分熟
- 全熟

---

do·mes·tic

[dəˈmɛstɪk]

形 國內的、家務的

英英 relating to a family or country affairs

例 Is it for **domestic** lines?
這是國內航班的嗎？

- 三分熟
- 五分熟
- 七分熟
- 全熟

---

dose [dos]

名 一劑（藥）、藥量
動 服藥

英英 a measured amount of a medicine or drug taken at one time

例 Give him a **dose** of opium.
給他一劑麻醉劑。

- 三分熟
- 五分熟
- 七分熟
- 全熟

D

doubt·ful [ˋdaʊtfəl]

形 有疑問的、可疑的

英英 uncertain about something; not known with certainty

例 This answer is **doubtful**.
這答案很可疑。

□三分熟
□五分熟
□七分熟
□全熟

---

drain [dren]

動 排出、流出、喝乾
名 排水管
同 dry 乾

英英 cause the liquid to run out or flow away

例 The factory **drained** lots of pollution.
這工廠排放很多污染。

□三分熟
□五分熟
□七分熟
□全熟

---

dra·mat·ic

[drəˋmætɪk]

形 戲劇性的
同 theatrical 戲劇性的

英英 relating to drama or acting; very sudden and striking

例 Life is always more **dramatic** than novel.
生活往往比小說更具有戲劇性。

□三分熟
□五分熟
□七分熟
□全熟

---

drip [drɪp]

動 滴下
名 滴、水滴
同 drop 水滴

英英 fall or let fall in drops of liquid

例 Some raindrop **drip** from the roof.
幾滴雨滴從屋頂上滴下來。

□三分熟
□五分熟
□七分熟
□全熟

---

drown [draʊn]

動 淹沒、淹死

英英 die or kill through submersion under water

例 He has been sad since his son was **drowned**.
從他的兒子被淹死之後，他總是很難過。

□三分熟
□五分熟
□七分熟
□全熟

---

drowsy [ˋdraʊzɪ]

形 沉寂的、懶洋洋的、
　 睏的
同 sleepy 睏的

英英 sleepy; between sleeping and being awake

例 I feel **drowsy** today.
我今天覺得懶洋洋的。

□三分熟
□五分熟
□七分熟
□全熟

---

drunk [drʌŋk]

形 酒醉的、著迷的
名 酒宴、醉漢

英英 unable to speak or act in the usual way because being affected by drinking too much alcohol

例 The man was too **drunk** to know what had been going on.
這男人喝太醉，都不知道發生什麼事。

□三分熟
□五分熟
□七分熟
□全熟

---

due [dju]

形 預定的
名 應付款、應得的東西
片 due to 因為……

英英 expected something to happen or planned for a certain time

例 When's the **due** time?
預定的時間是什麼時候？

□三分熟
□五分熟
□七分熟
□全熟

🎧 **Track 037**

dump [dʌmp]

動 拋下
名 垃圾場
片 dump truck 翻斗卡車

英英 a site for collecting rubbish or waste; to drop something with carelessness

例 He was **dumped** last month.
他上個月剛被甩了。

☐ 三分熟
☐ 五分熟
☐ 七分熟
☐ 全熟

dust [dʌst]

名 灰塵、灰
動 打掃、拂去灰塵
同 dirt 灰塵

英英 dry powder consisting of tiny particles of soil, sand or other substances

例 I am allergic to **dust**.
我對灰塵過敏。

☐ 三分熟
☐ 五分熟
☐ 七分熟
☐ 全熟

Ee

ea·ger [ˈigɚ]

形 渴望的

英英 keenly or strongly wanting to do or have something

例 I am **eager** to know the answer.
我很渴望知道答案。

☐ 三分熟
☐ 五分熟
☐ 七分熟
☐ 全熟

earn·ings [ˈɛnɪŋz]

名 收入
同 salary 薪水

英英 money or income paid for the work they do

例 Don't ask him about his **earnings**.
不要問他收入。

☐ 三分熟
☐ 五分熟
☐ 七分熟
☐ 全熟

ech·o [ˈɛko]

名 回音
動 發出回聲

英英 a sound that is reflected back from a wall or cliff

例 You can hear the **echo** in the valley.
你可以在山谷間聽到回音。

☐ 三分熟
☐ 五分熟
☐ 七分熟
☐ 全熟

ed·it [ˈɛdɪt]

動 編輯、發行

英英 prepare a film or text for publication by correcting, condensing, or modifying it

例 You can **edit** your file here.
你可以在這裡編輯文件。

☐ 三分熟
☐ 五分熟
☐ 七分熟
☐ 全熟

e·di·tion [ɪˈdɪʃən]

名 版本

英英 the form in which a book or newspaper is published

例 It is the first **edition**.
這是第一個版本。

☐ 三分熟
☐ 五分熟
☐ 七分熟
☐ 全熟

ed·i·tor [ˈɛdɪtɚ]

名 編輯者

英英 a person who modifies or corrects the text of newspaper or magazine and decides what should be included

例 Who's the **editor** of this book?
這本書的編輯者是誰？

☐ 三分熟
☐ 五分熟
☐ 七分熟
☐ 全熟

E

ed·u·cate

[ˈɛdʒəˌket]

動 教育
同 teach 教導

英英 to give intellectual and moral instruction to; to teach someone, usually with a formal system, such as a school

例 He **educated** his son to be honest.
他教育他的兒子要誠實。

☐ 三分熟
☐ 五分熟
☐ 七分熟
☐ 全熟

ed·u·ca·tion·al

[ˌɛdʒəˈkeʃənļ]

形 教育性的

英英 connected with education; relating to education

例 This museum is very **educational**.
這個博物館很有教育意義。

☐ 三分熟
☐ 五分熟
☐ 七分熟
☐ 全熟

ef·fi·cient

[ɪˈfɪʃənt]

形 有效率的

英英 working very productively and quickly with minimum wasted effort or expense

例 My boss asked me to be more **efficient**.
我的老闆要我更有效率。

☐ 三分熟
☐ 五分熟
☐ 七分熟
☐ 全熟

el·bow [ˈɛlˌbo]

名 手肘

英英 the joint in the arms where it bends in the middle

例 Her **elbow** was hurt.
她的手肘受傷了。

☐ 三分熟
☐ 五分熟
☐ 七分熟
☐ 全熟

eld·er·ly [ˈɛldəlɪ]

形 上了年紀的
同 old 老的

英英 old or ageing

例 Please yield your seat to the **elderly**.
請把座位讓給上了年紀的人。

☐ 三分熟
☐ 五分熟
☐ 七分熟
☐ 全熟

election [ɪˈlɛkʃən]

名 選舉
片 presidential election
總統大選

英英 voting for someone in order to choose a person or a group of people for a position, especially a political position

例 Who will win the **election**?
誰會贏得這次的選舉？

☐ 三分熟
☐ 五分熟
☐ 七分熟
☐ 全熟

e·lec·tric/ e·lec·tri·cal

[ɪˈlɛktrɪk]/[ɪˈlɛktrɪkļ]

形 電的

英英 connected with electricity or using or producing electricity for power

例 Is this device **electric**?
這裝置有電嗎？

☐ 三分熟
☐ 五分熟
☐ 七分熟
☐ 全熟

e·lec·tric·i·ty

[ɪlɛkˈtrɪsətɪ]

名 電

英英 a form of energy resulting from the existence of electrons, which provides devices that create light and heat

例 **Electricity** has changed human life.
電改變了人的生活。

☐ 三分熟
☐ 五分熟
☐ 七分熟
☐ 全熟

🎧 **Track 039**

e·lec·tron·ic
[ɪˋlɛkˋtrɑnɪk]

形 電子的
片 electronic device
電子產品

英英 using many small parts, such as microchips, that control and involve a small electric current

例 This cell phone is a charming **electronic** device.
這手機是個很迷人的電子用品。

☐ 三分熟
☐ 五分熟
☐ 七分熟
☐ 全熟

e·mer·gen·cy
[ɪˋmɛdʒənsɪ]

名 緊急情況
同 crisis 危機

英英 a sudden serious and urgent event or situation, such as unexpected accidents

例 Please write down your phone number just in case of any **emergency**.
請寫下你的電話，以免有任何緊急狀況。

☐ 三分熟
☐ 五分熟
☐ 七分熟
☐ 全熟

em·per·or
[ˋɛmpərɚ]

名 皇帝
同 sovereign 君主、元首

英英 the main ruler of an empire

例 The **emperor** is famous for his wits.
這皇帝以他的機智聞名。

☐ 三分熟
☐ 五分熟
☐ 七分熟
☐ 全熟

em·pha·size
[ˋɛmfəˏsaɪz]

動 強調
同 stress 強調

英英 to give special importance or attention to something

例 The manager **emphasized** the importance of this project.
經理強調這個計劃的重要性。

☐ 三分熟
☐ 五分熟
☐ 七分熟
☐ 全熟

em·ploy [ɪmˋplɔɪ]

動 從事、雇用
同 hire 雇用

英英 to provide work to someone and pay them for it; hire someone to work for you

例 We decided to **employ** an assistant.
我們決定要雇用一名助理。

☐ 三分熟
☐ 五分熟
☐ 七分熟
☐ 全熟

em·ploy·ment
[ɪmˋplɔɪmənt]

名 職業；受僱

英英 when someone earns money by working for a company

例 He found **employment** as a cook.
他找了一份廚師的工作。

☐ 三分熟
☐ 五分熟
☐ 七分熟
☐ 全熟

em·ploy·ee
[ˋɛmplɔɪˋi]

名 從業人員、職員
同 worker 工作人員

英英 a person who is employed for wages or salary

例 I am just an **employee** of the company.
我只是這家公司的職員而已。

☐ 三分熟
☐ 五分熟
☐ 七分熟
☐ 全熟

E

em·ploy·er
[ɪmˋplɔɪɚ]

名 老闆、雇主
同 boss 老闆

英英 a person or company that pays someone to work for them

例 Everyone in the company hates his **employer**.
這家公司的每個人都討厭他們的老闆。

☐ 三分熟
☐ 五分熟
☐ 七分熟
☐ 全熟

emp·ty [ˋɛmptɪ]

形 空的
動 倒空
同 vacant 空的

英英 without any people or things

例 Give me the **empty** box.
給我空的箱子。

☐ 三分熟
☐ 五分熟
☐ 七分熟
☐ 全熟

en·a·ble [ɪnˋebl̩]

動 使能夠

英英 to give effort with ability or means to do something

例 The oil will **enable** the machine to work.
加點油可以使這臺機器運作。

☐ 三分熟
☐ 五分熟
☐ 七分熟
☐ 全熟

en·er·ge·tic
[ˌɛnɚˋdʒɛtɪk]

形 有精力的
同 vigorous 精力旺盛的

英英 showing or involving a lot of energy or activity

例 Parents always feel their babies are too **energetic** at night.
父母總是覺得他們的小孩晚上還是太精力充沛了。

☐ 三分熟
☐ 五分熟
☐ 七分熟
☐ 全熟

en·gage [ɪnˋgedʒ]

動 雇用、允諾、訂婚
片 be engaged with
    跟……訂婚

英英 to give promise to someone; to hire or employ someone

例 I will be **engaged** with my girlfriend.
我將要跟我女朋友訂婚。

☐ 三分熟
☐ 五分熟
☐ 七分熟
☐ 全熟

en·gage·ment
[ɪnˋgedʒmənt]

名 預約、訂婚

英英 an agreement to married couples

例 The **engagement** makes him panic with regrets.
他們的婚約讓他後悔而焦慮。

☐ 三分熟
☐ 五分熟
☐ 七分熟
☐ 全熟

en·gine [ˋɛndʒən]

名 引擎

英英 the part of a machine that produces power to make the machine operate

例 There are some problems with the **engine**.
這臺引擎有點問題。

☐ 三分熟
☐ 五分熟
☐ 七分熟
☐ 全熟

en·gi·neer
[ˌɛndʒəˋnɪr]

名 工程師

英英 a person whose job is related to designing and building machines, roads, bridges, etc

例 **Engineers** are usually busy.
工程師通常都很忙。

☐ 三分熟
☐ 五分熟
☐ 七分熟
☐ 全熟

🎧 **Track 041**

en·joy·a·ble

[ɪnˈdʒɔɪəbl]

形 愉快的
同 delighyful 愉快的

英英 very pleasure and pleased
例 Wish you an **enjoyable** night.
祝你今晚玩得愉快。

☐ 三分熟
☐ 五分熟
☐ 七分熟
☐ 全熟

en·try [ˈɛntrɪ]

名 入口、進入

英英 a door, gate or passage where people enter a space or building
例 The weak girl's **entry** to military changes her life.
這體弱多病的女孩進入軍界後改變她的人生。

☐ 三分熟
☐ 五分熟
☐ 七分熟
☐ 全熟

en·vi·ron·men·tal

[ɪnˌvaɪrənˈmɛntl]

形 環境的

英英 connected with the environment
例 The **environmental** pollution harms our health.
環境汙染傷害我們的健康。

☐ 三分熟
☐ 五分熟
☐ 七分熟
☐ 全熟

en·vy [ˈɛnvɪ]

名 羨慕、嫉妒
動 對……羨慕
片 be the envy of 羨慕

英英 the feeling of wanting or having something in the same situation as somebody else
例 Everyone's the **envy** of his basketball skills.
大家都羨慕他的球技。

☐ 三分熟
☐ 五分熟
☐ 七分熟
☐ 全熟

e·rase [ɪˈres]

動 擦掉

英英 to remove something from something else completely
例 Would it be possible to **erase** my trauma?
我心中的創傷有可能擦拭掉嗎？

☐ 三分熟
☐ 五分熟
☐ 七分熟
☐ 全熟

es·cape [əˈskep]

動 逃走
名 逃脫
同 flee 逃走

英英 to run away from a place
例 I want to **escape** my familial duty.
我想要逃避我的家庭責任。

☐ 三分熟
☐ 五分熟
☐ 七分熟
☐ 全熟

e·vil [ˈivl]

形 邪惡的
名 邪惡

英英 people who are bad and cruel and enjoying harming others
例 You are such an **evil** businessman.
你真是邪惡的商人。

☐ 三分熟
☐ 五分熟
☐ 七分熟
☐ 全熟

ex·cel·lence

[`ɛksləns]

名 優點、傑出

英英 the quality of being good or excellent
例 Her **excellence** makes her the class leader.
她的傑出表現讓她成為班代。

□三分熟
□五分熟
□七分熟
□全熟

E

ex·change

[ɪksˋtʃendʒ]

名 交換
動 兌換、貿易

英英 an act of giving something to somebody and receiving something from somebody
例 Can I **exchange** money?
我可以換錢嗎？

□三分熟
□五分熟
□七分熟
□全熟

ex·hi·bi·tion

[ˌɛksəˋbɪʃən]

名 展覽

英英 the act of showing something, such as works of art or particular skill, to the public
例 I am going to an **exhibition** of Van Gogh.
我要去看一場梵谷的展覽。

□三分熟
□五分熟
□七分熟
□全熟

ex·is·tence

[ɪgˋzɪstəns]

名 存在

英英 the state of being real or living
例 Your **existence** makes my life perfect.
你的存在讓我的生命完美了。

□三分熟
□五分熟
□七分熟
□全熟

ex·it [`ɛgzɪt]

名 出口
動 離開
反 entrance 入口

英英 a way out of a public space or building or vehicle
例 Where's the **exit** of the cinema?
這間電影院的出口在哪裡？

□三分熟
□五分熟
□七分熟
□全熟

ex·pec·ta·tion

[ˌɛkspɛkˋteʃən]

名 期望

英英 a belief that good things will happen in the future
例 My parents' **expectation** on me makes me stressful.
我爸媽對我的期望讓我備感壓力。

□三分熟
□五分熟
□七分熟
□全熟

ex·pense

[ɪkˋspɛns]

名 費用
同 payment 付款

英英 the money that you spend on something
例 The **expense** of this trip is unaffordable.
這趟旅程的費用超過我可以負擔的。

□三分熟
□五分熟
□七分熟
□全熟

ex·per·i·ment

[ɪkˋspɛrəmənt]

名／動 實驗

英英 a scientific test that is done in order to study or discover what happens and to gain new knowledge
例 The **experiment** on animal is cruel.
動物實驗是很殘忍的。

□三分熟
□五分熟
□七分熟
□全熟

🎧 **Track 043**

ex·plode [ɪk`splod]

動 爆炸、推翻

英英 to burst something violently or break up something in pieces; causing damage

例 The bomb will **explode**.
這炸彈會爆炸。

☐ 三分熟
☐ 五分熟
☐ 七分熟
☐ 全熟

ex·port [`ɛksport]

動 輸出
名 出口貨、輸出

英英 to sell goods to another country

例 The country **exports** many dairy products.
這國家出口很多乳製品。

☐ 三分熟
☐ 五分熟
☐ 七分熟
☐ 全熟

ex·pres·sion
[ɪk`sprɛʃən]

名 表達

英英 things that people think, write, say or put into action in order to show their feelings and ideas

例 His **expression** always annoys his wife.
他的表達總是讓他妻子惱怒。

☐ 三分熟
☐ 五分熟
☐ 七分熟
☐ 全熟

ex·pres·sive
[ɪk`sprɛsɪv]

形 表達的

英英 able to show your thoughts and feelings

例 The **expressive** language is important.
表達的語言是很重要的。

☐ 三分熟
☐ 五分熟
☐ 七分熟
☐ 全熟

ex·treme
[ɪk`strim]

形 極度的
名 極端的事

英英 very great or large in degree

例 The heavy rain is an **extreme** one.
這是一場極度的大雨。

☐ 三分熟
☐ 五分熟
☐ 七分熟
☐ 全熟

Ff

fa·ble [`febl]

名 寓言
同 legend 傳說

英英 a traditional short story that teaches a moral lesson or general truth, especially one with animals as characters

例 I used to love **fable** in my childhood.
我童年時很喜歡寓言故事。

☐ 三分熟
☐ 五分熟
☐ 七分熟
☐ 全熟

fac·tor [`fæktɚ]

名 因素、要素
同 cause 原因

英英 a fact that causes or influences something

例 Tell me some **factors** of his failure.
告訴我他失敗的因素。

☐ 三分熟
☐ 五分熟
☐ 七分熟
☐ 全熟

fade [fed]

動 凋謝、變淡

英英 to become paler or less bright

例 Some flowers **fade** in autumn.
有些花在秋天凋謝。

☐ 三分熟
☐ 五分熟
☐ 七分熟
☐ 全熟

F

faint [fent]

形 暗淡的
名 昏厥

英英 not bright; the state of losing consciousness or feeling weak

例 She **fainted** in the morning.
她今天早上暈厥了。

☐ 三分熟
☐ 五分熟
☐ 七分熟
☐ 全熟

---

fair·ly [ˈfɛrlɪ]

副 相當地、公平地

英英 completely, extremely, very fair

例 It's a **fairly** good deal.
這是一個非常公平的交易。

☐ 三分熟
☐ 五分熟
☐ 七分熟
☐ 全熟

---

fair·y [ˈfɛrɪ]

名 仙子
形 神仙的
片 fairy tale 童話

英英 an imaginary creature like a small person, who has magical powers

例 I wish I could see the **fairy**.
我希望我可以看到這仙子。

☐ 三分熟
☐ 五分熟
☐ 七分熟
☐ 全熟

---

faith [feθ]

名 信任
同 trust 信任

英英 not bright; trust in somebody's ability or knowledge; trust in something or in someone without any doubts

例 Do you have **faith** in me?
你對我有信心嗎？

☐ 三分熟
☐ 五分熟
☐ 七分熟
☐ 全熟

---

fake [fek]

形 冒充的
動 仿造

英英 false; to make appear different from what it really is

例 It's just a **fake** brand.
這只是一個仿冒的牌子。

☐ 三分熟
☐ 五分熟
☐ 七分熟
☐ 全熟

---

fa·mil·iar [fəˈmɪljɚ]

形 熟悉的、親密的
片 be familiar with
　　對……熟悉

英英 well known to something or somebody

例 Are you **familiar** with this place?
你對這地方很熟悉嗎？

☐ 三分熟
☐ 五分熟
☐ 七分熟
☐ 全熟

---

fan/fa·nat·ic

[fæn]/[fəˈnætɪk]

名 狂熱者、迷（粉絲）
同 follower 跟隨者

英英 a person who admires or support somebody or something very much

例 I am not a **fan** of NBA.
我不是 NBA 的粉絲。

☐ 三分熟
☐ 五分熟
☐ 七分熟
☐ 全熟

---

fan·cy [ˈfænsɪ]

名 想像力、愛好

英英 something that you imagine or to think that something is so with your imagination

例 I have a **fancy** on this idea.
我很喜歡這主意。

☐ 三分熟
☐ 五分熟
☐ 七分熟
☐ 全熟

🎧 **Track 045**

fare [fɛr]

名 費用、運費
同 fee 費用

英英 the money that you spend on traveling by bus, plane, taxi, etc

例 What's the **fare** you would charge us?
你會跟我們索取多少費用？

☐ 三分熟
☐ 五分熟
☐ 七分熟
☐ 全熟

---

far·ther [ˈfɑrðɚ]

副 更遠地
形 更遠的
同 further 更遠的

英英 to a greater distance in space or time

例 Can you see the **farther** place?
你可以看到更遠的地方嗎？

☐ 三分熟
☐ 五分熟
☐ 七分熟
☐ 全熟

---

fash·ion [ˈfæʃən]

名 時髦、流行
同 style 時髦

英英 a popular style of clothes or hair at a particular period of time or place

例 What you can't understand is **fashion**.
你看不懂的東西就是時尚。

☐ 三分熟
☐ 五分熟
☐ 七分熟
☐ 全熟

---

fash·ion·a·ble
[ˈfæʃənəbl]

形 流行的、時髦的

英英 following a wearing or hair style that is popular at a particular time

例 Do you think her hat **fashionable**?
你覺得她的帽子很時髦嗎？

☐ 三分熟
☐ 五分熟
☐ 七分熟
☐ 全熟

---

fas·ten [ˈfæsn̩]

動 緊固、繫緊

英英 to fix or join together the two parts of something; to tie up tightly

例 Please **fasten** the seat belt.
請繫上安全帶。

☐ 三分熟
☐ 五分熟
☐ 七分熟
☐ 全熟

---

fate [fet]

名 命運、宿命

英英 the power that determines events; destiny

例 The ancient Greek believed that they couldn't change their **fate**.
古希臘人相信他們無法改變宿命。

☐ 三分熟
☐ 五分熟
☐ 七分熟
☐ 全熟

---

fau·cet/tap
[ˈfɔsɪt]/[tæp]

名 水龍頭
片 tap water 生飲水

英英 a device that controls the flow of liquid from a pipe

例 May I have some **tap** water?
可以給我一點生飲水嗎？

☐ 三分熟
☐ 五分熟
☐ 七分熟
☐ 全熟

---

fax [fæks]

名 傳真

英英 a document made by electronic scanning and transmitted through telephone line and printed on paper

例 We don't have any **fax** in the office.
我們辦公室沒有傳真。

☐ 三分熟
☐ 五分熟
☐ 七分熟
☐ 全熟

F

feath·er [ˈfɛðɚ]
名 羽毛、裝飾

英英 one of the many soft light parts which covers a bird's body

例 I am cleaning the **feathers** in the cage.
我在清理鳥籠中的羽毛。

☐ 三分熟
☐ 五分熟
☐ 七分熟
☐ 全熟

fea·ture [ˈfitʃɚ]
名 特徵、特色

英英 important part of something; interesting or typical of a place or thing

例 He has the **features** of a hero.
他有英雄的特徵。

☐ 三分熟
☐ 五分熟
☐ 七分熟
☐ 全熟

file [faɪl]
名 檔案
動 存檔、歸檔

英英 a folder or box for keeping written records or documents together and in order

例 They are **filing** for divorce.
他們正在申請離婚。

☐ 三分熟
☐ 五分熟
☐ 七分熟
☐ 全熟

fire·work
[ˈfaɪrˌwok]
名 煙火

英英 a small device containing explosive chemicals and produces bright colored lights and loud noises

例 The **fireworks** of New Year are fascinating.
新年的煙火非常漂亮。

☐ 三分熟
☐ 五分熟
☐ 七分熟
☐ 全熟

fist [fɪst]
名 拳頭、拳打、緊握

英英 a hand when it is tightly closed with the fingers and thumb bent into the palm

例 He gave him a **fist**.
他給他一拳。

☐ 三分熟
☐ 五分熟
☐ 七分熟
☐ 全熟

flame [flem]
名 火焰
動 燃燒

英英 a hot yellow light of burning gas that comes from something that is on fire

例 Did you see the **flame** in her eyes?
你看到她眼裡的火焰嗎？

☐ 三分熟
☐ 五分熟
☐ 七分熟
☐ 全熟

fla·vor [ˈflevɚ]
名 味道、風味
動 添情趣、添風味

英英 the taste of a food or drink

例 Mucha is my favorite **flavor**.
抹茶是我最愛的口味。

☐ 三分熟
☐ 五分熟
☐ 七分熟
☐ 全熟

flea [fli]
名 跳蚤

英英 a very tiny jumping insect without wings, that sucks human's or animals' blood

例 There are **fleas** on the stray dogs.
流浪狗身上有很多跳蚤。

☐ 三分熟
☐ 五分熟
☐ 七分熟
☐ 全熟

flesh [flɛʃ]
名 肉體、軀殼

英英 the soft part between the skin and bones of animal or human bodies

例 Which is more important for a relationship, **flesh** or soul?
在一段關係中，哪一個比較重要？肉體還是靈魂？

☐ 三分熟
☐ 五分熟
☐ 七分熟
☐ 全熟

🎧 **Track 047**

float [flot]

動 使漂浮

英英 to move slowly on the surface of water or in the air

例 The ice are **floating** on the soda.
冰塊在蘇打上漂浮。

☐ 三分熟
☐ 五分熟
☐ 七分熟
☐ 全熟

---

flock [flɑk]

名 禽群、人群

英英 a group of sheep, goats or birds or a group of people with the same type

例 There is a **flock** of chicken.
這裡有一群雞。

☐ 三分熟
☐ 五分熟
☐ 七分熟
☐ 全熟

---

fold [fold]

動 折疊

英英 to bend something, usually paper or fabric, so that one part lies on to another part

例 You can **fold** the chair.
你可以折疊這椅子。

☐ 三分熟
☐ 五分熟
☐ 七分熟
☐ 全熟

---

folk [fok]

名 人們
形 民間的

英英 people in general or in the same type

例 The **folk** song is popular.
這首民歌很受歡迎。

☐ 三分熟
☐ 五分熟
☐ 七分熟
☐ 全熟

---

fol·low·er [ˈfɑloɚ]

名 跟隨者、屬下

英英 a person who supports or believes a particular person or set of ideas

例 The king has some loyal **followers**.
這國王有一些忠臣的屬下。

☐ 三分熟
☐ 五分熟
☐ 七分熟
☐ 全熟

---

fond [fɑnd]

形 喜歡的
片 be fond of 喜歡

英英 feeling affection for somebody; something or someone you like very much

例 I am **fond** of you.
我喜歡你。

☐ 三分熟
☐ 五分熟
☐ 七分熟
☐ 全熟

---

fore·head/brow

[ˈfɔrˏhɛd]/[braʊ]

名 前額、額頭

英英 the flat part of the face above the eyes and below the hair

例 My girlfriend kissed my **forehead** when I slept.
當我睡著後，我女朋友親吻我的前額。

☐ 三分熟
☐ 五分熟
☐ 七分熟
☐ 全熟

---

for·ev·er [fɚˈɛvɚ]

副 永遠
同 always 永遠

英英 for good; for all time

例 This couple believes their love will last **forever**.
這對情侶相信他們的愛會永遠持續下去。

☐ 三分熟
☐ 五分熟
☐ 七分熟
☐ 全熟

---

forth [forθ]

副 向外、向前、在前方

英英 away from a place; out of a place

例 The teacher walks **forth** and pats the girl's head.
老師走向前，拍了這個小女孩的頭。

☐ 三分熟
☐ 五分熟
☐ 七分熟
☐ 全熟

F

for·tune [ˈfɔrtʃən]

名 運氣、財富
同 luck 幸運

英英 chance or luck which affects people's lives

例 It's a good **fortune** to be liked by somebody like you.
能被像你這樣的大人物喜歡，是何等的幸運。

☐ 三分熟
☐ 五分熟
☐ 七分熟
☐ 全熟

---

found [faʊnd]

動 建立、打基礎
同 establish 建立

英英 to establish a support in the ground for a building or road

例 He **founded** a company.
他創立了一家公司。

☐ 三分熟
☐ 五分熟
☐ 七分熟
☐ 全熟

---

foun·tain [ˈfaʊntn̩]

名 噴泉、噴水池

英英 a structure from which water is forced up into the air through a small hole, usually set in the garden or park

例 The **fountain** in the garden of Versailles is splendid.
凡爾賽宮的噴泉十分驚人。

☐ 三分熟
☐ 五分熟
☐ 七分熟
☐ 全熟

---

freeze [friz]

動 凍結

英英 to become hard, and often turn to ice because of low temperature

例 I was **frozen** when I heard the truth.
當我知道真相時，整個人凍結了。

☐ 三分熟
☐ 五分熟
☐ 七分熟
☐ 全熟

---

fre·quent
[ˈfrikwənt]

形 常有的、頻繁的
同 regular 經常的

英英 happening often; very common or usual

例 It's just a **frequent** problem.
這只是個常見的問題。

☐ 三分熟
☐ 五分熟
☐ 七分熟
☐ 全熟

---

friend·ship
[ˈfrɛndʃɪp]

名 友誼、友情

英英 a relationship between friends

例 Our **friendship** has lasted more than a decade.
我們的友情超過十年了。

☐ 三分熟
☐ 五分熟
☐ 七分熟
☐ 全熟

---

frus·trate
[ˈfrʌstret]

動 使受挫、擊敗
同 defeat 擊敗

英英 to make somebody feel annoyed or mad because they are not able to achieve what they want

例 I was **frustrated** by my grades.
我因為我的成績感到沮喪。

☐ 三分熟
☐ 五分熟
☐ 七分熟
☐ 全熟

---

fry [ˈfraɪ]

動 油炸、炸

英英 to cook something in hot oil to make food rich

例 I love **fried** dumplings.
我喜歡鍋貼。

☐ 三分熟
☐ 五分熟
☐ 七分熟
☐ 全熟

fund [fʌnd]

名 資金、財源
動 投資、儲蓄

英英 a sum of money that is saved or made available for a particular purpose

例 You need to have enough **fund** to invest.
你需要有足夠的資金才能投資。

☐ 三分熟
☐ 五分熟
☐ 七分熟
☐ 全熟

---

fur [fʊ]

名 毛皮、軟皮

英英 the soft thick mass of hair that grows on the body of some animals to cover their bodies

例 The **fur** of the rabbit is soft.
兔毛很柔軟。

☐ 三分熟
☐ 五分熟
☐ 七分熟
☐ 全熟

---

fur·ni·ture

[ˈfʊnɪtʃɚ]

名 家具、設備

英英 objects that can be moved in a house or work place, such as tables, chairs and beds

例 The style of the **furniture** shows the personality of the host.
這家具風格嶄露了主人的性格。

☐ 三分熟
☐ 五分熟
☐ 七分熟
☐ 全熟

Gg

gal·lon [ˈgælən]

名 加侖

英英 a unit of measuring volume for liquid, equal to eight pints

例 I want to add some **gallons** of gas.
我想要加幾加侖的油。

☐ 三分熟
☐ 五分熟
☐ 七分熟
☐ 全熟

---

gam·ble [ˈgæmbl̩]

動 賭博
名 賭博、投機
同 bet 打賭

英英 to bet on money or play games of chance for money

例 **Gambling** is a bad habit.
賭博是不好的嗜好。

☐ 三分熟
☐ 五分熟
☐ 七分熟
☐ 全熟

---

gang [gæŋ]

名 一隊（工人）、
一群（囚犯）

英英 an organized group of criminals or workers

例 A **gang** of labors dug the cave.
一群勞工挖掘山洞。

☐ 三分熟
☐ 五分熟
☐ 七分熟
☐ 全熟

---

gap [gæp]

名 差距、缺口
片 generation gap
代溝

英英 a space between two things or in the middle of something; a part which is missing

例 There is a generation **gap** between us.
我們之間有代溝。

☐ 三分熟
☐ 五分熟
☐ 七分熟
☐ 全熟

G

gar·lic [ˈɡɑrlɪk]

名 蒜

英英 a strong-smelling pungent-tasting plant of the onion family, which is used to add flavour while cooking

例 **Garlic** is essential for many Chinese dishes.
對於很多中式料理而言，蒜是不可或缺的。

☐ 三分熟
☐ 五分熟
☐ 七分熟
☐ 全熟

---

gas·o·line/ gas·o·lene/gas

[ˈɡæsḷˌin]/[ˌɡæsḷˈin]/[ɡæs]

名 汽油
同 petroleum 石油

英英 petrol or liquid fuel

例 We are running out of **gasoline**.
我們快要沒有汽油了。

☐ 三分熟
☐ 五分熟
☐ 七分熟
☐ 全熟

---

ges·ture [ˈdʒɛstʃɚ]

名 手勢、姿勢
動 打手勢
片 make a gesture
打手勢

英英 a movement made with your hands, your head or your face to express your feelings

例 When I make a **gesture**, please come to help me.
當我對你比手勢時，請來幫我。

☐ 三分熟
☐ 五分熟
☐ 七分熟
☐ 全熟

---

glance [ɡlæns]

動 瞥視、看一下
名 一瞥
同 glimpse 瞥見

英英 take a brief look in hurry

例 Would you have a **glance** at my work?
可以請你看一下我的作品嗎？

☐ 三分熟
☐ 五分熟
☐ 七分熟
☐ 全熟

---

glob·al [ˈɡlobḷ]

形 球狀的、全球的

英英 relating to the whole world; worldwide

例 **Global** warming is a big problem.
全球暖化是個大問題。

☐ 三分熟
☐ 五分熟
☐ 七分熟
☐ 全熟

---

glo·ry [ˈɡlorɪ]

名 榮耀、光榮
動 洋洋得意

英英 honor won by notable achievements or something you've done successfully

例 They fight for **glory**.
他們為了光榮而戰。

☐ 三分熟
☐ 五分熟
☐ 七分熟
☐ 全熟

---

glow [ɡlo]

動 熾熱、發光
名 白熱光
同 blaze 光輝

英英 give out steady light or heat without flame

例 People at the age were astonished to see the bulb **glow**.
當時人們看到白熾燈發亮十分意外。

☐ 三分熟
☐ 五分熟
☐ 七分熟
☐ 全熟

🎧 **Track 051**

gos·sip [ˈgɑsəp]

名 閒聊
動 說閒話
同 chat 閒聊

英英 casual, unimportant conversation about other people

例 She comes to her neighborhood to **gossip** every evening.
她每天晚上都到鄰居家閒聊。

☐ 三分熟
☐ 五分熟
☐ 七分熟
☐ 全熟

---

gov·er·nor

[ˈgʌvənə]

名 統治者
同 president 總統

英英 someone who is officially appointed to rule a town or region

例 We tried to elect the best **governor**.
我們試圖選出最好的統治者。

☐ 三分熟
☐ 五分熟
☐ 七分熟
☐ 全熟

---

gown [gaʊn]

名 長袍、長上衣

英英 a long loose dress worn by a woman on formal occasions

例 He wanted to be a pope because he thought the **gown** is beautiful.
他曾經想要當主教，因為他覺得主教的衣服很漂亮。

☐ 三分熟
☐ 五分熟
☐ 七分熟
☐ 全熟

---

grab [græb]

動 急抓、逮捕
同 snatch 抓住

英英 to seize suddenly and quickly

例 I just **grabbed** my cell phone and I rushed home.
我抓了手機就衝回家了。

☐ 三分熟
☐ 五分熟
☐ 七分熟
☐ 全熟

---

grad·u·al

[ˈgrædʒʊəl]

形 逐漸的、漸進的
反 sudden 突然的

英英 happening very slowly over a long period of time

例 It is a **gradual** habit.
這是個逐漸養成的習慣。

☐ 三分熟
☐ 五分熟
☐ 七分熟
☐ 全熟

---

grad·u·ate

[ˈgrædʒʊet]

名 畢業生
動 授予學位、畢業

英英 a person who has been awarded a first academic degree, or a high-school diploma

例 I **graduated** from MIT.
我從麻省理工學院畢業的。

☐ 三分熟
☐ 五分熟
☐ 七分熟
☐ 全熟

---

grain [gren]

名 穀類、穀粒

英英 wheat or seeds from other plants, which is used as food

例 **Grains** are important in our diet.
穀類對我們的飲食很重要。

☐ 三分熟
☐ 五分熟
☐ 七分熟
☐ 全熟

gram [græm]

名 公克

英英 a unit of mass equal to 0.001 kilograms

例 It's 100 **grams**.
這個一百公克。

☐三分熟
☐五分熟
☐七分熟
☐全熟

---

grasp [græsp]

動 掌握、領悟、抓牢
同 grab 抓住

英英 to seize and hold firmly

例 She can't **grasp** the main idea.
她無法掌握主要的要點。

☐三分熟
☐五分熟
☐七分熟
☐全熟

---

grass·hop·per

[ˋgræsˏhɑpɚ]

名 蚱蜢

英英 a plant-eating insect with long hind legs which are used for jumping and for making a sharp sound

例 Children in the city don't know what a **grasshopper** looks like.
都市裡的孩子不知道蚱蜢長怎樣。

☐三分熟
☐五分熟
☐七分熟
☐全熟

---

green·house

[ˋgrinˋhaʊs]

名 溫室
片 greenhouse effect
溫室效應

英英 a glass building in which plants that need protection and warm for growing

例 It's a **greenhouse** effect.
這是溫室效應。

☐三分熟
☐五分熟
☐七分熟
☐全熟

---

grin [grɪn]

動／名 露齒而笑

英英 smile broadly with your teeth being seen

例 The old man **grinned**.
這老男人露齒而笑。

☐三分熟
☐五分熟
☐七分熟
☐全熟

---

gro·cer·y

[ˋgrosərɪ]

名 雜貨店

英英 a grocer's shop or business

例 There are many **groceries** in the little town.
這小鎮裡面有很多雜貨店。

☐三分熟
☐五分熟
☐七分熟
☐全熟

---

guard·i·an

[ˋgɑrdɪən]

名 保護者、守護者

英英 a defender, protector, or keeper

例 He has been my **guardian** angel.
他一直是我的守護者。

☐三分熟
☐五分熟
☐七分熟
☐全熟

---

guid·ance

[ˋgaɪdn̩s]

名 引導、指導

英英 advice or information for resolving a problem or difficulty

例 My professor's **guidance** helps me a lot.
教授的引導幫了我很多。

☐三分熟
☐五分熟
☐七分熟
☐全熟

🎧 **Track 053**

---

gum [gʌm]

名 膠、口香糖

英英 a thick sticky substance produced by the stem of some trees or plants

例 I don't like to chew **gum**.
我不喜歡吃口香糖。

☐ 三分熟
☐ 五分熟
☐ 七分熟
☐ 全熟

---

gymnasium

[dʒɪmˋnezɪəm]

名 體育館、健身房

英英 a hall or large room equipped for exercising

例 We'll have PE class in the **gymnasium**.
我們會在體育館上體育課。

☐ 三分熟
☐ 五分熟
☐ 七分熟
☐ 全熟

Hh

hair·dres·ser

[ˋhɛrˌdrɛsɚ]

名 理髮師

英英 a person who cuts and styles people's hair

例 The **hairdresser** suggested me to have a haircut.
理髮師建議我應該要剪頭髮了。

☐ 三分熟
☐ 五分熟
☐ 七分熟
☐ 全熟

---

hall·way [ˋhɔlˌwe]

名 玄關、門廳

英英 another term for hall or a hall entrance

例 I put my keys at the **hallway**.
我將鑰匙放在玄關。

☐ 三分熟
☐ 五分熟
☐ 七分熟
☐ 全熟

---

hand·ful [ˋhændˌfəl]

形 少量、少數

英英 a small quantity that could be held in one hand

例 I gave him a **handful** of peanuts.
我給他一小把的花生。

☐ 三分熟
☐ 五分熟
☐ 七分熟
☐ 全熟

---

handy [ˋhændɪ]

形 手巧的、手邊的
同 convenient 方便的、隨手可得的

英英 using something very skillfully; convenient

例 You must be **handy** to make such a lovely rose.
你一定是手很巧才能做這麼一朵可愛的玫瑰。

☐ 三分熟
☐ 五分熟
☐ 七分熟
☐ 全熟

---

har·bor [ˋhɑrbɚ]

名 港灣
同 port 港口
片 harbor master 港務長

英英 a place next to the coast where ships and boats may moor in shelter

例 A ship is safe at the **harbor**, but it is not what it is made for.
船在港口邊是最安全的，但這不是造船的目的。

☐ 三分熟
☐ 五分熟
☐ 七分熟
☐ 全熟

---

harm [hɑrm]

名 損傷、損害
動 傷害、損害
同 damage 損害

英英 damage or injury that is caused by someone or something

例 She must have been **harmed** seriously.
她一定是被傷得很重。

☐ 三分熟
☐ 五分熟
☐ 七分熟
☐ 全熟

H

harm·ful [`hɑrmfəl]

形 引起傷害的、有害的
同 destructive 破壞的

英英 causing damage or injury to somebody or something; causing someone in danger

例 This kind of drug is **harmful** to people's health.
這種藥對人的健康有害。

☐ 三分熟
☐ 五分熟
☐ 七分熟
☐ 全熟

---

har·vest [`hɑrvɪst]

名 收穫
動 收穫、收割穀物

英英 the time of year when the crops are gathered from a farm or field

例 Only the diligent farmers know the pleasure of **harvest**.
只有勤奮的農夫才知道收穫的喜悅。

☐ 三分熟
☐ 五分熟
☐ 七分熟
☐ 全熟

---

hast·y [`hestɪ]

形 快速的

英英 made or done something very quickly or in a hurry without care

例 I can't hear his **hasty** words.
我無法聽得懂他快速講過的話。

☐ 三分熟
☐ 五分熟
☐ 七分熟
☐ 全熟

---

hatch [hætʃ]

動 計畫、孵化

英英 of an egg to break and open so that a young bird or fish can come out; to plan to do something

例 The hen is **hatching**.
母雞正在孵蛋。

☐ 三分熟
☐ 五分熟
☐ 七分熟
☐ 全熟

---

hawk [hɔk]

名 鷹

英英 a strong large bird, which is usually gray and catches small birds for food

例 The **hawk** is hovering.
老鷹正在盤旋。

☐ 三分熟
☐ 五分熟
☐ 七分熟
☐ 全熟

---

hay [he]

名 乾草

英英 dry grass (is) for feeding food animals

例 I put some **hay** into the stable.
我把乾草放在馬廄。

☐ 三分熟
☐ 五分熟
☐ 七分熟
☐ 全熟

---

head·line

[`hɛdˌlaɪn]

名 標題、寫標題
同 title 標題

英英 the title of an article or story printed in large and bold letters, usually at the top of the front page

例 What's the **headline** of this article?
這篇文章的標題是什麼？

☐ 三分熟
☐ 五分熟
☐ 七分熟
☐ 全熟

---

head·quar·ters

[`hɛdˌkwɔrtɚz]

名 總部、大本營

英英 the main place of an organization or a military, in which operation is controlled

例 The **headquarters** of our company is in Taipei.
我們公司的總部在臺北。

☐ 三分熟
☐ 五分熟
☐ 七分熟
☐ 全熟

🎧 **Track 055**

heal [hil]

動 治癒、復原
同 cure 治癒

英英 to become healthy again; to make someone recover

例 Trauma can never be **healed**.
創傷是永遠無法治療的。

☐ 三分熟
☐ 五分熟
☐ 七分熟
☐ 全熟

---

heap [hip]

名 積累
動 堆積

英英 an untidy pile or mass of something

例 I am **heaping** the hay.
我在堆積稻草。

☐ 三分熟
☐ 五分熟
☐ 七分熟
☐ 全熟

---

heav·en [ˈhɛvən]

名 天堂

英英 the place, which is believed to be the home of God and good people go when they die

例 No one knows what **heaven** looks like.
沒有人知道天堂長怎樣。

☐ 三分熟
☐ 五分熟
☐ 七分熟
☐ 全熟

---

heel [hil]

名 腳後跟

英英 the back part of the foot

例 The shoes bite my **heels**.
這雙鞋子會咬我的腳跟。

☐ 三分熟
☐ 五分熟
☐ 七分熟
☐ 全熟

---

hell [hɛl]

名 地獄、悲慘處境
同 misery 悲慘、苦難

英英 the place, which is believed to be the home of devils and where bad people go when they die

例 My life was like **hell** after she left me.
她離開後，我的生活就像是在地獄一樣糟糕。

☐ 三分熟
☐ 五分熟
☐ 七分熟
☐ 全熟

---

hel·met [ˈhɛlmɪt]

名 頭盔、安全帽

英英 a strong and hard hat that protects the head, usually wore by a police officer or a person playing some sports

例 Don't forget to wear a **helmet** when you ride a bike.
當你騎車的時候別忘了戴安全帽。

☐ 三分熟
☐ 五分熟
☐ 七分熟
☐ 全熟

---

hes·i·tate

[ˈhɛzəˌtet]

動 遲疑、躊躇

英英 to feel uncertain or nervous and don't know how to make decisions

例 When I asked him where he was last night, he **hesitated**.
當我問他昨晚去哪裡時，他遲疑了。

☐ 三分熟
☐ 五分熟
☐ 七分熟
☐ 全熟

---

hike [haɪk]

名 徒步旅行、健行
片 go hiking 健行

英英 a long walk in the countryside or in the mountain

例 We will go **hiking** this weekend.
我們這週末要去健行。

☐ 三分熟
☐ 五分熟
☐ 七分熟
☐ 全熟

hint [hɪnt]

名 暗示

同 imply 暗示

英英 words or gestures that you say or make in an indirect way for showing somebody what you are thinking

例 Please give me some **hints**.
請給我提示。

☐ 三分熟
☐ 五分熟
☐ 七分熟
☐ 全熟

---

his·to·ri·an

[hɪsˋtorɪən]

名 歷史學家

英英 a person who studies or writes about histories; or an expert in history

例 The **historians** don't really know what killed Napoleon.
歷史學家不太清楚拿破崙的死因。

☐ 三分熟
☐ 五分熟
☐ 七分熟
☐ 全熟

---

his·tor·ic

[hɪsˋtɔrɪk]

形 歷史性的

英英 important in history or likely to be important at some time in the future

例 It is not a **historic** fact.
這不是歷史事實。

☐ 三分熟
☐ 五分熟
☐ 七分熟
☐ 全熟

---

his·tor·i·cal

[hɪsˋtɔrɪk]

形 歷史的

英英 connected with or related to the past

例 Versailles is not merely important for its **historical** meaning.
凡爾賽宮不只是因為它的歷史意義而重要。

☐ 三分熟
☐ 五分熟
☐ 七分熟
☐ 全熟

---

hive [haɪv]

名 蜂巢、鬧區

英英 a structure where is for bees to live in

例 I am moving away the **hive**.
我搬離鬧區。

☐ 三分熟
☐ 五分熟
☐ 七分熟
☐ 全熟

---

hol·low [ˋhɑlo]

形 中空的、空的

同 empty 空的

片 hollow eyes
凹陷的眼睛

英英 having a hole or empty space inside

例 Without you, I feel my heart **hollow**.
沒有你，我覺得我的心是空洞的。

☐ 三分熟
☐ 五分熟
☐ 七分熟
☐ 全熟

---

ho·ly [ˋholɪ]

形 神聖的、聖潔的

英英 good in a moral and religious way, usually related to a religion or God

例 The ritual is **holy**.
這儀式很神聖。

☐ 三分熟
☐ 五分熟
☐ 七分熟
☐ 全熟

---

home·town

[ˋhomˏtaʊn]

名 家鄉

英英 the town where the people live or the town that they come from

例 It's my **hometown**.
這是我的家鄉。

☐ 三分熟
☐ 五分熟
☐ 七分熟
☐ 全熟

🎧 **Track 057**

---

hon·es·ty [ˋɑnɪstɪ]

名 正直、誠實

英英 the quality of being honest

例 **Honesty** may not be always the best policy.
誠實也許並不一定是上策。

□ 三分熟
□ 五分熟
□ 七分熟
□ 全熟

---

hon·or [ˋɑnə]

名 榮耀、尊敬
同 respect 尊敬

英英 great respect and admiration

例 The athlete is a man of **honor**.
這名運動員是個品德高尚的人。

□ 三分熟
□ 五分熟
□ 七分熟
□ 全熟

---

horn [hɔrn]

名 喇叭、號角

英英 a device in a car or on a vehicle which is for making a loud noise to warn other people

例 **Horn** plays an important role in the war.
號角在這場戰役中扮演很重要的角色。

□ 三分熟
□ 五分熟
□ 七分熟
□ 全熟

---

hor·ri·ble [ˋhɑrəb!]

形 可怕的

英英 very bad, unpleasant, frightening

例 How can you have such a **horrible** idea to kill him?
你怎麼可以有殺了他這種可怕的想法？

□ 三分熟
□ 五分熟
□ 七分熟
□ 全熟

---

horror [ˋhɑrə]

名 恐怖、恐懼、畏懼
同 panic 恐慌

英英 feeling of great shock or disgust

例 I don't like **horror** movies.
我不喜歡恐怖片。

□ 三分熟
□ 五分熟
□ 七分熟
□ 全熟

---

hour·ly [ˋaʊrlɪ]

形 每小時的
副 每小時地

英英 something is done or happening every hour

例 She asked me where I am **hourly**.
她每小時都問我在哪裡。

□ 三分熟
□ 五分熟
□ 七分熟
□ 全熟

---

house·keep·er

[ˋhaʊsˏkipə]

名 主婦、管家

英英 a person, usually a woman, whose job is to manage the shopping, cooking, cleaning, etc. in other's house

例 Fewer and fewer people want to be a **housekeeper** now.
現在越來越少人想當管家了。

□ 三分熟
□ 五分熟
□ 七分熟
□ 全熟

---

hug [hʌg]

動 抱、緊抱
名 緊抱、擁抱
同 embrace 擁抱

英英 to put your arms around somebody and hold them tightly, usually to show that you like them very much

例 Please give me a **hug**.
請抱抱我。

□ 三分熟
□ 五分熟
□ 七分熟
□ 全熟

hu·mor·ous
[ˋhjumərəs]

形 幽默的、滑稽的
同 funny 好笑的

英英 funny and make someone laugh very easily; showing a sense of humor
例 She has a crush on the **humorous** man.
她迷戀那個幽默的男人。

☐ 三分熟
☐ 五分熟
☐ 七分熟
☐ 全熟

hush [hʌʃ]

動 使靜寂
名 靜寂
同 silence 寂靜

英英 to make quiet or to stop talking, speaking or cry
例 **Hush**, someone is coming this way.
安靜，有人往這邊來了。

☐ 三分熟
☐ 五分熟
☐ 七分熟
☐ 全熟

hut [hʌt]

名 小屋、茅舍

英英 a small, simply built house, usual with one room only
例 The man walked from the **hut**.
這男人從小屋走出來。

☐ 三分熟
☐ 五分熟
☐ 七分熟
☐ 全熟

Ii

ic·y [ˋaɪsɪ]

形 冰的、冰冷的

英英 very cold
例 The air is **icy** cold today.
今天的空氣很冰冷。

☐ 三分熟
☐ 五分熟
☐ 七分熟
☐ 全熟

i·de·al [aɪˋdiəl]

形 理想的、完美的
同 perfect 完美的

英英 very perfect or most suitable
例 People seldom get married to their **ideal** lover.
很少有人是跟理想對象結婚的。

☐ 三分熟
☐ 五分熟
☐ 七分熟
☐ 全熟

i·den·ti·ty
[aɪˋdɛntətɪ]

名 身分

英英 who a person is or what something is
例 As her **identity** changed, her perspective changed.
當她的身分變了，她的觀點也變了。

☐ 三分熟
☐ 五分熟
☐ 七分熟
☐ 全熟

ig·no·rance
[ˋɪgnərəns]

名 無知、不學無術
反 knowledge 學識

英英 a lack of knowledge, common sense or information about something
例 Sometimes **ignorance** is a kind of blessing.
有時候無知就是福。

☐ 三分熟
☐ 五分熟
☐ 七分熟
☐ 全熟

im·age [ˋɪmɪdʒ]

名 影像、形象

英英 the impression or a picture in your mind
例 I still remember the **image** of my first love.
我仍記得初戀情人的長相。

☐ 三分熟
☐ 五分熟
☐ 七分熟
☐ 全熟

🎧 **Track 059**

---

i·mag·i·na·tion

[ɪˌmædʒəˈneʃən]

名 想像力、創作力

英英 the ability to create pictures or impression in your mind

例 It's **imagination** that makes his works great.
是想像力讓他的作品如此偉大。

☐ 三分熟 ☐ 五分熟 ☐ 七分熟 ☐ 全熟

---

im·me·di·ate

[ɪˈmidɪɪt]

形 直接的、立即的

英英 happening or done directly and instantly without delay

例 The **immediate** answer is not always the best answer.
立即的答覆未必就是最好的答案。

☐ 三分熟 ☐ 五分熟 ☐ 七分熟 ☐ 全熟

---

im·port

[ɪmˈport]/[ˈɪmport]

動 進口、輸入
名 輸入品、進口
反 export 出口

英英 a product or service that is brought or bought from another country

例 This country **imports** lots of gasoline.
這國家進口大量的石油。

☐ 三分熟 ☐ 五分熟 ☐ 七分熟 ☐ 全熟

---

im·press [ɪmˈprɛs]

動 留下深刻印象、
　使感動

英英 to have a great impression of something in mind

例 Which book **impressed** you the most?
哪一本書讓你最印象深刻？

☐ 三分熟 ☐ 五分熟 ☐ 七分熟 ☐ 全熟

---

im·pres·sive

[ɪmˈprɛsɪv]

形 印象深刻的

英英 of things or people making you feel unforgettable

例 When the girl made an **impressive** move, everyone clapped.
當這女孩做了讓人印象深刻的舉動，大家都鼓掌。

☐ 三分熟 ☐ 五分熟 ☐ 七分熟 ☐ 全熟

---

in·deed [ɪnˈdid]

副 實在地、的確

英英 surely or certainly, usually used for emphasizing something

例 **Indeed**, it is important.
真的，這很重要。

☐ 三分熟 ☐ 五分熟 ☐ 七分熟 ☐ 全熟

---

in·di·vid·u·al

[ˌɪndəˈvɪdʒʊəl]

形 個別的
名 個人

英英 a single item or a single person

例 Each **individual** is important for this country.
這國家的每個人都很重要。

☐ 三分熟 ☐ 五分熟 ☐ 七分熟 ☐ 全熟

---

in·door [ˈɪnˌdor]

形 屋內的、室內的
反 outdoor 戶外的

英英 situated, happening or used inside a building

例 I prefer **indoor** activity.
我偏好室內運動。

☐ 三分熟 ☐ 五分熟 ☐ 七分熟 ☐ 全熟

---

in·doors [`ɪn`dorz]

副 在室內
反 outdoors 在戶外

英英 situated, happening or used inside a building

例 I just love to stay **indoors**.
我只是喜歡待在室內。

□ 三分熟
□ 五分熟
□ 七分熟
□ 全熟

---

in·dus·tri·al

[ɪn`dʌstrɪəl]

形 工業的

英英 related to industry

例 The **industrial** pollution of this country is serious.
這國家的工業污染很嚴重。

□ 三分熟
□ 五分熟
□ 七分熟
□ 全熟

---

in·fe·ri·or [ɪn`fɪrɪɚ]

形 較低的、較劣的
同 worse 較差的
片 be inferior to
　　次於……

英英 not as good as somebody / something else; with lower quality

例 He always feels he's **inferior** to his elder brother.
他總是覺得自己比哥哥差。

□ 三分熟
□ 五分熟
□ 七分熟
□ 全熟

---

in·form [ɪn`fɔrm]

動 通知、報告

英英 to tell somebody about something officially

例 I was **informed** about the time of the class.
我被告知上課時間。

□ 三分熟
□ 五分熟
□ 七分熟
□ 全熟

---

in·jure [`ɪndʒɚ]

動 傷害、使受傷
同 hurt 傷害

英英 to harm yourself or somebody in an accident or in a purpose

例 The little girl was badly **injured** in the crash.
小女孩在車禍中受了重傷。

□ 三分熟
□ 五分熟
□ 七分熟
□ 全熟

---

in·ju·ry [`ɪndʒərɪ]

名 傷害、損害

英英 physical harm done to a person's or an animal's body, usually happened in an accident

例 This room is for patients who have accidental **injury**.
這房間是治療意外傷害的病人專用的。

□ 三分熟
□ 五分熟
□ 七分熟
□ 全熟

---

inn [ɪn]

名 旅社、小酒館

英英 a small pub; a small hotel where people can stay the night

例 I stayed in a small **inn** in Tokyo a year ago.
一年前，我待在東京的一間小酒館。

□ 三分熟
□ 五分熟
□ 七分熟
□ 全熟

---

in·ner [`ɪnɚ]

形 內部的、心靈的
同 outer 外部的

英英 inside; close to the centre of a place

例 She can see into the **inner** thoughts of him.
她可以看穿他內在的想法。

□ 三分熟
□ 五分熟
□ 七分熟
□ 全熟

🎧 **Track 061**

in·no·cent

[ˈɪnəsn̩t]

形 無辜的、純潔的
反 guilty 罪惡的

英英 not guilty of a crime; having done nothing wrong

例 The girl has **innocent** eyes.
這個女孩有著純潔的眼神。

☐ 三分熟
☐ 五分熟
☐ 七分熟
☐ 全熟

---

in·spect [ɪnˈspɛkt]

動 調查、檢查

英英 to check someone or something carefully for finding information

例 The police **inspected** the family of the suspect.
警察調查嫌疑犯的家庭。

☐ 三分熟
☐ 五分熟
☐ 七分熟
☐ 全熟

---

in·spec·tor

[ɪnˈspɛktɚ]

名 視察員、檢查者

英英 a person whose job is to check someone or something carefully for finding information

例 The **inspector** is coming.
視察員要來了。

☐ 三分熟
☐ 五分熟
☐ 七分熟
☐ 全熟

---

in·stead [ɪnˈstɛd]

副 替代
片 instead of...
取而代之……

英英 in the place of somebody or something else

例 I didn't choose the black puppy. I chose the white puppy **instead**.
我沒有選小黑狗，我選擇了小白狗來替代。

☐ 三分熟
☐ 五分熟
☐ 七分熟
☐ 全熟

---

instruction

[ɪnˈstrʌkʃən]

名 指令、教導

英英 detailed information guides people how to do or use something directions

例 You don't need to follow all the **instructions**.
你不需要聽從所有的指令。

☐ 三分熟
☐ 五分熟
☐ 七分熟
☐ 全熟

---

in·ter·nal [ɪnˈtɚnl̩]

形 內部的、國內的

英英 connected with or happening in the inside of something; inside of a country

例 The **internal** problem of the college is more serious.
這所大學內部的問題更嚴重。

☐ 三分熟
☐ 五分熟
☐ 七分熟
☐ 全熟

---

in·ter·rupt

[ˈɪntəˈrʌpt]

動 干擾、打斷
同 intrude 打擾

英英 saying or doing something makes somebody stop what they are saying or doing

例 Don't **interrupt** me.
不要打斷我。

☐ 三分熟
☐ 五分熟
☐ 七分熟
☐ 全熟

J

in·tro·duc·tion

[ˌɪntrəˈdʌkʃən]

名 引進、介紹

片 self-introduction
自我介紹

英英 the act of telling someone's name to another when they meet in the first time

例 I don't know how to make a self-**introduction**.
我不知道如何做自我介紹。

□ 三分熟
□ 五分熟
□ 七分熟
□ 全熟

in·ven·tor

[ɪnˈvɛntɚ]

名 發明家

英英 a person who invents something or whose job is inventing things

例 Some historians said Thomas Edison was not the **inventor** of the light bulb.
有些歷史學家說湯瑪斯·愛迪生不是燈泡的發明家。

□ 三分熟
□ 五分熟
□ 七分熟
□ 全熟

in·ves·ti·gate

[ɪnˈvɛstəˌget]

動 研究、調查

同 inspect 調查

英英 to carefully examine the facts of a situation, an event, a crime in order to find out the truth about it

例 This paper attempts to **investigate** the influence of childhood.
這篇論文試圖研究童年的影響。

□ 三分熟
□ 五分熟
□ 七分熟
□ 全熟

i·vo·ry [ˈaɪvərɪ]

名 象牙

形 象牙製的

英英 a hard yellowish-white substance like bone that forms the tusks, usually elephants and some other animals

例 These chopsticks are made of **ivory**.
這雙筷子是象牙做的。

□ 三分熟
□ 五分熟
□ 七分熟
□ 全熟

Jj

jail [dʒel]

名 監獄

同 prison 監獄

英英 a prison, a place where criminals are forced to live as a punishment

例 The criminal is put into **jail**.
這罪犯被關入監獄了。

□ 三分熟
□ 五分熟
□ 七分熟
□ 全熟

jar [dʒɑr]

名 刺耳的聲音、廣口瓶

英英 a round glass container, sometimes with a lid, used for storing food, such as jam or honey

例 I put the jam into a **jar**.
我把果醬放在廣口瓶中。

□ 三分熟
□ 五分熟
□ 七分熟
□ 全熟

jaw [dʒɔ]

名 顎、下巴

動 閒聊、嘮叨

英英 either of the two bones at the lower part of the face that contain the teeth and move when you open your mouth

例 Could you please stop your **jaw**?
你可以住嘴嗎？

□ 三分熟
□ 五分熟
□ 七分熟
□ 全熟

🎧 **Track 063**

---

jeal·ous [ˈdʒɛləs]

形 嫉妒的
同 envious 嫉妒的、
　羨慕的

英英 feeling angry or unhappy because somebody you like or love is not showing interest in you but in somebody else

例 Everyone's **jealous** of her beauty.
每個人都嫉妒她的美貌。

☐ 三分熟
☐ 五分熟
☐ 七分熟
☐ 全熟

---

jel·ly [ˈdʒɛlɪ]

名 果凍

英英 a cold sweet food made from gelatin, sugar and fruit juice, that shakes slightly when it is moved

例 Every kid loves **jelly**.
所有的小孩都喜歡果凍。

☐ 三分熟
☐ 五分熟
☐ 七分熟
☐ 全熟

---

jet [dʒɛt]

名 噴射機、噴嘴
動 噴出

英英 an aircraft driven by jet engines

例 The millionaire has a private **jet**.
這個百萬富豪有私人噴射機。

☐ 三分熟
☐ 五分熟
☐ 七分熟
☐ 全熟

---

jew·el [ˈdʒuəl]

名 珠寶

英英 a precious and valuable stone such as a diamond, ruby, etc

例 Ms. Su's husband gave her some **jewels**.
蘇老師的老公給她珠寶。

☐ 三分熟
☐ 五分熟
☐ 七分熟
☐ 全熟

---

jew·el·ry [ˈdʒuəlrɪ]

名 珠寶

英英 personal decorative objects, such as necklaces, rings, or bracelets, that are usually made from or contain jewels and precious metal

例 Not every girl loves **jewelry**.
不是所有的女孩都喜歡珠寶。

☐ 三分熟
☐ 五分熟
☐ 七分熟
☐ 全熟

---

jour·nal [ˈdʒɜnl̩]

名 期刊
同 magazine 雜誌

英英 a newspaper or magazine that deals with a particular subject or published regularly

例 I read a **journal** article about blue frogs.
我讀過一篇關於藍色青蛙的期刊文章。

☐ 三分熟
☐ 五分熟
☐ 七分熟
☐ 全熟

---

jour·ney [ˈdʒɜnɪ]

名 旅程
動 旅遊

英英 an act of travelling from one place to another, especially when they travel in a vehicle

例 Life is a **journey**.
人生就是趟旅程。

☐ 三分熟
☐ 五分熟
☐ 七分熟
☐ 全熟

---

joy·ful [ˈdʒɔɪfəl]

形 愉快的、喜悅的
同 glad 高興的

英英 very happy and pleasant; causing people to be happy and pleased

例 It was such a **joyful** day.
這真是一個愉快的一天。

☐ 三分熟
☐ 五分熟
☐ 七分熟
☐ 全熟

K

jun·gle [ˋdʒʌŋɡḷ]

名 叢林

英英 an area of tropical forest where trees and plants grow very thickly and with wild animals

例 I love to discover the secret of the **jungle**.
我想要探索叢林的祕密。

☐ 三分熟
☐ 五分熟
☐ 七分熟
☐ 全熟

---

junk [dʒʌŋk]

名 垃圾
同 trash 垃圾
片 junk food 垃圾食物

英英 things that are useless or with little value

例 Don't eat too much **junk** food.
不要吃太多垃圾食物。

☐ 三分熟
☐ 五分熟
☐ 七分熟
☐ 全熟

---

jus·tice [ˋdʒʌstɪs]

名 公平、公正

英英 the fair treatment of people; fairness

例 All we want is **justice**.
我們所要的一切是公正。

☐ 三分熟
☐ 五分熟
☐ 七分熟
☐ 全熟

Kk

kan·ga·roo
[͵kæŋɡəˋru]

名 袋鼠

英英 a large Australian mammal with a long stiff tail and back legs, that moves by jumping

例 It's dangerous to face a **kangaroo**.
面對袋鼠時是很危險的。

☐ 三分熟
☐ 五分熟
☐ 七分熟
☐ 全熟

---

ket·tle [ˋkɛtḷ]

名 水壺

英英 a cover metal or plastic container with a lid, handle and a spout, used for boiling water

例 I use a **kettle** to boil the water.
我用水壺燒水。

☐ 三分熟
☐ 五分熟
☐ 七分熟
☐ 全熟

---

key·board
[ˋki͵bord]

名 鍵盤

英英 the set of keys you press on a computer or typewriter to make it work

例 I can't type fast with this **keyboard**.
我用這鍵盤沒辦法打很快。

☐ 三分熟
☐ 五分熟
☐ 七分熟
☐ 全熟

---

kid·ney [ˋkɪdnɪ]

名 腎臟

英英 either of the two organs in the body that take away waste products from the blood and produce urine

例 This kind of diet is not good for your **kidney**.
這種飲食習慣對腎臟不好。

☐ 三分熟
☐ 五分熟
☐ 七分熟
☐ 全熟

---

ki·lo·gram/kg
[ˋkɪlə͵ɡræm]

名 公斤

英英 a unit for measuring weight; 1,000 grams, or 2.2 pounds

例 I gained one **kilogram** in this week.
我這週多了一公斤。

☐ 三分熟
☐ 五分熟
☐ 七分熟
☐ 全熟

🎧 **Track 065**

ki·lo·me·ter/km

[ˈkɪləˌmitə]

名 公里

英英 a unit for measuring distance, equals to 1,000 meters

例 It's less than a **kilometer** away from here.
距離這裡不到一公里遠。

☐ 三分熟
☐ 五分熟
☐ 七分熟
☐ 全熟

---

kit [kɪt]

名 工具箱

英英 a set of tools or equipment which are used for a particular purpose or activity

例 The carpenter forgot to bring a **kit**.
這木匠忘了帶工具箱。

☐ 三分熟
☐ 五分熟
☐ 七分熟
☐ 全熟

---

kneel [nil]

動 下跪
片 kneel down 下跪

英英 to move into a position where your body is supported on your knees on the ground

例 My mom punished me to **kneel** down.
我媽罰我跪。

☐ 三分熟
☐ 五分熟
☐ 七分熟
☐ 全熟

---

knight [naɪt]

名 騎士、武士
動 封……為爵士

英英 a man of high social rank or honor who had a duty to fight for his king, usually in the Middle Ages

例 A brave **knight** saving a princess is a common motif in romance.
浪漫故事中，勇敢的武士解救了公主是常見的題材。

☐ 三分熟
☐ 五分熟
☐ 七分熟
☐ 全熟

---

knit [nɪt]

動 編織
名 編織物

英英 to make clothes or scarves from woolen or cotton thread using two long thin knitting needles or a machine

例 I am **knitting** a scarf for my boyfriend.
我為我的男朋友編織一條圍巾。

☐ 三分熟
☐ 五分熟
☐ 七分熟
☐ 全熟

---

knob [nɑb]

名 圓形把手、球塊

英英 a round handle or small round device on a door or a drawer

例 The **knob** of the door is broken.
這門的圓形把手壞掉了。

☐ 三分熟
☐ 五分熟
☐ 七分熟
☐ 全熟

---

knot [nɑt]

名 結
動 打結

英英 a join made by tying or fastening together two pieces or ends of string, rope, etc

例 The **knot** on the box is too tight.
這箱子的結太緊了。

☐ 三分熟
☐ 五分熟
☐ 七分熟
☐ 全熟

la·bel [ˈlebl̩]

名 標籤
動 標明

英英 a small piece of paper which is attached to an object or a product and gives information about it

例 A teacher shouldn't **label** any student as problematic.
老師不該標明任何學生是有問題的。

☐ 三分熟
☐ 五分熟
☐ 七分熟
☐ 全熟

lace [les]

名 花邊、緞帶
動 用帶子打結

英英 a cloth or string which is made by weaving thin thread in delicate patterns with holes; to fasten something by tying a lace

例 I love the shirt with **lace** on the sleeves.
我喜歡這件袖子有蕾絲邊的襯衫。

☐ 三分熟
☐ 五分熟
☐ 七分熟
☐ 全熟

lad·der [ˈlædɚ]

名 梯子

英英 an equipment consisting of a series of bars or steps between two uprights, which is used for climbing up or down

例 I need a **ladder** to climb to the roof.
我需要一個梯子爬上屋頂。

☐ 三分熟
☐ 五分熟
☐ 七分熟
☐ 全熟

lat·ter [ˈlætɚ]

形 後者的

英英 nearer to the end of something

例 The **latter** is better.
後者比較好。

☐ 三分熟
☐ 五分熟
☐ 七分熟
☐ 全熟

laugh·ter [ˈlæftɚ]

名 笑聲

英英 the action or sound of laughing

例 **Laughter** is the best medicine.
歡笑是良藥。

☐ 三分熟
☐ 五分熟
☐ 七分熟
☐ 全熟

laun·dry [ˈlɔndrɪ]

名 洗衣店、送洗的衣服
片 do a laundry 洗衣服

英英 a place to help their customers do the washings; the dirty clothes that need to be washed or that have been washed

例 I will bring my clothes to the **laundry**.
我會帶衣服到洗衣店。

☐ 三分熟
☐ 五分熟
☐ 七分熟
☐ 全熟

lawn [lɔn]

名 草地

英英 an area of mown grass in a yard, garden or park

例 Children are chasing kites on the **lawn**.
孩子們在草地上追風箏。

☐ 三分熟
☐ 五分熟
☐ 七分熟
☐ 全熟

leak [lik]

動 洩漏、滲漏
名 漏洞

英英 accidentally allow a liquid or gas to escape or enter through a hole or crack; a hole or space which something can flow out of a container

例 Your water bottle is **leaking**.
你的水壺在漏水。

☐ 三分熟
☐ 五分熟
☐ 七分熟
☐ 全熟

🎧 Track 067

leap [lip]

動 使跳過
名 跳躍

英英 jump or spring suddenly; jump across or make a large movement

例 The frog **leaps** over the rock.
青蛙跳過那塊石頭。

☐三分熟
☐五分熟
☐七分熟
☐全熟

---

leath·er [ˋlɛðɚ]

名 皮革

英英 a material made from the skin of an animal; usually used to make shoes, bags or clothes

例 Don't buy **leather** products.
不要買皮革製品。

☐三分熟
☐五分熟
☐七分熟
☐全熟

---

lei·sure [ˋliʒɚ]

名 空閒

英英 free time which spent for relaxation or enjoyment

例 What do you do in your **leisure** time?
在你的空閒時間，你會做什麼？

☐三分熟
☐五分熟
☐七分熟
☐全熟

---

length·en

[ˋlɛŋθən]

動 加長

英英 make something longer or become longer

例 Please **lengthen** this skirt for my daughter.
請幫我女兒加長這條裙子。

☐三分熟
☐五分熟
☐七分熟
☐全熟

---

lens [lɛns]

名 透鏡、鏡片

英英 a piece of transparent material, such as glass, plastic, with one or both sides curved for concentrating or make the object seem closer, larger or smaller

例 The **lens** of your camera need cleaning.
照相機的鏡片需要清潔。

☐三分熟
☐五分熟
☐七分熟
☐全熟

---

li·ar [ˋlaɪɚ]

名 說謊者

英英 a person who tells a lie

例 Is it acceptable that your family members become **liars**?
你的家人變成說謊者是可以被接受的嗎？

☐三分熟
☐五分熟
☐七分熟
☐全熟

---

lib·er·al [ˋlɪbərəl]

形 自由主義的、
開明的、慷慨的
同 generous 慷慨的

英英 willing to respect and accept different behavior, opinions or religion; to be open-minded

例 My parents are **liberal** enough to allow gay marriage.
我的父母開明到可以允許同志婚姻。

☐三分熟
☐五分熟
☐七分熟
☐全熟

---

lib·er·ty [ˋlɪbɚtɪ]

名 自由
同 freedom 自由

英英 the state of being free from oppression or imprisonment

例 Individual **liberty** for independence is worthy of fighting for.
獨立的個人自由是值得爭取的。

☐三分熟
☐五分熟
☐七分熟
☐全熟

L

li·brar·i·an

[laɪˈbrɛrɪən]

名 圖書館員

英英 a person who works in a library

例 Some **librarians** are friendly, but some are mean.
有些圖書館員很友善，有些是很刻薄的。

☐ 三分熟
☐ 五分熟
☐ 七分熟
☐ 全熟

---

life·boat [ˈlaɪfˌbot]

名 救生艇

英英 a specially constructed large boat which is kept ready to go out to sea and to rescue people in distress

例 The **lifeboat** in Ang Lee's movie *Life of Pi* is impressive.
李安電影《少年 PI 的奇幻漂流》裡的救生艇令人印象深刻。

☐ 三分熟
☐ 五分熟
☐ 七分熟
☐ 全熟

---

life·guard

[ˈlaɪfˌgɑrd]

名 救生員

英英 a person who works to rescue bathers who get into difficulty at a beach or swimming pool

例 The **lifeguard** of the swimming pool saved Grandpa in time.
游泳池的救生員及時救了爺爺。

☐ 三分熟
☐ 五分熟
☐ 七分熟
☐ 全熟

---

life·time

[ˈlaɪfˌtaɪm]

名 一生

英英 the duration of someone's life

例 James Joyce spent almost one third of his **lifetime** writing Finnegans Wake.
詹姆斯・喬伊斯花了他近三分之一的人生寫作《芬尼根守靈記》。

☐ 三分熟
☐ 五分熟
☐ 七分熟
☐ 全熟

---

light·house

[ˈlaɪtˈhaʊs]

名 燈塔

英英 a tower or a tall building containing a flashing light to warn ships at sea

例 Virginia Woolf's famous novel To the **Lighthouse** deals with the relationship between men and women.
維吉尼亞・吳爾芙的知名小說《燈塔行》處理關於女人與男人之間的問題。

☐ 三分熟
☐ 五分熟
☐ 七分熟
☐ 全熟

---

limb [lɪm]

名 枝幹、肢體

英英 an arm or a leg of a person or animal; a large branch of a tree

例 The old solider lost a **limb** in the battlefield.
老士兵在戰場上失去了一條腿。

☐ 三分熟
☐ 五分熟
☐ 七分熟
☐ 全熟

---

lin·en [ˈlɪnɪn]

名 亞麻製品

英英 articles such as sheets or clothes, which are made from linen

例 The pattern of the **linen** is designed by a famous designer.
亞麻製品的格式是有名的設計師所設計的。

☐ 三分熟
☐ 五分熟
☐ 七分熟
☐ 全熟

🎧 Track 069

lip·stick [ˈlɪpˌstɪk]

名 口紅、唇膏

英英 colored substance applied to the lips of women from a small solid stick

例 The **lipstick** is a kind of cosmetics.
口紅是化粧品的一種。

☐三分熟
☐五分熟
☐七分熟
☐全熟

lit·ter [ˈlɪtɚ]

名 雜物、一窩（小豬或小狗）、廢物
動 散置
同 rubbish 廢物、垃圾

英英 rubbish that left in an public place or on the ground

例 **Litter** was left all over the house.
這間房子裡的廢棄物堆的到處都是。

☐三分熟
☐五分熟
☐七分熟
☐全熟

live·ly [ˈlaɪvlɪ]

形 有生氣的
同 bright 有生氣的

英英 full of life or having a lot energy; very active

例 The tiger's eyes are **lively**, full of spirit.
這隻老虎的眼睛很有生氣，充滿了精神。

☐三分熟
☐五分熟
☐七分熟
☐全熟

liv·er [ˈlɪvɚ]

名 肝臟

英英 a large organ in the abdomen that produces bile and cleans blood

例 Some scientists are doing researches on **liver** cancer.
有些科學家在做關於肝癌的研究。

☐三分熟
☐五分熟
☐七分熟
☐全熟

load [lod]

名 負載
動 裝載

英英 a heavy or bulky thing being or about to be carried, such as an animal

例 Are you aware of their heavy work **load**?
你難道沒有察覺到他們的工作負擔很重嗎？

☐三分熟
☐五分熟
☐七分熟
☐全熟

lob·by [ˈlɑbɪ]

名 休息室、大廳
同 entrance 入口

英英 a large room out of which one or more other rooms, typically forming a small entrance hall in a hotel or other large building

例 The Korean movie star invites his fans to play a game with him in the **lobby**.
韓國電影明星邀請他的粉絲到大廳去跟他玩遊戲。

☐三分熟
☐五分熟
☐七分熟
☐全熟

lob·ster [ˈlɑbstɚ]

名 龍蝦

英英 a large sea animals with stalked eyes, large pincers, hard shell and eight legs

例 The **lobster** in the fish tank looks unhappy.
在魚缸裡的龍蝦看起來不太開心。

☐三分熟
☐五分熟
☐七分熟
☐全熟

lol·li·pop [ˈlɑlɪˌpɑp]

名 棒棒糖

英英 a large, flat, rounded boiled sweet on a stick

例 The **lollipop** looks like a snowman, and tastes like milk.
這枝棒棒糖看起來像雪人，嚐起來像牛奶。

☐三分熟
☐五分熟
☐七分熟
☐全熟

L

loose [lus]
形 寬鬆的

英英 not tight or not tied or packaged together
例 My pants become too **loose** to wear after three month's dieting.
我的褲子在三個月的節食後，變得太鬆而不能穿。

☐ 三分熟
☐ 五分熟
☐ 七分熟
☐ 全熟

loos·en [ˈlusn̩]
動 鬆開、放鬆
同 relax 放鬆

英英 make something loose become looses; to release something
例 **Loosen** the tie and you'll feel better.
鬆開領帶，你會感覺好點。

☐ 三分熟
☐ 五分熟
☐ 七分熟
☐ 全熟

lord [lɔrd]
名 領主、統治者
同 owner 物主

英英 a man of noble rank or high office with a lot of power
例 The director of *The **Lord** of the Rings* films was Peter Jackson.
《魔戒》系列電影的導演是彼得‧傑克森。

☐ 三分熟
☐ 五分熟
☐ 七分熟
☐ 全熟

loud·speak·er
[ˈlaʊdˌspikɚ]
名 擴音器

英英 an equipment that converts electrical impulses into sounds
例 The head of the village uses a **loudspeaker** to speak to all the villagers.
村長用擴音器對著全部的村民講話。

☐ 三分熟
☐ 五分熟
☐ 七分熟
☐ 全熟

lug·gage [ˈlʌgɪdʒ]
名 行李
同 baggage 行李

英英 suitcases or other bags which are carried while travelling
例 The new **luggage** with Hello Kitty is my favorite.
有凱蒂貓的新行李箱是我的最愛。

☐ 三分熟
☐ 五分熟
☐ 七分熟
☐ 全熟

lull·a·by [ˈlʌləˌbaɪ]
名 搖籃曲
動 唱催眠曲

英英 a soothing song sung to make a child to sleep
例 Mother often hummed **lullaby** beside me when I was a kid.
當我還是小孩時，母親時常在我身邊哼唱搖籃曲。

☐ 三分熟
☐ 五分熟
☐ 七分熟
☐ 全熟

lung [lʌŋ]
名 肺臟

英英 each of the pair of organs in the chest with which people and some animals breathe
例 A healthy **lung** seems to be pink.
健康的肺臟看起來似乎是粉紅色的。

☐ 三分熟
☐ 五分熟
☐ 七分熟
☐ 全熟

Mm

🎧 Track 071

mag·i·cal
[`mædʒɪkl̩]
形 有魔術的、神奇的

英英 having supernatural powers or using magic

例 Moonstones are **magical** stones for ancient Romans.
月光石對古代的羅馬人來說是神奇的石頭。

☐ 三分熟
☐ 五分熟
☐ 七分熟
☐ 全熟

mag·net [`mægnɪt]
名 磁鐵

英英 an object of iron or other material that has the property of attracting similar objects

例 These letters with **magnets** inside can stick to the whiteboard.
這些有磁鐵的字母可以黏到白板上。

☐ 三分熟
☐ 五分熟
☐ 七分熟
☐ 全熟

maid [med]
名 女僕、少女

英英 a female servant; a girl or young woman who is unmarried

例 The **maid** is clever enough to know how to help Mrs. Simpson.
女僕很聰慧，知道如何幫助辛普森太太。

☐ 三分熟
☐ 五分熟
☐ 七分熟
☐ 全熟

ma·jor [`medʒɚ]
形 較大的、主要的
動 主修

英英 more important or serious

例 Vito did the **major** work of the museum design, but his boss took all the credits.
維托做了主要的博物館設計工作，但他的老闆卻搶走了所有的功勞。

☐ 三分熟
☐ 五分熟
☐ 七分熟
☐ 全熟

ma·jor·i·ty
[mə`dʒɔrətɪ]
名 多數
反 minority 少數

英英 the large number of something

例 We should be careful about the opinions of the **majority**.
我們要留心多數人的意見。

☐ 三分熟
☐ 五分熟
☐ 七分熟
☐ 全熟

mall [mɔl]
名 購物中心

英英 a large shopping area from which traffic is busy

例 The **mall** is full of people, ready to buy and win that red sports car.
購物中心滿是人群，準備好大肆採購，贏得那輛紅色的跑車。

☐ 三分熟
☐ 五分熟
☐ 七分熟
☐ 全熟

man·age
[`mænɪdʒ]
動 管理、處理

英英 to be in charge of or run an organization; to handle or deal with something

例 **Managing** a department is certainly not an easy task.
管理一個部門絕非一個簡單的任務。

☐ 三分熟
☐ 五分熟
☐ 七分熟
☐ 全熟

man·age·ment

[ˈmænɪdʒmənt]

名 處理、管理

英英 the process of managing or dealing with something in an organization

例 It takes time to learn financial **management**.
學財務管理需要時間。

M

man·age·a·ble

[ˈmænɪdʒəbl]

形 可管理的、易處理的、易辦的

英英 can be in charge of or possible to deal with

例 To finish writing this computer program in a week is tough but **manageable**.
要在一星期內完成這個電腦程式的撰寫雖然艱難，但做得到。

man·ag·er

[ˈmænɪdʒɚ]

名 經理

英英 a person who succeeds in doing or dealing with business or something

例 Our **manager** is not always mean. Actually, she is sometimes generous.
我們經理並不是吝嗇。事實上，她有時還滿大方的。

man·kind/ hum·an·kind

[mænˈkaɪnd]/[ˈhjumənˌkaɪnd]

名 人類
同 humanity 人類

英英 human beings or the human race

例 **Mankind** is sometimes very cruel to animals.
人類有時對動物非常的殘忍。

man·ners

[ˈmænɚz]

名 禮貌、風俗
同 custom 風俗

英英 polite ways of treating other people and behaving in public

例 Mind your **manners** with elders.
留意你對長者的禮貌。

mar·ble [ˈmɑrbl]

名 大理石

英英 a hard rock, which may be polished and is used in sculpture and building

例 Unbelievably, this **marble** statue of Apollo is smiling at me.
真是不敢相信，這座阿波羅大理石雕像竟對我微笑。

march [mɑrtʃ]

動 前進、行軍
名 行軍、長途跋涉
同 hike 健行

英英 walk or move towards in a military manner with a regular measured tread

例 The troop prepared to **march** to the capital of France.
軍隊準備前進至法國首都。

🎧 **Track 073**

---

mar·vel·ous

[ˋmɑrvələs]

形 令人驚訝的

英英 causing great wonder or surprising; extremely good or excellent

例 Look at the building made up with banned books. It's truly **marvelous**.
看看那座用禁書所組成的建築物。真是令人驚訝。

☐ 三分熟 ☐ 五分熟 ☐ 七分熟 ☐ 全熟

---

math·e·mat·i·cal

[͵mæθəˋmætɪk!]

形 數學的

英英 the study of numbers, shapes and space using a special system of symbols and rules for organizing them

例 This complex **mathematical** formula is hard to understand.
這一則複雜的數學算式很難懂。

☐ 三分熟 ☐ 五分熟 ☐ 七分熟 ☐ 全熟

---

math·e·mat·ics/ math

[͵mæθəˋmætɪks]/[mæθ]

名 數學

英英 the study of the properties, relationships and measurement of quantities and sets, using numbers and symbols

例 **Mathematics** is a piece of cake for Monica.
對莫妮卡來講，數學真的太簡單。

☐ 三分熟 ☐ 五分熟 ☐ 七分熟 ☐ 全熟

---

ma·ture [məˋtjʊr]

形 成熟的
同 adult 成熟的、成年的

英英 a person acts like an adult that shows they are fully grown or physically developed

例 Why does Aunt Sally always blame Tom for being not **mature** enough?
為什麼莎莉姑姑總是責怪湯姆不夠成熟？

☐ 三分熟 ☐ 五分熟 ☐ 七分熟 ☐ 全熟

---

may·or [ˋmeɚ]

名 市長

英英 the head or leader of a city or borough council

例 The **mayor** is giving a speech in front of the citizens in this plaza.
市長面對廣場上的市民們演講。

☐ 三分熟 ☐ 五分熟 ☐ 七分熟 ☐ 全熟

---

mead·ow [ˋmɛdo]

名 草地

英英 an area or a field of grassland and usually grows wild flowers

例 Having a picnic on the **meadow** is wonderful.
在草地上野餐真是太棒了。

☐ 三分熟 ☐ 五分熟 ☐ 七分熟 ☐ 全熟

---

mean·ing·ful

[ˋminɪŋfəl]

形 有意義的
同 significant 有意義的

英英 having meaning; worthwhile or meaningful

例 Helping people in need is **meaningful**.
幫助有需要的人是件有意義的事。

☐ 三分熟 ☐ 五分熟 ☐ 七分熟 ☐ 全熟

---

mean·while

[`min`hwaɪl]

副 同時
名 期間
同 meantime 同時

英英 at the same time

例 Cindy is starting college in March. **Meanwhile**, she's having a part-time job.
辛蒂在三月將開始大學生活。同時，她也要打工。

☐ 三分熟
☐ 五分熟
☐ 七分熟
☐ 全熟

med·al [`mɛdl]

名 獎章

英英 a small metal disc with an inscription or pictures, which is awarded for achievement in the event or competition

例 Winning **medals** is a must if you plan to become a coach some day.
如果您計劃有一天成為一名教練，則必須獲得獎章。

☐ 三分熟
☐ 五分熟
☐ 七分熟
☐ 全熟

med·i·cal

[`mɛdɪkl]

形 醫學的

英英 relating to the treatment or practice of medicine

例 Some **medical** researches takes years to have break-through development.
有些醫學研究要花數年的時間才會有突破性的發展。

☐ 三分熟
☐ 五分熟
☐ 七分熟
☐ 全熟

me·di·um/me·di·a

[`midɪəm]/[`midɪə]

名 媒體

英英 the means of mass communication, especially television, radio, and newspapers

例 Social **media**, like Facebook or Line, are quite popluar these days.
現今像臉書或 Line 這種社群媒體是非常流行的。

☐ 三分熟
☐ 五分熟
☐ 七分熟
☐ 全熟

mem·ber·ship

[`mɛmbɚʃɪp]

名 會員

英英 a person who belongs to a group or society

例 I'd like to apply for the **membership** of the gym.
我想申請成為這間健身房的會員。

☐ 三分熟
☐ 五分熟
☐ 七分熟
☐ 全熟

mem·o·rize

[`mɛməˌraɪz]

動 記憶

英英 to learn something by heart

例 You'd better **memorize** the steps of planting these purple roses.
你最好記一下種植這些紫色玫瑰的步驟。

☐ 三分熟
☐ 五分熟
☐ 七分熟
☐ 全熟

mend [mɛnd]

動 修補、修改
同 repair 修理

英英 to restore or repair something which is broken; to improve something

例 How efficiently the plumber **mended** this burst pipe!
這個水電工修理爆裂水管真有效率！

☐ 三分熟
☐ 五分熟
☐ 七分熟
☐ 全熟

🎧 Track 075

men·tal [ˋmɛntl̩]

形 心理的、心智的
片 mental cruelty
精神虐待

英英 relating to disorders, the process of thinking or illnesses of the mind

例 It's quite hard to judge if the criminal's **mental** state is normal.
要判斷這個罪犯的心理狀態是否正常是困難的。

☐ 三分熟
☐ 五分熟
☐ 七分熟
☐ 全熟

---

men·tion [ˋmɛnʃən]

動 提起
名 提及

英英 to speak about something with few words

例 Don't ever **mention** the name of Julia. I warn you!
千萬不要提茱莉亞的名字。我警告你！

☐ 三分熟
☐ 五分熟
☐ 七分熟
☐ 全熟

---

mer·chant [ˋmɝtʃənt]

名 商人

英英 a retail trader; a businessman

例 Steve Jobs is a well-known American **merchant**.
史蒂夫‧賈伯斯是有名的美國商人。

☐ 三分熟
☐ 五分熟
☐ 七分熟
☐ 全熟

---

mer·ry [ˋmɛrɪ]

形 快樂的

英英 very cheerful and pleasant

例 Mike's **merry** sound of laughter turns his mother's sadness to smiles.
麥克快樂的笑聲讓他母親的悲傷轉為笑容。

☐ 三分熟
☐ 五分熟
☐ 七分熟
☐ 全熟

---

mess [mɛs]

名 雜亂
動 弄亂

英英 a state of confusion or untidiness

例 Clean up this **mess**!
把這堆雜亂的東西清乾淨！

☐ 三分熟
☐ 五分熟
☐ 七分熟
☐ 全熟

---

mi·cro·phone/ mike [ˋmaɪkrəˌfon]/[maɪk]

名 麥克風

英英 an instrument for converting sound waves into electrical energy which makes your voice louder or recorded

例 Should I use the **microphone**?
我應該用麥克風嗎？

☐ 三分熟
☐ 五分熟
☐ 七分熟
☐ 全熟

---

mi·cro·wave [ˋmaɪkrəˌwev]

名 微波爐
動 微波

英英 an electric device that uses waves of energy to cook or heat food quickly

例 How much is the **microwave**?
這個微波爐多少錢？

☐ 三分熟
☐ 五分熟
☐ 七分熟
☐ 全熟

---

might [maɪt]

名 權力、力氣
同 power 權力

英英 used to express possibility or make a suggestion; the power or the strength

例 The girl cried with all her **might** to get someone to help her.
女孩用盡力氣大叫，希望能有個人來救她。

☐ 三分熟
☐ 五分熟
☐ 七分熟
☐ 全熟

M

might·y [ˋmaɪtɪ]
形 強大的、有力的

英英 very great power or strength

例 **Mighty** will power leads her to succeed in the fashion model career.
強大的意志力讓她在時尚模特兒的職場上取得成功。

---

mill [mɪl]
名 磨坊、工廠
動 研磨

英英 a building equipped with machinery for crushing grain into flour

例 The job in the **mill** is tiring.
磨坊裡的工作讓人疲累。

---

mil·lion·aire [ˋmɪljənɛr]
名 百萬富翁

英英 a person whose assets are worth one million pounds at least

例 If you became a **millionaire**, what would you do first?
如果你是百萬富翁，你會先做什麼？

---

min·er [ˋmaɪnɚ]
名 礦夫、礦工

英英 a person who works in a mine

例 This exhibition is about the past life of the **miners**.
這個展覽是關於礦工過去的生活。

---

mi·nor [ˋmaɪnɚ]
形 較小的、次要的
名 未成年者

英英 less important or with a little important; smaller type

例 Compared to the safety of life, money is **minor**.
跟生命的安全相比，金錢是次要的。

---

mi·nor·i·ty [maɪˋnɔrətɪ]
名 少數
反 majority 多數

英英 the smaller number or part; small group of people

例 We need to respect the rights of the **minority** groups.
我們必需尊重少數團體的權利。

---

mir·a·cle [ˋmɪrəkl̩]
名 奇蹟
同 marvel 令人驚奇的事物

英英 an extraordinary and unusual event which is thought to be caused by a god or any surprising event

例 To see you again after the tsunami is a **miracle**.
海嘯過後還能再見到你，真的是奇蹟。

---

mis·er·y [ˋmɪzərɪ]
名 悲慘
同 distress 悲痛

英英 very painful or unhappiness

例 Marriage without love is a **misery**.
沒有愛的婚姻是悲慘的。

Track 077

---

mis·sile [`mɪsḷ]

名 發射物、飛彈

英英 an object which can travel a long distance to hit the target

例 Japanese **missiles** angered the Americans in the World War II.
在二次大戰期間，日本人的飛彈惹惱了美國人。

☐ 三分熟　☐ 五分熟　☐ 七分熟　☐ 全熟

---

miss·ing [`mɪsɪŋ]

形 失蹤的、缺少的

英英 something is gone or shortage

例 The lovely parrot is **missing**.
可愛的鸚鵡失蹤了。

☐ 三分熟　☐ 五分熟　☐ 七分熟　☐ 全熟

---

mis·sion [`mɪʃən]

名 任務

英英 an important job which requires more care or efforts

例 **Mission** *Impossible* is one of Tom Cruise's most famous movies.
湯姆・克魯斯主演的《不可能的任務》是他最有名的影視作品之一。

☐ 三分熟　☐ 五分熟　☐ 七分熟　☐ 全熟

---

mist [mɪst]

名 霧
動 被霧籠罩
同 fog 霧

英英 a cloud of tiny water droplets in the atmosphere, more like thin fog; to cover something with very small drops of liquid

例 The **mist** in Ali Mountain adds certain spiritual mystery.
阿里山的白霧讓這座山增添某種靈性氣息。

☐ 三分熟　☐ 五分熟　☐ 七分熟　☐ 全熟

---

mix·ture [`mɪkstʃɚ]

名 混合物

英英 a substance which is mixed with other substances

例 The mansion is a **mixture** of the new and the old.
這棟大廈混合新舊的元素。

☐ 三分熟　☐ 五分熟　☐ 七分熟　☐ 全熟

---

mob [mɑb]

名 民眾
動 群集

英英 a crowd of people; people come together around someone or something to express their emotions, such as admiration, interest or anger

例 The **mob** has rushed into the president's house.
民眾已經衝進總統府。

☐ 三分熟　☐ 五分熟　☐ 七分熟　☐ 全熟

---

mo·bile [`mobɪl]

形 可動的
同 movable 可動的

英英 able to move or be moved freely or easily; portable

例 The **mobile** home in the Alps keeps the climbers warm.
阿爾卑斯山的可動式房屋讓登山客得以溫暖。

☐ 三分熟　☐ 五分熟　☐ 七分熟　☐ 全熟

M

moist [mɔɪst]

形 潮濕的
同 damp 潮濕的

英英 slightly wet or damp

例 The soil is not **moist** enough.
土壤不夠潮濕。

---

mois·ture [ˈmɔɪstʃɚ]

名 溼氣

英英 water or other liquid in the form of very small drops, which appears in the air, in a substance, or on a surface

例 The **moisture** here is perfect for your skin.
這裡的溼氣對你的皮膚來講真是太好不過了。

---

monk [mʌŋk]

名 僧侶、修道士

英英 man belonging to a religion, who keeps single and usually live together in a monastery

例 He became a **monk** ten years ago.
他十年前成了僧侶。

---

mood [mud]

名 心情
同 feeling 感覺

英英 a temporary state of mind, temper or depression

例 Singing aloud turned her bad **mood** into good **mood**.
大聲歌唱讓她原先的壞心情轉好。

---

mop [mɑp]

名 拖把
動 擦拭
同 wipe 擦

英英 a bundle of thick loose strings or a sponge attached to a handle, used for wiping or washing floors or dishes; to rub with a mop

例 Return the **mop** to Mr. Li and you may go home.
把拖把交給李先生，你便可以回家。

---

mor·al [ˈmɔrəl]

形 道德上的
名 寓意

英英 concerned with the principles of good and bad behavior and the goodness or badness of human character; a practical lesson about what to do or how to behave, which you learn from a fable

例 Stealing money is not **moral**.
偷錢是件不道德的事。

---

mo·tel [moˈtɛl]

名 汽車旅館

英英 a roadside hotel, in which cars have space for parking in each room

例 The **motel** has a stature of Cupid and Psyche inside.
汽車旅館內有座丘比特和賽姬的雕像。

🎧 Track 079

mo·tor [`motɚ]

名 馬達、發電機

英英 a machine that supplies power to make vehicle or other device work

例 Ride on the **motor** boat and you'll reach the other side of the lake.
乘坐這艘馬達發動的船，你將可抵達湖的另一邊。

☐ 三分熟
☐ 五分熟
☐ 七分熟
☐ 全熟

mur·der [`mɝdɚ]

名 謀殺
動 謀殺、殘害
同 assassinate 暗殺

英英 the crime of intentionally killing someone; to kill somebody

例 The **murder** case of prostitutes attracted the public's attention.
妓女的謀殺案引起大眾的注意。

☐ 三分熟
☐ 五分熟
☐ 七分熟
☐ 全熟

mus·cle [`mʌsl̩]

名 肌肉

英英 a band of fibrous tissue in the body that has the ability to tighten and relax to produce movement

例 Weight lifters usually have **muscles**.
舉重者通常有肌肉。

☐ 三分熟
☐ 五分熟
☐ 七分熟
☐ 全熟

mush·room [`mʌʃrum]

名 蘑菇
動 急速生長

英英 a spore-producing body of a fungus, usually with a round top and short stem; to increase or grow up very quickly

例 In the cartoon, blue fairies live in the **mushroom** village.
在卡通影片裡，藍色精靈住在蘑菇村裡。

☐ 三分熟
☐ 五分熟
☐ 七分熟
☐ 全熟

mu·si·cal [`mjuzɪkl̩]

形 音樂的
名 音樂劇

英英 relating to music or fond of music or good at music; a performance that includes singing and dancing

例 The Phantom of the Opera is a famous **musical**.
《歌劇魅影》是有名的音樂劇。

☐ 三分熟
☐ 五分熟
☐ 七分熟
☐ 全熟

mys·ter·y [`mɪstərɪ]

名 神祕
片 mystery play 神祕劇

英英 something that is hard or impossible to be understood or explained

例 The legend of the monkey god adds certain **mystery** to the town.
猴神的傳說為這個城鎮添加一些神祕感。

☐ 三分熟
☐ 五分熟
☐ 七分熟
☐ 全熟

nan·ny [ˈnænɪ]

名 奶媽

英英 a woman who is hired to look after a child in its own home

例 **Nanny**, the baby is crying.
奶媽，寶寶在哭。

☐三分熟
☐五分熟
☐七分熟
☐全熟

---

nap [næp]

名 小睡、打盹

英英 short sleep during the day time

例 If you're tired, take a **nap** for a while.
如果你累了，可以小睡一會兒。

☐三分熟
☐五分熟
☐七分熟
☐全熟

---

na·tive [ˈnetɪv]

形 本國的、天生的

英英 a person born in a specific place

例 Some **native** speakers here are from Canada.
這裡的一些本國人是從加拿大來的。

☐三分熟
☐五分熟
☐七分熟
☐全熟

---

na·vy [ˈnevɪ]

名 海軍、艦隊

英英 the branch of a state's armed services which operate military at sea

例 How lovely are those **navy**'s uniform!
那些海軍的制服好美啊！

☐三分熟
☐五分熟
☐七分熟
☐全熟

---

ne·ces·si·ty

[nəˈsɛsətɪ]

名 必需品

英英 something that is required or needed

例 Before the typhoon, we need to buy some **necessities**.
在颱風來臨前，我們必須買些必需品。

☐三分熟
☐五分熟
☐七分熟
☐全熟

---

neck·tie [ˈnɛkˌtaɪ]

名 領帶

英英 a long narrow piece of cloth worn around the neck or under a shirt collar

例 The **necktie** is used in formal occasions.
在正式場合中才需要用到領帶。

☐三分熟
☐五分熟
☐七分熟
☐全熟

---

neigh·bor·hood

[ˈnebɚˌhʊd]

名 社區

英英 a community within a town or city, where the people are living in

例 People avoided visiting the **neighborhood** at night time.
人們避免在晚間時分造訪這個社區。

☐三分熟
☐五分熟
☐七分熟
☐全熟

---

nerve [nɝv]

名 神經

英英 a fiber or bundle of fibers in the body that carry information or transmits impulses of sensation between the brain and other parts of the body

例 **Nerve** damage can be avoided.
神經損傷是可以避免的。

☐三分熟
☐五分熟
☐七分熟
☐全熟

🎧 Track 081

nerv·ous [ˋnɝvəs]

形 神經質的、膽怯的、緊張不安的

英英 apprehensive or anxious; not brave

例 To deliver a public speech makes me **nervous**.
要在大眾面前演講讓我好緊張。

□ 三分熟
□ 五分熟
□ 七分熟
□ 全熟

---

net·work

[ˋnɛtˌwɝk]

名 網路

英英 to connect computers together for sharing information or data

例 Computer **network** offered great help to modern people.
電腦網路提供現代人很多的協助。

□ 三分熟
□ 五分熟
□ 七分熟
□ 全熟

---

nick·name

[ˋnɪkˌnem]

名 綽號
動 取綽號

英英 a familiar or informal name for a person or thing; to call someone in an informal name

例 He is smart and his **nickname** is Conan.
他很聰明，他的綽號是柯南。

□ 三分熟
□ 五分熟
□ 七分熟
□ 全熟

---

no·ble [ˋnobḷ]

形 高貴的
名 貴族

英英 having fine personal qualities or high moral principles or social rank

例 Sara is a real princess with a **noble** mind.
莎拉是個擁有高貴心靈的真正的公主。

□ 三分熟
□ 五分熟
□ 七分熟
□ 全熟

---

nor·mal [ˋnɔrmḷ]

形 標準的、正常的
同 regular 正常的、規律的

英英 standard, usual, normal, or expected

例 **Normal** people will laugh out loud, but some people just don't.
正常人會放聲大笑，但有些人就是不笑。

□ 三分熟
□ 五分熟
□ 七分熟
□ 全熟

---

nov·el·ist [ˋnɑvḷɪst]

名 小說家

英英 a person who writes novels

例 E. Nesbit is one of J.K. Rowling's favorite **novelists**.
意蒂絲·內斯比特是 J.K. 羅琳最喜歡的小說家之一。

□ 三分熟
□ 五分熟
□ 七分熟
□ 全熟

---

nun [nʌn]

名 修女、尼姑

英英 women belong to a religion, who usually live together in a convent

例 Mother Teresa is a **nun** who helps many poor people.
德蕾莎是名幫助過很多窮人的修女。

□ 三分熟
□ 五分熟
□ 七分熟
□ 全熟

Oo

O

oak [ok]
名 橡樹、橡葉

英英 a large tree which bears acorns and typically has lobed leaves and hard wood, usually grows in northern countries

例 The **oak** tree produces squirrel's food, acrons.
橡樹生產松鼠的食物—橡實。

□ 三分熟
□ 五分熟
□ 七分熟
□ 全熟

ob·serve [əbˋzɝv]
動 觀察、評論

英英 to notice or perceive; watch or monitor attentively

例 **Observe** the night sky and see if any shooting star is coming.
觀察夜空，看看是否有流星要來。

□ 三分熟
□ 五分熟
□ 七分熟
□ 全熟

ob·vi·ous [ˋɑbvɪəs]
形 顯然的、明顯的
同 evident 明顯的

英英 very clear or easily understood

例 After a summer holiday, there's an **obvious** change of Elizabeths' skin color.
一個暑假過後，伊莉莎白的膚色有明顯的變化。

□ 三分熟
□ 五分熟
□ 七分熟
□ 全熟

oc·ca·sion
[əˋkeʒən]
名 事件、場合
動 引起

英英 a particular event or the time at which something is happening; to cause something happen

例 Sam put on black suit on special **occasions**.
山姆在特殊的場合穿黑色西裝。

□ 三分熟
□ 五分熟
□ 七分熟
□ 全熟

odd [ɑd]
形 單數的、殘餘的、怪異的

英英 can't be divided by two; very unusual or strange

例 If the last petal you count is **odd**, stop one-sided love.
如果你數的最後一片花瓣是奇數，停止單相思。

□ 三分熟
□ 五分熟
□ 七分熟
□ 全熟

on·to [ˋɑntu]
介 在……之上

英英 in contact with a surface of something

例 The boxes were loaded **onto** the van.
箱子裝載到貨車上。

□ 三分熟
□ 五分熟
□ 七分熟
□ 全熟

op·er·a·tor
[ˋɑpəˏretɚ]
名 操作者

英英 a person who operates a machine

例 The **operator** of the cookie-making machine takes a day off.
製作餅乾機器的操作員請了一天假。

□ 三分熟
□ 五分熟
□ 七分熟
□ 全熟

🎧 **Track 083**

op·por·tu·ni·ty

[ˌɑpɚˈtjunətɪ]

名 機遇、機會

英英 a possibility for people to succeed something they want to do

例 Grasp the **opportunity** and sing for the world.
把握這個機會，為這個世界唱歌吧。

☐ 三分熟
☐ 五分熟
☐ 七分熟
☐ 全熟

---

op·po·site

[ˈɑpəsɪt]

形 相對的、對立的
同 contrary 對立的

英英 situated on the different side

例 The lady sitting **opposite** to you is Jolin Tsai.
坐在你對面的那名女士就是蔡依林。

☐ 三分熟
☐ 五分熟
☐ 七分熟
☐ 全熟

---

op·ti·mis·tic

[ˌɑptəˈmɪstɪk]

形 樂觀（主義）的
反 pessimistic 悲觀的

英英 be very confident about the future or the things will happen

例 Rita is **optimistic** about her chances of winning the game.
麗塔對於贏得這場比賽感到樂觀。

☐ 三分熟
☐ 五分熟
☐ 七分熟
☐ 全熟

---

or·i·gin [ˈɔrədʒɪn]

名 起源

英英 the point where something start or begin with

例 The **origin** of the vampire legend is related to a kind of terrible bat.
吸血鬼傳說的起源跟某種可怕的蝙蝠有關。

☐ 三分熟
☐ 五分熟
☐ 七分熟
☐ 全熟

---

o·rig·i·nal

[əˈrɪdʒən!]

形 起初的
名 原作

英英 existing from the very beginning; being the earliest form of something

例 The palace was restored to its **original** glory.
這座皇宮恢復了原先的輝煌。

☐ 三分熟
☐ 五分熟
☐ 七分熟
☐ 全熟

---

or·phan [ˈɔrfən]

名 孤兒
動 使（孩童）成為孤兒

英英 a child who doesn't have parents

例 Due to the war, children become **orphans**.
由於戰爭的緣故，小孩成為孤兒。

☐ 三分熟
☐ 五分熟
☐ 七分熟
☐ 全熟

---

ought to [ɔt tu]

助 應該

英英 used to indicate duty or correctness

例 You **ought to** be in bed before 10 p.m.
晚上十點前你就該上床了。

☐ 三分熟
☐ 五分熟
☐ 七分熟
☐ 全熟

---

out·door [ˈaʊtˌdor]

形 戶外的
反 indoor 室內的

英英 done, situated, or used outside a building

例 Why don't you do some **outdoor** activity in your free time?
在你空閒時，為什麼不做一些戶外活動呢？

☐ 三分熟
☐ 五分熟
☐ 七分熟
☐ 全熟

out·doors
[`aʊt`dorz]

副 在戶外、在屋外

英英 outside of a space or a house

例 If it's not rainy, we'll eat **outdoors**.
如果沒有下雨的話，我們會在戶外用餐。

☐ 三分熟
☐ 五分熟
☐ 七分熟
☐ 全熟

out·er [`aʊtɚ]
形 外部的、外面的

英英 at a long distance from the centre

例 The **outer** space is the setting of most sci-fi movies.
外太空是多數科幻電影的場景。

☐ 三分熟
☐ 五分熟
☐ 七分熟
☐ 全熟

out·line [`aʊt`laɪn]
名 外形、輪廓
動 畫出輪廓
同 sketch 畫草圖、草擬

英英 the main shape of something or someone, without any details; to draw the main shape of something or someone

例 The **outline** of the creature seems to be a mermaid.
生物的外形看起來好像美人魚。

☐ 三分熟
☐ 五分熟
☐ 七分熟
☐ 全熟

o·ver·coat
[`ovɚ͵kot]

名 大衣、外套

英英 a long warm coat worn in cold weather

例 Men's **overcoats** are 30% off.
男士大衣七折。

☐ 三分熟
☐ 五分熟
☐ 七分熟
☐ 全熟

owe [o]
動 虧欠、欠債

英英 be required to pay someone money or goods that you have borrowed

例 The taxi driver **owed** his boss 50,000 dollars.
計程車司機欠他的老闆 5 萬元。

☐ 三分熟
☐ 五分熟
☐ 七分熟
☐ 全熟

own·er·ship
[`onɚ͵ʃɪp]

名 主權、所有權
同 possession 所有物

英英 sole right of possession

例 The **ownership** of the private library is still a mystery.
這間私人圖書館的主權仍然是個謎。

☐ 三分熟
☐ 五分熟
☐ 七分熟
☐ 全熟

Pp

pad [pæd]
名 墊子、印臺
動 填塞
同 cushion 墊子

英英 a thick piece of soft material; to fill something with a soft material in order to protect it

例 The shoulder's **pad** is taken away from the woman's coat.
這件女用大衣裡的墊肩已經拿掉了。

☐ 三分熟
☐ 五分熟
☐ 七分熟
☐ 全熟

🎧 **Track 085**

---

pail [pel]

名 桶

英英	a bucket; a metal, plastic or wooden container with a handle, used for carrying liquids
例	This **pail** of water is really heavy. 這桶水真的好重。

☐ 三分熟
☐ 五分熟
☐ 七分熟
☐ 全熟

---

pal [pæl]

名 夥伴
同 companion 同伴
片 old pal 老友

英英	a friend; a person who usually accompanies you
例	Clara is my best **pal**. 克萊拉是我最好的夥伴。

☐ 三分熟
☐ 五分熟
☐ 七分熟
☐ 全熟

---

pal·ace [ˈpælɪs]

名 宮殿

英英	a large, impressive building forming the official residence of a king, queen or other person of high social rank
例	The baroque **palace** in Austria looks magnificent. 奧地利的巴洛克宮殿看起來高雅非凡。

☐ 三分熟
☐ 五分熟
☐ 七分熟
☐ 全熟

---

pale [pel]

形 蒼白的

英英	describe someone's skin or face is approaching white
例	The backpacker's face turned **pale** when he saw the ghost in the castle. 當背包客看到城堡裡的鬼魂，他的臉變得好蒼白。

☐ 三分熟
☐ 五分熟
☐ 七分熟
☐ 全熟

---

pan·cake

[ˈpænˌkek]

名 薄煎餅

英英	a thin, flat cake, made from a mixture of flour, milk and egg, which is fried and turned in a pan
例	The **pancakes** with creams taste delicious. 上面有奶油的薄煎餅嚐起來很美味。

☐ 三分熟
☐ 五分熟
☐ 七分熟
☐ 全熟

---

pan·ic [ˈpænɪk]

名 驚恐
動 恐慌
同 scare 驚嚇

英英	fear or anxiety; to feel frightened
例	Alice got into a **panic** because she forgot to bring her report to school. 愛麗絲陷入恐慌，怕自己忘記把報告帶來學校。

☐ 三分熟
☐ 五分熟
☐ 七分熟
☐ 全熟

---

pa·rade [pəˈred]

名 遊行
動 參加遊行、閱兵
片 parade ground 閱兵場

英英	a large number of people walking in the same direction, usually as part of a public celebration of something; to walk or march somewhere, to celebrate or protest about something
例	The **parade** of huge cartoon figures affects the traffic. 大型卡通人物的遊行影響了交通。

☐ 三分熟
☐ 五分熟
☐ 七分熟
☐ 全熟

---

par·a·dise

[`pærə͵daɪs]

名 天堂

英英 heaven as the place where the good live after people die

例 It is said that the phoenix lives in the **paradise**.
據說鳳凰住在天堂。

☐ 三分熟
☐ 五分熟
☐ 七分熟
☐ 全熟

par·cel [`pɑrsl̩]

名 包裹
動 捆成

英英 an object or collection of objects wrapped in paper for being carried or sent by post; to cover or surround something completely in paper or other material

例 This **parcel** has some Chinese herbs.
這個包裹裡有些中國藥草。

☐ 三分熟
☐ 五分熟
☐ 七分熟
☐ 全熟

par·tic·i·pate

[pɑr`tɪsə͵pet]

動 參與

英英 take part, attend or join

例 Kim can't **participate** in the race as she broke her legs two days ago.
金無法參加賽跑，因為她兩天前摔斷了自己的腿。

☐ 三分熟
☐ 五分熟
☐ 七分熟
☐ 全熟

pas·sage

[`pæsɪdʒ]

名 通道

英英 a way or path through something or a passageway

例 The **passage** to the outside of White House is a secret.
這條通往白宮外面的通道是個祕密。

☐ 三分熟
☐ 五分熟
☐ 七分熟
☐ 全熟

pas·sion [`pæʃən]

名 熱情
同 emotion 情感

英英 strong and intense emotion

例 If you have **passion** for artistic creation, go for it.
如果你對藝術創作有熱情，就去追吧。

☐ 三分熟
☐ 五分熟
☐ 七分熟
☐ 全熟

pass·port

[`pæs͵port]

名 護照

英英 an official government document certifying the holder's personal information which allow a person to travel abroad under its protection

例 Show your **passport** to the staff in the airport and get your plane ticket.
把你的護照秀給機場的工作人員看，然後拿機票。

☐ 三分熟
☐ 五分熟
☐ 七分熟
☐ 全熟

pass·word

[`pæs͵wɝd]

名 口令、密碼

英英 secret word or code used to gain admission or for entering a space

例 The **password** to enter the computer system is your birthday.
要進入電腦系統的密碼就是你的生日。

☐ 三分熟
☐ 五分熟
☐ 七分熟
☐ 全熟

🎧 **Track 087**

pa·tience

[ˈpeʃəns]

名 耐心

英英 the capacity to tolerate delay, trouble, or suffering without anger

例 Have some **patience** to Amy when she's crying.
艾咪哭的時候，對她有點耐心。

☐ 三分熟
☐ 五分熟
☐ 七分熟
☐ 全熟

---

pause [pɔz]

名 暫停、中止
同 cease 停止

英英 to stop in the middle of something or in operating status

例 Press the button of **pause** if you need to go somewhere else for a while.
如果你需要去別的地方一會兒，按一下暫停鍵。

☐ 三分熟
☐ 五分熟
☐ 七分熟
☐ 全熟

---

pave [pev]

動 鋪築

英英 to cover the surface of ground or a path with concrete or bricks

例 Workers will **pave** the road with white stones.
工人會用白色石頭鋪築這條路。

☐ 三分熟
☐ 五分熟
☐ 七分熟
☐ 全熟

---

pave·ment

[ˈpevmənt]

名 人行道

英英 sidewalk for people to work on at the side of a road

例 The **pavement** is wet and slippery after raining.
人行道在下過雨後就變得溼滑。

☐ 三分熟
☐ 五分熟
☐ 七分熟
☐ 全熟

---

paw [pɔ]

名 腳掌
動 以掌拍擊

英英 an animal's foot having claws or nails, such as a dog or cat

例 The **paw** prints of polar bears seem to be clear in the snow.
北極熊的腳掌印在雪地裡看起來很清晰。

☐ 三分熟
☐ 五分熟
☐ 七分熟
☐ 全熟

---

pay/sal·a·ry/ wage

[pe]/[ˈsælərɪ]/[wedʒ]

名 薪水

英英 a fixed amount of money that is paid to someone for work

例 The **pay** of my last part-time job is not good.
我上一個兼差工作的薪水並不好。

☐ 三分熟
☐ 五分熟
☐ 七分熟
☐ 全熟

---

pea [pi]

名 豌豆

英英 a round green seed eaten as a vegetable

例 "The Princess and the **Pea**" is a famous Andersen's fairy tale.
〈豌豆公主〉是有名的童話。

☐ 三分熟
☐ 五分熟
☐ 七分熟
☐ 全熟

P

peak [pik]

名 山頂
動 豎起、達到高峰
同 top 頂端

英英 the highest top of a mountain; to reach the highest or best point, value or level

例 Did you reach to the highest **peak** of the Alps?
你有攻下阿爾卑斯山最高的山頂嗎？

☐三分熟
☐五分熟
☐七分熟
☐全熟

---

pearl [pɝl]

名 珍珠

英英 a hard, round, shiny object, formed within the shell of an oyster or other mollusk and is used to make jewelry

例 Clams can produce **pearls**.
蛤蜊可以產出珍珠。

☐三分熟
☐五分熟
☐七分熟
☐全熟

---

peel [pil]

名 果皮
動 剝皮

英英 the skin of fruits or vegetables; remove the skin of fruits or vegetables

例 Why did you throw the **peel** of the banana on the sidewalk?
你為什麼要把香蕉皮丟在人行道上？

☐三分熟
☐五分熟
☐七分熟
☐全熟

---

peep [pip]

動 窺視、偷看

英英 look quickly and secretly

例 A strange man **peeped** into the warehouse.
有一位奇怪的男子窺視倉庫。

☐三分熟
☐五分熟
☐七分熟
☐全熟

---

pen·ny [ˈpɛnɪ]

名 便士、分

英英 a British bronze coin equals to one hundredth of a pound; or a small coin worth this much

例 The bun is 3 **pennies**.
這個小圓麵包 3 便士。

☐三分熟
☐五分熟
☐七分熟
☐全熟

---

per·form [pɚˈfɔrm]

動 執行、表演

英英 to accomplish, or fulfill an action, task, or performance

例 Grandma's operation will be **performed** after the Chinese New Year.
奶奶會在春節（農曆新年）後動手術。

☐三分熟
☐五分熟
☐七分熟
☐全熟

---

per·form·ance
[pɚˈfɔrməns]

名 演出

英英 the action of doing something or the process of performing

例 The **performance** of the band is held in the year-end party.
樂團的表演在尾牙餐會中舉行。

☐三分熟
☐五分熟
☐七分熟
☐全熟

🎧 Track 089

per·mis·sion
[pə`mɪʃən]

名 許可
同 approval 許可

英英 the allowance for someone to do something

例 Henry needs his parent's **permission** to join the school trip to a theme park.
哈利需要父母的許可，才能參加校外的主題樂園。

☐ 三分熟
☐ 五分熟
☐ 七分熟
☐ 全熟

per·mit
[pə`mɪt]/[`pɝmɪt]

動 容許、許可
名 批准
同 allow 允許

英英 to give permission to allow someone to do something

例 You're not **permitted** to leave the classroom before the bell rings.
在鐘聲響起前，你們不許離開教室。

☐ 三分熟
☐ 五分熟
☐ 七分熟
☐ 全熟

per·son·al·i·ty
[ˌpɝsṇ`ælətɪ]

名 個性、人格

英英 the characteristics or qualities of a person

例 The tour guide has a **warm** personality.
導遊有著熱情的個性。

☐ 三分熟
☐ 五分熟
☐ 七分熟
☐ 全熟

per·suade
[pə`swed]

動 說服
同 convince 說服

英英 induce a person to do something by giving reasons

例 **Persuading** your father to agree that the marriage is difficult.
說服你父親同意這門婚事是有困難的。

☐ 三分熟
☐ 五分熟
☐ 七分熟
☐ 全熟

pest [pɛst]

名 害蟲、令人討厭的人

英英 destructive animals which are harmful and attacks crops, food, or livestock; or someone who is annoying

例 The locusts are deemed as **pests** for farmers.
蝗蟲對農夫而言被視為害蟲。

☐ 三分熟
☐ 五分熟
☐ 七分熟
☐ 全熟

pick·le [`pɪkḷ]

名 醃菜
動 醃製

英英 vegetables or fruit which are preserved in vinegar, brine, or mustard

例 **Pickles** are not healthy food.
醃菜不是健康的食物。

☐ 三分熟
☐ 五分熟
☐ 七分熟
☐ 全熟

pill [pɪl]

名 藥丸

英英 a small round piece of solid medicine for swallowing without chewing

例 Take 2 **pills** with warm water.
配開水吃 2 顆藥丸。

☐ 三分熟
☐ 五分熟
☐ 七分熟
☐ 全熟

pi·lot [ˈpaɪlət]
名 飛行員、領航員

英英 a person who flies an aircrafts
例 The **pilot** checks her airplane before flying.
飛行員飛行前檢查飛機。

□ 三分熟
□ 五分熟
□ 七分熟
□ 全熟

P

pine [paɪn]
名 松樹

英英 an evergreen coniferous tree having clusters of long needle-shaped leaves and grows in cooler areas of the world
例 The **pine** often serves as one popular motif in Chinese paintings.
松樹經常是出現在國畫裡的一個受歡迎的主題。

□ 三分熟
□ 五分熟
□ 七分熟
□ 全熟

pint [paɪnt]
名 品脫

英英 a measure for liquid, such as beer or milk, equal to about half a liter
例 Add two **pints** of milk into the egg juice.
把兩品脫的牛奶加進蛋汁裡。

□ 三分熟
□ 五分熟
□ 七分熟
□ 全熟

pit [pɪt]
名 坑洞
動 挖坑

英英 a large hole in the surface of the ground; to make small marks or holes in the surface of something
例 A snake is in the **pit**.
蛇在坑洞裡。

□ 三分熟
□ 五分熟
□ 七分熟
□ 全熟

pit·y [ˈpɪtɪ]
名 同情、可惜的事
動 憐憫

英英 a feeling of sorrow and compassion caused by the sufferings of others
例 It was a **pity** that you missed the bus.
真可惜，你錯過公車了。

□ 三分熟
□ 五分熟
□ 七分熟
□ 全熟

plas·tic [ˈplæstɪk]
名 塑膠
形 塑膠的

英英 a synthetic substance made from organic polymers, that can be shaped while soft and then set into a rigid or slightly elastic form
例 Why can't we use less **plastic** products?
為什麼我們不能少用一些塑膠製品？

□ 三分熟
□ 五分熟
□ 七分熟
□ 全熟

plen·ty [ˈplɛntɪ]
名 豐富
形 充足的

英英 a large or sufficient quantity or more than enough
例 Paul got a cold and he needed to drink **plenty** of water.
保羅感冒了，他需要喝很多水。

□ 三分熟
□ 五分熟
□ 七分熟
□ 全熟

plug [plʌg]
名 插頭
動 接插頭

英英 a piece of solid object fitting tightly into a hole for connect the equipment to a supply of electricity
例 Don't touch the **plug**. It might be dangerous.
不要碰插頭，可能會有危險。

□ 三分熟
□ 五分熟
□ 七分熟
□ 全熟

🎧 **Track 091**

plum [plʌm]

名 李子

英英 a soft round fruit with smooth red or purple skin, which tastes sweet and with a flat hard seed inside

例 **Plum** cake is Grandma's favorite.
李子糕是奶奶的最愛。

☐三分熟
☐五分熟
☐七分熟
☐全熟

---

plumb·er [ˈplʌmɚ]

名 水管工

英英 a person who works to fit and repair the pipes or toilets, etc.

例 Mario in this video game looks like a **plumber**.
這款電玩遊戲裡的瑪力歐看起來就像個水管工人。

☐三分熟
☐五分熟
☐七分熟
☐全熟

---

pole [pol]

名 杆

英英 a long thin straight stick which is made by wood or metal for supporting a person to stand up in the ground

例 The drunk driver's car crashed onto a telephone **pole**.
喝醉酒司機的車撞上電線杆。

☐三分熟
☐五分熟
☐七分熟
☐全熟

---

pol·i·ti·cal

[pəˈlɪtɪkḷ]

形 政治的

英英 relating to the government issue or public affairs of a country

例 Professor Huang pays lots of attention to the **political** matters.
黃教授很關注政治事務。

☐三分熟
☐五分熟
☐七分熟
☐全熟

---

pol·i·ti·cian

[ˌpɑləˈtɪʃən]

名 政治家

英英 a person active in politics or a law-making organization

例 **Politicians** tend to be eloquent in delivering speeches.
政治家在演講時通常都是滔滔不絕，口齒伶俐。

☐三分熟
☐五分熟
☐七分熟
☐全熟

---

pol·i·tics

[ˈpɑləˌtɪks]

名 政治學

英英 the study associated with governing a country or area, and with the political relations between states

例 George studied **politics** when he was a college student.
當喬治是大學生時，他研讀政治學。

☐三分熟
☐五分熟
☐七分熟
☐全熟

---

poll [pol]

名 投票、民調
動 得票、投票
同 vote 投票

英英 the process of asking people's opinions about an issue or person; to get a particular number of votes in an election

例 They'll carry out a **poll** to find out how many people agree to same-sex marriage.
他們會進行民意調查，調查多少人同意同性婚姻。

☐三分熟
☐五分熟
☐七分熟
☐全熟

pol·lute [pəˈlut]

動 污染

英英 to make land, air, water, etc. dirty or harmful so that it is no longer safe to use

例 Stop **polluting** the river with dead pigs.
不要再用死豬來污染河川了。

☐ 三分熟
☐ 五分熟
☐ 七分熟
☐ 全熟

po·ny [ˈponɪ]

名 小馬

英英 a small young horse

例 Be careful when you ride the **pony**.
騎小馬時要小心點。

☐ 三分熟
☐ 五分熟
☐ 七分熟
☐ 全熟

pop/pop·u·lar

[pɑp]/[ˈpɑpjələ]

形 流行的
名 流行

英英 related to modern popular music

例 Korean clothes are pretty **poplular**.
韓系服飾很流行的。

☐ 三分熟
☐ 五分熟
☐ 七分熟
☐ 全熟

porce·lain/chi·na

[ˈpɔrslɪn]/[ˈtʃaɪnə]

名 瓷器

英英 articles made of clay in high temperature, such as cups, plates, etc.

例 When I think of Qing dynasty, I think of **porcelain**.
當我想到清朝，我就想到瓷器。

☐ 三分熟
☐ 五分熟
☐ 七分熟
☐ 全熟

por·tion [ˈpɔrʃən]

名 部分
動 分配

英英 one part of something; to divide something into parts and give it to several people

例 A **portion** of the company profits goes into the project of the theme park.
有一部分公司的利潤投入到這座主題樂園的案子裡。

☐ 三分熟
☐ 五分熟
☐ 七分熟
☐ 全熟

por·trait [ˈportret]

名 肖像

英英 an artistic representation of a person or a group of people, especially one representing only the face or head and shoulders

例 The **portrait** of the lady looks like a princess.
這位女士的肖像看起來像一位公主。

☐ 三分熟
☐ 五分熟
☐ 七分熟
☐ 全熟

post·age [ˈpostɪdʒ]

名 郵資

英英 the money you pay for sending a letter, etc. by post

例 We should pay the **postage**.
我們應該要付郵資。

☐ 三分熟
☐ 五分熟
☐ 七分熟
☐ 全熟

post·er [ˈpostə]

名 海報

英英 a large printed picture or notice used for decoration or advertisement

例 Jay Chou signed his name on my **poster**.
周杰倫在我的海報上簽名。

☐ 三分熟
☐ 五分熟
☐ 七分熟
☐ 全熟

P

🎧 Track 093

post·pone

[post`pon]

動 延緩、延遲
同 delay 延遲

英英 to delay an event or make an event take place at a later time or date

例 The rock'n roll concert is **postponed**.
搖滾樂演唱會又往後延了。

☐ 三分熟
☐ 五分熟
☐ 七分熟
☐ 全熟

---

post·pone·ment

[post`ponmənt]

名 延後

英英 the act of delaying an event or an activity happening or arranging for it to take place at a later time

例 Repeated **postponement** is not allowed.
持續的延後是不被允許的。

☐ 三分熟
☐ 五分熟
☐ 七分熟
☐ 全熟

---

pot·ter·y/ ce·ram·ics

[`pɑtəɪ]/[sə`ræmɪks]

名 陶器

英英 articles made of clay in high temperature, such as cups, plates, etc.

例 Making **pottery** is fun.
捏陶是有趣的。

☐ 三分熟
☐ 五分熟
☐ 七分熟
☐ 全熟

---

pour [por]

動 澆、倒
片 pour one's heart out 傾訴

英英 cause to flow in a steady stream into a container

例 The rain is **pouring** heavily.
下了傾盆大雨。

☐ 三分熟
☐ 五分熟
☐ 七分熟
☐ 全熟

---

pov·er·ty [`pɑvətɪ]

名 貧窮

英英 the state of being very poor

例 **Poverty** tries your will power.
貧窮考驗你的意志力。

☐ 三分熟
☐ 五分熟
☐ 七分熟
☐ 全熟

---

pow·der [`paʊdə]

名 粉
動 灑粉

英英 a dry solid substance in the form of very small grains; to use a soft dry substance on someone's skin or hair

例 Have you bought our baby's milk **powder**?
你買了我們寶寶的奶粉了嗎？

☐ 三分熟
☐ 五分熟
☐ 七分熟
☐ 全熟

---

prac·ti·cal

[`præktɪkḷ]

形 實用的
同 useful 有用的

英英 very useful, very effective

例 Professor Liang's advice is **practical**.
梁教授的建議是實用的。

☐ 三分熟
☐ 五分熟
☐ 七分熟
☐ 全熟

---

prayer [prɛr]

名 禱告

英英 a request which is asking for help or expression from God or another deity

例 Say your **prayer** before bedtime.
睡覺前要禱告。

☐ 三分熟
☐ 五分熟
☐ 七分熟
☐ 全熟

pre·cious [ˋprɛʃəs]

形 珍貴的
同 valuable 珍貴的

英英 extremely rare and valuable

例 The painting your mother left to you is **precious**.
你母親留給你的畫作很珍貴。

P

prep·a·ra·tion

[ˌprɛpəˋreʃən]

名 準備

英英 the action of preparing or getting ready for something

例 Make **preparation** for the wedding earlier, or it will be too late.
早點準備婚禮，否則會太晚。

pres·sure [ˋprɛʃɚ]

名 壓力
動 施壓

英英 the force or weight made by pressing or pushing someone by someone else

例 Why did you always give Fanny **pressure**?
你為什麼總是要給芬妮壓力呢？

pre·tend [prɪˋtɛnd]

動 假裝

英英 to fake something as it is real or it's happening in this way

例 **Pretend** to smile and then you can smile without pretending.
假裝微笑，然後你就可以不用假裝，也會不禁微笑。

pre·vent [prɪˋvɛnt]

動 預防、阻止

英英 to stop somebody from doing something or to stop something happens

例 Nothing can **prevent** me from gaining success.
沒有任何事可以阻止我取得成功。

pre·vi·ous

[ˋprivɪəs]

形 先前的
同 prior 先前的

英英 occurring or happening before in time or order

例 Max had no **previous** experience in sales.
麥克斯以前沒有業務方面的經驗。

priest [prist]

名 神父

英英 a person, usually a male, who is qualified to perform religious duties in the Roman Catholic or Anglican Churches

例 The **priest** delivers a speech and moves the church goers.
神父發表了演說，感動了去教堂的人。

🎧 **Track 095**

---

pri·mar·y

[ˈpraɪˌmɛrɪ]

形 主要的

英英 being the most important of all

例 The **primary** task of yours is to take care of your daughter.
你的主要任務是照顧你的女兒。

☐ 三分熟
☐ 五分熟
☐ 七分熟
☐ 全熟

---

prob·a·ble

[ˈprɑbəbḷ]

形 可能的

英英 likely to happen or to be true

例 The **probable** solution to this problem is rewriting a new computer program.
這個問題的可能解決之道是重寫新的電腦程式。

☐ 三分熟
☐ 五分熟
☐ 七分熟
☐ 全熟

---

proc·ess [ˈprɑsɛs]

名 過程
動 處理

英英 a series of things or actions that are done in order to achieve a result; to deal with something

例 The **process** of dealing with the contract is quite complex.
處理這份合約的流程相當複雜的。

☐ 三分熟
☐ 五分熟
☐ 七分熟
☐ 全熟

---

prod·uct [ˈprɑdəkt]

名 產品

英英 an article or substance manufactured to be sold

例 Consumers love this brand of medical **products**.
消費者喜歡這個品牌的醫藥產品。

☐ 三分熟
☐ 五分熟
☐ 七分熟
☐ 全熟

---

prof·it [ˈprɑfɪt]

名 利潤
動 獲利

英英 the money that you earn by selling things or business, especially after paying the costs involved; to get money or something useful from a situation

例 Technology industry tends to make **profits** fast.
科技業傾向於快速獲得利潤。

☐ 三分熟
☐ 五分熟
☐ 七分熟
☐ 全熟

---

pro·gram

[ˈprogræm]

名 節目

英英 a radio or television show; or a series of planned events

例 The new TV **program** starts at 8 p.m.
新的電視節目八點開播。

☐ 三分熟
☐ 五分熟
☐ 七分熟
☐ 全熟

---

pro·mote

[prəˈmot]

動 提倡

英英 to help something or someone to develop or upgrade

例 Naomi Klein **promotes** the further understanding of ecological crisis.
娜歐米・克萊因提倡對生態危機的進一步瞭解。

☐ 三分熟
☐ 五分熟
☐ 七分熟
☐ 全熟

proof [pruf]
名 證據
同 evidence 證據

英英 evidence makes a fact or the truth of a statement

例 The key **proof** will be sent to the police soon.
關鍵證據很快會寄給警察。

☐ 三分熟
☐ 五分熟
☐ 七分熟
☐ 全熟

---

prop·er [ˈprɑpɚ]
形 適當的

英英 appropriate, suitable or real

例 A **proper** meal is what you need now.
好好吃一頓飯是你現在所需要的。

☐ 三分熟
☐ 五分熟
☐ 七分熟
☐ 全熟

---

prop·er·ty [ˈprɑpɚlɪ]
名 財產

英英 a thing or things which belong to someone

例 The vases and furniture are personal **properties**.
這些花瓶和家具是個人的財產。

☐ 三分熟
☐ 五分熟
☐ 七分熟
☐ 全熟

---

pro·pos·al [prəˈpozl̩]
名 提議、求婚

英英 a plan or suggestion for something

例 It is said that Prince Charles' **proposal** to Diana is not out of his free will.
據說查爾斯王子向黛安娜求婚一事並非出於他個人的自由意志。

☐ 三分熟
☐ 五分熟
☐ 七分熟
☐ 全熟

---

pro·tec·tion [prəˈtɛkʃən]
名 保護

英英 the act of protecting somebody or something to keep them safe

例 Children need parents' **protection**.
小孩需要父母的保護。

☐ 三分熟
☐ 五分熟
☐ 七分熟
☐ 全熟

---

pro·tec·tive [prəˈtɛktɪv]
形 保護的

英英 providing protection intently

例 Wear the **protective** knee pad.
穿上這副護膝。

☐ 三分熟
☐ 五分熟
☐ 七分熟
☐ 全熟

---

pub [pʌb]
名 酒館

英英 a place for people to relax themselves and have beer and other drinks

例 Let's go to the **pub** and have a drink.
一起去酒館喝一杯吧。

☐ 三分熟
☐ 五分熟
☐ 七分熟
☐ 全熟

---

punch [pʌntʃ]
動 以拳頭重擊
名 打、擊

英英 to hit somebody or something strongly with your fist closed

例 The audience cried out loud, "**Punch** him."
觀眾大喊：「用力給他一拳。」

☐ 三分熟
☐ 五分熟
☐ 七分熟
☐ 全熟

P

🎧 **Track 097**

pure [pjʊr]

形 純粹的

英英 not mixed with any other substance or material, keeping pure and clear

例 Buy **pure** honey instead of fake one you usually see in the supermarket.
買純蜂蜜，不要超市裡常見的假蜂蜜。

☐ 三分熟
☐ 五分熟
☐ 七分熟
☐ 全熟

pur·sue [pəˋsu]

動 追捕、追求

英英 try to make something happen or achieve something over a period of time

例 **Pursuing** the criminal is not just the police's duty.
追捕犯人不只是警察的責任。

☐ 三分熟
☐ 五分熟
☐ 七分熟
☐ 全熟

Qq

quar·rel [ˋkwɔrəl]

名／動 爭吵

英英 an angry argument with someone, often about a personal matter

例 Stop **quarreling** with your younger brother.
不要再跟弟弟吵架。

☐ 三分熟
☐ 五分熟
☐ 七分熟
☐ 全熟

queer [kwɪr]

形 違背常理的、奇怪的

英英 very strange, odd or annoying

例 What a **queer** dream!
好奇怪的夢啊！

☐ 三分熟
☐ 五分熟
☐ 七分熟
☐ 全熟

quote [kwot]

動 引用、引證

英英 to repeat the exact words that other person has said or written

例 Can I **quote** what you just said?
我可否引用你剛才說的話？

☐ 三分熟
☐ 五分熟
☐ 七分熟
☐ 全熟

Rr

ra·cial [ˋreʃəl]

形 種族的

英英 connected with people or differences between races

例 **Racial** prejudice is not allowed.
種族歧視是不被允許的。

☐ 三分熟
☐ 五分熟
☐ 七分熟
☐ 全熟

ra·dar [ˋredɑr]

名 雷達

英英 a system that uses radio waves to find the position and movement of objects, which cannot be seen

例 The airplane disappeared from the **radar**.
飛機從雷達上消失。

☐ 三分熟
☐ 五分熟
☐ 七分熟
☐ 全熟

rag [ræg]
名 破布、碎片

英英 a torn piece of old cloth, especially one from a larger piece
例 The mop is made of **rags**.
這支拖把是破布做的。

☐ 三分熟
☐ 五分熟
☐ 七分熟
☐ 全熟

Q R

---

rai·sin [ˋrezn̩]
名 葡萄乾

英英 a dried grape, usually used in cakes
例 Eat the **raisin** and get iron and vitamin A.
吃葡萄乾，取得鐵質和維他命 A。

☐ 三分熟
☐ 五分熟
☐ 七分熟
☐ 全熟

---

rank [ræŋk]
名 行列、等級、
社會地位

英英 a position in an organization, especially in armed forces, showing the importance of the person having it
例 Show respect to people no matter what their **rank** is.
不管人們社會階級為何，對人要表示尊重。

☐ 三分熟
☐ 五分熟
☐ 七分熟
☐ 全熟

---

rate [ret]
名 比率
動 估價

英英 a measurement of the number of times something happens; to have or think that someone or something has a particular level of value
例 The success **rate** of you being a pianist is high.
你能成為鋼琴家的成功比率是很高的。

☐ 三分熟
☐ 五分熟
☐ 七分熟
☐ 全熟

---

raw [rɔ]
形 生的、原始的

英英 not cooked
例 Eating **raw** meat may be harmful to your health.
吃生肉可能對你的健康有害。

☐ 三分熟
☐ 五分熟
☐ 七分熟
☐ 全熟

---

ray [re]
名 光線

英英 a narrow beam of light, heat or other energy
例 The **ray** comes into the living room from the window.
光線從客廳的窗戶透了進來。

☐ 三分熟
☐ 五分熟
☐ 七分熟
☐ 全熟

---

ra·zor [ˋrezɚ]
名 剃刀、刮鬍刀

英英 an instrument with a sharp blade, which is used to shave unwanted hair from the face or head
例 The **razor** is sharp.
刮鬍刀好銳利。

☐ 三分熟
☐ 五分熟
☐ 七分熟
☐ 全熟

---

re·act [rɪˋækt]
動 反應、反抗
同 respond 回應

英英 to act or behave in a particular way as a result of or in response to something
例 Tim's girlfriend wanted to leave him, but he didn't **react**.
提姆的女朋友想離開他，但他不予回應。

☐ 三分熟
☐ 五分熟
☐ 七分熟
☐ 全熟

🎧**Track 099**

---

re·ac·tion

[rɪˋækʃən]

名 反應

英英 what you react as a result of something that has happened on you

例 The baby's **reaction** is fun when his mother tickles him.
當媽媽搔癢寶寶時，寶寶的反應很有趣。

☐三分熟
☐五分熟
☐七分熟
☐全熟

---

rea·son·a·ble

[ˋriznəbl̩]

形 合理的

英英 very fair, sensible or reasonable

例 The charge for this car washing service is **reasonable**.
洗車服務的收費是合理的。

☐三分熟
☐五分熟
☐七分熟
☐全熟

---

re·ceipt [rɪˋsit]

名 收據

英英 a piece of paper that you get to show that you've paid for the goods or services you bought

例 Pay the credit card bill at the 7-11, and you'll receive a **receipt**.
在 7-11 付信用卡的帳單，你可以拿到一張收據。

☐三分熟
☐五分熟
☐七分熟
☐全熟

---

re·ceiv·er [rɪˋsivɚ]

名 收受者

英英 a person or thing that receives or takes something

例 The **receiver** of the gift you sent has signed her name on the document.
你所寄送禮物的收件人已經在這份文件上簽名。

☐三分熟
☐五分熟
☐七分熟
☐全熟

---

rec·og·nize

[ˋrɛkəɡ͵naɪz]

動 認知
同 know 知道

英英 to acknowledge something which is existing

例 It's hard to **recognize** the manager's signature.
很難認出經理人的簽名。

☐三分熟
☐五分熟
☐七分熟
☐全熟

---

re·cord·er

[rɪˋkɔrdɚ]

名 紀錄員

英英 a person who records sounds or picture or data, etc

例 The **recorder** in this sports game is a Canadian.
運動比賽的紀錄員是加拿大人。

☐三分熟
☐五分熟
☐七分熟
☐全熟

---

re·cov·er [rɪˋkʌvɚ]

動 恢復、重新獲得

英英 to become well or better again after being ill or sick

例 Uncle Bob **recovered** gradually after the surgery.
鮑伯舅舅在手術後逐漸康復。

☐三分熟
☐五分熟
☐七分熟
☐全熟

---

re·duce [rɪˋdjus]

動 減輕

英英 to become smaller or less in amount, degree, or size

例 Her weight was **reduced** after one-month dieting.
一個月的節食後，她的重量減輕了。

☐三分熟
☐五分熟
☐七分熟
☐全熟

R

re·gion·al

[ˈridʒənl̩]

形 區域性的

英英 used to describe things which connecting to a particular area of a country

例 **Regional** sales representatives had a meeting this morning.
區域業務代表們今天早上開過會。

☐ 三分熟
☐ 五分熟
☐ 七分熟
☐ 全熟

---

re·gret [rɪˈgrɛt]

動 後悔、遺憾
名 悔意

英英 to feel sorrow or disappointed because something you've done or you haven't done

例 Don't say anything when you're angry, or you'll **regret.**
當你生氣時，不要講話，不然你會後悔。

☐ 三分熟
☐ 五分熟
☐ 七分熟
☐ 全熟

---

re·late [rɪˈlet]

動 敘述、有關係

英英 to describe or to show a connection between things

例 This story is **related** to the motif of conversations between trees.
這個故事跟樹之間的對話主題有關。

☐ 三分熟
☐ 五分熟
☐ 七分熟
☐ 全熟

---

re·lax [rɪˈlæks]

動 放鬆

英英 to make or become less tense, anxious and feel more comfortable

例 Listen to the bird's singing and **relax** yourself.
聆聽鳥兒的歌聲，放鬆自己。

☐ 三分熟
☐ 五分熟
☐ 七分熟
☐ 全熟

---

re·lease [rɪˈlis]

動 解放
名 釋放

英英 to let somebody or something come out of a place where they have been kept

例 His father was **released** from prison last week.
他的父親上星期便被釋放出獄。

☐ 三分熟
☐ 五分熟
☐ 七分熟
☐ 全熟

---

re·li·a·ble

[rɪˈlaɪəbl̩]

形 可靠的
同 dependable 可靠的

英英 able to be relied on

例 We can trust Paul as he's a **reliable** person.
我們可以信任保羅，因為他是個可靠的人。

☐ 三分熟
☐ 五分熟
☐ 七分熟
☐ 全熟

---

re·lief [rɪˈlif]

名 解除、減輕

英英 a feeling of happiness that something unpleasant has not happened or has ended

例 Drinking can give her some **relief**.
喝酒可以減輕她一些痛苦。

☐ 三分熟
☐ 五分熟
☐ 七分熟
☐ 全熟

🎧 Track 101

---

re·li·gion

[rɪˋlɪdʒən]

名 宗教

英英 the belief in and worship of a superhuman controlling power, especially a God or gods

例 **Religion** brings lucky and unlucky things to humankind.
宗教為人類帶來了幸運和不幸運的事。

☐三分熟
☐五分熟
☐七分熟
☐全熟

---

re·li·gious

[rɪˋlɪdʒəs]

形 宗教的

英英 related to religion or with a particular religion

例 Priests, monks, and nuns are all **religious** people.
修士、和尚和修女都是宗教人士。

☐三分熟
☐五分熟
☐七分熟
☐全熟

---

re·ly [rɪˋlaɪ]

動 依賴

英英 to depend on with full trust or be dependant on something

例 Can old people **rely** on their memory?
可以依賴老人家他們的記憶力嗎？

☐三分熟
☐五分熟
☐七分熟
☐全熟

---

re·main [rɪˋmen]

動 殘留、仍然、繼續

英英 to keep the same state or condition

例 **Remain** hopeful even though you're in a situation without hope.
即便在一個沒有希望的情況下，仍然要保有希望。

☐三分熟
☐五分熟
☐七分熟
☐全熟

---

re·mind [rɪˋmaɪnd]

動 提醒

英英 to say something to cause someone to remember something or to do something

例 **Remind** me to send a Christmas card to Judy.
提醒我送一張聖誕卡給茱蒂。

☐三分熟
☐五分熟
☐七分熟
☐全熟

---

re·mote [rɪˋmot]

形 遠程的、遙遠的

英英 far away from places, distant

例 The prince who had been cursed lived in a **remote** country.
被詛咒的王子住在遙遠的國度。

☐三分熟
☐五分熟
☐七分熟
☐全熟

---

re·move [rɪˋmuv]

動 移動

英英 to take off or away from the position occupied

例 My son helped me to **remove** the shoe cabinet to our basement.
我的兒子幫我把鞋櫃移到地下室。

☐三分熟
☐五分熟
☐七分熟
☐全熟

---

re·new [rɪˋnju]

動 更新、恢復、補充

英英 to recover or re-establish after an interruption

例 Remember to **renew** the passport if you'd like to go to Japan this year.
如果你今年想要去日本，記得要更新護照。

☐三分熟
☐五分熟
☐七分熟
☐全熟

R

---

rent [rɛnt]

名 租金
動 租借

英英 an amount of money that you regularly pay so that you can use a house or a space, etc.

例 We can't afford the **rent** of the apartment in this area.
我們無法負擔這個區域的公寓租金。

☐ 三分熟
☐ 五分熟
☐ 七分熟
☐ 全熟

---

re·pair [rɪˋpɛr]

動 修理
名 修理

英英 to restore or fix something damaged or worn to a good condition

例 The shopkeeper of the bicycles is **repairing** Miss Chen's bicycle.
腳踏車店鋪的老闆正在修理陳老師的腳踏車。

☐ 三分熟
☐ 五分熟
☐ 七分熟
☐ 全熟

---

re·place [rɪˋples]

動 代替

英英 to be used or to do something instead of something or somebody else

例 Would you mind **replacing** the spaghetti with fried rice?
你介意用炒飯取代義大利麵嗎？

☐ 三分熟
☐ 五分熟
☐ 七分熟
☐ 全熟

---

re·place·ment
[rɪˋplesmənt]

名 取代、更新

英英 the action or process of replacing someone or something

例 The **Replacement** faucet looks more fashionable.
新換的水龍頭愈看愈有時尚感了。

☐ 三分熟
☐ 五分熟
☐ 七分熟
☐ 全熟

---

rep·re·sent
[ˏrɛprɪˋzɛnt]

動 代表、象徵

英英 to be a member of a group of people and act or speak on their behalf at an event or a meeting

例 The picture of Cupid shooting the heart **represents** romantic love.
丘比特射心的圖案象徵浪漫的愛情。

☐ 三分熟
☐ 五分熟
☐ 七分熟
☐ 全熟

---

rep·re·sent·a·tive
[rɛprɪˋzɛntətɪv]

形 典型的、代表的
名 典型、代表人員

英英 typical of a large group of people

例 New Zealand's trade **representative** came to visit our office.
紐西蘭的貿易代表來訪我們的辦公室。

☐ 三分熟
☐ 五分熟
☐ 七分熟
☐ 全熟

---

re·pub·lic
[rɪˋpʌblɪk]

名 共和國

英英 a country without a king or queen, which is held by the people and their elected representatives, and which has an elected president rather than a monarch

例 The old lady who is famous for painting the white buildings is from the Czech **republic**.
以在白色建築物上作畫而聞名的老奶奶來自捷克共和國。

☐ 三分熟
☐ 五分熟
☐ 七分熟
☐ 全熟

🎧 **Track 103**

re·quest [rɪˋkwɛst]
名 要求
動 請求
同 beg 乞求

英英 the action of asking for something politely

例 Is the **request** of having a diaper too much for the restaurant?
要求一片尿布對餐廳來講會不會太過份？

☐ 三分熟
☐ 五分熟
☐ 七分熟
☐ 全熟

re·serve [rɪˋzɝv]
動 保留
名 儲藏、保留

英英 to keep for future use or other use; arrange for a seat or ticket to be kept for a particular person

例 The duke of the castle loves to **reserve** the best wine in the basement.
這座城堡的公爵喜歡把最好的酒儲藏到地下室。

☐ 三分熟
☐ 五分熟
☐ 七分熟
☐ 全熟

re·sist [rɪˋzɪst]
動 抵抗

英英 to refuse to accept something and try to fight back

例 Emily tried her best to **resist** the impulse of eating fried chicken.
愛蜜莉傾盡全力抵抗吃炸雞的衝動。

☐ 三分熟
☐ 五分熟
☐ 七分熟
☐ 全熟

re·source [rɪˋsors]
名 資源

英英 a supply of something that is owned and used by a country, an organization or a person

例 The major **resource** of this country is oil.
這個國家的主要資源是石油。

☐ 三分熟
☐ 五分熟
☐ 七分熟
☐ 全熟

re·spond
[rɪˋspɑnd]
動 回答

英英 to act, say or do something in reply

例 It's hard to **respond** to such an embarrassing question.
要回答這樣一個讓人尷尬的問題真的很難。

☐ 三分熟
☐ 五分熟
☐ 七分熟
☐ 全熟

re·sponse
[rɪˋspɑns]
名 回應、答覆

英英 a reaction or written answer

例 His **response** of blushing seems to suggest that he has a crush on Miss Tien.
他臉紅的反應，似乎暗示他對田小姐的愛慕之意。

☐ 三分熟
☐ 五分熟
☐ 七分熟
☐ 全熟

re·spon·si·bil·i·ty
[rɪˏspɑnsəˋbɪlətɪ]
名 責任

英英 something you take as your job or duty to manage or handle

例 Your **responsibility** is to help the manager translate business documents.
你的責任是協助經理翻譯商業文件。

☐ 三分熟
☐ 五分熟
☐ 七分熟
☐ 全熟

re·strict [rɪˋstrɪkt]
動 限制

英英 to limit the actions for someone or the size, amount or range of something

例 **Restricting** the children's actions here may not be right as they love to play around.
限制小孩在此區域的行動可能不太對，因為他們喜歡到處玩耍。

☐ 三分熟
☐ 五分熟
☐ 七分熟
☐ 全熟

R

re·veal [rɪˋvil]

動 顯示

英英 to make something known or appeared to somebody

例 The survey **revealed** that women lived longer than men.
這份調查報告顯示，女人比男人活得久。

☐ 三分熟
☐ 五分熟
☐ 七分熟
☐ 全熟

---

rib·bon [ˋrɪbən]

名 絲帶、破碎條狀物

英英 a narrow strip of material which is used to tie things together or for decoration

例 The **ribbons** on the wedding dress add certain dreaming color.
這件結婚禮服的絲帶增添了某種夢幻的色彩。

☐ 三分熟
☐ 五分熟
☐ 七分熟
☐ 全熟

---

rid [rɪd]

動 使擺脫、除去

英英 to set someone or something free

例 It's time to get **rid** of the bad habit of drinking the soda every day.
該是擺脫每天喝汽水的壞習慣的時候了。

☐ 三分熟
☐ 五分熟
☐ 七分熟
☐ 全熟

---

rid·dle [ˋrɪdḷ]

名 謎語

英英 a question which is requiring ingenuity in knowing its answer or meaning

例 Sphinx the monster loves to test travelers with **riddles**.
斯芬克斯這隻怪物喜歡出謎語考旅客。

☐ 三分熟
☐ 五分熟
☐ 七分熟
☐ 全熟

---

ripe [raɪp]

形 成熟的

英英 ready for harvesting and eating, such as fruits or vegetables

例 The apple is **ripe** and you can pick it off the tree.
蘋果成熟了，你可以把它從樹上摘下來了。

☐ 三分熟
☐ 五分熟
☐ 七分熟
☐ 全熟

---

risk [rɪsk]

名 危險
動 冒險

英英 the possibility of something bad happening or putting someone in danger

例 Sometimes you have to take **risks** to gain what you want in life.
有時你必須冒險才能得到你所想要獲得的東西。

☐ 三分熟
☐ 五分熟
☐ 七分熟
☐ 全熟

---

roar [ror]

名 吼叫
動 怒吼

英英 to make a very loud, deep sound

例 The lion **roared** and the deer remained still.
獅子吼叫，鹿不敢亂動。

☐ 三分熟
☐ 五分熟
☐ 七分熟
☐ 全熟

Track 105

roast [rost]

動 烘烤
形 烘烤的
名 烘烤的肉

英英 to cook or be cooked by the heat of an oven or over a fire

例 Leslie went camping with his girlfriend and **roasted** chicken for her.
萊斯利跟他的女朋友去露營，烤雞給她吃。

☐ 三分熟
☐ 五分熟
☐ 七分熟
☐ 全熟

rob [rɑb]

動 搶劫

英英 to take money or property illegally from a person or place

例 The middle-aged man **robbed** the woman of her purse at night.
這名中年男子在晚上搶了該名女子的錢包。

☐ 三分熟
☐ 五分熟
☐ 七分熟
☐ 全熟

rob·ber [ˈrɑbə]

名 強盜

英英 a person who takes money or property illegally from a person or place

例 It was said that the **robbers** were hidden in this forest.
據說強盜藏身在樹林裡。

☐ 三分熟
☐ 五分熟
☐ 七分熟
☐ 全熟

rob·ber·y [ˈrɑbərɪ]

名 搶案

英英 the crime of stealing money or goods from somewhere or someone

例 It takes five years to detect the **robbery**.
偵破這樁搶案要花五年的時間。

☐ 三分熟
☐ 五分熟
☐ 七分熟
☐ 全熟

robe [rob]

名 長袍
動 穿長袍

英英 a long loose outer piece of clothing, especially one worn on very formal occasions; to dress somebody or yourself in long loose clothes

例 The wizard wearing the white **robe** is Gandolf.
穿白袍的巫師是甘道夫。

☐ 三分熟
☐ 五分熟
☐ 七分熟
☐ 全熟

rock·et [ˈrɑkɪt]

名 火箭
動 發射火箭

英英 a cylindrical projectile that move to a great height or distance by the combustion of its contents

例 The new type of **rocket** is on the process of researching.
新型的火箭還在研發的階段。

☐ 三分熟
☐ 五分熟
☐ 七分熟
☐ 全熟

ro·man·tic [roˈmæntɪk]

形 浪漫的
名 浪漫主義者
片 romantic novel 言情小說

英英 relating to love or a sexual relationship; someone who is not practical , and bases their ideas too much on an imagined idea

例 John Keats is one of the most **romantic** poets in the 19th century.
約翰·濟慈是十九世紀最浪漫的詩人之一。

☐ 三分熟
☐ 五分熟
☐ 七分熟
☐ 全熟

rot [rɑt]
動 腐敗
名 腐壞

英英 to make something decay naturally and gradually
例 The berries **rotted** on the table of the hut.
莓果在小屋的桌上腐爛。

☐ 三分熟 ☐ 五分熟 ☐ 七分熟 ☐ 全熟

rot·ten [ˈrɑtṇ]
形 腐化的

英英 suffering from decay; corrupt
例 The **rotten** meat has certain bad smell.
腐肉有某種不好的味道。

☐ 三分熟 ☐ 五分熟 ☐ 七分熟 ☐ 全熟

rough [rʌf]
形 粗糙的
名 粗暴的人、草圖

英英 having a surface that is not even or smooth; a violent person
例 The **rough** drawing of the little elephant attracted Disney's attention.
小飛象的概略草圖吸引了迪士尼的注意力。

☐ 三分熟 ☐ 五分熟 ☐ 七分熟 ☐ 全熟

rou·tine [ruˈtin]
名 慣例
形 例行的

英英 a sequence of actions regularly followed; a usual way of doing things
例 Cooking coffee for the whole family is Ginny's daily **routine**.
為全家人煮咖啡是金妮每天的例行事務。

☐ 三分熟 ☐ 五分熟 ☐ 七分熟 ☐ 全熟

rug [rʌg]
名 地毯
同 carpet 地毯

英英 a piece of thick material like a small carpet that is used for covering the floor for decoration
例 I bought the red **rug** for the new apartment.
我為新公寓買了一條紅地毯。

☐ 三分熟 ☐ 五分熟 ☐ 七分熟 ☐ 全熟

ru·mor [ˈrumɚ]
名 謠言
動 謠傳

英英 a currently circulating story or news of unverified or doubtful truth
例 **Rumor** has it that he had a son who's deaf.
謠言是說他有個耳朵聽不見的兒子。

☐ 三分熟 ☐ 五分熟 ☐ 七分熟 ☐ 全熟

rust [rʌst]
名 鐵鏽
動 生鏽

英英 a reddish-brown substance which is formed on the metals by reacting with water and air
例 Don't touch the **rust**.
不要碰鐵鏽 。

☐ 三分熟 ☐ 五分熟 ☐ 七分熟 ☐ 全熟

rust·y [ˈrʌstɪ]
形 生鏽的、生疏的

英英 affected or covered by rust
例 The door key to the basement is **rusty**.
要進入地下室的大門鑰匙生鏽了。

☐ 三分熟 ☐ 五分熟 ☐ 七分熟 ☐ 全熟

Ss

🎧 Track 107

sack [sæk]

名 大包、袋子

英英 a large bag made of a material such as cloth, paper or thick paper, used to store and carry something

例 The **sacks** were full of all Christmas gifts to the orphanages.
袋子裡裝滿了要寄到孤兒院的聖誕節禮物。

☐ 三分熟　☐ 五分熟　☐ 七分熟　☐ 全熟

---

sake [sek]

名 緣故、理由

英英 for the reason; or in the interest of

例 For the **sake** of safety, swimming is not allowed in this river.
為了安全的緣故，這條溪不准游泳。

☐ 三分熟　☐ 五分熟　☐ 七分熟　☐ 全熟

---

sat·is·fac·to·ry
[ˌsætɪsˈfæktərɪ]

形 令人滿意的

英英 good enough for a particular purpose or need; absolutely acceptable

例 The art design of the lantern festival is not **satisfactory**.
燈節的藝術設計並不令人滿意。

☐ 三分熟　☐ 五分熟　☐ 七分熟　☐ 全熟

---

sau·cer [ˈsɔsɚ]

名 托盤、茶碟

英英 a small shallow round dish that you make a cup stand on

例 The green **saucer** matches the pink tea cup.
綠色的茶碟與粉紅色的茶杯搭配的很好。

☐ 三分熟　☐ 五分熟　☐ 七分熟　☐ 全熟

---

sau·sage [ˈsɔsɪdʒ]

名 臘腸、香腸

英英 a short tube of raw minced meat encased in a skin, which is usually grilled or fried before eating

例 The **sausage** made of pork is a traditional food.
豬肉香腸是種傳統食物。

☐ 三分熟　☐ 五分熟　☐ 七分熟　☐ 全熟

---

sav·ing(s)
[ˈsevɪŋ(z)]

名 拯救、救助、存款

英英 an amount of money that you save or keep in the account of a bank

例 Miss Chen donated a half of her **savings** to the elementary school.
陳女士捐了一半的存款給這間小學。

☐ 三分熟　☐ 五分熟　☐ 七分熟　☐ 全熟

---

scale(s) [skel(z)]

名 刻度、尺度、天秤

英英 a set of numbers, amounts etc., used to measure or compare the level of something

例 The weight **scale** is on sale.
體重計特價中。

☐ 三分熟　☐ 五分熟　☐ 七分熟　☐ 全熟

scarce [skɛrs]

形 稀少的
同 rare 稀有的

英英 very rare; not easy to find or get

例 The red bean is **scarce** in this bowl of dessert.
在這碗甜點裡，紅豆很稀少。

☐ 三分熟
☐ 五分熟
☐ 七分熟
☐ 全熟

S

---

scare·crow [ˈskɛrˌkro]

名 稻草人

英英 a figure made to look like a person, which is dressed in old clothes and put in a field to frighten birds away

例 The **scarecrow** in the rice field looks real.
在稻田中的稻草人看起來像真人。

☐ 三分熟
☐ 五分熟
☐ 七分熟
☐ 全熟

---

scarf [skɑrf]

名 圍巾、頸巾

英英 length of fabric worn around the neck or head to keep a person warm

例 Vivian's mother **weaved** a scarf for her.
薇薇安的母親為她編織了一條圍巾。

☐ 三分熟
☐ 五分熟
☐ 七分熟
☐ 全熟

---

scar·y [ˈskɛrɪ]

形 駭人的

英英 frightening

例 The vampire fiction is pretty **scary**.
這本吸血鬼小說是很嚇人的。

☐ 三分熟
☐ 五分熟
☐ 七分熟
☐ 全熟

---

scat·ter [ˈskætɚ]

動 散佈
名 散播物

英英 to spread something in a place; a small amount or number of things spread over an area

例 To **scatter** the rumor will not do us any good.
散佈這則謠言並不會對我們有任何好處。

☐ 三分熟
☐ 五分熟
☐ 七分熟
☐ 全熟

---

sched·ule [ˈskɛdʒʊl]

名 時刻表
動 將……列表
同 list 列表

英英 a plan that lists all the work that you have to do in a certain period of time or a date; to plan that something will happen at a particular time

例 Would you mind waiting for us near the flight **schedule**?
你介不介意在飛行時刻表附近等我們？

☐ 三分熟
☐ 五分熟
☐ 七分熟
☐ 全熟

---

schol·ar [ˈskɑlɚ]

名 有學問的人、學者

英英 a specialist in a particular field of study, especially the humanities or a distinguished academic

例 Some **scholars** did further research on white swan's courting behavior.
有些學者針對白天鵝的求偶行為做進一步的研究。

☐ 三分熟
☐ 五分熟
☐ 七分熟
☐ 全熟

🎧 **Track 109**

---

schol·ar·ship

[ˈskɑləˌʃɪp]

名 獎學金

英英 an amount of money given to students by an organization in order to help pay for their education

例 **Scholarship** from the Boston University helps Wayne study for doctor's degree.
來自波士頓大學的獎學金幫助偉恩攻讀博士學位。

☐ 三分熟
☐ 五分熟
☐ 七分熟
☐ 全熟

---

sci·en·tif·ic

[ˌsaɪənˈtɪfɪk]

形 科學的、有關科學的

英英 related to science; connected with science

例 Students are curious about the **scientific** study of dolphin communication.
學生們對海豚溝通的科學研究感到好奇。

☐ 三分熟
☐ 五分熟
☐ 七分熟
☐ 全熟

---

scoop [skup]

名 舀取的器具
動 挖、掘、舀取

英英 a spoon with a short handle and a deep bowl which is used to move a soft substance

例 One **scoop** of sugar water is enough for the bowl of bean curd.
舀一勺的糖水就足夠配這碗豆花了。

☐ 三分熟
☐ 五分熟
☐ 七分熟
☐ 全熟

---

scout [skaʊt]

名 斥候、偵查
動 斥候、偵查

英英 a person, an aircraft, etc. sent ahead to get the enemy's information

例 Erin **scouted** around for somewhere to continue the poetry course.
艾倫到處偵查，想找出某地可以繼續上詩的課程。

☐ 三分熟
☐ 五分熟
☐ 七分熟
☐ 全熟

---

scream [skrim]

動 大聲尖叫、作出尖叫聲
名 大聲尖叫

英英 to make a long, loud, creepy sound

例 **Scream** out loud if you're in danger.
如果陷入危險，就放聲大叫。

☐ 三分熟
☐ 五分熟
☐ 七分熟
☐ 全熟

---

screw [skru]

名 螺絲
動 旋緊、轉動

英英 a thin pointed piece of metal that you push and turn in order to fasten things together; to twist something around in order to fasten it in a place

例 Could you buy me some **screws**?
可否幫我買些螺絲？

☐ 三分熟
☐ 五分熟
☐ 七分熟
☐ 全熟

---

scrub [skrʌb]

動 擦拭、擦洗
名 擦洗、灌木叢

英英 to rub something very hard for cleaning it

例 My mother was angry and she **scrubbed** the pot so hard.
我媽很生氣，她用力的擦洗這個鍋子。

☐ 三分熟
☐ 五分熟
☐ 七分熟
☐ 全熟

---

seal [sil]

名 海豹、印章
動 獵海豹、蓋章、密封

英英 a sea animal that eats fish and lives around coasts or on land or ice; a mark made with wax for official use; to close an envelope

例 The way the **seal** plays with the ball is entertaining.
海豹玩球的樣子很有娛樂性。

☐ 三分熟
☐ 五分熟
☐ 七分熟
☐ 全熟

---

sec·ond·a·r·y
[ˈsɛkənˌdɛrɪ]

形 第二的

英英 less important than related things

例 This set of sofa is the most important, and the table is the **secondary** of importance.
這組沙發是最重要的，而這張桌子是次重要的。

☐ 三分熟
☐ 五分熟
☐ 七分熟
☐ 全熟

se·cu·ri·ty
[sɪˈkjʊrətɪ]

名 安全
同 safety 安全

英英 the state of feeling happy and safe

例 The **security** of the car depends on the place you place it.
車子是否安全，要看你把它放在哪個地方。

☐ 三分熟
☐ 五分熟
☐ 七分熟
☐ 全熟

seek [sik]

動 尋找

英英 to try to find or get; to search for something or someone

例 **Seeking** the yellow parrot is not an easy task.
尋找那隻黃色的鸚鵡並不是件簡單的任務。

☐ 三分熟
☐ 五分熟
☐ 七分熟
☐ 全熟

seize [siz]

動 抓、抓住

英英 to take or grab somebody or something in your hand

例 **Seize** the opportunity.
抓住機會。

☐ 三分熟
☐ 五分熟
☐ 七分熟
☐ 全熟

sel·dom [ˈsɛldəm]

副 不常地、難得地

英英 not often, very hardly

例 The writer **seldom** returns to his homeland.
這名作家很少返回祖國。

☐ 三分熟
☐ 五分熟
☐ 七分熟
☐ 全熟

sen·si·ble
[ˈsɛnsəbl]

形 可感覺的、理性的

英英 being able to feel or sense

例 Calm down and be **sensible**.
冷靜下來，理性一點。

☐ 三分熟
☐ 五分熟
☐ 七分熟
☐ 全熟

sen·si·tive
[ˈsɛnsətɪv]

形 敏感的

英英 being influenced or change easily, such as one's mood

例 Some parents are not **sensitive** to their children's needs.
有些父母對孩子的需求不太敏感。

☐ 三分熟
☐ 五分熟
☐ 七分熟
☐ 全熟

sep·a·ra·tion
[ˌsɛpəˈreʃən]

名 分離、隔離

英英 the state of being apart

例 The **separation** of David and his family left him a scar.
大衛和家人的分離在他心上留下一道疤痕。

☐ 三分熟
☐ 五分熟
☐ 七分熟
☐ 全熟

🎧 Track 111

sew [so]
動 縫、縫上

英英 to use a needle and thread to make stitches in fabric

例 The elves **sew** a pair of shoes for the shoe maker at night.
小精靈們在晚上幫鞋匠縫製一雙鞋。

☐ 三分熟
☐ 五分熟
☐ 七分熟
☐ 全熟

sex [sɛks]
名 性、性別

英英 gender of being male or female

例 What's the **sex** of your boss' baby?
你老闆的寶寶是男是女？

☐ 三分熟
☐ 五分熟
☐ 七分熟
☐ 全熟

sex·u·al [ˈsɛkʃʊəl]
形 性的

英英 relating to the physical activity of sex

例 **Sexual** education is necessary for junior high school students.
性教育對國中生來講是有必要的。

☐ 三分熟
☐ 五分熟
☐ 七分熟
☐ 全熟

sex·y [ˈsɛksɪ]
形 性感的

英英 very attractive or aroused

例 **Sexy** models triggered men's desire.
性感的模特兒引發男人的慾望。

☐ 三分熟
☐ 五分熟
☐ 七分熟
☐ 全熟

shade [ʃed]
名 陰涼處、樹蔭
動 遮住、使陰暗

英英 an area that is little dark and cool under something, such as a large tree; to cover or hide from injury

例 You'd better take a rest under the **shade** of the tree.
你最好在樹蔭下休息。

☐ 三分熟
☐ 五分熟
☐ 七分熟
☐ 全熟

shad·ow [ˈʃædo]
名 陰暗之處、影子
動 使有陰影

英英 a dark area or shape produced by an object coming between light rays and a surface; to cover something to make it dark

例 The **shadow** puppets look like the characters in The Journey to the West.
皮影戲偶看起來像是《西遊記》裡的角色。

☐ 三分熟
☐ 五分熟
☐ 七分熟
☐ 全熟

shad·y [ˈʃedɪ]
形 多蔭的、成蔭的

英英 sheltered from direct light from the sun

例 It's good to have a picnic on the **shady** grasss.
在陰涼的草地上野餐挺好的。

☐ 三分熟
☐ 五分熟
☐ 七分熟
☐ 全熟

shal·low [ˈʃælo]
形 淺的、淺薄的、膚淺的

英英 of little depth or not deep

例 Why are you so **shallow**?
你為什麼如此的膚淺？

☐ 三分熟
☐ 五分熟
☐ 七分熟
☐ 全熟

shame [ʃem]

名 羞恥、羞愧
動 使羞愧

英英 the feelings of guilt or embarrassment that you have because something you have done is wrong or bad

例 "**Shame** on you," Mrs. Wu said to her son.
吳太太對她的兒子說：「真以你為恥。」

S

sham·poo [ʃæmˋpu]

名 洗髮精
動 清洗

英英 a liquid for washing the hair; using liquid soap to wash hair, carpets, etc

例 The bottle of **shampoo** smells like rose.
這瓶洗髮精聞起來像玫瑰。

shave [ʃev]

動 刮鬍子、剃

英英 to cut the hair off one's face with a razor

例 My father **shaves** every morning.
我父親每天早晨都刮鬍子。

shep·herd [ˋʃɛpɚd]

名 牧羊人、牧師

英英 a person who takes care of sheep

例 The **shepherd** is good at taking care of the goats.
牧羊人很擅於照顧山羊。

shin·y [ˋʃaɪnɪ]

形 發光的、晴朗的

英英 reflecting light because very smooth, clean, or polished

例 The sun is **shiny**.
太陽閃耀著光芒。

short·en [ˋʃɔrtn̩]

動 縮短、使變短

英英 to make something shorter; to become shorter

例 Love messages **shortened** the distance of heart between the couple.
愛的訊息縮短了這對情侶之間心的距離。

short·ly [ˋʃɔrtlɪ]

副 不久、馬上
同 soon 不久

英英 in a short time; soon; right away

例 **Shortly**, the ambulance arrived.
不久，救護車就到了。

shov·el [ˋʃʌvl̩]

名 鏟子
動 剷除

英英 a tool with a long handle and a broad blade with curved edges which is used for moving earth, snow, etc.; to lift and move soil, stones etc. with a tool

例 Clara's child was playing the sand with the **shovel**.
克萊拉的小孩正在用鏟子玩沙。

🎧 **Track 113**

shrink [ʃrɪŋk]

動 收縮、退縮

英英 to become or make smaller in size or amount; contract

例 The shirt **shrinks**.
這件襯衫縮水了。

☐ 三分熟
☐ 五分熟
☐ 七分熟
☐ 全熟

---

sigh [saɪn]

動／名 嘆息

英英 to make a long breath to show that you are disappointed, sad or tired

例 "I wish I could see Romeo tonight," Juliet **signed**.
茱麗葉嘆了口氣說：「我希望我今晚能見到羅密歐。」

☐ 三分熟
☐ 五分熟
☐ 七分熟
☐ 全熟

---

sig·nal [ˈsɪgn̩]

名 信號、號誌
動 打信號

英英 a movement or sound that you make for giving somebody information or a warning

例 The policeman gave a **signal** and the truck driver turned right.
警察打了個信號，貨車司機便轉向右邊。

☐ 三分熟
☐ 五分熟
☐ 七分熟
☐ 全熟

---

sig·nif·i·cant

[sɪgˈnɪfəkənt]

形 有意義的

英英 important enough or noticeable

例 The wedding ring is **significant** for most women.
結婚戒指對大多數女人而言都是有意義的。

☐ 三分熟
☐ 五分熟
☐ 七分熟
☐ 全熟

---

sim·i·lar·i·ty

[ˌsɪməˈlærətɪ]

名 類似、相似
同 resemblance 相似

英英 the state of being like somebody or something but not the same one

例 We're wondering why there're so many **similarities** between the two butterflies.
我們在想，為什麼這兩隻蝴蝶有如此多的相似之處。

☐ 三分熟
☐ 五分熟
☐ 七分熟
☐ 全熟

---

sin [sɪn]

名 罪、罪惡
動 犯罪

英英 to break law or do something illegally

例 There's not much difference between breaking a law and committing a **sin**.
違反法律與犯罪之間沒有太大的不同。

☐ 三分熟
☐ 五分熟
☐ 七分熟
☐ 全熟

---

sin·cere [sɪnˈsɪr]

形 真實的、誠摯的
同 genuine 真誠的

英英 of feelings, beliefs or behavior showing what you really think or feel and not pretend or tell lies

例 **Sincere** loving tears change the beast into a prince.
真誠的愛的淚水，把野獸變成王子。

☐ 三分熟
☐ 五分熟
☐ 七分熟
☐ 全熟

---

sip [sɪp]

動 啜飲、小口地喝
同 drink 喝

英英 to drink something by taking small mouthfuls

例 **Sip** the hot coffee carefully.
小心啜飲熱咖啡。

☐ 三分熟
☐ 五分熟
☐ 七分熟
☐ 全熟

S

sit·u·a·tion

[ˌsɪtʃʊˋeʃən]

名 情勢
同 condition 情況

英英 all the things that are happening at a particular time and place

例 After he became the city mayor, economical **situation** of the citizens improved.
自從他變成市長後，市民的經濟狀況改善了。

□ 三分熟
□ 五分熟
□ 七分熟
□ 全熟

skate [sket]

動 溜冰、滑冰

英英 to move or glide along on skates

例 The way she **skated** on the ice amazed everyone.
她在冰上溜冰的樣子讓每個人感到吃驚。

□ 三分熟
□ 五分熟
□ 七分熟
□ 全熟

ski [ski]

名 滑雪板
動 滑雪

英英 one of a pair of long narrow pieces of wood or plastic that attached to boots so that one can move on snow; to move on show with some particular equipments

例 **Skiing** down the hill is fun.
由這座小丘陵往下滑是很有趣的。

□ 三分熟
□ 五分熟
□ 七分熟
□ 全熟

skip [skɪp]

動 略過、跳過
名 略過、跳過
同 omit 省略

英英 to leave out something to the next when you're reading or doing something

例 **Skip** pork if you really like to buy some meat.
如果你真想買些肉，跳過豬肉。

□ 三分熟
□ 五分熟
□ 七分熟
□ 全熟

sky·scrap·er

[ˋskaɪˌskrepɚ]

名 摩天大樓

英英 a very tall building, usually in a city

例 Taipei 101 is a famous **skyscraper**.
臺北 101 是棟有名的摩天大樓。

□ 三分熟
□ 五分熟
□ 七分熟
□ 全熟

slave [slev]

名 奴隸
動 做苦工

英英 a person who works for a person and is legally owned by them; to work very hard

例 **Slaves** worked hard in order to have something to eat.
奴隸辛勤工作才能有點東西吃。

□ 三分熟
□ 五分熟
□ 七分熟
□ 全熟

sleeve [sliv]

名 衣袖、袖子

英英 a part of a piece of clothing that covers all or part of your arm

例 The **sleeves** of this pink dress need to be shortened.
這件粉紅色洋裝的衣袖需要改短。

□ 三分熟
□ 五分熟
□ 七分熟
□ 全熟

slice [slaɪs]

名 片、薄的切片
動 切成薄片

英英 a thin piece of food or something cut from a larger portion; to cut something into thin flat pieces

例 Give a **slice** of chocolate cake to your aunt.
把這塊巧克力蛋糕拿給你阿姨。

□ 三分熟
□ 五分熟
□ 七分熟
□ 全熟

Track 115

slip·per·y [ˋslɪpərɪ]
形 滑溜的

英英 smooth and wet so that is difficult to hold or to stand or move on
例 The **slippery** slide in the playground is children's favorite.
遊樂場中滑溜的溜滑梯是孩子們的最愛。

☐三分熟 ☐五分熟 ☐七分熟 ☐全熟

slope [slop]
名 坡度、斜面

英英 a surface of which one end or side is at a higher level than others
例 The apartment is at a **slope** of 90 degrees.
這棟公寓 90 度傾斜。

☐三分熟 ☐五分熟 ☐七分熟 ☐全熟

smooth [smuð]
形 平滑的
動 使平滑、使平和

英英 completely flat and even, without any holes or rough areas; to make something flat and even
例 TV ads often promote products, which are used to keep women's skin **smooth**.
電視廣告總是宣傳能用來保持讓女人皮膚光滑的產品。

☐三分熟 ☐五分熟 ☐七分熟 ☐全熟

snap [snæp]
動 折斷、迅速抓住

英英 to break something suddenly and quickly; to hold or grab quickly
例 How dare you **snap** Mrs. Huang's stick!
你怎麼敢折斷黃老師的棍子！

☐三分熟 ☐五分熟 ☐七分熟 ☐全熟

sol·id [ˋsɑlɪd]
形 固體的

英英 firm and stable in shape
例 Ghosts can pass through **solid** walls.
鬼魂可以穿過固體的牆。

☐三分熟 ☐五分熟 ☐七分熟 ☐全熟

some·day [ˋsʌmˏde]
副 將來有一天、來日

英英 at some time in the future which is unknown or that has not yet been decided
例 **Someday** you'll understand why some people are not fit to be friends.
有一天你會知道為什麼有些人不適合當朋友。

☐三分熟 ☐五分熟 ☐七分熟 ☐全熟

some·how [ˋsʌmˏhaʊ]
副 不知何故

英英 in a way which is not known or certain
例 **Somehow** I have the feeling that he'll leave us.
不知道為什麼，我有種他會離開我們的感覺。

☐三分熟 ☐五分熟 ☐七分熟 ☐全熟

some·time [ˋsʌmˏtaɪm]
副 某些時候、來日

英英 at some unknown time
例 You'll come to visit us **sometime**, right?
你會找個時間來看我們，對吧？

☐三分熟 ☐五分熟 ☐七分熟 ☐全熟

some·what

[ˋsʌmˏhwɑt]

副 多少、幾分

英英 to some degree; slightly

例 The project is **somewhat** difficult to complete.
這個案子要完成是有幾分困難的。

☐ 三分熟
☐ 五分熟
☐ 七分熟
☐ 全熟

---

sore [sor]

形 疼痛的
名 痛處
同 painful 疼痛的

英英 painful or aching; suffering from pain

例 My nephew has a **sore** throat.
我姪子喉嚨痛。

☐ 三分熟
☐ 五分熟
☐ 七分熟
☐ 全熟

---

sor·row [ˋsɑro]

名 悲傷、感到哀傷
同 grief 悲傷

英英 a feeling of great sadness because something bad has happened

例 It takes time to heal the **sorrow** of losing a family.
療癒失去親人的悲傷需要時間。

☐ 三分熟
☐ 五分熟
☐ 七分熟
☐ 全熟

---

spade [sped]

名 鏟子
片 call a spade a spade
實話實說

英英 a garden tool which is used for digging, with a broad metal flat blade and a long handle, used for digging

例 The ice cream **spade** is easy to use.
冰淇淋鏟子很好用。

☐ 三分熟
☐ 五分熟
☐ 七分熟
☐ 全熟

---

spa·ghet·ti

[spəˋgɛtɪ]

名 義大利麵

英英 pasta made in long solid strings

例 Which type of **spaghetti** do you want to order?
你想點哪一種義大利麵？

☐ 三分熟
☐ 五分熟
☐ 七分熟
☐ 全熟

---

spe·cif·ic

[sprˋsɪfɪk]

形 具體的、特殊的、
明確的
同 precise 明確的

英英 detailed or exact

例 Without **specific** evidence, you can't send him to jail.
如果沒有確切的證據，你是無法讓他坐牢的。

☐ 三分熟
☐ 五分熟
☐ 七分熟
☐ 全熟

---

spice [spaɪs]

名 香料

英英 powder or seed that tastes or small strong used in cooking for giving a special flavor

例 The fried rice with special **spice** tastes good.
加了特殊香料的炒飯嚐起來很美味。

☐ 三分熟
☐ 五分熟
☐ 七分熟
☐ 全熟

---

spill [spɪl]

動 使溢流
名 溢出

英英 to flow or cause to flow over the edge of a container

例 Can you pour the coffee without **spilling** it?
你能不能把咖啡倒出來，而不讓它灑出來？

☐ 三分熟
☐ 五分熟
☐ 七分熟
☐ 全熟

spin [spɪn]

動 旋轉、紡織
名 旋轉

英英 to turn round and round quickly very fast

例 **Spinning** the huge top is almost an impossible mission for a child.
旋轉這個巨型的陀螺，對小孩來說，幾乎是不可能的任務。

☐ 三分熟
☐ 五分熟
☐ 七分熟
☐ 全熟

---

spit [spɪt]

動 吐、吐口水
名 唾液

英英 to expel saliva from one's mouth; the liquid that is produced in one's mouth

例 Don't **spit** out the gum carelessly when finishing chewing.
嚼完口香糖後，不要隨便亂吐。

☐ 三分熟
☐ 五分熟
☐ 七分熟
☐ 全熟

---

spite [spaɪt]

名 惡意

英英 a feeling of wanting to hurt or harm somebody

例 Lee stole Amy's cellphone out of **spite**.
李出於惡意，偷了艾美的手機。

☐ 三分熟
☐ 五分熟
☐ 七分熟
☐ 全熟

---

splash [splæʃ]

動 濺起來
名 飛濺聲

英英 to cause to fall in scattered drops, especially liquid; a noise made by striking upon a liquid

例 The car rushed by me and the mud water **splashed** on my pants.
車子從我身旁急馳而過，泥漿水飛濺到我的褲子上。

☐ 三分熟
☐ 五分熟
☐ 七分熟
☐ 全熟

---

spoil [spɔɪl]

動 寵壞、損壞

英英 to change things good into bad or unpleasant, useless

例 Don't buy little George so many toys, you'll **spoil** him.
不要買給小喬治那麼多的玩具，你會寵壞他。

☐ 三分熟
☐ 五分熟
☐ 七分熟
☐ 全熟

---

sprain [spren]

動／名 扭傷

英英 to cause pain and injury to a joint

例 What should I do if I **sprain** my ankle?
如果我扭傷了腳踝，我該怎麼做？

☐ 三分熟
☐ 五分熟
☐ 七分熟
☐ 全熟

---

spray [spre]

名 噴霧器
動 噴、濺

英英 a device that is used to make very small drops of liquid from a special container; very small drops of a liquid that are sent through the air

例 Why not using a **spray** of perfume?
為什麼不噴一些香水？

☐ 三分熟
☐ 五分熟
☐ 七分熟
☐ 全熟

---

sprin·kle [ˈsprɪŋkl̩]

動 灑、噴淋

英英 to scatter or pour small drops or particles over

例 **Sprinkle** some candies on top of the doughnut.
在甜甜圈上灑一些糖果。

☐ 三分熟
☐ 五分熟
☐ 七分熟
☐ 全熟

spy [spaɪ]

名 間諜

英英 a person who tries to get information secretly about another country, organization, or person

例 The **spy** was discovered and shot to death.
間諜被發現了，一槍斃命。

□ 三分熟
□ 五分熟
□ 七分熟
□ 全熟

---

squeeze [skwiz]

動 壓擠、擠壓
名 緊抱、擁擠
同 crush 壓、榨

英英 to firmly press something from all sides

例 The French chef is good at **squeezing** rose-like cream on top of the pudding.
法國主廚擅於在布丁的上面擠出玫瑰般的奶油。

□ 三分熟
□ 五分熟
□ 七分熟
□ 全熟

---

stab [stæb]

動 刺、戳
名 刺傷

英英 to push a sharp, pointed object to a person in order to kill them or injure them

例 Her heart was deeply **stabbed** by a knife.
小刀深深的刺入她的心臟。

□ 三分熟
□ 五分熟
□ 七分熟
□ 全熟

---

sta·ble [ˈstebl̩]

形 穩定的
同 steady 穩定的

英英 firmly fixed; not likely to move or fail

例 Marriage helps their children to have a **stable** home.
婚姻幫助他們的孩子有個穩定的家。

□ 三分熟
□ 五分熟
□ 七分熟
□ 全熟

---

sta·di·um [ˈstedɪəm]

名 室外運動場

英英 an athletic or sports ground with rows of seats around the sites

例 Let's go to the **stadium** to play tennis, shall we?
讓我們去室外運動場打網球，好嗎？

□ 三分熟
□ 五分熟
□ 七分熟
□ 全熟

---

staff [stæf]

名 棒、竿子、全體人員

英英 the employees who work in an organization

例 The company's **staff** are nice and polite.
這間公司的員工人很好，也很有禮貌。

□ 三分熟
□ 五分熟
□ 七分熟
□ 全熟

---

stale [stel]

形 不新鮮的、陳舊的
同 old 老舊的

英英 of food, especially bread and cake are not fresh for eating

例 The eggs have been **stale**.
這些蛋已經不新鮮了。

□ 三分熟
□ 五分熟
□ 七分熟
□ 全熟

---

stare [stɛr]

動／名 盯、凝視

英英 to look fixedly at someone or something with the eyes wide open

例 Why do you **stare** at me?
你為什麼要盯著我看？

□ 三分熟
□ 五分熟
□ 七分熟
□ 全熟

---

starve [stɑrv]

動 餓死、饑餓

英英 to suffer or die because you don't have enough food to eat; very hungry

例 Give me rice; I'm **starving**.
給我飯，我快餓死了。

□ 三分熟
□ 五分熟
□ 七分熟
□ 全熟

🎧 **Track 119**

---

stat·ue [ˈstætʃʊ]

名 鑄像、雕像

片 put up a statue
設一尊雕像

英英 a carved or cast figure of a person or animal

例 The **statue** of Apollo seems to smile at me.
阿波羅的雕像似乎在對我微笑。

□ 三分熟
□ 五分熟
□ 七分熟
□ 全熟

---

stead·y [ˈstɛdɪ]

形 穩固的

副 穩固地

英英 very even and stable; fixed and not easy to move

例 **Steady** flow of Gilbert's salary brings his wife a sense of safety.
吉伯特穩定的薪水帶給他的太太一種安全感。

□ 三分熟
□ 五分熟
□ 七分熟
□ 全熟

---

steep [stip]

形 險峻的

英英 rising or falling sharply

例 The road to the Heaven's Lake is **steep**.
要到天湖的路陰峻不平。

□ 三分熟
□ 五分熟
□ 七分熟
□ 全熟

---

step·child [ˈstɛpˌtʃɪld]

名 前夫（妻）所生的孩子

英英 a child of your husband or wife by a previous marriage

例 Angela gets along with her **stepchild** very well.
安琪拉跟前夫所生的孩子相處的很好。

□ 三分熟
□ 五分熟
□ 七分熟
□ 全熟

---

step·father [ˈstɛpˌfɑðɚ]

名 繼父、後父

英英 the man who is married to a person's mother but who is not their real father

例 Stanley got married and became the **stepfather** of a boy.
史丹利結婚了，變成一個小男孩的繼父。

□ 三分熟
□ 五分熟
□ 七分熟
□ 全熟

---

step·mother [ˈstɛpˌmʌðɚ]

名 繼母、後母

英英 a woman who is married to a person's father but who is not their real father

例 Angela is a **stepmother**.
安琪拉是後母。

□ 三分熟
□ 五分熟
□ 七分熟
□ 全熟

---

ster·e·o [ˈstɛrɪo]

名 立體音響

英英 a machine that plays CDs or cassettes, or a radio, etc. which has two separate speakers so that you can hear nature sounds from each

例 With this set of **stereo**, classic music sounds more powerful.
有了這組立體音響，古典樂聽起來更有力道。

□ 三分熟
□ 五分熟
□ 七分熟
□ 全熟

---

stick·y [ˈstɪkɪ]

形 黏的、棘手的

英英 designed to stick and fix to any surface of an object easily; very tough

例 The **sticky** ball is popular in the English class.
黏黏球在英語課堂中很受歡迎。

□ 三分熟
□ 五分熟
□ 七分熟
□ 全熟

S

stiff [stɪf]

形 僵硬的

英英 firm and difficult to bend or move

例 My neck is **stiff**.
我的脖子僵硬。

☐ 三分熟
☐ 五分熟
☐ 七分熟
☐ 全熟

---

sting [stɪŋ]

動 刺、叮

英英 to prick or wound with a sharp point

例 Put on this and avoid being **stung** by bees.
把這穿上，避免被蜜蜂叮咬。

☐ 三分熟
☐ 五分熟
☐ 七分熟
☐ 全熟

---

stir [stɜ]

動 攪拌

英英 to move a liquid or substance around with a spoon in order to mix it completely

例 Add some milk and **stir** your coffee gently.
加一些牛奶，慢慢的輕攪你的咖啡。

☐ 三分熟
☐ 五分熟
☐ 七分熟
☐ 全熟

---

stitch [stɪtʃ]

名 編織、一針
動 縫、繡

英英 to sew two things together with a single pass of the needle

例 No **stitch** is missing in the weaving of this wool hat.
這頂羊毛帽在編織上沒有漏掉一針。

☐ 三分熟
☐ 五分熟
☐ 七分熟
☐ 全熟

---

stock·ing(s)

[ˋstɑkɪŋ(z)]

名 長襪

英英 one of a pair of thin pieces of clothing that fits closely over feet

例 These **stockings** will keep you warm.
這些長襪會讓你覺得溫暖。

☐ 三分熟
☐ 五分熟
☐ 七分熟
☐ 全熟

---

stool [stul]

名 凳子

英英 a seat with legs but has nothing to support your back or arms

例 Max is a smart kid as he knows how to use a **stool** to help him reach the cookie.
麥克斯是個聰明的孩子，因為他知道如何用凳子來幫他搆到餅乾。

☐ 三分熟
☐ 五分熟
☐ 七分熟
☐ 全熟

---

storm·y [ˋstɔrmɪ]

形 暴風雨的、多風暴的

英英 with strong wild and heavy rain

例 Why did he insist on leaving for the hospital on this **stormy** weather?
為什麼他堅持要在這種暴風雨的天氣前往醫院？

☐ 三分熟
☐ 五分熟
☐ 七分熟
☐ 全熟

---

strat·e·gy

[ˋstrætədʒɪ]

名 戰略、策略

英英 a plan designed to achieve a particular aim

例 The **strategy** guide is helpful.
這戰略是有幫助的。

☐ 三分熟
☐ 五分熟
☐ 七分熟
☐ 全熟

🎧 **Track 121**

strength [strɛŋθ]

名 力量、強度

英英 requiring physical or mental power or effort

例 Hercules is said to have great **strength**.
海克力士據説有很大的力氣。

☐三分熟
☐五分熟
☐七分熟
☐全熟

---

strip [strɪp]

名 條、臨時跑道
動 剝、剝除

英英 a long narrow piece of something; to tear off the thread from a nut or something

例 The **strips** of paper are here for you to write three sentences you make.
放在這裡的這些紙條是讓你寫三句自創的句子。

☐三分熟
☐五分熟
☐七分熟
☐全熟

---

struc·ture

[ˈstrʌktʃɚ]

名 構造、結構
動 建立組織

英英 a particular arrangement of parts; something are connected together from parts

例 The **structure** of the mansion is nearly perfect.
這棟大廈的構造近乎完美。

☐三分熟
☐五分熟
☐七分熟
☐全熟

---

stub·born

[ˈstʌbən]

形 頑固的
同 obstinate 頑固的

英英 determined not to change one's attitude or behavior

例 My father is a **stubborn** old man.
我父親是個頑固的老人家。

☐三分熟
☐五分熟
☐七分熟
☐全熟

---

stu·di·o [ˈstjudɪo]

名 工作室、播音室

英英 a room where radio or television programmers are recorded or where music is recorded

例 Jolin Tsai is in the **studio**.
蔡依林就在錄音室裡。

☐三分熟
☐五分熟
☐七分熟
☐全熟

---

stuff [stʌf]

名 東西、材料
動 填塞、裝填

英英 substance, material, articles, or activities of a specified or indeterminate kind; to fill something in

例 This kind of plastic **stuff** is cheap and harmful to the environment.
這種塑膠做的東西很廉價，對環境又有害。

☐三分熟
☐五分熟
☐七分熟
☐全熟

---

style [staɪl]

名 風格、時尚

英英 fashion, especially in clothing or hair

例 Emma is a novel with Jane Austen's humorous writing **style**.
愛瑪是一本有珍·奧斯汀幽默寫作風格的小説。

☐三分熟
☐五分熟
☐七分熟
☐全熟

---

sub·stance

[ˈsʌbstəns]

名 物質、物體、實質

英英 a type of solid, liquid or gas which has particular qualities

例 The drug contains chemical **substances**.
這種藥含有化學物質。

☐三分熟
☐五分熟
☐七分熟
☐全熟

S

sub·urb [ˈsʌbɝb]

名 市郊、郊區

英英 an outlying residential area of a city

例 Her uncle lives in the **suburb** of Taipei city.
她的舅舅住在臺北市的郊區。

☐ 三分熟
☐ 五分熟
☐ 七分熟
☐ 全熟

suck [sʌk]

動 吸、吸取、吸收

英英 to take liquid or air into your mouth by using a straw

例 The baby is **sucking** the milk from his mother's breast.
寶寶從母親的乳房中吸吮出牛奶。

☐ 三分熟
☐ 五分熟
☐ 七分熟
☐ 全熟

suf·fer [ˈsʌfɚ]

動 受苦、遭受
同 endure 忍受

英英 to be badly affected by a disease, pain, sadness

例 Stop blaming yourself and you won't **suffer**.
不要再自責，你就不會受苦了。

☐ 三分熟
☐ 五分熟
☐ 七分熟
☐ 全熟

sufficient

[səˈfɪʃənt]

形 充足的
同 enough 充足的

英英 enough or plenty

例 The tulips in the flower field have **sufficient** sunshine.
花田裡的鬱金香有充足的陽光。

☐ 三分熟
☐ 五分熟
☐ 七分熟
☐ 全熟

sug·gest [səˈdʒɛst]

動 提議、建議
同 hint 建議

英英 to offer an idea or a plan for other people to think about

例 I **suggest** we take a trip to Korea.
我提議我們到韓國去旅行。

☐ 三分熟
☐ 五分熟
☐ 七分熟
☐ 全熟

su·i·cide

[ˈsuəˌsaɪd]

名 自殺、自滅

英英 the action of killing oneself intentionally

例 It's stupid to commit **suicide** for someone who doesn't even understand you.
為一個根本就不瞭解你的人自殺，簡直愚蠢。

☐ 三分熟
☐ 五分熟
☐ 七分熟
☐ 全熟

suit·a·ble [ˈsutəbḷ]

形 適合的
同 fit 適合的

英英 right or appropriate for a particular thing or occasion

例 Wearing casual clothes to the party is not **suitable**.
穿輕便的衣服去那場派對並不合適。

☐ 三分熟
☐ 五分熟
☐ 七分熟
☐ 全熟

sum [sʌm]

名 總數
動 合計

英英 the amount you get when you are adding two or more numbers together

例 A large **sum** of money was spent on this motorcycle.
有一大筆錢是花在這輛摩托車上。

☐ 三分熟
☐ 五分熟
☐ 七分熟
☐ 全熟

🎧 Track 123

sum·ma·ry

[ˋsʌmərɪ]

名 摘要

英英 a brief statement of the main points of something

例 Write a **summary** of the story.
為這則故事寫摘要。

☐三分熟
☐五分熟
☐七分熟
☐全熟

---

sum·mit [ˋsʌmɪt]

名 頂點、高峰

英英 the highest point of something or the top of something

例 The **summit** between American president and Korean leader is going to be held.
美國總統與韓國領導的高峰會將要舉行了。

☐三分熟
☐五分熟
☐七分熟
☐全熟

---

su·pe·ri·or

[səˋpɪrɪə]

形 上級的
名 長官

英英 higher in status, quality, or power; a person of higher position

例 Bob planned to report this news to his **superior**.
鮑伯計畫要向上級長官呈報這則消息。

☐三分熟
☐五分熟
☐七分熟
☐全熟

---

sup·pose [səˋpoz]

動 假定

英英 to think or believe that something is true or possible

例 Miss Chang **supposes** we all know there is a quiz.
張老師假定我們都知道有小考。

☐三分熟
☐五分熟
☐七分熟
☐全熟

---

sur·round

[səˋraʊnd]

動 圍繞

英英 to be all around something or somebody

例 The white clouds **surround** the green mountain.
白雲圍繞著綠山。

☐三分熟
☐五分熟
☐七分熟
☐全熟

---

sur·vey [ˋsɝve] /
[sɝˋve]

動／名 考察、測量、實地調查

英英 to make some questions for getting the information or opinions from people

例 The government did some **survey** on the local villagers' health.
政府針對當地村民的健康做了一些調查。

☐三分熟
☐五分熟
☐七分熟
☐全熟

---

sur·viv·al

[səˋvaɪvl]

名 殘存、倖存

英英 something left or stayed to live or exist, often in spite of difficulty or danger

例 In the battlefield, **survival** is the key question.
在戰場上，倖存與否是關鍵問題。

☐三分熟
☐五分熟
☐七分熟
☐全熟

sur·vi·vor

[sə`vaɪvɚ]

名 生還者

英英 a person who continues to live, especially in the great danger

例 **Survivors** are requested to stay in this activity center.
生還者被要求要待在這個活動中心。

□三分熟
□五分熟
□七分熟
□全熟

---

sus·pect [`sʌspɛkt]
[sə`spɛkt]

動 懷疑
名 嫌疑犯

英英 to doubt or distrust something that is not true; a person who is thought to be guilty of a crime

例 We **suspect** that the woman who came to visit us is the baby's mother.
我們懷疑來造訪我們的女子是寶寶的母親。

□三分熟
□五分熟
□七分熟
□全熟

---

sus·pi·cion

[sə`spɪʃəs]

名 懷疑

英英 a feeling of wondering or doubting that somebody has done something wrong, illegal or dishonest but without proof

例 I have a **suspicion** that my parents asked my boyfriend to buy a house.
我懷疑是我爸媽要求我男友買棟房子。

□三分熟
□五分熟
□七分熟
□全熟

---

swear [swɛr]

動 發誓、宣誓

英英 to give a promise or state oath

例 How dare he **swore** that he would love me forever?
他怎麼敢發誓他會永遠愛我？

□三分熟
□五分熟
□七分熟
□全熟

---

sweat [swɛt]

名 汗水
動 出汗

英英 drops of liquid that appear on the surface of your skin when you are hot or after exercise

例 The mother wiped the **sweat** beads from her child's forehead.
母親拭去小孩額頭上的汗珠。

□三分熟
□五分熟
□七分熟
□全熟

---

swell [swɛl]

動 膨脹

英英 to become bigger or rounder

例 The little girl's heart **swelled** with pride.
小女孩的心胸脹滿了驕傲。

□三分熟
□五分熟
□七分熟
□全熟

---

swift [swɪft]

形 迅速的

英英 happening or moving very quickly or promptly

例 The police officer's action is **swift**.
警員的動作是迅速的。

□三分熟
□五分熟
□七分熟
□全熟

---

switch [swɪtʃ]

名 開關
動 轉換

英英 a device for making and breaking an electrical connection; to change suddenly, especially from one thing to another

例 The **switch** of the bathroom's light is on your right side.
浴室電燈的開關在你的右手邊。

□三分熟
□五分熟
□七分熟
□全熟

Track 125

sword [sord]

名 劍、刀

英英 a weapon with a handle and a long sharp metal blade

例 The **sword** is shining.
這把劍閃燿著光芒。

☐ 三分熟
☐ 五分熟
☐ 七分熟
☐ 全熟

sys·tem [ˋsɪstəm]

名 系統
片 the immune system
免疫系統

英英 a set of things working together as a mechanism or interconnecting network

例 The train **system** was out of function this morning.
火車系統今天早上故障。

☐ 三分熟
☐ 五分熟
☐ 七分熟
☐ 全熟

Tt

tab·let [`tæblɪt]

名 塊、片、碑、牌

英英 a square slab of stone, clay, or wood, usually used for writing inscription on

例 The vitamin C **tablets** are on the table.
維他命 C 片在桌上。

□三分熟
□五分熟
□七分熟
□全熟

---

tack [tæk]

名 大頭釘
動 釘住

英英 a small, sharp nail with a flat end

例 Butterflies are **tacked**.
蝴蝶被釘住了。

□三分熟
□五分熟
□七分熟
□全熟

---

tag [tæg]

名 標籤
動 加標籤、尾隨
同 label 標籤

英英 a label providing identification or information of products, goods, etc.; to stick a piece of paper as a label; to follow closely after someone or something

例 The price **tag** of the dress is missing.
洋裝的價錢標不見了。

□三分熟
□五分熟
□七分熟
□全熟

---

tai·lor [`telɚ]

名 裁縫師
動 裁製

英英 a person who makes suits, jackets for people or individual customers; to make one's clothes

例 The **tailor** of the wedding gown worked hard day and night.
這名結婚禮服的裁縫師日以繼夜的辛勤工作。

□三分熟
□五分熟
□七分熟
□全熟

---

tame [tem]

形 馴服的、單調的
動 馴服

英英 an animal which is not dangerous because of training; to train a wild animal to obey you and not to attack anyone

例 The elephant in Thailand seems **tame**.
泰國的大象看起來是溫順的。

□三分熟
□五分熟
□七分熟
□全熟

---

tap [tæp]

名 輕拍聲
動 輕打

英英 the noise made by knocking or touching something gently; to hit somebody or something gently and lightly

例 **Tap** the door three times and I'll know it's you.
輕輕敲打這扇門三次，我就會知道是你。

□三分熟
□五分熟
□七分熟
□全熟

---

tax [tæks]

名 稅

英英 money paid to the government, which is based on your salary or the cost of products or services you have bought

例 The tea **tax** greatly angered some people in the 18th century.
十八世紀的茶葉稅讓一些人非常的生氣。

□三分熟
□五分熟
□七分熟
□全熟

🎧 Track 126

tease [tiz]

動 嘲弄、揶揄
名 揶揄

英英 to laugh at somebody and make fun of them in order to annoy or embarrass them

例 Don't **tease** the boy.
不要嘲弄該名男孩。

☐三分熟
☐五分熟
☐七分熟
☐全熟

---

tech·ni·cal

[ˈtɛknɪkl̩]

形 技術上的、技能的

英英 of or relating to a particular skill or its techniques

例 There are some **technical** problems
有一些技術上的問題。

☐三分熟
☐五分熟
☐七分熟
☐全熟

---

tech·nique

[tɛkˋnik]

名 技術、技巧

英英 a particular way or skill of doing something or making something

例 The **technique** of building is excellent.
建築的技術真好。

☐三分熟
☐五分熟
☐七分熟
☐全熟

---

tech·nol·o·gy

[tɛkˋnɑlədʒɪ]

名 技術學、工藝學

英英 the study of scientific or industrial knowledge, use of scientific discoveries

例 **Technology** of making a car has been quite advanced.
造車的技術已經很先進了。

☐三分熟
☐五分熟
☐七分熟
☐全熟

---

tem·per [ˈtɛmpɚ]

名 脾氣

英英 if somebody has a temper, they become angry very easily and quickly

例 Grandfather's **temper** is bad.
爺爺的脾氣不好。

☐三分熟
☐五分熟
☐七分熟
☐全熟

---

tem·per·a·ture

[ˈtɛmprərətʃɚ]

名 溫度、氣溫

英英 the measured amount of heat or degree in a place or in the body

例 The **temperature** in the mountain area is around 10 to 15 degrees.
山區的氣溫大概 10 到 15 度。

☐三分熟
☐五分熟
☐七分熟
☐全熟

---

tem·po·ra·ry

[ˈtɛmpərɛrɪ]

形 暫時的

英英 lasting only for a short period of time

例 The popularity of silver shoes is **temporary**.
銀色鞋的受歡迎只是暫時的。

☐三分熟
☐五分熟
☐七分熟
☐全熟

---

tend [tɛnd]

動 傾向、照顧
同 incline 傾向

英英 to frequently behave in a particular way or have a particular characteristic

例 Peter's roommate **tends** to wake him up in the very early morning.
彼得的室友往往在一大清早把他吵醒。

☐三分熟
☐五分熟
☐七分熟
☐全熟

ten·der [ˈtɛndɚ]
形 溫柔的、脆弱的、幼稚的
同 soft 輕柔的

英英 kind, gentle and sympathetic
例 Be **tender** to the white cat.
對這隻白色貓咪要溫柔點。

☐三分熟 ☐五分熟 ☐七分熟 ☐全熟

T

ter·ri·to·ry [ˈtɛrəˌtorɪ]
名 領土、版圖

英英 an area or land which belongs to a particular country or person
例 The **territory** of the duke was given by the king.
這名公爵的領土是國王所給的。

☐三分熟 ☐五分熟 ☐七分熟 ☐全熟

text [tɛkst]
名 課文、本文

英英 the printed or written part of a book or magazine, not the notes or pictures
例 The **text** of the lesson is about penguins.
這課的本文是關於企鵝。

☐三分熟 ☐五分熟 ☐七分熟 ☐全熟

thank·ful [ˈθæŋkfəl]
形 欣慰的、感謝的
同 grateful 感謝的

英英 pleased, relieved or grateful
例 I'm **thankful** for the gentleman's kind act.
我感謝這位先生的善行。

☐三分熟 ☐五分熟 ☐七分熟 ☐全熟

the·o·ry [ˈθiərɪ]
名 理論、推論
同 inference 推論

英英 a system of ideas to explain something, usually based on general principles
例 It's my **theory** about their relationship.
這是我對他們之間的關係的推論。

☐三分熟 ☐五分熟 ☐七分熟 ☐全熟

thirst [θɝst]
名 口渴、渴望

英英 a feeling of wanting something to drink; a feeling of wanting something
例 Many boys have a **thirst** for adventures.
有許多男孩子都渴望冒險。

☐三分熟 ☐五分熟 ☐七分熟 ☐全熟

thread [θrɛd]
名 線
動 穿線

英英 a thin string of cotton or wood, which is used for sewing or making fabric; to put a thin string through a narrow hold
例 I need some **threads** and a needle.
我需要一根針和一些線。

☐三分熟 ☐五分熟 ☐七分熟 ☐全熟

threat [θrɛt]

名 威脅、恐嚇

英英 a statement in which you tell somebody that you will harm them or do some damage

例 The **threat** is terrifying.
這樣的威脅很嚇人。

☐ 三分熟
☐ 五分熟
☐ 七分熟
☐ 全熟

threat·en [ˈθrɛtn̩]

動 威脅

英英 to make a threat to a person to do something

例 The robber **threatened** the banker to take out all the cash.
搶匪威脅銀行行員拿出所有的現金。

☐ 三分熟
☐ 五分熟
☐ 七分熟
☐ 全熟

tick·le [ˈtɪkl̩]

動 搔癢、呵癢

英英 to lightly touch a person in a way that causes itching and making them laugh

例 **Tickle** the baby and it'll laugh.
搔寶寶癢，寶寶會笑。

☐ 三分熟
☐ 五分熟
☐ 七分熟
☐ 全熟

tide [taɪd]

名 潮、趨勢

英英 a regular rise and fall of the sea, which happens twice a day

例 You will see a bridge when the **tide** is out.
退潮時，你會看到一座橋。

☐ 三分熟
☐ 五分熟
☐ 七分熟
☐ 全熟

ti·dy [ˈtaɪdɪ]

形 整潔的
動 整頓

英英 very neat and clean without dirt; to make a place look neat and clean

例 The room of the hotel is **tidy**.
旅館的房間是很整潔的。

☐ 三分熟
☐ 五分熟
☐ 七分熟
☐ 全熟

tight [taɪt]

形 緊的、緊密的
副 緊緊地、安穩地

英英 very closed or fastened firmly

例 The pants are **tight**.
褲子很緊。

☐ 三分熟
☐ 五分熟
☐ 七分熟
☐ 全熟

tight·en [ˈtaɪtn̩]

動 勒緊、使堅固

英英 to make something become tight or firm

例 **Tighten** the rope.
勒緊這條繩子。

☐ 三分熟
☐ 五分熟
☐ 七分熟
☐ 全熟

tim·ber [ˈtɪmbɚ]

名 木材、樹林
同 wood 木材、樹林

英英 wood that are grown and used in building

例 These **timbers** catch fire easily.
這些木材容易著火。

☐ 三分熟
☐ 五分熟
☐ 七分熟
☐ 全熟

tis·sue [ˈtɪʃʊ]

名 面紙

英英 a piece of soft paper that usually used to absorb liquids or clean something

例 Give me a box of **tissues**.
給我一盒面紙。

☐ 三分熟
☐ 五分熟
☐ 七分熟
☐ 全熟

T

to·bac·co

[tə`bæko]

名 菸草

| 英英 | a substance which is made from the dried leaves of a particular plant for smoking or chewing |
| 例 | Could you fill the pipe with some **tobacco**? |

你可否在這隻菸斗裡裝些菸草？

□ 三分熟
□ 五分熟
□ 七分熟
□ 全熟

---

ton [tʌn]

名 噸

| 英英 | a unit for measuring weight equal to one thousand kilograms |
| 例 | Half a **ton** of sands are poured into the dump truck. |

半噸的砂倒入砂石車裡。

□ 三分熟
□ 五分熟
□ 七分熟
□ 全熟

---

tor·toise [`tɔrtəs]

名 烏龜

| 英英 | a slow-moving land reptile with a scaly and hard shell into which it can retract its head and legs |
| 例 | The **tortoises** in the Shou Shan Zoo look like huge stones if they don't move. |

壽山動物園的烏龜如果不動，看起來就像巨石。

□ 三分熟
□ 五分熟
□ 七分熟
□ 全熟

---

toss [tɔs]

動 投、擲
名 投、擲
同 throw 投、丟

| 英英 | to throw something gently or carelessly |
| 例 | **Toss** the coin into the fountain and make a wish. |

把硬幣丟進泉水裡許願。

□ 三分熟
□ 五分熟
□ 七分熟
□ 全熟

---

tour·ism [`tʊrɪzəm]

名 觀光、遊覽

| 英英 | the business which provides services such as transport or entertainment for people who are on holiday |
| 例 | **Tourism** suddenly becomes a hot topic in this city. |

觀光突然間就變成關於這座城市的熱門話題。

□ 三分熟
□ 五分熟
□ 七分熟
□ 全熟

---

tour·ist [`tʊrɪst]

名 觀光客

| 英英 | a person who is travelling or visiting a place for pleasure or in interest |
| 例 | Some **tourists** just don't know how to behave themselves. |

有些觀光客就是不知道該如何守規矩。

□ 三分熟
□ 五分熟
□ 七分熟
□ 全熟

---

tow [to]

動 拖曳
名 拖曳
同 pull 拖、拉

| 英英 | to pull a car or boat behind another vehicle with a rope or chain |
| 例 | Lucky **tows** the bone to its house. |

阿福把骨頭拖到牠的屋子裡。

□ 三分熟
□ 五分熟
□ 七分熟
□ 全熟

🎧 Track 130

trace [tres]

動 追溯
名 蹤跡

英英 to draw back or find by investigation; a mark that shows that somebody or something existed

例 The history of this theater can be **traced** back to the 19th century.
這座劇院的歷史可以回溯到十九世紀。

☐三分熟
☐五分熟
☐七分熟
☐全熟

trad·er [ˋtredɚ]

名 商人

英英 a person whose job is to buy and sell things or products

例 The **trader** of furs would not be happy if the law was passed.
如果這條法律通過了，毛皮商人會不太開心。

☐三分熟
☐五分熟
☐七分熟
☐全熟

trail [trel]

名 痕跡、小徑
動 拖著、拖著走

英英 a long line or a path through the countryside, often used for a particular purpose; to pull something behind somebody or something

例 The **trail** on the sand tells us that a beach motorcycle has passed.
沙上的痕跡告訴我們海灘摩托車剛經過。

☐三分熟
☐五分熟
☐七分熟
☐全熟

trans·port
[ˋtrænsport]

動 輸送、運輸
名 輸送

英英 to take or carry something or someone from one place to another place by a vehicle, aircraft, or ship

例 **Transport** the furniture to the restaurant.
把家具運到餐廳去。

☐三分熟
☐五分熟
☐七分熟
☐全熟

trash [træʃ]

名 垃圾

英英 useless things that you throw away because you don't want or need them

例 Can you take out the **trash** please?
可以請你把垃圾拿出去丟嗎？

☐三分熟
☐五分熟
☐七分熟
☐全熟

trav·el·er [ˋtrævlɚ]

名 旅行者、旅客
片 traveler's check
　　旅行者支票

英英 someone who is travelling or who travels a lot

例 The **traveler** takes a photo of the Egyptian pyramid.
旅客拍了張埃及金字塔的照片。

☐三分熟
☐五分熟
☐七分熟
☐全熟

tray [tre]

名 托盤

英英 a flat piece of wood which is used for carrying or holding things, such as food or drinks

例 Put the dishes you want on the **tray**.
把要的菜放在托盤上。

☐三分熟
☐五分熟
☐七分熟
☐全熟

T

trem·ble [ˈtrɛmbḷ]

名 顫抖、發抖
動 顫慄

英英 shake slightly, usually resulted in anxiety, excitement, or frailty

例 The woman in the horror film **trembled** with fear.
恐怖片中的女人因恐懼而顫抖。

☐ 三分熟
☐ 五分熟
☐ 七分熟
☐ 全熟

---

trend [trɛnd]

名 趨勢、傾向

英英 a general direction or development in which a situation is changing

例 The **trend** of drinking bubble milk tea is common nowadays.
喝珍珠奶茶的趨勢在現在是很普遍的。

☐ 三分熟
☐ 五分熟
☐ 七分熟
☐ 全熟

---

tribe [traɪb]

名 部落、種族

英英 a group of people who live together and share the same language, culture and history, especially in the mountain regions

例 The **tribe** worshipped the sun.
這個部落崇拜太陽。

☐ 三分熟
☐ 五分熟
☐ 七分熟
☐ 全熟

---

trick·y [ˈtrɪkɪ]

形 狡猾的、狡詐的

英英 of people clever but likely to do something sneaky

例 The hero's way to win the lady's heart is **tricky**.
男主角贏得女士芳心的方法好狡詐。

☐ 三分熟
☐ 五分熟
☐ 七分熟
☐ 全熟

---

troop [trup]

名 軍隊

英英 soldiers or armed forces in a large group

例 The general leads his **troop** to go across the dark forest.
將軍領著他的軍隊通過黑暗森林。

☐ 三分熟
☐ 五分熟
☐ 七分熟
☐ 全熟

---

trop·i·cal [ˈtrɑpɪkḷ]

形 熱帶的

英英 coming from, relating to or typical of the tropics

例 The fish tank is full of beautiful **tropical** fish.
魚缸裡滿是漂亮的熱帶魚。

☐ 三分熟
☐ 五分熟
☐ 七分熟
☐ 全熟

---

trunk [trʌŋk]

名 樹幹、大行李箱、象鼻

英英 the thick main stem of a tree; a storage in the back of a car; an elephant's nose which is long and its shape like a tube

例 There is a heart mark carved on the **trunk**.
有個心型標誌刻在樹幹上。

☐ 三分熟
☐ 五分熟
☐ 七分熟
☐ 全熟

---

truth·ful [ˈtruθfəl]

形 誠實的
同 honest 誠實的

英英 telling the truth; being very honest

例 Was your husband **truthful** with you?
妳的老公對妳誠實嗎？

☐ 三分熟
☐ 五分熟
☐ 七分熟
☐ 全熟

🎧 Track 132

tub [tʌb]

名 桶、盆、盤

英英 a large round container without a lid, used for storing food

例 A **tub** of pudding smells good.
一桶的布丁聞起來不錯。

☐ 三分熟
☐ 五分熟
☐ 七分熟
☐ 全熟

---

tug [tʌg]

動 用力拉
名 拖拉
同 pull 拖、拉

英英 to pull hard or with great efforts

例 **Tug** the rope as hard as you can.
盡你所能，用力拉繩。

☐ 三分熟
☐ 五分熟
☐ 七分熟
☐ 全熟

---

tulip [ˈtjuləp]

名 鬱金香

英英 a large, brightly colored spring flower, shaped like a bell, on a tall stem

例 If you're deep in love, you may send red **tulips** to the person you love.
如果你陷入熱戀，你可以送紅色鬱金香給你所愛的人。

☐ 三分熟
☐ 五分熟
☐ 七分熟
☐ 全熟

---

tum·ble [ˈtʌmbḷ]

動 摔跤、跌落

英英 move and fall suddenly or clumsily

例 The egg man **tumbled** down the wall.
蛋人摔下牆。

☐ 三分熟
☐ 五分熟
☐ 七分熟
☐ 全熟

---

tune [tjun]

名 調子、曲調
動 調整音調

英英 a series of musical notes usually sung or played in a easy and pleasant way to form a piece of music; to make a musical instrument play at the right pitch

例 The **tune** of the song he hummed sounds funny.
他哼唱的曲調聽起來滿滑稽的。

☐ 三分熟
☐ 五分熟
☐ 七分熟
☐ 全熟

---

tutor [ˈtjutɚ]

名 家庭教師、導師
動 輔導

英英 a private teacher who usually teaches an individual student or a very small group; to teach someone as a teacher

例 The **tutor** teaches Jack French.
家庭教師教傑克法文。

☐ 三分熟
☐ 五分熟
☐ 七分熟
☐ 全熟

---

twig [twɪg]

名 小枝、嫩枝

英英 a thin woody shoot growing from a branch of a tree

例 There are some pink buds on the **twigs**.
嫩枝上有些粉紅色的花苞。

☐ 三分熟
☐ 五分熟
☐ 七分熟
☐ 全熟

twin [twɪn]

名 雙胞胎

英英 one of two children born at the same time from the same mother

例 The **twin** brothers look exactly the same.
這對雙胞胎看起來完全一模一樣。

□ 三分熟
□ 五分熟
□ 七分熟
□ 全熟

---

twist [twɪst]

動 扭曲

英英 to bend or turn something repeatedly into a particular shape

例 Although Daniel **twisted** the truth, his wife believed him anyway.
雖然丹尼爾扭曲事實，他的太太無論如何還是相信他。

□ 三分熟
□ 五分熟
□ 七分熟
□ 全熟

---

type·writ·er

[ˋtaɪpˌraɪtɚ]

名 打字機

英英 a machine with keys for producing print-like letters and numbers

例 **Typewriters** were commonly used before the popularity of computers.
在電腦普及前，使用打字機很普遍。

□ 三分熟
□ 五分熟
□ 七分熟
□ 全熟

---

typ·i·cal [ˋtɪpɪk!]

形 典型的

英英 having the distinctive qualities of a particular type

例 Turnip cake is a **typical** traditional food during the Chinese New Year.
蘿蔔糕是農曆新年期間的典型傳統食物。

□ 三分熟
□ 五分熟
□ 七分熟
□ 全熟

T

Uu

un·ion [ˋjunjən]

名 聯合、組織

英英 an association or organizations which are formed with the same interest or purpose

例 We need to select some representatives of the Labor **Union**.
我們必須要選出一些工會代表。

☐三分熟
☐五分熟
☐七分熟
☐全熟

---

u·nite [juˋnaɪt]

動 聯合、合併

英英 to combine or bring together for a common purpose or to make a whole

例 The women **united** to stop their husbands from going to the war.
女人團結起來，阻止他們的丈夫去打仗。

☐三分熟
☐五分熟
☐七分熟
☐全熟

---

u·ni·ty [ˋjunətɪ]

名 聯合、統一

英英 the state of being stayed together; the state of being joined together to form one unit

例 A call for national **unity** is necessary.
號召全民團結是有必要的。

☐三分熟
☐五分熟
☐七分熟
☐全熟

---

u·ni·verse

[ˋjunəˏvɝs]

名 宇宙、天地萬物

英英 all existing matters or creatures in space

例 The viewpoint of the **universe** changes constantly along the historical times.
隨著歷史時代，宇宙觀不斷的在改變。

☐三分熟
☐五分熟
☐七分熟
☐全熟

---

un·less [ənˋlɛs]

連 除非

英英 if; used to express that something can only happen in a particular situation

例 **Unless** you called me, I'll wait for you in that café.
除非你打給我，要不然我會在那家咖啡廳等你。

☐三分熟
☐五分熟
☐七分熟
☐全熟

---

up·set [ʌpˋsɛt] [ˋʌpsɛt]

動 顛覆、使心煩
名 顛覆、煩惱
同 overturn 顛覆

英英 to make unhappy or disappointed

例 Don't **upset** your elder brother.
不要惹你哥生氣。

☐三分熟
☐五分熟
☐七分熟
☐全熟

Vv

---

va·cant [ˋvekənt]

形 空閒的、空虛的

英英 being empty or hollow; not being used

例 The company has no **vacant** warehouse.
這家公司沒有空的倉庫。

☐ 三分熟
☐ 五分熟
☐ 七分熟
☐ 全熟

---

val·u·a·ble

[ˋvæljʊəbl̩]

形 貴重的

英英 worth a great deal of money; very useful or important

例 These pearls are **valuable**.
這些珍珠是貴重的。

☐ 三分熟
☐ 五分熟
☐ 七分熟
☐ 全熟

---

van [væn]

名 貨車

英英 a vehicle with no side windows in its back half, which is used for carrying things or people

例 The new toaster is still in the **van**.
新的烤吐司機還在貨車裡。

☐ 三分熟
☐ 五分熟
☐ 七分熟
☐ 全熟

---

van·ish [ˋvænɪʃ]

動 消失、消逝

英英 to disappear suddenly and completely; gradually stop being existing

例 The girl seems to **vanish** on the stage of the magic show.
這個女孩似乎從魔術的舞臺上消失。

☐ 三分熟
☐ 五分熟
☐ 七分熟
☐ 全熟

---

va·ri·e·ty

[vəˋraɪətɪ]

名 多樣化

英英 several different kinds of the same thing

例 A **variety** of scarves are displayed on the table.
桌上陳列了各式各樣的圍巾。

☐ 三分熟
☐ 五分熟
☐ 七分熟
☐ 全熟

---

var·i·ous [ˋvɛrɪəs]

形 多種的

英英 of different or varied kinds or sorts

例 You need to have **various** drawing skills to gain that job.
你需要有不同的繪畫技巧才能獲得那份工作。

☐ 三分熟
☐ 五分熟
☐ 七分熟
☐ 全熟

---

var·y [ˋvɛrɪ]

動 使變化、改變

英英 to make something different; to change something in amount or level

例 His facial expressions **vary** greatly from this moment to the next moment.
他的臉上表情從此刻到下一刻有著劇烈的變化。

☐ 三分熟
☐ 五分熟
☐ 七分熟
☐ 全熟

---

vase [ves]

名 花瓶

英英 a decorative glass container which is used for displaying cut flowers

例 The **vase** is broken.
花瓶破了。

☐ 三分熟
☐ 五分熟
☐ 七分熟
☐ 全熟

🎧 Track 135

ve·hi·cle [ˋviɪkl̩]

名 交通工具、車輛

英英 a thing that is used for transporting people or things, such as a car or trunk

例 Technology made impossible **vehicles** possible.
科技讓不可能的交通工具成為可能。

☐ 三分熟
☐ 五分熟
☐ 七分熟
☐ 全熟

---

verse [vɝs]

名 詩、詩句

英英 poetry or words written in short lines with a metrical rhythm

例 Almost all the school children can recite Li Bai's **verse**.
幾乎所有的學童都可以朗誦李白的詩。

☐ 三分熟
☐ 五分熟
☐ 七分熟
☐ 全熟

---

vest [vɛst]

名 背心、馬甲
動 授給

英英 a type of underwear worn to cover the upper part of the body

例 The red **vest** is my nephew's favorite.
這件紅背心是我姪子的最愛。

☐ 三分熟
☐ 五分熟
☐ 七分熟
☐ 全熟

---

vice-pres·i·dent

[vaɪs ˋprɛzədənt]

名 副總統

英英 the person has a position below the president of a country in rank, who takes control of the country if the president is not able to

例 Miss Liu was the **vice-president** then.
呂小姐是當時的副總統。

☐ 三分熟
☐ 五分熟
☐ 七分熟
☐ 全熟

---

vic·tim [ˋvɪktɪm]

名 受害者

英英 a person harmed or killed as a result of a crime or accident

例 **Victims** should have the justice they deserve.
受害者應該討回應有的正義。

☐ 三分熟
☐ 五分熟
☐ 七分熟
☐ 全熟

---

vi·o·lence

[ˋvaɪələns]

名 暴力
同 force 暴力

英英 violent behavior which is intended to hurt or kill people

例 **Violence** against **violence** is wrong.
以暴制暴是錯的。

☐ 三分熟
☐ 五分熟
☐ 七分熟
☐ 全熟

---

vi·o·lent [ˋvaɪələnt]

形 猛烈的

英英 sudden and powerful

例 A **violent** storm is coming soon.
有個猛烈的暴風雨即將來臨。

☐ 三分熟
☐ 五分熟
☐ 七分熟
☐ 全熟

vi·o·let [ˋvaɪəlɪt]

名 紫羅蘭
形 紫羅蘭色的

英英 a small wild plant which is usually purple or white flowers with a sweet smell; a bluish-purple color

例 **Violet** pillow matches perfectly with the yellow bed sheet.
紫羅蘭色的枕頭與黃色床單完美搭配。

☐ 三分熟
☐ 五分熟
☐ 七分熟
☐ 全熟

---

vis·i·ble [ˋvɪzəb!]

形 可看見的

英英 capable to be seen or noticed

例 Germs are not **visible**.
細菌是看不見的。

☐ 三分熟
☐ 五分熟
☐ 七分熟
☐ 全熟

---

vi·sion [ˋvɪʒən]

名 視力、視覺、洞察力

英英 the state of being able to see

例 Your **vision** is excellent.
你的視力很好。

☐ 三分熟
☐ 五分熟
☐ 七分熟
☐ 全熟

---

vi·ta·min

[ˋvaɪtəmɪn]

名 維他命

英英 a natural substance in food that is an essential part of what humans and animals eat to help them stay good healthy

例 Eat some carrots which contain **vitamin** A.
吃些含有維他命 A 的紅蘿蔔吧。

☐ 三分熟
☐ 五分熟
☐ 七分熟
☐ 全熟

---

viv·id [ˋvɪvɪd]

形 閃亮的、生動的

英英 of memories, a description, etc. producing very clear and detailed images pictures in your mind

例 Anne has **vivid** imagination.
安有生動的想像力。

☐ 三分熟
☐ 五分熟
☐ 七分熟
☐ 全熟

---

vol·ume [ˋvɑljəm]

名 卷、冊、音量、容積

英英 the amount of space that an object fills; the level of sound produced by a television, MP3 player, etc

例 The last **volume** of martial arts fiction is the most appealing.
最後一冊的武俠小説是最引人入勝的。

☐ 三分熟
☐ 五分熟
☐ 七分熟
☐ 全熟

V

Ww

🎧 **Track 137**

wag [wæg]

動 搖擺
名 搖擺、搖動

英英 to move rapidly from side to side
例 The puppy is **wagging** its tail happily.
這隻小狗開心得搖著尾巴。

☐ 三分熟
☐ 五分熟
☐ 七分熟
☐ 全熟

wage [wedʒ]

名 週薪、工資

英英 a regular amount of money that you are paid weekly because the work you do or the services provide in an organization
例 The **wage** of the workers from Philippines in this factory is pretty low.
這家工廠來自菲律賓的工人工資相當低。

☐ 三分熟
☐ 五分熟
☐ 七分熟
☐ 全熟

wag·on [ˈwægən]

名 四輪馬車、貨車

英英 a horse-drawn vehicle for transporting goods
例 The **wagon** often reminds me of Cinderella.
四輪馬車總讓我想到灰姑娘。

☐ 三分熟
☐ 五分熟
☐ 七分熟
☐ 全熟

wak·en [ˈwekən]

動 喚醒、醒來

英英 to wake or make somebody wake from sleep
例 **Waken** your younger brother at six.
六點時叫醒你弟弟。

☐ 三分熟
☐ 五分熟
☐ 七分熟
☐ 全熟

wan·der [ˈwɑndɚ]

動 徘徊、漫步

英英 to walk slowly around a place, often without any particular purpose or direction
例 Lily **wanders** along the lake.
莉莉沿著湖泊徘徊。

☐ 三分熟
☐ 五分熟
☐ 七分熟
☐ 全熟

warmth [wɔrmθ]

名 暖和、溫暖、熱忱
同 zeal 熱忱

英英 the state of being warm
例 It is hard to forget the **warmth** of this family's kind act.
這家人善舉的溫暖難以忘懷。

☐ 三分熟
☐ 五分熟
☐ 七分熟
☐ 全熟

warn [wɔrn]

動 警告、提醒

英英 to tell somebody about something which may be dangerous or unpleasant
例 Don't move; I **warned** you.
我警告你，不要動。

☐ 三分熟
☐ 五分熟
☐ 七分熟
☐ 全熟

wax [wæks]

名 蠟、蜂蠟、月盈
片 ear wax 耳垢

英英 a soft solid substance that contains much fat and melts easily, usually used for making candles
例 The floor **wax** does not smell good.
地板蠟不好聞。

☐ 三分熟
☐ 五分熟
☐ 七分熟
☐ 全熟

weak·en [ˈwikən]
動 使變弱、減弱

英英 to make somebody or something less strong or powerful; to become less strong or powerful

例 The soldiers' morale has been **weakened**.
士兵的士氣變弱。

☐ 三分熟
☐ 五分熟
☐ 七分熟
☐ 全熟

---

wealth [wɛlθ]
名 財富、財產

英英 a large amount of money or valuable property that a person has

例 The **wealth** of the rich man is beyond our imagination.
有錢人的財富是超乎我們想像的。

☐ 三分熟
☐ 五分熟
☐ 七分熟
☐ 全熟

---

wealth·y [ˈwɛlθɪ]
形 富裕的、富有的

英英 rich or having a lot of money, property, etc.

例 All of my uncles were **wealthy**.
我的叔叔們全都是有錢人。

☐ 三分熟
☐ 五分熟
☐ 七分熟
☐ 全熟

---

weave [wiv]
名 織法、編法、織物、編織、編造

英英 a way or style in which fabric is woven; to form fabric by repeatedly crossing a single thread through two sets of long threads on a loom

例 The boy in this tribe needs to learn the **weave** of the basket.
這個部落裡的男孩需要學習籃子的編法。

☐ 三分熟
☐ 五分熟
☐ 七分熟
☐ 全熟

---

web [wɛb]
名 網、蜘蛛網

英英 a net which is made by a spider to catch insects

例 Charlotte's **Web** is certainly one of E. B. White's best novels.
《夏綠蒂的網》絕對是 E. B. 懷特所寫過最好的小說之一。

☐ 三分熟
☐ 五分熟
☐ 七分熟
☐ 全熟

---

weed [wid]
名 野草、雜草

英英 a wild plant growing which grows in an unwanted zone or place, usually in the garden or field

例 Get rid of those **weeds** in our garden.
除掉我們花園裡的那些雜草。

☐ 三分熟
☐ 五分熟
☐ 七分熟
☐ 全熟

---

weep [wip]
動 哭泣，哭
同 cry 哭

英英 to cry when you are sad

例 Mrs. Smith was **weeping** because she missed her son.
史密斯太太在哭，因為她思念她的兒子。

☐ 三分熟
☐ 五分熟
☐ 七分熟
☐ 全熟

🎧 **Track 139**

---

wheat [hwit]
名 小麥、麥子

英英 a plant grown for its grain that is for producing the flour to make bread, cakes, pasta, etc.

例 This bottle of drink tastes like the flavor of **wheat**.
這瓶飲料嚐起來有麥子的味道。

☐ 三分熟
☐ 五分熟
☐ 七分熟
☐ 全熟

---

whip [hwɪp]
名 鞭子
動 鞭打

英英 a strip of leather or rope fastened to a handle, used for hitting a person or urging on an animal; to hit or strike somebody with a thong

例 The **whip** serves as a tool of punishing the sinner.
鞭子為用以懲罰犯罪者的工具。

☐ 三分熟
☐ 五分熟
☐ 七分熟
☐ 全熟

---

whis·tle [ˈhwɪsl̩]
名 口哨、汽笛
動 吹口哨

英英 a small metal or plastic tube that you blow through the hold to make a loud high sound, used to attract attention or as a signal; to make a clear high-pitched sound through pursed lips

例 The **whistle** could be used when you're in danger.
當你有危險時，可以吹口哨。

☐ 三分熟
☐ 五分熟
☐ 七分熟
☐ 全熟

---

wick·ed [ˈwɪkɪd]
形 邪惡的、壞的

英英 very bad or morally wrong

例 In fairy tales, most stepmothers are **wicked**.
在童話故事中，多數的繼母都是邪惡的。

☐ 三分熟
☐ 五分熟
☐ 七分熟
☐ 全熟

---

wil·low [ˈwɪlo]
名 柳樹

英英 a tree has long thin branches and long thin leaves, that usually grows by the water

例 **Willows** were planted along the river bank.
沿河岸種植柳樹。

☐ 三分熟
☐ 五分熟
☐ 七分熟
☐ 全熟

---

wink [wɪŋk]
動 眨眼、使眼色
名 眨眼、使眼色

英英 to close and open one eye quickly as a signal to transfer a message

例 How come you **wink** at me?
為什麼你向我眨眼？

☐ 三分熟
☐ 五分熟
☐ 七分熟
☐ 全熟

---

wipe [waɪp]
動 擦拭
名 擦拭、擦

英英 to rub a surface with a piece of cloth, in order to remove dirt or liquid

例 I have to **wipe** the table.
我必須要擦這張桌子。

☐ 三分熟
☐ 五分熟
☐ 七分熟
☐ 全熟

---

wis·dom [ˈwɪzdəm]
名 智慧

英英 the ability of making good decisions with your knowledge or experience

例 I admired the **wisdom** of the master.
我佩服這位師父的智慧。

☐ 三分熟
☐ 五分熟
☐ 七分熟
☐ 全熟

---

wrap [ræp]

動 包裝
名 包裝紙

英英 to cover something completely with paper or other material, especially when preparing a gift; a piece of paper used to cover objects

例 **Wrap** the gift quickly.
快點包這份禮物。

☐ 三分熟
☐ 五分熟
☐ 七分熟
☐ 全熟

---

wrist [rɪst]

名 腕關節、手腕

英英 the joint part between the hand and the arm

例 Her **wrist** was hurt.
她的手腕受傷了。

☐ 三分熟
☐ 五分熟
☐ 七分熟
☐ 全熟

W

🎧 Track 140

yawn [jɔn]

動 打呵欠
名 打呵欠

英英	to open one's mouth wide and inhale deeply because of tiredness or boredom
例	Boring classes make students **yawn**. 無聊的課讓學生打呵欠。

☐ 三分熟
☐ 五分熟
☐ 七分熟
☐ 全熟

yell [jɛl]

動 大叫、呼喊

英英	to shout out loudly to get the attention or express the emotion
例	I heard somebody **yelling** help. 我聽到某個人在喊救命。

☐ 三分熟
☐ 五分熟
☐ 七分熟
☐ 全熟

yolk [jok]

名 蛋黃、卵黃

英英	the yellow center part of a bird's egg
例	The **yolk** cookie tastes delicious. 蛋黃餅好吃。

☐ 三分熟
☐ 五分熟
☐ 七分熟
☐ 全熟

Zz

Z
Y

zip·per [ˋzɪpɚ]

名 拉鏈

英英 a device used to open or fasten parts of clothes and bags

例 You fogot to zip your **zipper** up.
你忘記拉上拉鏈了。

☐ 三分熟
☐ 五分熟
☐ 七分熟
☐ 全熟

zone [zon]

名 地區、地帶、
　 劃分地區

英英 an area or a region with a particular feature or characteristics

例 The village is in an earthquake **zone**.
這個村落位於地震區。

☐ 三分熟
☐ 五分熟
☐ 七分熟
☐ 全熟

LEVEL 4 音檔雲端連結

因各家手機系統不同，若無法直接掃描，
仍可以至以下電腦雲端連結下載收聽。
（https://tinyurl.com/bdfcvmda）

Level 4

中級進階
英文能力

挑戰
4200單字

Aa

🎧 Track 141

a·ban·don

[əˋbændən]

動 放棄
同 desert 遺棄

英英 to give up something before you have finished it
例 How could she **abandon** her new-born baby?
她怎麼可以遺棄她的新生兒？

☐ 三分熟
☐ 五分熟
☐ 七分熟
☐ 全熟

ab·do·men

[ˋæbdəmən]

名 腹部

英英 the lower part of the body containing the stomach and other organs; the belly
例 Some food stayed in the abdomen of the **ladybug**.
一些食物留在瓢蟲的腹部。

☐ 三分熟
☐ 五分熟
☐ 七分熟
☐ 全熟

ab·so·lute

[ˋæbsəˏlut]

形 絕對的
同 complete 絕對的

英英 very great or to the largest degree possible
例 The **absolute** answer is "no" even if you ask me one hundred times.
即便你問我一百次這種問題，絕對的答案就是「不准」。

☐ 三分熟
☐ 五分熟
☐ 七分熟
☐ 全熟

ab·sorb [əbˋsɔrb]

動 吸收

英英 to soak up a liquid or another substance
例 Children are quick to **absorb** knowledge.
小孩吸收知識很快。

☐ 三分熟
☐ 五分熟
☐ 七分熟
☐ 全熟

ab·stract

[ˋæbstrækt]

形 抽象的
反 concrete 具體的

英英 existing as theoretical rather than physical or concrete
例 Could you give us several examples to explain the **abstract** concept?
您可否給我們幾個例子解釋抽象的概念？

☐ 三分熟
☐ 五分熟
☐ 七分熟
☐ 全熟

ac·a·dem·ic

[ˏækəˋdɛmɪk]

形 學院的、大學的

英英 relating to education and scholarship
例 **Academic** researches are important in improving intelligence and mind.
學術研究在改善智力和心靈方面有其重要性。

☐ 三分熟
☐ 五分熟
☐ 七分熟
☐ 全熟

A

---

ac·cent [ˈæksɛnt]

名 口音、腔調

英英 a way of pronouncing a language, associated with a country or an area

例 The salesman's **accent** confuses his guest.
這個銷售員的口音讓他的客人感到困惑。

☐ 三分熟
☐ 五分熟
☐ 七分熟
☐ 全熟

---

ac·cep·tance

[əkˈsɛptəns]

名 接受

英英 agreement that something is right could be to received

例 Kim's idea gained **acceptance** in the design department.
金的想法得到設計部門的認可。

☐ 三分熟
☐ 五分熟
☐ 七分熟
☐ 全熟

---

ac·cess [ˈæksɛs]

名 接近、會面、進入
動 接近、會面

英英 to approach or enter a place

例 The only **access** to my office is getting through the department store.
要進我辦公室的唯一入口是穿過百貨公司。

☐ 三分熟
☐ 五分熟
☐ 七分熟
☐ 全熟

---

ac·ci·den·tal

[ˌæksəˈdɛntl̩]

形 偶然的、意外的

英英 happening by accident, happening unexpectedly

例 Seeing this black-and-white bird was quite **accidental**.
看見這隻黑白相間的鳥是很偶然的。

☐ 三分熟
☐ 五分熟
☐ 七分熟
☐ 全熟

---

ac·com·pa·ny

[əˈkʌmpənɪ]

動 隨行、陪伴、伴隨

英英 to go somewhere with someone

例 Should we **accompany** the manager to go to Shanghai?
我們要陪經理去上海嗎？

☐ 三分熟
☐ 五分熟
☐ 七分熟
☐ 全熟

---

ac·com·plish

[əˈkɑmplɪʃ]

動 達成、完成
同 finish 完成

英英 to achieve or complete something successfully

例 Sometimes people need a bit of luck to **accomplish** their dreams.
有時候人們需要點運氣才能完成夢想。

☐ 三分熟
☐ 五分熟
☐ 七分熟
☐ 全熟

---

ac·com·plish·ment

[əˈkɑmplɪmənt]

名 達成、成就

英英 something that has been achieved by something successfully

例 Not everyone can have this great **accomplishment**.
不是每個人都可以有這樣偉大的成就。

☐ 三分熟
☐ 五分熟
☐ 七分熟
☐ 全熟

---

ac·coun·tant

[əˈkaʊntənt]

名 會計師

英英 a person whose job is to keep or inspect financial accounts

例 The **accountant** works extra hours during the weekend.
會計師在週末時加班。

☐ 三分熟
☐ 五分熟
☐ 七分熟
☐ 全熟

🎧 **Track 143**

---

ac·cu·ra·cy

[ˋækjərəsɪ]

名 正確、精密

英英 very correct in all details

例 The **accuracy** of this hand-made watch is amazing.
這隻手工製手錶的準確度讓人吃驚。

☐ 三分熟
☐ 五分熟
☐ 七分熟
☐ 全熟

---

ac·cuse [əˋkjuz]

動 控告
同 denounce 控告

英英 to express that someone has done something illegal, such as an offence or crime

例 Jack was **accused** of murdering his wife.
傑克被控謀殺他的太太。

☐ 三分熟
☐ 五分熟
☐ 七分熟
☐ 全熟

---

ac·id [ˋæsɪd]

名 酸性物質
形 酸的

英英 a liquid substance which can dissolve some metals or other materials; containing acid

例 Stomach **acid** helps to break down the food.
胃酸幫忙分解食物。

☐ 三分熟
☐ 五分熟
☐ 七分熟
☐ 全熟

---

ac·quaint

[əˋkwent]

動 使熟悉、告知

英英 to make someone aware of something or familiar with something

例 You'd better **acquaint** yourself with the use of this app.
你最好去熟悉手機應用程式的使用。

☐ 三分熟
☐ 五分熟
☐ 七分熟
☐ 全熟

---

ac·quain·tance

[əˋkwentəns]

名 認識的人、熟人
同 companion 同伴

英英 someone who you are familiar with

例 The mysterious woman living in the beach house is an **acquaintance** of Tim.
住在海邊度假屋的那個神祕女子是提姆的舊識。

☐ 三分熟
☐ 五分熟
☐ 七分熟
☐ 全熟

---

ac·quire [əˋkwaɪr]

動 取得、獲得
同 obtain 獲得

英英 to come to possess; to get or obtain

例 Some scholars believe that children can naturally **acquire** fluency in any language.
有些學者相信，孩子能自然而然的習得任一語言的流暢度。

☐ 三分熟
☐ 五分熟
☐ 七分熟
☐ 全熟

---

a·cre [ˋekə]

名 英畝

英英 a unit of measuring a land or an area, equal to 4,840 square yards

例 The vacation village is said to be more than 500 **acres**.
這個度假村據說超過 500 英畝。

☐ 三分熟
☐ 五分熟
☐ 七分熟
☐ 全熟

---

a·dapt [əˋdæpt]

動 使適應

英英 to become adjusted to new conditions or environment

例 Did your children **adapt** themselves well to the new school?
你的孩子們新學校的適應狀況良好嗎？

☐ 三分熟
☐ 五分熟
☐ 七分熟
☐ 全熟

A

ad·e·quate

[`ædəkwɪt]

形 適當的、足夠的
同 enough 足夠的

英英 satisfactory or acceptable

例 We need **adequate** information to solve this problem.
我們需要足夠的資訊解決問題。

□ 三分熟
□ 五分熟
□ 七分熟
□ 全熟

ad·jec·tive

[`ædʒɪktɪv]

名 形容詞

英英 a word used to describe or modify a noun

例 "Poor" and "rich" are opposite **adjectives**.
「貧窮」和「富有」是相對立的形容詞。

□ 三分熟
□ 五分熟
□ 七分熟
□ 全熟

ad·just [ə`dʒʌst]

動 調節、對準

英英 to alter slightly so as to achieve the goal or a desired result

例 Could you **adjust** the temperature of the air-conditioner?
你可否調節冷氣機的溫度？

□ 三分熟
□ 五分熟
□ 七分熟
□ 全熟

ad·just·ment

[ə`dʒʌstmənt]

名 調整、調節

英英 a small change

例 The **adjustment** of class schedule seems to be not quite well-accepted by teachers.
課程表的調整，似乎不太被教師們所接受。

□ 三分熟
□ 五分熟
□ 七分熟
□ 全熟

ad·mi·ra·ble

[`ædmərəbl̩]

形 令人欽佩的

英英 deserving respect and admiration

例 The boy's courage of beating the robbers is **admirable**.
男孩打敗搶匪的勇氣是令人欽佩的。

□ 三分熟
□ 五分熟
□ 七分熟
□ 全熟

ad·mi·ra·tion

[ˌædmə`reʃən]

名 欽佩、讚賞

英英 regard with respect or warm approval

例 People's **admiration** for their leader is beyond words.
人們對領袖的景仰是筆墨也難以形容的。

□ 三分熟
□ 五分熟
□ 七分熟
□ 全熟

ad·mis·sion

[əd`mɪʃən]

名 准許進入、入場費、承認

英英 when something is allowed to enter a place; an amount of money that a person paid for entering a place

例 The **admission** fee to the Taipei zoo is $60.
到臺北動物園的入場費是 60 元。

□ 三分熟
□ 五分熟
□ 七分熟
□ 全熟

ad·verb [`ædvɚb]

名 副詞

英英 word or phrase that modifies the meaning of an adjective, verb, or other adverb, or of a sentence

例 "Well" is a commonly used **adverb**.
「Well（很好地）」是很常用的副詞。

□ 三分熟
□ 五分熟
□ 七分熟
□ 全熟

a·gen·cy [ˋedʒənsɪ]

名 代理商

英英 a business organization providing a particular service

例 The local **agency** of sports cars is holding a car exhibition.
當地的跑車代理公司舉辦車展。

☐ 三分熟　☐ 五分熟　☐ 七分熟　☐ 全熟

---

a·gent [ˋedʒənt]

名 代理人

英英 a person who provides a particular service or information, typically liaising between two other parties

例 The insurance **agent** is going to visit us.
保險代理人要來拜訪我們。

☐ 三分熟　☐ 五分熟　☐ 七分熟　☐ 全熟

---

ag·gres·sive [əˋgrɛsɪv]

形 侵略的、攻擊的

英英 behaving in an angry way toward another person

例 Ted has an **aggressive** personality, which makes him not quite popular at school.
泰德有侵略性的人格特質，讓他在學校不那麼有人緣。

☐ 三分熟　☐ 五分熟　☐ 七分熟　☐ 全熟

---

a·gree·a·ble [əˋgriəb!]

形 令人愉快的、宜人的

英英 very pleasant and acceptable

例 The weather is **agreeable**.
天氣是很好的。

☐ 三分熟　☐ 五分熟　☐ 七分熟　☐ 全熟

AIDS/ac·quired im·mune de·fi·cien·cy syn·drome [edz]/[əˋkwaɪrd iˋmjun dɪˋfɪʃənsɪ ˋsɪnˏdrom]

名 愛滋病

英英 a disease, caused by the HIV virus and transmitted in body fluids, in which destroys the body's natural protection from infection, even death

例 **AIDS** is often associated with improper sexual behavior.
愛滋病經常與不恰當的性行為做聯想。

☐ 三分熟　☐ 五分熟　☐ 七分熟　☐ 全熟

---

al·co·hol [ˋælkəˏhɔl]

名 酒精

英英 a colorless volatile liquid compound which is the intoxicating ingredient in drinks such as wine, beer, and spirits

例 This brand of wine contains 20% of **alcohol**.
這個品牌的紅酒含有百分之二十的酒精。

☐ 三分熟　☐ 五分熟　☐ 七分熟　☐ 全熟

---

a·lert [əˋlɝt]

名 警報
形 機警的
片 stay alert 保持警覺

英英 a warning sound of danger; describes someone acts or understands something very quickly

例 **Alert** of fire rings, and everyone runs out of the restaurant.
火警響起，每個人都衝出餐廳。

☐ 三分熟　☐ 五分熟　☐ 七分熟　☐ 全熟

al·low·ance/
pock·et mon·ey

[əˋlaʊəns]/[ˋpɑkɪtˋmʌnɪ]

名 津貼、補助

英英 a sum of money that you are paid regularly

例 **Allowance** of transportation is included in your salary.
交通津貼包含在你的薪水裡。

☐ 三分熟
☐ 五分熟
☐ 七分熟
☐ 全熟

A

---

a·lu·mi·num

[əˋlumɪnəm]

名 鋁

英英 a strong, light, corrosion-resistant silvery-grey metallic element

例 Put these **aluminum** bottles in that paper box.
把這些鋁罐放在那個紙箱裡。

☐ 三分熟
☐ 五分熟
☐ 七分熟
☐ 全熟

---

a.m. [ˋeˋɛm]

副 上午

英英 before noon

例 How about having a brunch with me at 10:30 **a.m.**?
早上 10 點半來個早午餐如何？

☐ 三分熟
☐ 五分熟
☐ 七分熟
☐ 全熟

---

am·a·teur

[ˋæmətʃʊr]

名 業餘愛好者
形 業餘的
反 professional 專業的

英英 a person who takes part an activity without being paid; not professional

例 **Amateur** writers sometimes write better than professional writers.
業餘寫作者有時寫的比專業作者更好。

☐ 三分熟
☐ 五分熟
☐ 七分熟
☐ 全熟

---

am·bi·tious

[æmˋbɪʃəs]

形 有野心的

英英 having or showing ambition

例 **Men** are encouraged to be ambitious in the career field.
男士被鼓勵要在職場上有野心。

☐ 三分熟
☐ 五分熟
☐ 七分熟
☐ 全熟

---

a·mid/a·midst

[əˋmɪd]/[əˋmɪdst]

連 在……之中

英英 surrounded by, in the middle of; among

例 The ocean park sits **amid** the town and the ocean.
海洋公園座落於城鎮與海洋之中。

☐ 三分熟
☐ 五分熟
☐ 七分熟
☐ 全熟

---

a·muse [əˋmjuz]

動 娛樂、消遣

英英 to cause someone to laugh or smile

例 The brown cat **amused** the Huang family.
棕色貓咪娛樂了黃氏一家。

☐ 三分熟
☐ 五分熟
☐ 七分熟
☐ 全熟

---

a·muse·ment

[əˋmjuzmənt]

名 娛樂、有趣

英英 the feeling of being amused or made to laugh

例 Natalie's favorite **amusement** park is located in Tokyo.
娜塔莉最喜歡的遊樂園位於東京。

☐ 三分熟
☐ 五分熟
☐ 七分熟
☐ 全熟

🎧 **Track 147**

---

a·nal·y·sis

[ə`næləsɪs]

名 分析

英英 when you analyze something with a detailed examination

例 The **analysis** of the data shows that the population of this country is going down.

資料分析顯示，這個國家的人口數下滑。

☐ 三分熟
☐ 五分熟
☐ 七分熟
☐ 全熟

---

an·a·lyze [`ænḷˌaɪz]

動 分析、解析

英英 to examine in detail the elements

例 Write an essay to **analyze** the main plot of the novel.

寫一篇文章分析這本小說的主要情節。

☐ 三分熟
☐ 五分熟
☐ 七分熟
☐ 全熟

---

an·ces·tor

[`ænsɛstə]

名 祖先、祖宗

英英 a person, typically one more remote than a grandparent, related to you who lived a long time ago

例 Most people believe humankind's **ancestors** are apes.

多數人相信人類的祖先是猿猴。

☐ 三分熟
☐ 五分熟
☐ 七分熟
☐ 全熟

---

an·ni·ver·sa·ry

[ˌænə`vɝsərɪ]

名 週年紀念日

英英 the date on which an event happened in a previous year

例 My parents wedding **anniversary** is on Valentine's Day.

我父母的結婚紀念日是在情人節。

☐ 三分熟
☐ 五分熟
☐ 七分熟
☐ 全熟

---

an·noy [ə`nɔɪ]

動 煩擾、使惱怒
同 irritate 使惱怒

英英 to make someone slightly angry

例 What the clerk just said **annoyed** me a lot.

店員剛才講的話大大地惹惱了我。

☐ 三分熟
☐ 五分熟
☐ 七分熟
☐ 全熟

---

an·nu·al [`ænjʊəl]

形 一年的、年度的

英英 happening once a year

例 It is necessary to take an **annual** leave for office workers.

對辦公室職員來講，請年假是有必要的。

☐ 三分熟
☐ 五分熟
☐ 七分熟
☐ 全熟

---

anx·i·e·ty

[æŋ`zaɪətɪ]

名 憂慮、不安、渴望
片 deep anxiety 深刻憂慮

英英 an anxious feeling or worry

例 The news of plane crash caused some **anxiety** of my boyfriend.

撞機的消息引起我男友的不安。

☐ 三分熟
☐ 五分熟
☐ 七分熟
☐ 全熟

---

anx·ious [`æŋkʃəs]

形 憂心的、擔憂的

英英 very worried or anxious

例 They are **anxious** to know the result of the basketball game.

他們急著想知道籃球比賽的結果。

☐ 三分熟
☐ 五分熟
☐ 七分熟
☐ 全熟

A

a·po·l·o·gize
[əˋpɑləˏdʒaɪz]

動 道歉、認錯

英英 to express regret to someone for the wrong thing you have done

例 It is unfair to **apologize** for the mistake that is not made by you.
為你沒有犯的錯道歉是不公平的。

□ 三分熟
□ 五分熟
□ 七分熟
□ 全熟

a·pol·o·gy
[əˋpɑlədʒɪ]

名 謝罪、道歉

英英 an act of saying sorry or apologizing

例 Make **apology** now or never.
現在就道歉，要不然就都不用了。

□ 三分熟
□ 五分熟
□ 七分熟
□ 全熟

ap·pli·ance
[əˋplaɪəns]

名 器具、家電用品

英英 a device, especially an electrical one, designed to perform a specific task

例 The prize drawing this time offers a variety of household **appliances**.
這次的抽獎活動提供各式各樣的家電用品。

□ 三分熟
□ 五分熟
□ 七分熟
□ 全熟

ap·pli·cant
[ˋæpləkənt]

名 申請人、應徵者

英英 a person who applies for something, such as a job

例 The job **applicants** for the position of secretary are waiting in the meeting room.
祕書這個職位的申請人在會議室等著。

□ 三分熟
□ 五分熟
□ 七分熟
□ 全熟

ap·pli·ca·tion
[ˏæpləˋkeʃən]

名 應用、申請

英英 the action of applying

例 Fill in the **application** form if you'd like to apply for the part-time job.
如果你想申請這份兼差工作，請填寫申請表。

□ 三分熟
□ 五分熟
□ 七分熟
□ 全熟

ap·point [əˋpɔɪnt]
動 任命、約定、指派、任用

英英 to assign someone a job or role

例 To **appoint** Frank to be in charge of this project needs a second thought.
任命法蘭克負責這個計畫案需要再想想。

□ 三分熟
□ 五分熟
□ 七分熟
□ 全熟

ap·point·ment
[əˋpɔɪntmənt]

名 指定、約定、指派、任用

英英 an arrangement to meet or a job or position

例 I have an **appointment** with my dentist.
我跟牙醫有約。

□ 三分熟
□ 五分熟
□ 七分熟
□ 全熟

ap·pre·ci·a·tion
[əˏpriʃɪˋeʃən]

名 賞識、鑑識

英英 recognition of the value or significance of something, such as paintings

例 It takes time to cultivate the ability of painting **appreciation**.
培養欣賞畫作的能力需要時間。

□ 三分熟
□ 五分熟
□ 七分熟
□ 全熟

🎧 **Track 149**

---

ap·pro·pri·ate

[əˋproprɪˌet]

形 適當的、適切的
同 proper 適當的

英英 suitable or right for a particular situation

例 To shake legs while eating is not quite **appropriate**.
一邊吃飯一邊抖腿，是很不恰當的。

☐ 三分熟
☐ 五分熟
☐ 七分熟
☐ 全熟

---

ap·prov·al

[əˋpruv!]

名 承認、同意

英英 the opinion that something is good or suitable

例 To sign this contract or not needs our manager's **approval**.
是否要簽這份合約需要我們經理的同意。

☐ 三分熟
☐ 五分熟
☐ 七分熟
☐ 全熟

---

arch [ɑrtʃ]

名 拱門、拱形
動 變成拱形

英英 a curved structure spanning an opening or supporting the weight of something; to make something in the shape of arch

例 When we're sitting on the boat, we can take a picture of the **arch** of the trees.
當我們坐在船上時，我們可以拍拱形樹的照片。

☐ 三分熟
☐ 五分熟
☐ 七分熟
☐ 全熟

---

a·rise [əˋraɪz]

動 出現、發生

英英 to happen or occur

例 When the opportunity **arises**, I'd like to visit the castle in France.
當機會出現，我想造訪法國的城堡。

☐ 三分熟
☐ 五分熟
☐ 七分熟
☐ 全熟

---

arms [ɑrmz]

名 武器、兵器

英英 guns and other weapons

例 We need continued supply of **arms**.
我們需要持續不斷的武器供應。

☐ 三分熟
☐ 五分熟
☐ 七分熟
☐ 全熟

---

a·rouse [əˋrauz]

動 喚醒

英英 to make someone have a special feeling; bring about a feeling or response in someone

例 This picture book **aroused** our curiosity in the life of the Japanese artist.
這本繪本喚醒我們對這位日本藝術家生平的好奇心。

☐ 三分熟
☐ 五分熟
☐ 七分熟
☐ 全熟

---

ar·ti·cle [ˋɑrtɪk!]

名 論文、物件

英英 a particular object; a piece of writing

例 This **article** on the subject of the mermaid is quite interesting.
這篇討論美人魚主題的論文還挺有趣的。

☐ 三分熟
☐ 五分熟
☐ 七分熟
☐ 全熟

---

artificial

[ˌɑrtəˋfɪʃəl]

形 人工的

英英 made as a copy of something natural by people

例 Some carps are bred in this **artificial** fish pond.
一些鯉魚被飼養在這座人工魚池裡。

☐ 三分熟
☐ 五分熟
☐ 七分熟
☐ 全熟

A

ar·tis·tic [ɑrˋtɪstɪk]

形 藝術的、美術的

英英 relating to creative skill or art

例 The **artistic** design of this pair of earrings amazes everyone.
這副耳環的藝術設計讓每個人感到吃驚。

☐ 三分熟
☐ 五分熟
☐ 七分熟
☐ 全熟

a·shamed

[əˋʃemd]

形 以……為恥

英英 feeling embarrassed or guilty about something

例 The man is **ashamed** of himself because he can't stop drinking.
這個人為自己感到羞恥，因為他無法停止飲酒。

☐ 三分熟
☐ 五分熟
☐ 七分熟
☐ 全熟

as·pect [ˋæspɛkt]

名 方面、外貌、外觀

英英 particular part of a matter, problem, subjects, etc

例 The most important **aspect** to consider is the light in this house.
最重要的考量方面是這棟房子的燈光。

☐ 三分熟
☐ 五分熟
☐ 七分熟
☐ 全熟

as·pi·rin [ˋæspərɪn]

名 （藥）阿斯匹靈

英英 a medicine used in tablet form for reducing pain and fever

例 If you have a headache, you may consider taking some **aspirin**.
如果你頭痛，你可以考量吃些阿斯匹靈。

☐ 三分熟
☐ 五分熟
☐ 七分熟
☐ 全熟

as·sem·ble

[əˋsɛmbl]

動 聚集、集合

英英 to come or bring together in a place

例 The soldiers are **assembled** to clean the mud in the basement.
士兵集合起來清理地下室的泥巴。

☐ 三分熟
☐ 五分熟
☐ 七分熟
☐ 全熟

as·sem·bly

[əˋsɛmblɪ]

名 集會、集合、會議

英英 a group of people gathered together

例 We wear uniforms to attend school **assembly**.
我們穿制服參加學校的集會。

☐ 三分熟
☐ 五分熟
☐ 七分熟
☐ 全熟

as·sign [əˋsaɪn]

動 分派、指定

英英 to allocate a task or duty to someone or to give someone a job

例 Mrs. Wang **assigned** different tasks to each group of the students.
王老師指派任務給各組學生。

☐ 三分熟
☐ 五分熟
☐ 七分熟
☐ 全熟

as·sign·ment

[əˋsaɪnmənt]

名 分派、任命、工作 [C]

英英 a task assigned to someone as part of a job

例 The reading **assignment** in the summer vacation includes three novels.
暑假的閱讀工作包含三本小説。

☐ 三分熟
☐ 五分熟
☐ 七分熟
☐ 全熟

Track 151

as·sist·ance
[əˋsɪstəns]

名 幫助、援助

英英 help or support

例 The researching department needs more financial **assistance**.
研發部門需要更多的財務援助。

☐ 三分熟 ☐ 五分熟 ☐ 七分熟 ☐ 全熟

as·so·ci·ate
[əˋsoʃɪˏet]/[əˋsoʃɪt]

名 同事、夥伴
動 聯合

英英 a work partner or colleague; to join together

例 Our boss' business **associate** is coming to see him.
我們老闆的生意夥伴要來見他。

☐ 三分熟 ☐ 五分熟 ☐ 七分熟 ☐ 全熟

as·so·ci·a·tion
[əˏsosɪˋeʃən]

名 協會、聯合會

英英 a group of people organized for a particular purpose

例 Ski **association** of Hong Kong was founded sixteen years ago.
香港的滑雪協會是在十六年前成立。

☐ 三分熟 ☐ 五分熟 ☐ 七分熟 ☐ 全熟

as·sume [əˋsum]

動 假定、擔任、以為

英英 to accept something to be true without proof

例 Peter **assumed** that we two knew each other.
彼得以為我們兩個彼此認識。

☐ 三分熟 ☐ 五分熟 ☐ 七分熟 ☐ 全熟

as·sur·ance
[əˋʃurəns]

名 保證、保險
同 insurance 保險
片 seek an assurance 尋找保證

英英 giving confidence

例 The agent gave us **assurance** that our daughter would become a famous actress soon.
經紀人給我們保證，我們的女兒很快就會變成有名的女演員。

☐ 三分熟 ☐ 五分熟 ☐ 七分熟 ☐ 全熟

as·sure [əˋʃur]

動 向……保證、使確信
同 guarantee 向……保證

英英 to tell someone something positively and confidently, so that they do not worry

例 I **assure** you the car has never been driven by anyone.
我向你保證，這輛車從不曾被任何人開過。

☐ 三分熟 ☐ 五分熟 ☐ 七分熟 ☐ 全熟

ath·let·ic
[æθˋlɛtɪk]

形 運動的、強健的

英英 fit, strong and good at sports

例 The **athletic** meeting will take place next Friday.
運動會下週五舉行。

☐ 三分熟 ☐ 五分熟 ☐ 七分熟 ☐ 全熟

ATM/au·to·mat·ic tell·er ma·chine
[ˌɔtəˈmætɪk ˈtɛlɚ məˈʃin]

名 自動櫃員機

英英 abbreviation for automated teller machine: a machine, in or out of the bank, from which you can take money out of your bank with your bank card

例 The **ATM** of Hua-Nan Bank is not far from here.
華南銀行的提款機離這裡不遠。

☐ 三分熟
☐ 五分熟
☐ 七分熟
☐ 全熟

at·mos·phere
[ˈætməsˌfɪr]

名 大氣、氣氛

英英 the mixture of gases surrounding the earth or another planet

例 The **atmosphere** in this restaurant relaxes customers.
這家餐廳的氣氛讓顧客感到放鬆。

☐ 三分熟
☐ 五分熟
☐ 七分熟
☐ 全熟

at·om [ˈætəm]

名 原子

英英 the smallest particle of a chemical element, consisting of a positively charged nucleus surrounded by negative electrons

例 It is said that the earliest **atoms** in the universe are mainly hydrogen and helium.
據說宇宙中最早的原子主要是氫氣和氦氣。

☐ 三分熟
☐ 五分熟
☐ 七分熟
☐ 全熟

a·tom·ic [əˈtɑmɪk]

形 原子的

英英 relating to an atom or atoms

例 One organization in Japan aims to find ways to promote peaceful use of **atomic** energy.
日本有個組織，試圖要找出促進和平使用原子能的方法。

☐ 三分熟
☐ 五分熟
☐ 七分熟
☐ 全熟

at·tach [əˈtætʃ]

動 連接、附屬、附加

英英 to fasten or join

例 The new printer is **attached** to your computer.
新的印表機連接你的電腦。

☐ 三分熟
☐ 五分熟
☐ 七分熟
☐ 全熟

at·tach·ment
[əˈtætʃmənt]

名 連接、附著

英英 an extra part or condition attached to something

例 The **attachment** to the bottle of the soda is used to open the bottle.
汽水瓶的附屬物是用來打開這個瓶子的。

☐ 三分熟
☐ 五分熟
☐ 七分熟
☐ 全熟

at·trac·tion
[əˈtrækʃən]

名 魅力、吸引力

英英 the action or power of attracting

例 The **attraction** of the new type of cellphone is beyond description.
新型手機的吸引力是筆墨所難以形容的。

☐ 三分熟
☐ 五分熟
☐ 七分熟
☐ 全熟

🎧 **Track 153**

au·di·o [ˈɔdɪˌo]

名 聲音

英英 the sound within the acoustic range available to humans

例 We went to the **audio**-visual room to view a Disney movie.
我們到視聽教室去看一部迪士尼的電影。

☐ 三分熟
☐ 五分熟
☐ 七分熟
☐ 全熟

---

au·thor·i·ty
[əˈθɔrətɪ]

名 權威、當局

英英 the power or right to give orders or control

例 Miller is determined to rebel against the **authority**.
米勒決意要反抗權威。

☐ 三分熟
☐ 五分熟
☐ 七分熟
☐ 全熟

---

au·to·bi·og·ra·phy
[ˌɔtəbaɪˈɑgrəfɪ]

名 自傳

英英 a book or story that about a person's life written by that person

例 Benjamin Franklin's **autobiography** is a famous example of this genre.
班傑明・富蘭克林的自傳，是這種文體中的有名例子之一。

☐ 三分熟
☐ 五分熟
☐ 七分熟
☐ 全熟

---

a·wait [əˈwet]

動 等待

英英 to wait for something or someone

例 Daniel is anxiously **awaiting** the news of his missing girlfriend.
丹尼爾焦急的等待他失蹤女友的消息。

☐ 三分熟
☐ 五分熟
☐ 七分熟
☐ 全熟

---

awk·ward
[ˈɔkwəd]

形 笨拙的、不熟練的

英英 hard to do or deal with; not familiar with

例 When Sunny tried to explain the concept of love, he seemed to be **awkward**.
當桑尼試著要解釋愛的概念，他似乎顯得笨拙。

☐ 三分熟
☐ 五分熟
☐ 七分熟
☐ 全熟

Bb

back·pack
[ˈbækˌpæk]

名 背包
動 把⋯⋯放入背包、
背負簡便行李旅行

英英 a rucksack, that is worn on a person's back

例 Carry your **backpack** and we can go mountain climbing.
背上你的背包，我們就可以去爬山了。

☐ 三分熟
☐ 五分熟
☐ 七分熟
☐ 全熟

---

bald [bɔld]

形 禿頭的、禿的

英英 having very little or no hair

例 My uncle is **bald**, but he wears a straw hat on the beach.
我舅舅禿頭，但在海灘上他戴了頂草帽。

☐ 三分熟
☐ 五分熟
☐ 七分熟
☐ 全熟

bal·let [ˋbæle]
名 芭蕾

英英 an artistic dance form performed to music, usually tells a story or express an idea

例 Black Swan features the competition between **ballet** dancers.
《黑天鵝》以芭蕾舞者之間的競爭為主。

☐ 三分熟
☐ 五分熟
☐ 七分熟
☐ 全熟

B

bank·rupt
[ˋbæŋkrʌpt]
名 破產者
形 破產的

英英 a person who is legally declared as bankrupt

例 TV celebrities sometimes made risky investment and went **bankrupt**.
電視名人有時會做有風險的投資，然後以破產收尾。

☐ 三分熟
☐ 五分熟
☐ 七分熟
☐ 全熟

bar·gain [ˋbɑrgɪn]
名 協議、成交
動 討價還價

英英 an agreement made between two people as to what each gives promises to do something for the other

例 I made a **bargain** of an elegant blouse yesterday.
我昨天以便宜的價格買到一件優雅的女性上衣。

☐ 三分熟
☐ 五分熟
☐ 七分熟
☐ 全熟

bar·ri·er [ˋbærɪɚ]
名 障礙
片 the language barrier
語言的隔閡

英英 anything that prevents movement or access

例 The doctor tried her best to break down the psychological **barrier** of Cathy.
醫生盡其所能要破除凱蒂的心理障礙。

☐ 三分熟
☐ 五分熟
☐ 七分熟
☐ 全熟

ba·sin [ˋbes]
名 盆、水盆

英英 a large bowl or open container for preparing food or holding liquid

例 Put some yellow ducks into the **basin**.
把一些黃色小鴨放到水盆裡。

☐ 三分熟
☐ 五分熟
☐ 七分熟
☐ 全熟

bat·ter·y [ˋbætərɪ]
名 電池

英英 a device containing one or more electrical cells, which is used as a source of power

例 The **battery** is dead.
電池沒電了。

☐ 三分熟
☐ 五分熟
☐ 七分熟
☐ 全熟

beak [bik]
名 鳥嘴

英英 a hard part of bird's mouth

例 The **beak** of the bird changes on the process of evolution.
在演化的過程中鳥嘴會有所改變。

☐ 三分熟
☐ 五分熟
☐ 七分熟
☐ 全熟

🎧 **Track 155**

beam [bim]

名 光線、容光煥發、樑
動 照耀、微笑

英英 a line of life from a bright thing; a long piece of timber or metal used to support building; to show a smile pleasantly

例 The **beam** comes through the window on top of the roof.
光線從屋頂的窗戶照射進來。

☐ 三分熟
☐ 五分熟
☐ 七分熟
☐ 全熟

---

be·hav·ior

[bɪ'hevjɚ]

名 舉止、行為
同 action 行為

英英 the way in which someone or something behaves; manners

例 The courting **behaviors** of some birds are amusing.
有些鳥類的求偶行為是有趣的。

☐ 三分熟
☐ 五分熟
☐ 七分熟
☐ 全熟

---

bi·og·ra·phy

[baɪ'ɑgrəfɪ]

名 傳記

英英 a story of a person's life written by someone else

例 The **biography** of J. K. Rowling reveals sad events Rowling experienced.
J. K. 羅琳的傳記顯示出羅琳所經歷過的悲傷事件。

☐ 三分熟
☐ 五分熟
☐ 七分熟
☐ 全熟

---

bi·ol·o·gy

[baɪ'ɑlədʒɪ]

名 生物學

英英 the scientific study of living organisms and natural processes of living things

例 The **biology** teacher is good at arousing learning interest.
生物學老師擅長於引起學習興趣。

☐ 三分熟
☐ 五分熟
☐ 七分熟
☐ 全熟

---

blade [bled]

名 刀鋒

英英 the flat cutting edge of a knife or other weapon

例 The **blade** of the sward is not sharp anymore.
這把劍的刀鋒不再銳利了。

☐ 三分熟
☐ 五分熟
☐ 七分熟
☐ 全熟

---

blend [blɛnd]

名 混合
動 使混合、使交融

英英 a mixture of different things; to mix different things together

例 The **blend** of strawberry and chocolate adds flavor to the cake.
草莓和巧克力的混合為這塊蛋糕增添了美味。

☐ 三分熟
☐ 五分熟
☐ 七分熟
☐ 全熟

---

bless·ing ['blɛsɪŋ]

名 恩典、祝福

英英 God's favor and care; to ask for God's help or protection

例 The beautiful voice of singing well is God's **blessing**.
唱歌好聽的美妙嗓音是上帝的恩典。

☐ 三分熟
☐ 五分熟
☐ 七分熟
☐ 全熟

B

blink [blɪŋk]

名 眨眼
動 使眨眼、閃爍

英英 to close and open the eyes quickly

例 The doll's **blinking** eyes scared my niece.
娃娃眨眼，嚇到我的姪女了。

☐ 三分熟
☐ 五分熟
☐ 七分熟
☐ 全熟

bloom [blum]

名 開花期
動 開花

英英 a period of time which plants produces flowers

例 The **bloom** of cherry flowers is usually in the spring.
櫻花的開花期通常是在春天。

☐ 三分熟
☐ 五分熟
☐ 七分熟
☐ 全熟

blos·som [ˋblɑsəm]

名 花、花簇
動 開花、生長茂盛

英英 a flower or a mass of flowers on a tree or bush

例 The peach **blossoms** in this mountain have pink petals.
這座山裡的桃花有粉紅色的花瓣。

☐ 三分熟
☐ 五分熟
☐ 七分熟
☐ 全熟

blush [blʌʃ]

名 羞愧、慚愧
動 臉紅

英英 embarrassment; to feel embarrassed and become pink in the face

例 David **blushed** when he saw Lily's eyes.
當大衛與莉莉的眼神相遇，他不禁臉紅了。

☐ 三分熟
☐ 五分熟
☐ 七分熟
☐ 全熟

boast [bost]

名／動 自誇

英英 to speak too proudly about what you have or what you have done

例 Why did Grandpa love to **boast** of his past adventures?
為什麼爺爺喜歡自誇他過去的冒險經驗？

☐ 三分熟
☐ 五分熟
☐ 七分熟
☐ 全熟

bond [bɑnd]

名 契約、束縛、抵押、聯繫

英英 a written agreement; a thing used to fasten things together; to give in pledge when you want to borrow money or something valuable

例 The **bond** of love leads the heroine to go back to the past life.
愛的聯繫引領女主角返回前世。

☐ 三分熟
☐ 五分熟
☐ 七分熟
☐ 全熟

bounce [baʊns]

名 彈、跳
動 彈回

英英 to cause something move up and down

例 The colored ball **bounces** up and down in the game.
在這款遊戲裡，彩球上下彈跳。

☐ 三分熟
☐ 五分熟
☐ 七分熟
☐ 全熟

brace·let [ˋbreslɪt]

名 手鐲

英英 an piece of jewelry or chain worn on the wrist or arm

例 The **bracelet** is stored in Grandma's safety box.
那只手鐲保存在奶奶的保險箱裡。

☐ 三分熟
☐ 五分熟
☐ 七分熟
☐ 全熟

🎧 Track 157

bras·siere/bra

[brəˋzɪr]/[brɑ]

名 胸罩、內衣

英英 a piece of women's underwear that supports the breasts

例 The **brassiere** at the night market is cheap but has good design.
夜市的胸罩雖然便宜，但設計的不錯。

☐三分熟
☐五分熟
☐七分熟
☐全熟

---

breed [brid]

動 生育、繁殖
名 品種

英英 to give a birth to or produce offspring; a distinctive type of animal or plants

例 The baby kangaroo is **bred** in mother kangaroo's pouch.
寶寶袋鼠養在媽媽袋鼠的育兒袋裡。

☐三分熟
☐五分熟
☐七分熟
☐全熟

---

bride·groom/ groom

[ˋbraɪdˌgrum]/[grum]

名 新郎

英英 a man who is about to get married or after getting married

例 "Beauty and the Beast" features animal **bridegroom** and human bride.
《美女與野獸》的故事以動物新郎和人類新娘為其特色。

☐三分熟
☐五分熟
☐七分熟
☐全熟

---

broil [brɔɪl]

動 烤、炙

英英 to cook meat or fish with direct heat

例 I'd like to **broil** some pork chops.
我想要烤一些豬排。

☐三分熟
☐五分熟
☐七分熟
☐全熟

---

broke [brok]

形 一無所有的、破產的

英英 without money or anything

例 My boss is **broke**.
我老闆破產了。

☐三分熟
☐五分熟
☐七分熟
☐全熟

---

bru·tal [ˋbrutl̩]

形 野蠻的、殘暴的

英英 very cruel and savagely violent

例 The emperor is **brutal**.
這個皇帝殘暴不仁。

☐三分熟
☐五分熟
☐七分熟
☐全熟

---

bul·le·tin [ˋbʊlətɪn]

名 公告、告示

英英 a short official statement or summary of news printed by an organization

例 Take a look at the **bulletin** board.
看一下公告欄。

☐三分熟
☐五分熟
☐七分熟
☐全熟

cab·i·net
[ˈkæbənɪt]

名 小櫥櫃、內閣

英英 cupboard with drawers or shelves for storing or showing things

例 Could you fetch the cup in the **cabinet** for me?
你可否幫我拿一下小櫥櫃裡的杯子？

□三分熟
□五分熟
□七分熟
□全熟

cal·cu·late
[ˈkælkjəˌlet]

動 計算

英英 to determine mathematically

例 The team leader is **calculating** the days of finishing the whole project.
團隊領導正在計算要完成這整個計畫的天數。

□三分熟
□五分熟
□七分熟
□全熟

cal·cu·la·tion
[ˌkælkjəˈleʃən]

名 計算

英英 a process of using information to add, multiplying, subtracting or dividing numbers to judge the number or amount of something

例 I need time to do that **calculation** for the math question.
我需要時間完成那道數學題的計算。

□三分熟
□五分熟
□七分熟
□全熟

cal·cu·la·tor
[ˈkælkjəˌletɚ]

名 計算機

英英 something used for making mathematical calculations

例 This pink Hello Kitty **calculator** is lovely.
這臺粉紅色凱蒂貓的計算機好可愛。

□三分熟
□五分熟
□七分熟
□全熟

cal·o·rie [ˈkælərɪ]

名 卡、卡路里

英英 a unit of energy which is used as a measurement for the amount of energy that food offers

例 Three bites of ice cream provide you 100 **calories**.
三口冰淇淋提供你 100 卡的熱量。

□三分熟
□五分熟
□七分熟
□全熟

cam·paign
[kæmˈpen]

名 戰役、活動
動 作戰、從事活動

英英 a series of military or business activities intended to achieve an objective in a particular area

例 To win this election, we need an effective promotional **campaign**.
為了打贏這場選戰，我們需要有效的行銷活動。

□三分熟
□五分熟
□七分熟
□全熟

can·di·date
[ˈkændəˌdet]

名 候選人

英英 a person who is nominated for an election

例 The **candidate** is boasting about what he did for the city.
候選人誇耀他以前為這座城市所做的事。

□三分熟
□五分熟
□七分熟
□全熟

🎧 Track 159

ca·pac·i·ty
[kə`pæsətɪ]

名 容積、能力
同 size 容量

英英 the total amount that something can contain or produce

例 Sometimes people will doubt if they have the **capacity** to solve problems.
有時候人們會懷疑自身是否具備可以解決問題的能力。

☐ 三分熟
☐ 五分熟
☐ 七分熟
☐ 全熟

cape [kep]

名 岬、海角

英英 a large piece of land sticking out into the sea

例 **Cape** No. 7 describes a touching love story.
《海角七號》描寫動人的愛情故事。

☐ 三分熟
☐ 五分熟
☐ 七分熟
☐ 全熟

cap·i·tal·(ism)
[`kæpətl̩]/[`kæpətl̩ɪzəm]

名 資本（資本主義）、首都

英英 a large amount of money which is used for producing more wealth or for starting a new business

例 Does **capitalism** make people live a better life?
資本主義讓人們活得更好嗎？

☐ 三分熟
☐ 五分熟
☐ 七分熟
☐ 全熟

cap·i·tal·ist
[`kæpətl̩ɪst]

名 資本家

英英 someone who supports capitalism

例 Even though a **capitalist** loves money, he can't solve all problems with it.
即便一位資本家喜歡錢，他也不能用錢解決所有問題。

☐ 三分熟
☐ 五分熟
☐ 七分熟
☐ 全熟

ca·reer [kə`rɪr]

名 （終身的）職業、生涯

英英 an occupation or job undertaken a person's work life, usually with opportunities for progress

例 You need to think about how to make the best choice in your **career** life.
你需要思考如何在你的職涯中做出最好的選擇。

☐ 三分熟
☐ 五分熟
☐ 七分熟
☐ 全熟

car·go [`kɑrgo]

名 貨物、船貨

英英 goods which is carried on a ship, aircraft, or truck

例 The **cargo** of shoes in our ship weighs 200 tons.
我們船裡的鞋子的貨物重 200 噸。

☐ 三分熟
☐ 五分熟
☐ 七分熟
☐ 全熟

car·ri·er [`kærɪɚ]

名 運送者

英英 a person who carries or holds something

例 The freight **carrier** will handle the shipment this afternoon.
這家貨運公司今天下午會處理這貨物。

☐ 三分熟
☐ 五分熟
☐ 七分熟
☐ 全熟

carve [`kɑrv]

動 切、切成薄片

英英 to cut something into slight pieces

例 Jason demonstrates how to **carve** a carrot into a rose.
傑森示範如何把蘿蔔切成玫瑰。

☐ 三分熟
☐ 五分熟
☐ 七分熟
☐ 全熟

**cat·a·logue/
cat·a·log**

[ˈkætələɡ]

名 目錄
動 編輯目錄
同 list 目錄

英英 a list of items arranged in alphabetical or other systematic order; to make a list of

例 Show me the latest **catalogue** of the party dresses.
拿宴會服的最新目錄給我看。

☐ 三分熟
☐ 五分熟
☐ 七分熟
☐ 全熟

cease [sis]

名 停息
動 終止、停止

英英 to stop or to end up

例 Jeff can't **cease** making too much investment on the stock market.
傑夫無法停止投資太多資金在股票市場。

☐ 三分熟
☐ 五分熟
☐ 七分熟
☐ 全熟

cel·e·bra·tion

[ˌsɛləˈbreʃən]

名 慶祝、慶祝典禮

英英 mark a significant event with an enjoyable activity

例 **Celebration** of Tina's promotion is in this afternoon.
提娜的促銷慶祝會在今天下午。

☐ 三分熟
☐ 五分熟
☐ 七分熟
☐ 全熟

ce·ment [səˈmɛnt]

名 水泥
動 用水泥砌合、強固

英英 a powdery substance made by coalmining lime and clay, used in making concrete; to make something strong; to stick together with cement

例 Most houses in this area are built with **cement**.
這個區域內多數房屋都可用水泥建造。

☐ 三分熟
☐ 五分熟
☐ 七分熟
☐ 全熟

CD/com·pac disk

[ˈsiˈdi]/[ˈkɑmpækt dɪsk]

名 光碟

英英 a small plastic disc on which information or high quality sound is recorded

例 The nature music **CD** helps me to relax.
這張自然音樂的光碟幫助我放鬆。

☐ 三分熟
☐ 五分熟
☐ 七分熟
☐ 全熟

cham·ber

[ˈtʃembɚ]

名 房間、寢室
同 room 房間

英英 a large room of a house, especially a bedroom

例 Annie's diary is in the **chamber**.
《安妮的日記》在那間房間裡。

☐ 三分熟
☐ 五分熟
☐ 七分熟
☐ 全熟

cham·pion·ship

[ˈtʃæmpɪənʃɪp]

名 冠軍賽

英英 a sporting contest or competition for the position of champion

例 The world **championships** will be held next month.
世界冠軍賽下個月即將舉行。

☐ 三分熟
☐ 五分熟
☐ 七分熟
☐ 全熟

C

177

Track 161

---

char·ac·ter·is·tic

[ˌkærɪktəˈrɪstɪk]

名 特徵
形 有特色的

英英 a feature or quality typical of someone or something; pertaining to the moral nature of

例 The **characteristic** of this set of headphone is sound quality.
這組耳機的特徵是聲音品質。

☐ 三分熟
☐ 五分熟
☐ 七分熟
☐ 全熟

---

char·i·ty [ˈtʃærətɪ]

名 慈悲、慈善、寬容
同 generosity 寬宏大量

英英 kindness and generosity

例 Lisa did a lot of work of **charity**.
麗莎做了很多慈善工作。

☐ 三分熟
☐ 五分熟
☐ 七分熟
☐ 全熟

---

chem·is·try

[ˈkɛmɪstrɪ]

名 化學

英英 the basic characteristics of substances and the different ways in which they react or combine with other substances

例 **Chemistry** is an interesting subject.
化學是一門有趣的學科。

☐ 三分熟
☐ 五分熟
☐ 七分熟
☐ 全熟

---

cher·ish [ˈtʃɛrɪʃ]

動 珍愛、珍惜

英英 to protect and care for something or someone you love

例 **Cherish** your family.
珍愛你的家人。

☐ 三分熟
☐ 五分熟
☐ 七分熟
☐ 全熟

---

chirp [tʃɝp]

名 蟲鳴鳥叫聲
動 蟲鳴鳥叫

英英 shot high sound made by birds

例 The birds in this forest were **chirping**.
這座森林裡的鳥在吱吱喳喳的叫。

☐ 三分熟
☐ 五分熟
☐ 七分熟
☐ 全熟

---

chore [tʃor]

名 雜事、打雜

英英 a routine or piece of work, especially a household one

例 Andy's house **chore** is to take out the trash.
安迪所負責的家事是丟垃圾。

☐ 三分熟
☐ 五分熟
☐ 七分熟
☐ 全熟

---

cho·rus [ˈkorəs]

名 合唱團、合唱

英英 a part of a song which is repeated several times after each verse

例 The **chorus** is made up of twelve women.
這個合唱團是由十二個女人所組成。

☐ 三分熟
☐ 五分熟
☐ 七分熟
☐ 全熟

---

ci·gar [sɪˈgɑr]

名 雪茄

英英 a cylinder of tobacco rolled in tobacco leaves for smoking

例 This pack of **cigar** is expensive.
這包雪茄很貴的。

☐ 三分熟
☐ 五分熟
☐ 七分熟
☐ 全熟

---

ci·ne·ma [ˈsɪnəmə]

名 電影院、電影

英英 a theater where films are on

例 Let's go to the **cinema** tonight.
我們今晚來去電影院吧。

☐ 三分熟
☐ 五分熟
☐ 七分熟
☐ 全熟

C

---

cir·cu·lar

[ˈsɝkjələ]

形 圓形的

英英 like a circle shape

例 The theater features **circular** seat arrangement.
這個劇院以圓形座位安排為其特色。

☐ 三分熟
☐ 五分熟
☐ 七分熟
☐ 全熟

---

cir·cu·late

[ˈsɝkjəˌlet]

動 傳佈、循環

英英 to move continuously through a closed system

例 Linda **circulated** the birthday card for everyone to sign.
琳達把這張生日卡傳出去讓大家簽名。

☐ 三分熟
☐ 五分熟
☐ 七分熟
☐ 全熟

---

cir·cu·la·tion

[ˌsɝkjəˈleʃən]

名 通貨、循環、發行量

英英 movement around something

例 This memorial CD has a **circulation** of 2000.
這張紀念版 CD 有 2000 張的發行量。

☐ 三分熟
☐ 五分熟
☐ 七分熟
☐ 全熟

---

cir·cum·stance

[ˈsɝkəmˌstæns]

名 情況
同 condition 情況

英英 a fact or situation connected with an event or action

例 Under that dangerous **circumstance**, what would you do?
在那危急的情況下，你會怎麼做？

☐ 三分熟
☐ 五分熟
☐ 七分熟
☐ 全熟

---

ci·vil·ian [səˈvɪljən]

名 平民、一般人
形 平民的

英英 an ordinary person

例 560 **civilians** died in that war.
560 個平民在那場戰役中喪失性命。

☐ 三分熟
☐ 五分熟
☐ 七分熟
☐ 全熟

---

civ·i·li·za·tion

[ˌsɪvḷəˈzeʃən]

名 文明、開化
同 culture 文化

英英 human society with its great development

例 **Civilization** turns bloody wars into different kinds of competitions.
文明將血淋淋的戰爭變成不同類別的競爭。

☐ 三分熟
☐ 五分熟
☐ 七分熟
☐ 全熟

---

clar·i·fy [ˈklærəˌfaɪ]

動 澄清、變得明晰

英英 to make something more comprehensible

例 Professor Huang has already **clarified** this point.
黃教授已經澄清了這個點。

☐ 三分熟
☐ 五分熟
☐ 七分熟
☐ 全熟

🎧 **Track 163**

clash [klæʃ]

名 衝突、猛撞
動 衝突、猛撞
片 a clash of opinions
　意見衝突

英英 an act or sound of clashing

例 The severe **clash** with different points of view surprised me.
不同觀點的嚴重衝突讓我感到吃驚。

☐ 三分熟
☐ 五分熟
☐ 七分熟
☐ 全熟

clas·si·fi·ca·tion
[ˌklæsəfəˈkeʃən]

名 分類

英英 the action or process of classifying

例 The **classification** of novels in this bookstore is clear.
這家店裡小說的分類滿清楚的。

☐ 三分熟
☐ 五分熟
☐ 七分熟
☐ 全熟

clas·si·fy
[ˈklæsəˌfaɪ]

動 分類

英英 arrange something in a group according to shared characteristics

例 **Classify** the garbage and throw it into the right garbage box.
做好垃圾分類，把垃圾丟到合適的垃圾箱。

☐ 三分熟
☐ 五分熟
☐ 七分熟
☐ 全熟

cliff [klɪf]

名 峭壁、斷崖

英英 a steep rock side, especially at the edge of the sea

例 A black goat almost fell off the **cliff**.
一隻黑羊險些從陡峭的山崖上跌落。

☐ 三分熟
☐ 五分熟
☐ 七分熟
☐ 全熟

cli·max [ˈklaɪmæks]

名 頂點、高潮
動 達到頂點

英英 the highest or most important point of something; to reach a climax

例 The **climax** of the Lantern Festival was when the main lantern was lit.
燈節的高潮就在點主燈的那一刻。

☐ 三分熟
☐ 五分熟
☐ 七分熟
☐ 全熟

clum·sy [ˈklʌmzɪ]

形 笨拙的

英英 awkward in movement or performance

例 The new waiter is a bit **clumsy**.
新來的服務生有點笨拙。

☐ 三分熟
☐ 五分熟
☐ 七分熟
☐ 全熟

coarse [kors]

形 粗糙的
同 rough 粗糙的

英英 rough or harsh in something

例 How come the elegant lady has **coarse** hands?
為什麼這個優雅的女士有粗糙的雙手？

☐ 三分熟
☐ 五分熟
☐ 七分熟
☐ 全熟

code [kod]

名 代號、編碼
片 break the code
　破譯密碼

英英 a system of words, letters, or symbols used to represent others

例 The important messages are written in **code** words.
重要的訊息是用代號寫的。

☐ 三分熟
☐ 五分熟
☐ 七分熟
☐ 全熟

C

col·lapse

[kə`læps]

動 崩潰、倒塌

英英 to fall down suddenly or give way

例 The mansion in the earthquake **collapsed** quickly.
地震中的大廈快速地倒塌。

☐ 三分熟
☐ 五分熟
☐ 七分熟
☐ 全熟

com·bi·na·tion

[ˌkɑmbə`neʃən]

名 結合

英英 the action of combining two or more different things

例 The perfect **combination** of pudding and wine delights everyone at the party.
布丁和紅酒的完美結合取悅了派對裡的每個人。

☐ 三分熟
☐ 五分熟
☐ 七分熟
☐ 全熟

com·e·dy

[`kɑmədɪ]

名 喜劇

英英 film, play or book consisting of jokes and makes audiences laugh intentionally

例 A Midsummer Night's Dream is a **comedy** written by Shakespeare.
《仲夏夜之夢》是莎士比亞所寫的喜劇。

☐ 三分熟
☐ 五分熟
☐ 七分熟
☐ 全熟

com·ic [`kɑmɪk]

形 滑稽的、喜劇的
名 漫畫

英英 causing or meant to make someone laugh; a book or magazine which contains a set of funny stories in pictures

例 **Comic** books are 75% off.
漫畫書二五折。

☐ 三分熟
☐ 五分熟
☐ 七分熟
☐ 全熟

com·mand·er

[kə`mændɚ]

名 指揮官

英英 a person in high rank, especially in a military context

例 The **commander** of the ship was shot.
這艘船的指揮官被射殺。

☐ 三分熟
☐ 五分熟
☐ 七分熟
☐ 全熟

com·ment

[`kɑmɛnt]

名 評語、評論
動 做註解、做評論

英英 a remark expressing an opinion or reaction of an issue

例 The illustrator made revisions according to the editor's **comments**.
插畫家根據編者的評語做了修改。

☐ 三分熟
☐ 五分熟
☐ 七分熟
☐ 全熟

com·merce

[`kɑmɝs]

名 商業、貿易
同 trade 貿易

英英 the activity of buying and selling, like trading

例 The **commerce** of the country develops rapidly.
這個國家的商業貿易快速發展。

☐ 三分熟
☐ 五分熟
☐ 七分熟
☐ 全熟

🎧 **Track 165**

---

com·mit [kə`mɪt]

動 委任、承諾、使作出保證

英英 to carry out or perform a crime, immoral act, or mistake what a person made

例 Be sure to **commit** yourself to something meaningful.
確定你投入的是有意義的事。

□三分熟
□五分熟
□七分熟
□全熟

---

com·mu·ni·ca·tion

[kə͵mjunə`keʃən]

名 通信、溝通、交流

英英 the action of communicating

例 **Communication** between trees are said to be possible.
樹木之間的交流溝通據說是有可能的。

□三分熟
□五分熟
□七分熟
□全熟

---

com·mu·ni·ty

[kə`mjunətɪ]

名 社區

英英 a group of people living together at the place

例 A group of married women volunteered to do cleaning work for their **community**.
一群婦女志願為社區做清潔工作。

□三分熟
□五分熟
□七分熟
□全熟

---

com·pan·ion

[kəm`pænjən]

名 同伴

英英 a person you spend much time with while travelling together

例 Some pets serve as human beings' best **companions**.
有些寵物可當做人類的最好同伴。

□三分熟
□五分熟
□七分熟
□全熟

---

com·pe·ti·tion

[͵kɑmpə`tɪʃən]

名 競爭、競爭者
同 rival 對手

英英 the activity of competing against other person

例 Does **competition** truly makes a more advanced society?
競爭真的造就了更為進步的社會嗎？

□三分熟
□五分熟
□七分熟
□全熟

---

com·pet·i·tive

[kəm`pɛtətɪv]

形 競爭的

英英 relating to or involving competition

例 There is certain **competitive** atmosphere between the two basketball teams.
在這兩個籃球團隊間有某種競爭的氣氛。

□三分熟
□五分熟
□七分熟
□全熟

---

com·pet·i·tor

[kəm`pɛtətɚ]

名 競爭者

英英 a person who takes part in a sporting contest or competition

例 The number of the **competitors** for winning the game is on the increase.
要贏得這場比賽的競爭者人數在增加中。

□三分熟
□五分熟
□七分熟
□全熟

---

com·pli·cate

[`kɑmpləͺket]

動 使複雜

英英 make something more complex or confusing

例 I don't understand why some people like to **complicate** things.
我不明白為什麼有些人喜歡把事情複雜化。

□三分熟
□五分熟
□七分熟
□全熟

---

com·pose
[kəmˋpoz]
動 組成、作曲

英英 to create a work of art, especially music or poetry

例 The group is **composed** of Africans, Americans, and Japanese.
這支隊伍是由非洲人、美國人和日本人所組成。

☐ 三分熟
☐ 五分熟
☐ 七分熟
☐ 全熟

com·pos·er
[kəmˋpozɚ]
名 作曲家、設計者

英英 a person who writes music

例 Mozart is a famous **composer**.
莫札特是有名的作曲家。

☐ 三分熟
☐ 五分熟
☐ 七分熟
☐ 全熟

com·po·si·tion
[ˌkɑmpəˋzıʃən]
名 組合、作文、混合物
片 chemical composition 化學組成

英英 the constitution of something made up from different parts or substances

例 **Composition** classes for some students are a kind of daydreaming practice.
作文課對某些學生來講是一種做白白夢的練習。

☐ 三分熟
☐ 五分熟
☐ 七分熟
☐ 全熟

con·cen·trate
[ˋkɑnsˌtret]
動 集中

英英 to focus completely one's attention or mental effort on something

例 You need to **concentrate** on the details of this topic.
你必需集中你的注意力在這個主題的細節。

☐ 三分熟
☐ 五分熟
☐ 七分熟
☐ 全熟

con·cen·tra·tion
[ˌkɑnsˋtreʃən]
名 集中、專心

英英 the action or power of concentrating

例 Jews were forced to stay in the **concentration** camps.
猶太人被迫待在集中營。

☐ 三分熟
☐ 五分熟
☐ 七分熟
☐ 全熟

con·cept
[ˋkɑnsɛpt]
名 概念

英英 an abstract idea or principle

例 The **concept** is so hard that students pay all their attention to the teacher.
這個概念難到學生對老師付出所有的注意力。

☐ 三分熟
☐ 五分熟
☐ 七分熟
☐ 全熟

con·cern·ing
[kənˋsɝnıŋ]
連 關於

英英 about; relating to

例 Have you found the data **concerning** the origin of "Little Red Riding Hood"?
你找到關於「小紅帽」這個故事起源的資料了嗎？

☐ 三分熟
☐ 五分熟
☐ 七分熟
☐ 全熟

con·crete
[ˋkɑnkrit]
名 水泥、混凝土
形 具體的、混凝土的
反 abstract 抽象的

英英 a building material made by mixing gravel, sand, cement, and water; very real and existing in a form which can be seen or felt

例 This art gallery is built with **concrete**.
這棟美術館是水泥建造的。

☐ 三分熟
☐ 五分熟
☐ 七分熟
☐ 全熟

C

con·duc·tor
[kən`dʌktɚ]

名 指揮、指導者

英英 a person who directs an orchestra or choir

例 The **conductor** of the band perfoms well.
這個樂團的指揮表演的很好。

□ 三分熟
□ 五分熟
□ 七分熟
□ 全熟

con·fer·ence
[`kɑnfərəns]

名 招待會、會議
同 meeting 會議

英英 a meeting for discussion or debate which is held formally

例 The **conference** of comparative literature was held last Friday.
比較文學會議上個星期五舉辦過了。

□ 三分熟
□ 五分熟
□ 七分熟
□ 全熟

con·fess [kən`fɛs]

動 承認、供認

英英 to admit to a crime or mistake

例 I **confessed** to my mother that the necklace was lost.
我跟母親承認那條項鍊遺失了。

□ 三分熟
□ 五分熟
□ 七分熟
□ 全熟

con·fi·dence
[`kɑnfədəns]

名 信心、信賴
片 in confidence 私下地

英英 the belief that one can have faith in someone or something

例 If anyone said something that made you lose your **confidence**, ignore it.
如果任何人說了某件讓你失去信心的事，忽略它。

□ 三分熟
□ 五分熟
□ 七分熟
□ 全熟

con·fine [kən`faɪn]

動 限制、侷限

英英 to limit someone or something's space, scope, or time

例 **Confine** yourself in this circle won't do you any good.
把你自己侷限在這個圈圈裡對你不會有好處。

□ 三分熟
□ 五分熟
□ 七分熟
□ 全熟

con·fu·sion
[kən`fjuʒən]

名 迷惑、混亂

英英 the state of being confused or uncertainty

例 Vincent's accent caused some **confusion**.
文生的口音造成了一些混亂。

□ 三分熟
□ 五分熟
□ 七分熟
□ 全熟

con·grat·u·late
[kən`grætʃəlet]

動 恭喜

英英 to express good wishes or praise at the happiness, success, or good fortune to someone

例 Bring this gift to George and Mary and **congratulate** them for me.
把這份禮物帶給喬治和瑪麗，並替我向他們表達祝賀之意。

□ 三分熟
□ 五分熟
□ 七分熟
□ 全熟

C

con·gress
[ˈkɑŋgrəs]

名 國會

英英 a formal meeting or series of meetings from countries

例 The **congress** won't allow the president to do that.
國會不會允許總統做那件事。

☐ 三分熟
☐ 五分熟
☐ 七分熟
☐ 全熟

con·junc·tion
[kənˈdʒʌŋkʃən]

名 連接、關聯

英英 when some things combine or happen together

例 The scientists are working in **conjunction** to do the virus researching project.
科學家們聯合起來做病毒的研發案。

☐ 三分熟
☐ 五分熟
☐ 七分熟
☐ 全熟

con·quer [ˈkɑŋkɚ]

動 征服

英英 to overcome or take control of by force

例 The English **conquered** the kingdom in the 19th century.
英國人在十九世紀時征服了這個王國。

☐ 三分熟
☐ 五分熟
☐ 七分熟
☐ 全熟

con·science
[ˈkɑnʃəns]

名 良心
片 have a clear conscience
問心無愧

英英 a person's moral sense of right and wrong

例 **Conscience** tells us what is the right thing to do.
良心告訴我們什麼才是應當要做的對的事。

☐ 三分熟
☐ 五分熟
☐ 七分熟
☐ 全熟

con·se·quence
[ˈkɑnsəˌkwɛns]

名 結果、影響

英英 a result, effect or influence

例 The **consequence** is not good.
結果不太好。

☐ 三分熟
☐ 五分熟
☐ 七分熟
☐ 全熟

con·se·quent
[ˈkɑnsəˌkwɛnt]

形 必然的、隨之引起的

英英 following as a consequence of something

例 The **consequent** ocean wastes need more environmental activities.
隨之而來的海洋廢棄物，需要更多的環保活動。

☐ 三分熟
☐ 五分熟
☐ 七分熟
☐ 全熟

con·ser·va·tive
[kənˈsɚvətɪv]

名 保守主義者
形 保守的、保守黨的

英英 someone keeps traditional values and not willing to change

例 Some people seem to be **conservative** in expressing opinions.
有些人在表達意見上似乎是很保守的。

☐ 三分熟
☐ 五分熟
☐ 七分熟
☐ 全熟

con·sist [kənˈsɪst]

動 組成、構成

英英 to be made of or formed from something

例 The committee of school **consists** of 15 people.
學校的委員會由十五人組成。

☐ 三分熟
☐ 五分熟
☐ 七分熟
☐ 全熟

🎧 Track 169

con·sis·tent

[kənˋsɪstənt]

形 一致的、調和的

英英 always behaving or happening in a similar, not changing

例 Parents' discipline principles should be **consistent** when they teach children.
教小孩時，父母的管教原則應該要一致。

☐ 三分熟
☐ 五分熟
☐ 七分熟
☐ 全熟

---

con·so·nant

[ˋkɑnsənənt]

名 子音
形 和諧的
反 vowel 母音

英英 a speech sound in which the breath is at least partly obstructed and which forms a syllable when combined with a vowel; in agreement or harmony with

例 The **consonant** letters of the word "cat" are "c" and "t".
"cat" 這個字的子音字母是 "c" 和 "t"。

☐ 三分熟
☐ 五分熟
☐ 七分熟
☐ 全熟

---

con·sti·tute

[ˋkɑnstəˏtjut]

動 構成、組成、制定

英英 be a part of a whole; to be considered as something

例 Canadians **constitute** 50% of the army.
這支軍隊由百分之五十的加拿大人所組成。

☐ 三分熟
☐ 五分熟
☐ 七分熟
☐ 全熟

---

con·sti·tu·tion

[ˏkɑnstəˋtjuʃən]

名 憲法、章程、構造
片 strong constitution 堅固的構造

英英 the set of political principles by which a state or organization is governed, especially in relation to the rights of the people it governs

例 Some laws in the **constitution** aim to protect the rights of the people.
憲法中有些法律旨在保障人民的權利。

☐ 三分熟
☐ 五分熟
☐ 七分熟
☐ 全熟

---

con·struct

[kənˋstrʌkt]

動 建造、構築

英英 to build something by assembling or combining parts

例 The French palace was **constructed** as a luxurious restaurant.
這座法國宮殿被建造成奢華的餐廳。

☐ 三分熟
☐ 五分熟
☐ 七分熟
☐ 全熟

---

con·struc·tion

[kənˋstrʌkʃən]

名 建築、結構

英英 the action or process of constructing

例 My brother-in-law works in the **construction** industry.
我的妹夫在建築業工作。

☐ 三分熟
☐ 五分熟
☐ 七分熟
☐ 全熟

---

con·struc·tive

[kənˋstrʌktɪv]

形 有建設性的

英英 serving a useful purpose or idea

例 I hope your feedback is **constructive**.
我希望你的意見回饋是有建設性的。

☐ 三分熟
☐ 五分熟
☐ 七分熟
☐ 全熟

con·sult [kənˋsʌlt]

動 請教、諮詢
同 confer 協商

英英 to seek information or advice from someone

例 **Consult** your teacher if you can't solve the difficult question.
如果你無法解決這個困難的問題，請教你的老師。

□ 三分熟
□ 五分熟
□ 七分熟
□ 全熟

con·sul·tant

[kənˋsʌltənt]

名 諮詢者

英英 a person who provides advice professionally

例 The publisher hired **consultants** to educate editors.
出版商聘請顧問，以教育編輯。

□ 三分熟
□ 五分熟
□ 七分熟
□ 全熟

con·sume

[kənˋsum]

動 消耗、耗費
同 waste 耗費

英英 to use fuel, energy, or time, especially in large amounts

例 A gallon of petrol is **consumed** every 20 miles.
每 20 英哩就消耗掉一加侖的汽油。

□ 三分熟
□ 五分熟
□ 七分熟
□ 全熟

con·sum·er

[kənˋsumɚ]

名 消費者

英英 a person who buys a product or service for personal use

例 The **consumer** should be wise and reject the products with plastic substances.
消費者應該要有智慧，拒絕含有塑膠物質的產品。

□ 三分熟
□ 五分熟
□ 七分熟
□ 全熟

con·tain·er

[kənˋtenɚ]

名 容器

英英 a box, cylinder, or similar object for storing something

例 The **container** is designed as a peach.
這個容器設計的像顆桃子。

□ 三分熟
□ 五分熟
□ 七分熟
□ 全熟

con·tent

[ˋkɑntɛnt]/[kənˋtɛnt]

名 內容、滿足、目錄
形 滿足的、願意的

英英 a state of being happy or satisfied; something that is contained; a list of subjects contained in a book, with the page number they begin on

例 Martin won't be **content** to this position.
馬丁對這個職位不會覺得滿意的。

□ 三分熟
□ 五分熟
□ 七分熟
□ 全熟

con·tent·ment

[kənˋtɛntmənt]

名 滿足

英英 very pleased with what you already have and not hoping for change or improvement

例 Happiness consists in **contentment**.
知足常樂。

□ 三分熟
□ 五分熟
□ 七分熟
□ 全熟

con·test

[ˋkɑntɛst]/[kənˋtɛst]

名 比賽
動 與……競爭、爭奪

英英 an event in which people compete for supremacy; to try to win; to struggle to gain, as a victory

例 My daughter is going to perform a magic trick during the talent **contest**.
我的女兒將在才藝賽中表演變魔術。

□ 三分熟
□ 五分熟
□ 七分熟
□ 全熟

C

con·text
[ˈkɑntɛkst]

名 上下文、文章脈絡

英英 the parts of a written or spoken statement that follow a specific word or passage

例 Use the **context** to decode the word.
利用上下文來解碼這個字。

□ 三分熟
□ 五分熟
□ 七分熟
□ 全熟

con·tin·u·al
[kənˈtɪnjʊəl]

形 連續的

英英 happening constantly or frequently

例 The **continual** winning record turns the singer into a popular performer.
連續的得獎紀錄把歌手變成了受歡迎的表演者。

□ 三分熟
□ 五分熟
□ 七分熟
□ 全熟

con·tin·u·ous
[kənˈtɪnjʊəs]

形 不斷的、連續的

英英 without interruption

例 It is necessary to make **continuous** efforts to keep the house clean.
持續的努力讓這棟房子保持乾淨是有必要的。

□ 三分熟
□ 五分熟
□ 七分熟
□ 全熟

con·trar·y
[ˈkɑntrɛrɪ]

名 矛盾
形 反對的

英英 the opposite; opposite in nature, direction, or meaning; in a different way from what people act or believe

例 Don't judge people even if they have **contrary** opinions.
不要評斷人，即便他們持反對意見。

□ 三分熟
□ 五分熟
□ 七分熟
□ 全熟

con·trast
[ˈkɑnˌtræst]/[kənˈtræst]

名 對比
動 對照

英英 the difference which is obvious between two or more things; to compare in order to show unlikeness

例 The **contrast** of colors highlights the beauty of the painting.
對比色強調出這幅畫的美。

□ 三分熟
□ 五分熟
□ 七分熟
□ 全熟

con·trib·ute
[kənˈtrɪbjʊt]

動 貢獻

英英 to give in order to help achieve something

例 We did appreciate what you **contributed** to the association.
我們著實感謝您對協會的貢獻。

□ 三分熟
□ 五分熟
□ 七分熟
□ 全熟

con·tri·bu·tion
[ˌkɑntrəˈbjuʃən]

名 貢獻、捐獻

英英 something that you do or give to help achieve one thing

例 Jing-yong has great **contribution** to the genre of wuxia novels.
金庸對武俠小說這種文藝作品的類型有很大的貢獻。

□ 三分熟
□ 五分熟
□ 七分熟
□ 全熟

con·ve·nience
[kənˈvinjəns]

名 便利

英英 freedom from effort or without difficulty

例 Have a cup of coffee at the **convenience** store.
在便利商店喝杯咖啡吧。

□ 三分熟
□ 五分熟
□ 七分熟
□ 全熟

con·ven·tion
[kən`vɛnʃən]

名 會議、條約、傳統

英英 a formal meeting with a group of people who have the same or similar interest

例 Eating rice dumplings on Dragon Boat Festival is a **convention**.
在端午節吃粽子是一項傳統習俗。

☐ 三分熟
☐ 五分熟
☐ 七分熟
☐ 全熟

con·ven·tion·al
[kən`vɛnʃənl]

形 會議的、傳統的

英英 based on convention

例 Some people like to wear **conventional** clothes during the wedding.
有些人喜歡在婚禮上穿傳統的衣服。

☐ 三分熟
☐ 五分熟
☐ 七分熟
☐ 全熟

con·verse
[kən`vɝs]

動 談話

英英 to hold a conversation

例 **Conversing** with the guest tries our patience.
跟這些客人交談考驗我們的耐心。

☐ 三分熟
☐ 五分熟
☐ 七分熟
☐ 全熟

con·vey [kən`ve]

動 傳達、運送

英英 to express a thought, feeling, or idea so that it is understood by other people

例 Actors use body language to **convey** emotions.
演員們用身體語言傳達情緒。

☐ 三分熟
☐ 五分熟
☐ 七分熟
☐ 全熟

con·vince
[kən`vɪns]

動 說服、信服

英英 to cause someone to believe firmly in the truth of something

例 How can we **convince** our parents that we did see the aliens?
我們該如何讓爸媽相信我們確實看到外星人了？

☐ 三分熟
☐ 五分熟
☐ 七分熟
☐ 全熟

co·op·er·ate
[ko`ɑpəˌret]

名 協力、合作

英英 to work together towards the same end

例 Brothers and sisters should **cooperate** when solving problems.
當解決問題時，兄弟姊妹要一起合作。

☐ 三分熟
☐ 五分熟
☐ 七分熟
☐ 全熟

co·op·er·a·tion
[koˌɑpə`reʃən]

名 合作、協力

英英 when you work together with someone

例 "Ten Brothers" describes the **cooperation** of ten brothers with different abilities.
「十兄弟」描述十個擁有不同能力的兄弟之間的通力合作。

☐ 三分熟
☐ 五分熟
☐ 七分熟
☐ 全熟

co·op·er·a·tive
[ko`ɑpəˌretɪv]

名 合作社
形 合作的

英英 a cooperative organization; willing to work together or help

例 Profess Cory asked them not to close the door so hard, but they were not **cooperative**.
科瑞教授要求他們不要太用力關門，但他們就是不想合作。

☐ 三分熟
☐ 五分熟
☐ 七分熟
☐ 全熟

C

🎧 **Track 173**

cope [kop]
動 處理、對付

英英 to deal with something difficult effectively
例 I need to **cope** with house chores tonight.
我今晚需要處理家務事。

☐ 三分熟 ☐ 五分熟 ☐ 七分熟 ☐ 全熟

cop·per [ˈkɑpɚ]
名 銅
形 銅製的

英英 a red-brown metallic chemical substance which is used for electrical wiring and as a component of brass and bronze
例 The **copper** medal will be given to the third place.
銅製獎牌會頒給第三名。

☐ 三分熟 ☐ 五分熟 ☐ 七分熟 ☐ 全熟

cord [kɔrd]
名 電線、繩

英英 long thin rope made from several twisted strands
例 Some sparrows are on the electric **cord**.
有些麻雀在電線上。

☐ 三分熟 ☐ 五分熟 ☐ 七分熟 ☐ 全熟

cork [kɔrk]
名 軟木塞
動 用軟木塞栓緊

英英 the light brown substance from the bark of the cork oak; to close a bottle or a container with a cork
例 The policeman looks for the **cork** of the wine.
警方在找那瓶紅酒的軟木塞。

☐ 三分熟 ☐ 五分熟 ☐ 七分熟 ☐ 全熟

cor·re·spond [ˌkɔrəˈspɑnd]
動 符合、相當

英英 to match something or agree something almost exactly
例 It is strange that Dr Jekyll's signature **corresponds** to the one on the check.
奇怪的是傑奇博士的簽名符合支票上的簽名。

☐ 三分熟 ☐ 五分熟 ☐ 七分熟 ☐ 全熟

cos·tume [ˈkɑstjum]
名 服裝、服飾、劇裝

英英 a set of clothes in a style in a particular country or historical period
例 The clown **costume** is stolen.
小丑服被偷了。

☐ 三分熟 ☐ 五分熟 ☐ 七分熟 ☐ 全熟

cot·tage [ˈkɑtɪdʒ]
名 小屋、別墅

英英 a small house, typically one in the countryside
例 The **cottage** is beside the lake.
那棟小屋在湖邊。

☐ 三分熟 ☐ 五分熟 ☐ 七分熟 ☐ 全熟

coun·cil [ˈkaʊnsl̩]
名 議會、會議

英英 a formal meeting with group of people who chosen to make decisions or give advice on an event or subject
例 The City **Council** provides good community services.
市議會提供優質的社區服務。

☐ 三分熟 ☐ 五分熟 ☐ 七分熟 ☐ 全熟

count·er [ˈkaʊntɚ]
名 櫃檯、計算機
動 反對、反抗

英英 a machine that counts; to protect yourself against something

例 The **counter** of the post office is on your left.
郵局的櫃檯在你的左邊。

☐三分熟 ☐五分熟 ☐七分熟 ☐全熟

---

cou·ra·geous [kəˈredʒəs]
形 勇敢的

英英 having courage, very brave

例 Generally speaking, knights are **courageous**.
一般而言，武士是勇敢的。

☐三分熟 ☐五分熟 ☐七分熟 ☐全熟

---

cour·te·ous [ˈkɝtjəs]
形 有禮貌的

英英 very polite, respectful, and considerate

例 My mother is fond of **courteous** people.
我母親喜愛有禮貌的人。

☐三分熟 ☐五分熟 ☐七分熟 ☐全熟

---

cour·te·sy [ˈkɝtəsɪ]
名 禮貌

英英 courteous behavior; politeness

例 Confucius emphasized the importance of **courtesy**.
孔子強調禮節的重要。

☐三分熟 ☐五分熟 ☐七分熟 ☐全熟

---

crack [kræk]
名 裂縫、瑕疵
動 使爆裂、使破裂

英英 a narrow opening between two parts of something which either has split or been broken; to break something suddenly and abruptly

例 The water is leaking from the **crack** of the wall.
水從牆縫滲了出來。

☐三分熟 ☐五分熟 ☐七分熟 ☐全熟

---

craft [kræft]
名 手工藝

英英 an activity involving skill in making things by hand

例 People were marveled at the weaving **craft** of the boy.
人們驚嘆於這個男孩的手工藝。

☐三分熟 ☐五分熟 ☐七分熟 ☐全熟

---

cram [kræm]
動 把……塞進、狼吞虎嚥地吃東西

英英 to force too many things into something

例 The monkey **crammed** the bananas into his mouth.
這隻猴子往嘴裡塞進香蕉。

☐三分熟 ☐五分熟 ☐七分熟 ☐全熟

---

cre·a·tion [krɪˈeʃən]
名 創造、創世

英英 the action or process of creating

例 A cockroach is hidden in the paper art **creation** of Tim Budden.
在提姆·巴頓的紙藝創造品裡藏著一隻蟑螂。

☐三分熟 ☐五分熟 ☐七分熟 ☐全熟

🎧 Track 175

---

cre·a·tiv·i·ty

[ˌkrieˋtɪvətɪ]

名 創造力

英英 involving the use of the imagination for create something

例 Tim is a great artist with lots of **creativity**.
提姆是個很有創造力的偉大藝術家。

☐ 三分熟
☐ 五分熟
☐ 七分熟
☐ 全熟

---

crip·ple [ˋkrɪpl̩]

名 瘸子、殘疾人

英英 a person who is unable to walk or move properly

例 Helen had a car accident and became a **cripple**.
海倫出了車禍，變成了瘸子。

☐ 三分熟
☐ 五分熟
☐ 七分熟
☐ 全熟

---

crit·ic [ˋkrɪtɪk]

名 批評家、評論家

英英 a person who expresses that they do not approve of something

例 The movie **critic** was harsh on the movie director.
這個影評家對電影導演好嚴苛。

☐ 三分熟
☐ 五分熟
☐ 七分熟
☐ 全熟

---

crit·i·cal [ˋkrɪtɪkl̩]

形 評論的、愛挑剔的

英英 expressing adverse or disapproving opinion

例 Why was your father so **critical** about the article you wrote?
為什麼你的父親對你寫的這篇文章如此挑剔？

☐ 三分熟
☐ 五分熟
☐ 七分熟
☐ 全熟

---

crit·i·cism

[ˋkrɪtəˌsɪzəm]

名 評論、批評的論文

英英 expression of disapproval, finding fault

例 I don't think anybody can take that **criticism** without anger.
我不認為有人可以心平氣和的接受那樣的評論。

☐ 三分熟
☐ 五分熟
☐ 七分熟
☐ 全熟

---

crit·i·cize

[ˋkrɪtəˌsaɪz]

動 批評、批判

英英 to indicate the faults of in a disapproving way

例 Do you dare to **criticize** him?
你敢批評他嗎？

☐ 三分熟
☐ 五分熟
☐ 七分熟
☐ 全熟

---

cru·el·ty [ˋkruəltɪ]

名 冷酷、殘忍

英英 cruel behavior or manner

例 Human beings' **cruelty** to animals angered the staff in the animal shelter.
人類對動物的殘忍讓動物收容所的工作人員感到氣憤。

☐ 三分熟
☐ 五分熟
☐ 七分熟
☐ 全熟

---

crush [krʌʃ]

名 毀壞、壓榨
動 壓碎、壓壞

英英 breaking something with violence; to press a crowd of people or things closely together

例 The cane juice is made by **crushing** the canes.
甘蔗汁是藉由壓榨甘蔗做成的。

☐ 三分熟
☐ 五分熟
☐ 七分熟
☐ 全熟

C

cube [kjub]

名 立方體、正六面體
片 ice cube 冰塊

英英 a symmetrical three-dimensional shape contained by six equal squares
例 The ice **cubes** are added to the orange juice.
冰塊加到柳橙汁裡。

☐ 三分熟
☐ 五分熟
☐ 七分熟
☐ 全熟

cu·cum·ber [ˈkjukʌmbɚ]

名 小黃瓜、黃瓜

英英 the long, pale-green fruit of a climbing plant, which has watery flesh and usually is eaten raw in salads
例 It is suggested putting some slices of **cucumber** on your face.
建議把一些小黃瓜切片放在你臉上。

☐ 三分熟
☐ 五分熟
☐ 七分熟
☐ 全熟

cue [kju]

名 暗示

英英 a signal to an actor to start their action in the performance
例 The waitress is mopping the floor, which is the **cue** of asking the customers to leave.
女侍者在拖地，這是請客人離開的暗示。

☐ 三分熟
☐ 五分熟
☐ 七分熟
☐ 全熟

cun·ning [ˈkʌnɪŋ]

形 精明的、狡猾的

英英 describes a person who is clever at planning something in order to get what they want
例 The **cunning** fox stole the chicken.
狡猾的狐狸偷了雞。

☐ 三分熟
☐ 五分熟
☐ 七分熟
☐ 全熟

cu·ri·os·i·ty [ˌkjʊrɪˈɑsətɪ]

名 好奇心

英英 a strong desire to know or learn something
例 Children are born with plenty of **curiosity**.
孩子們天生就有很多的好奇心。

☐ 三分熟
☐ 五分熟
☐ 七分熟
☐ 全熟

curl [kɝl]

名 捲髮、捲曲
動 使捲曲
片 loose curls
蓬鬆的捲髮

英英 something in the shape of a spiral or coil; to twist into ringlets
例 Lady Gaga's hair fell in **curls** over her shoulder.
女神卡卡的頭髮捲曲著垂在肩上。

☐ 三分熟
☐ 五分熟
☐ 七分熟
☐ 全熟

curse [kɝs]

動 詛咒、罵

英英 to use obscene words against someone
例 There's no use **cursing** your fate.
咒罵你的命運沒有用。

☐ 三分熟
☐ 五分熟
☐ 七分熟
☐ 全熟

curve [kɝv]

名 曲線
動 使彎曲

英英 a line which gradually deviates from being straight for its length; to bend or crook something
例 The **curve** of the woman in silver dress attracts many men's attention.
身穿銀色洋裝的女人的曲線吸引了很多男人的注意。

☐ 三分熟
☐ 五分熟
☐ 七分熟
☐ 全熟

🎧 **Track 177**

---

cush·ion [ˈkʊʃən]

名 墊子
動 緩和……衝擊

英英 a bag of cloth stuffed with a mass of soft material, which is used as a comfortable support for sitting on; to soften something and make less impact

例 The papering cat sits comfortably on the **cushion**.
被嬌寵的貓咪很舒服地坐在墊子上。

☐ 三分熟
☐ 五分熟
☐ 七分熟
☐ 全熟

Dd

---

damn [dæm]

動 指責、輕蔑

英英 to blame or criticize something or someone strongly

例 The public **damned** the parents for abusing their children.
大眾指責這對虐待自己小孩的父母。

☐ 三分熟
☐ 五分熟
☐ 七分熟
☐ 全熟

---

damp [dæmp]

形 潮濕的
動 使潮濕
同 moist 潮濕的

英英 slightly wet; to make something wet

例 The curtain in the living room feels a bit **damp**.
客廳的窗簾摸起來有點潮濕。

☐ 三分熟
☐ 五分熟
☐ 七分熟
☐ 全熟

---

dead·line

[ˈdɛdˌlaɪn]

名 限期

英英 the latest time or date by which something should be completed by someone

例 The **deadline** of this project is on the fifth of March.
這個案子的限期是三月五日。

☐ 三分熟
☐ 五分熟
☐ 七分熟
☐ 全熟

---

de·clare [dɪˈklɛr]

動 宣告、公告

英英 announce officially

例 Miss Lin **declared** that there's a charity party this weekend.
林小姐宣告這週有個慈善派對。

☐ 三分熟
☐ 五分熟
☐ 七分熟
☐ 全熟

---

dec·o·ra·tion

[ˌdɛkəˈreʃən]

名 裝飾

英英 the process or art of decorating

例 Judy is good at the art **decoration** of restaurants.
茱蒂擅長餐廳的藝術裝飾。

☐ 三分熟
☐ 五分熟
☐ 七分熟
☐ 全熟

---

de·crease [dɪˈkris]

動 減少、減小
名 減少、減小
反 increase 增加

英英 the process of decreasing

例 People have the responsibility to help with the **decreasing** of pollution.
人們有責任協助減少污染。

☐ 三分熟
☐ 五分熟
☐ 七分熟
☐ 全熟

---

de·feat [dɪˈfit]

名 挫敗、擊敗
動 擊敗、戰勝

英英 a state of defeating or being defeated

例 **Defeating** the enemy takes courage.
打敗敵人需要勇氣。

☐ 三分熟
☐ 五分熟
☐ 七分熟
☐ 全熟

D

---

de·fend [dɪˈfɛnd]

動 保衛、防禦

英英 to protect from harm or danger or resist an attack

例 The soldiers are **defending** the country.
士兵保衛國家。

☐ 三分熟
☐ 五分熟
☐ 七分熟
☐ 全熟

---

de·fense [dɪˈfɛns]

名 防禦、辯護

英英 the action of defending from danger or risk

例 The oral **defense** is required if you'd like to obtain a master degree.
如果你想取得碩士學位，論文答辯是必要的。

☐ 三分熟
☐ 五分熟
☐ 七分熟
☐ 全熟

---

de·fen·si·ble
[dɪˈfɛnsəbl]

形 可辯護的、可防禦的

英英 justifiable by argument

例 It is important for the Israel government to seek for a **defensible** border.
對以色列政府來說，找尋防禦的邊界是重要的。

☐ 三分熟
☐ 五分熟
☐ 七分熟
☐ 全熟

---

de·fen·sive
[dɪˈfɛnsɪv]

形 防禦的、保衛的

英英 used or intended to defend or protect

例 Lori is **defensive** of her privacy.
羅莉很保護自己的隱私。

☐ 三分熟
☐ 五分熟
☐ 七分熟
☐ 全熟

---

def·i·nite [ˈdɛfənɪt]

形 確定的
同 precise 確切的

英英 very certain or clear

例 There's no **definite** answer to the question of what appears first.
對於這種什麼東西先出現的問題，並沒有確定的答案。

☐ 三分熟
☐ 五分熟
☐ 七分熟
☐ 全熟

---

del·i·cate
[ˈdɛləkət]

形 精細的、精巧的

英英 very fine in texture or structure

例 The chain bracelet is so **delicate**.
這條手鍊好精巧。

☐ 三分熟
☐ 五分熟
☐ 七分熟
☐ 全熟

---

de·light [dɪˈlaɪt]

名 欣喜
動 使高興

英英 great pleasure or joy; to make someone happy

例 Angie got the first prize, which **delighted** her parents.
安琪得了第一名，這件事讓她的父母很高興。

☐ 三分熟
☐ 五分熟
☐ 七分熟
☐ 全熟

Track 179

de·light·ful
[dɪˋlaɪtfəl]

形 令人欣喜的

英英 causing delight, very pleasant

例 The news of being chosen as a cheerleader is **delightful**.
被選為啦啦隊隊長的消息是令人欣喜的。

☐ 三分熟　☐ 五分熟　☐ 七分熟　☐ 全熟

de·mand
[dɪˋmænd]

名 要求
動 要求

英英 an insistent request or ask

例 The **demand** for more budget for the project is rejected.
要求給予這個案子更多的預算被拒絕了。

☐ 三分熟　☐ 五分熟　☐ 七分熟　☐ 全熟

dem·on·strate
[ˋdɛmənˏstret]

動 展現、表明

英英 to clearly show that something is true or right

例 He drew a process picture to **demonstrate** how to cook curry rice.
他畫了一張流程圖以展示煮咖哩的步驟。

☐ 三分熟　☐ 五分熟　☐ 七分熟　☐ 全熟

dem·on·stra·tion
[ˏdɛmənˋstreʃən]

名 證明、示範

英英 the action or an instance of demonstrating

例 Teaching **demonstration** is required if you'd like to be a teacher.
如果你想成為老師，教學示範是必要的。

☐ 三分熟　☐ 五分熟　☐ 七分熟　☐ 全熟

dense [dɛns]

形 密集的、稠密的
片 dense fog 濃霧

英英 very crowded closely together

例 The population in Taipei city is quite **dense**.
臺北市的人口是相當密集的。

☐ 三分熟　☐ 五分熟　☐ 七分熟　☐ 全熟

de·part [dɪˋpart]

動 離開、走開
同 leave 離開

英英 to leave or go away, especially to start a journey

例 The plane **departs** at 10:20 a.m.
飛機於早上 10 點 20 分離境。

☐ 三分熟　☐ 五分熟　☐ 七分熟　☐ 全熟

de·par·ture
[dɪˋpartʃɚ]

名 離去、出發

英英 the action or an instance of departing, usually to start a journey

例 There are several **departures** of trains to Taichung.
有好幾班開往臺中的火車。

☐ 三分熟　☐ 五分熟　☐ 七分熟　☐ 全熟

de·pend·a·ble
[dɪˋpɛndəbl̩]

形 可靠的

英英 very trustworthy and reliable

例 My father needs a **dependable** agent to help handle his land selling.
我的父親需有一個可靠的經紀人幫忙處理他賣土地的事。

☐ 三分熟　☐ 五分熟　☐ 七分熟　☐ 全熟

D

de·pend·ent

[dɪˈpɛndənt]

名 從屬者
形 從屬的、依賴的、受撫養者

英英 relying on someone or something for the support

例 A weak wage will provide for my **dependents**.
我靠微薄的工資供養家人。

☐ 三分熟
☐ 五分熟
☐ 七分熟
☐ 全熟

de·press [dɪˈprɛs]

動 壓下、降低

英英 to cause to feel utterly dispirited or dejected

例 The rise in the value of euro **depressed** our company's earnings last year.
去年歐元升值導致我們公司營業額降低。

☐ 三分熟
☐ 五分熟
☐ 七分熟
☐ 全熟

de·pres·sion

[dɪˈprɛʃən]

名 下陷、降低

英英 the feeling of being down and unhappy without hope

例 The rain falls into the depression in the sand.
雨下進凹陷的沙坑中。

☐ 三分熟
☐ 五分熟
☐ 七分熟
☐ 全熟

de·serve [dɪˈzɝv]

動 值得、應得

英英 to get something because you're supportive to have

例 Take a trip to Italy since you **deserve** a qualified vacation.
去義大利旅行，因為你值得一個有質感的假期。

☐ 三分熟
☐ 五分熟
☐ 七分熟
☐ 全熟

des·per·ate

[ˈdɛspərɪt]

形 絕望的

英英 feeling, showing, or involving hopeless

例 Don't give up hope even though you're in a **desperate** situation.
即便在絕望的情境中，也不要放棄希望。

☐ 三分熟
☐ 五分熟
☐ 七分熟
☐ 全熟

de·spite [dɪˈspaɪt]

介 不管、不顧、儘管

英英 in spite of

例 **Despite** the icy-cold seawater, Jack jumped into the ocean to save Rose.
儘管海水冰冷，傑克仍跳進海裡，援救蘿絲。

☐ 三分熟
☐ 五分熟
☐ 七分熟
☐ 全熟

de·struc·tion

[dɪˈstrʌkʃən]

名 破壞、損壞

英英 the action of destroying something

例 The **destruction** of the rainforest results in many homeless animals.
雨林的破壞造成了很多無家可歸的動物。

☐ 三分熟
☐ 五分熟
☐ 七分熟
☐ 全熟

de·tec·tive

[dɪˈtɛktɪv]

名 偵探、探員
形 偵探的

英英 a person, especially a police officer, whose job is to investigate crimes

例 The **detective** hides himself behind the wall.
偵探藏身在那道牆之後。

☐ 三分熟
☐ 五分熟
☐ 七分熟
☐ 全熟

🎧 **Track 181**

de·ter·mi·na·tion

[dɪˌtɝməˋneʃən]

名 決心

英英 firmness of purpose and mind

例 Are you a man of **determination**?
你是個有決心的人嗎？

- [ ] 三分熟
- [ ] 五分熟
- [ ] 七分熟
- [ ] 全熟

---

de·vice [dɪˋvaɪs]

名 裝置、設計

英英 an object that has been invented for a particular purpose

例 The electrical **device** is purchased to track down criminals.
這臺電子裝置是買來追蹤罪犯的。

- [ ] 三分熟
- [ ] 五分熟
- [ ] 七分熟
- [ ] 全熟

---

de·vise [dɪˋvaɪz]

動 設計、想出

英英 to plan or invent something

例 The robot is **devised** to answer the travelers' questions.
這臺機器人是設計來回答旅客的問題。

- [ ] 三分熟
- [ ] 五分熟
- [ ] 七分熟
- [ ] 全熟

---

de·vote [dɪˋvot]

動 貢獻、奉獻

英英 to give time or resources to someone or something

例 Albert Schweitzer **devotes** himself to the medical work in Africa.
阿爾伯特・史懷哲奉獻自己給非洲的醫療工作。

- [ ] 三分熟
- [ ] 五分熟
- [ ] 七分熟
- [ ] 全熟

---

di·a·per [ˋdaɪəpɚ]

名 尿布

英英 a baby's nappy

例 This brand of **diaper** is recommend by most mothers on this website.
這個網站上大多數的媽媽們都推薦這個品牌的尿布。

- [ ] 三分熟
- [ ] 五分熟
- [ ] 七分熟
- [ ] 全熟

---

dif·fer [ˋdɪfɚ]

動 不同、相異

英英 to be unlike or dissimilar; disagree with

例 The two sisters **differ** not only in appearance but also in personality.
這兩姊妹非但外表不同，個性也不一樣。

- [ ] 三分熟
- [ ] 五分熟
- [ ] 七分熟
- [ ] 全熟

---

di·gest

[daɪˋdʒɛst]/[ˋdaɪdʒɛst]

動 瞭解、消化
名 摘要、分類

英英 to understand new information; to change food in your stomach into different substances that your body can use; classifying and summarizing

例 This kind of peanut candy is hard to **digest**.
這種花生糖難以消化。

- [ ] 三分熟
- [ ] 五分熟
- [ ] 七分熟
- [ ] 全熟

---

di·ges·tion

[dəˋdʒɛstʃən]

名 領會、領悟、消化

英英 the process of digesting; a person's ability to digest food

例 Fried chicken and French fries are not good for **digestion**.
炸雞和炸薯條不利於消化。

- [ ] 三分熟
- [ ] 五分熟
- [ ] 七分熟
- [ ] 全熟

dig·i·tal [ˋdɪdʒɪtl̩]

形 數字的、數位的

英英 relating to information represented as digits using particular values of a physical quantity such as voltage or magnetic polarization

例 **Digital** devices will gradually take over our life.
數位裝置將逐漸掌控我們的生活。

☐三分熟
☐五分熟
☐七分熟
☐全熟

dig·ni·ty [ˋdɪgnətɪ]

名 威嚴、尊嚴

英英 serious behavior or attitude that makes people respect you

例 The old man in Hemingway's Old Man and the Sea demonstrates human **dignity**.
海明威小說《老人與海》展現了人的尊嚴。

☐三分熟
☐五分熟
☐七分熟
☐全熟

di·li·gence [ˋdɪlədʒəns]

名 勤勉、勤奮

英英 care and conscientiousness in one's work

例 Nina is a college student of **diligence**.
妮娜是個勤勉的大學生。

☐三分熟
☐五分熟
☐七分熟
☐全熟

di·plo·ma [dɪˋplomə]

名 文憑、畢業證書

英英 a certificate which you get by an educational establishment for passing an examination or completing a course of study

例 The **diploma** of master is earned with great efforts for Annie.
安妮用最大的努力取得碩士文憑。

☐三分熟
☐五分熟
☐七分熟
☐全熟

dip·lo·mat [ˋdɪpləmæt]

名 外交官

英英 an official who represents a country abroad

例 The **diplomat** likes to make friends from different countries.
外交官喜歡結交來自不同國家的朋友。

☐三分熟
☐五分熟
☐七分熟
☐全熟

dis·ad·van·tage [ˌdɪsədˋvæntɪdʒ]

名 缺點、不利
反 advantage 優點

英英 an unfavorable condition which causes problems

例 The **disadvantage** of taking a ship to Penghu is the sea sickness.
坐船到澎湖的缺點就是會暈船。

☐三分熟
☐五分熟
☐七分熟
☐全熟

dis·as·ter [dɪzˋæstɚ]

名 天災、災害

英英 an unexpected accident or a natural catastrophe that causes great damage or loss of life

例 Natural **disasters** can't be avoided.
自然災害無法避免。

☐三分熟
☐五分熟
☐七分熟
☐全熟

🎧 **Track 183**

dis·ci·pline

[ˈdɪsəplɪn]

名 紀律、訓練
動 懲戒
片 school discipline 校規

英英 the practice of training people to obey rules; to punish someone

例 The football team lacks **discipline**.
這個橄欖球隊缺乏紀律。

☐ 三分熟
☐ 五分熟
☐ 七分熟
☐ 全熟

dis·con·nect

[ˌdɪskəˈnɛkt]

動 斷絕、打斷

英英 to break the connection of or between; to interrupt

例 The communication of my cellphone is **disconnected** in this mountain.
我的手機在這座山裡訊號中斷。

☐ 三分熟
☐ 五分熟
☐ 七分熟
☐ 全熟

dis·cour·age

[dɪsˈkɝɪdʒ]

動 使沮喪、阻止、妨礙

英英 to cause a loss of confidence or enthusiasm in

例 Ryan is **discouraged** because he didn't win the first prize this time.
因為萊恩這次沒有得到第一名，他感到心灰意冷。

☐ 三分熟
☐ 五分熟
☐ 七分熟
☐ 全熟

dis·cour·age·ment

[dɪsˈkɝɪdʒmənt]

名 失望、氣餒

英英 when you have lost your confidence or hope for something

例 **Discouragement** signifies admitting one's weakness.
失望代表承認某人的弱點。

☐ 三分熟
☐ 五分熟
☐ 七分熟
☐ 全熟

dis·guise

[dɪsˈgaɪz]

名 掩飾
動 喬裝、假扮

英英 to change the appearance of someone or something in order to hide its true form

例 In this stage play, some women **disguised** themselves as black cats.
在這個舞臺劇裡，有些女人把自己喬裝為黑貓。

☐ 三分熟
☐ 五分熟
☐ 七分熟
☐ 全熟

dis·gust [dɪsˈgʌst]

名 厭惡
動 使厭惡

英英 a strong feeling of dislike at something or someone's behavior

例 Mrs. Wu was **disgusted** by her husband's nose-picking habit.
吳太太對老公挖鼻孔的習慣感到厭惡。

☐ 三分熟
☐ 五分熟
☐ 七分熟
☐ 全熟

dis·miss [dɪsˈmɪs]

動 摒除、解散

英英 to allow to leave, send away

例 Jimmy **dismissed** the band.
吉米解散了樂團。

☐ 三分熟
☐ 五分熟
☐ 七分熟
☐ 全熟

D

dis·or·der

[dɪsˈɔrdɚ]

名 無秩序
動 使混亂

英英 a lack of order, out of control

例 The room was obviously in a state of **disorder**.
這個房間顯然是在一片混亂的狀態。

☐ 三分熟
☐ 五分熟
☐ 七分熟
☐ 全熟

dis·pute [dɪˈspjut]

名 爭論
動 爭論

英英 to argue or question about something

例 Concerning the car accident, the legal **dispute** has to be solved.
關於車禍，法律糾紛必須要解決。

☐ 三分熟
☐ 五分熟
☐ 七分熟
☐ 全熟

dis·tinct [dɪˈstɪŋkt]

形 個別的、獨特的

英英 unique or individual

例 The Russian doll has its own **distinct** characteristics.
這個俄國的娃娃有其獨特的特色。

☐ 三分熟
☐ 五分熟
☐ 七分熟
☐ 全熟

dis·tin·guish

[dɪˈstɪŋgwɪʃ]

動 辨別、分辨

英英 to recognize, show, or treat as different

例 It is important to teach children to **distinguish** good and bad behaviors.
教導小孩分辨好行為和壞行為是重要的。

☐ 三分熟
☐ 五分熟
☐ 七分熟
☐ 全熟

dis·tin·guished

[dɪˈstɪŋgwɪʃt]

形 卓越的

英英 successful and outstanding

例 Professor Liang has **distinguished** academic performance in animal studies.
梁教授在動物研究上有卓越的學術表現。

☐ 三分熟
☐ 五分熟
☐ 七分熟
☐ 全熟

dis·trib·ute

[dɪˈstrɪbjut]

動 分配、分發

英英 to give something out to a group of people, or to spread something

例 **Distribute** these sweets to your friends.
把這些甜食分給你的朋友。

☐ 三分熟
☐ 五分熟
☐ 七分熟
☐ 全熟

dis·tri·bu·tion

[ˌdɪstrəˈbjuʃən]

名 分配、配給

英英 the action of distributing

例 Paul is busy on the **distribution** of watermelons to different areas.
保羅忙著把西瓜分發到不同的地區。

☐ 三分熟
☐ 五分熟
☐ 七分熟
☐ 全熟

dis·trict [ˈdɪstrɪkt]

名 區域
同 region 區域

英英 an area of a town or region, especially one regarded as a unit because of a particular feature

例 In the 19th century London **district**, Jack the Ripper committed serial murders.
在十九世紀的倫敦區，開膛手傑克連續殺人。

☐ 三分熟
☐ 五分熟
☐ 七分熟
☐ 全熟

🎧 Track 185

dis·turb [dɪˋstɝb]

動 使騷動、使不安

同 annoy 惹惱、打擾

英英 to interrupt when someone is doing something

例 The pop quiz **disturbs** us.
隨堂測驗讓我們不安。

□ 三分熟
□ 五分熟
□ 七分熟
□ 全熟

di·vine [dəˋvaɪn]

形 神的、神聖的

英英 like God or a god; holy

例 The mountain shaped like a Chinese goddess offers **divine** impression.
這座形狀像中國女神的山給人神聖的印象。

□ 三分熟
□ 五分熟
□ 七分熟
□ 全熟

di·vorce [dəˋvors]

名 離婚、解除婚約
動 使離婚、離婚

英英 to end a marriage legally

例 You need to take some time to consider the consequence of **divorce**.
你需要花些時間考慮離婚的後果。

□ 三分熟
□ 五分熟
□ 七分熟
□ 全熟

dom·i·nant
[ˋdɑmənənt]

形 支配的

英英 most important, powerful, or strong

例 It is hard not to be **dominant** by emotions.
很難不被情緒所支配。

□ 三分熟
□ 五分熟
□ 七分熟
□ 全熟

dom·i·nate
[ˋdɑmə͵net]

動 支配、統治

英英 to have a commanding or controlling influence over

例 The Leos like to be leaders **dominating** the decision-making process.
獅子座的人喜歡成為支配做決策過程的領導者。

□ 三分熟
□ 五分熟
□ 七分熟
□ 全熟

dor·mi·to·ry/
dorm

[ˋdɔrmə͵torɪ]/[dɔrm]

名 宿舍

英英 a large room with many beds for a number of people in a school or university

例 The **dormitory** is offered but you have to take a draw.
有提供宿舍，但是你必須要抽籤。

□ 三分熟
□ 五分熟
□ 七分熟
□ 全熟

down·load
[ˋdaʊn͵lod]

動 下載、往下傳送

英英 to copy data from one computer system to another

例 **Download** the file from the Google Cloud Platform.
從谷歌雲端平臺下載檔案。

□ 三分熟
□ 五分熟
□ 七分熟
□ 全熟

doze [doz]

名 打瞌睡
動 打瞌睡

英英 a short sleep

例 Grandpa is **dozing** off in front of the TV.
爺爺在電視機前面打瞌睡。

□ 三分熟
□ 五分熟
□ 七分熟
□ 全熟

draft [dræft]

名 草稿
動 撰寫、草擬
同 sketch 草稿、草擬

英英 a preliminary piece of writing or plan

例 The **draft** of the first chapter should be revised.
第一章的草稿應該要修改。

三分熟
五分熟
七分熟
全熟

dread [drɛd]

名 非常害怕
動 敬畏、恐怖
同 fear 恐怖

英英 great fear or worry; to feel frightened about something that is going to happen

例 My girlfriend is **dreading** to see my parents.
我的女朋友害怕見我的父母。

三分熟
五分熟
七分熟
全熟

drift [drɪft]

名 漂流物
動 漂移

英英 an object flowing on the water from one place to another

例 The **drifting** garbage on the river disgusts everyone.
河上漂流的垃圾讓每個人都覺得噁心。

三分熟
五分熟
七分熟
全熟

drill [drɪl]

名 鑽、錐、操練
動 鑽孔

英英 a tool or machine which is used for boring holes

例 The **drill** of the dentist terrified me.
牙醫的鑽頭嚇壞我了。

三分熟
五分熟
七分熟
全熟

du·ra·ble [ˈdjʊrəbl̩]

形 耐穿的、耐磨的

英英 to describe clothes or shoes are hard-wearing

例 This pair of leather shoes is **durable**.
這雙皮鞋很耐穿。

三分熟
五分熟
七分熟
全熟

dust·y [ˈdʌstɪ]

形 覆著灰塵的

英英 covered with dust

例 The white piano in the basement is **dusty**.
地下室的白色鋼琴覆著灰塵。

三分熟
五分熟
七分熟
全熟

DVD/dig·it·al vid·e·o disk/ dig·it·al ver·sa·tile disk

[ˈdɪdʒɪtl̩ ˈvɪdɪ‚o dɪsk]/
[ˈdɪdʒɪtl̩ ˈvɝsətɪl dɪsk]

名 影音光碟

英英 abbreviation for digital video disc: a disc used for storing and playing music or movies

例 Renting **DVDs** used to be my hobby.
租借影碟是我以前的嗜好。

三分熟
五分熟
七分熟
全熟

dye [daɪ]

名 染料
動 染、著色

英英 to change the color of something by using a special liquid

例 **Dying** hair is not good for our body.
染頭髮對我們的身體不好。

三分熟
五分熟
七分熟
全熟

🎧 **Track 187**

dy·nam·ic
[`daɪnəˏmaɪt]

形 動能的、動力的
同 energetic 有力的

英英 having a lot of energy or enthusiasm

例 Ted becomes **dynamic** when talking about football.
當談及橄欖球，泰德充滿了動力。

□三分熟
□五分熟
□七分熟
□全熟

dyn·as·ty
[`daɪnəstɪ]

名 王朝、朝代

英英 a period when a country is ruled by the same family

例 The soap drama often sets the story in Qing **dynasty**.
連續劇經常把故事安排在清朝。

□三分熟
□五分熟
□七分熟
□全熟

Ee

ear·nest [`ɝnɪst]

名 認真
形 認真的

英英 very serious or determined

例 What's wrong with a person being so **earnest**?
一個如此認真的人有什麼不對勁？

□三分熟
□五分熟
□七分熟
□全熟

ear·phone
[`ɪrˏfon]

名 耳機

英英 an electrical device worn on the ear to receive the sound of radio or telephone

例 The **earphone** is hung around her ears.
耳機就垂掛在她耳邊。

□三分熟
□五分熟
□七分熟
□全熟

ec·o·nom·ic
[ˏikə`nɑmɪk]

形 經濟上的

英英 relating to economics or the economy

例 **Economic** burden almost drives him crazy.
經濟上的壓力幾乎把他逼瘋。

□三分熟
□五分熟
□七分熟
□全熟

ec·o·nom·i·cal
[ˏikə`nɑmɪk!]

形 節儉的

英英 giving good value on the money you spent

例 Grandma is so **economical**.
奶奶好節儉。

□三分熟
□五分熟
□七分熟
□全熟

ec·o·nom·ics
[ˏikə`nɑmɪks]

名 經濟學

英英 the branch of study concerned with the production, consumption, and transfer of wealth

例 In the business college, **economics** is a must read.
在經濟學院，經濟學是必讀。

□三分熟
□五分熟
□七分熟
□全熟

E

e·con·o·mist

[ɪˈkɑnəmɪst]

名 經濟學家

英英 an expert in economics

例 An **economist** predicted the dollar would rise in value soon.
經濟學家預測美元很快就會漲。

□三分熟
□五分熟
□七分熟
□全熟

e·con·o·my

[ɪˈkɑnəmɪ]

名 經濟

英英 the system of trade and industry by which the wealth of a country is made and used

例 The city mayor invited experts of **economy** to have an afternoon tea.
市長邀請經濟專家喝下午茶。

□三分熟
□五分熟
□七分熟
□全熟

efficiency

[əˈfɪʃənsɪ]

名 效率

英英 state or quality of being efficient

例 Emily got promoted because of her working **efficiency**.
艾蜜莉因為工作效率而升遷。

□三分熟
□五分熟
□七分熟
□全熟

e·las·tic [ɪˈlæstɪk]

名 橡皮筋
形 有彈性的

英英 a type of rubber which can be stretch and be returned to its original shape or size; capable of forming shake after stretching

例 Use an **elastic** rope to tie the gift box.
用一條有彈性的繩子把禮物盒綁好。

□三分熟
□五分熟
□七分熟
□全熟

e·lec·tri·cian

[ɪˌlɛkˈtrɪʃən]

名 電機工程師

英英 a person who works related to electrical equipment

例 The **electrician** is fixing the light.
電機工程師正在修電燈。

□三分熟
□五分熟
□七分熟
□全熟

e·lec·tron·ics

[ɪˌlɛktˈtrɑniks]

名 電機工程學

英英 the branch of study concerned with the behavior and movement of electrons

例 Stanley studied **electronics** hard.
史丹利認真的唸電機工程學。

□三分熟
□五分熟
□七分熟
□全熟

el·e·gant [ˈɛləgənt]

形 優雅的

英英 very graceful and stylish

例 The lady dressing in blue dress looks **elegant**.
穿著藍色洋裝的女士看起來很優雅。

□三分熟
□五分熟
□七分熟
□全熟

el·e·men·ta·ry

[ˌɛləˈmɛntərɪ]

形 基本的、初級的

英英 basic

例 **Elementary** school kids are having fun on the playground.
小學生在操場玩得很開心。

□三分熟
□五分熟
□七分熟
□全熟

🎧 **Track 189**

e·lim·i·nate
[ɪˈlɪməˌnet]

動 消除

英英 to get ride of or to remove

例 You can **eliminate** a mark by using the carpet cleaner.
藉由使用地毯清潔劑，你可以消除標記。

□ 三分熟
□ 五分熟
□ 七分熟
□ 全熟

else·where
[ˈɛlsˌhwɛr]

副 在別處

英英 at some other place or other places

例 Let's look **elsewhere** for a nice T-shirt.
讓我們到別的地方看看有沒有好穿的 T 恤。

□ 三分熟
□ 五分熟
□ 七分熟
□ 全熟

e-mail/email
[ˈimel]

名 電子郵件
動 發電子郵件

英英 the mail sent from computer user via the Internet

例 I write **emails** to my friend every weekend.
我每個週末都寫電子郵件給我朋友。

□ 三分熟
□ 五分熟
□ 七分熟
□ 全熟

em·bar·rass
[ɪmˈbærəs]

動 使困窘

英英 to cause to feel awkward or ashamed

例 What Monica just said **embarrassed** us.
莫妮卡剛剛說的讓我們感到很不好意思。

□ 三分熟
□ 五分熟
□ 七分熟
□ 全熟

em·bar·rass·ment
[ɪmˈbærəsmənt]

名 困窘

英英 when you feel embarrassed, or something that makes you feel embarrassed

例 The error of the report caused certain **embarrassment**.
報告的錯誤造成了某些困窘。

□ 三分熟
□ 五分熟
□ 七分熟
□ 全熟

em·bas·sy
[ˈɛmbəsɪ]

名 大使館

英英 the official residence or offices of an ambarrassed

例 The **embassy** is behind the park.
大使館在公園後面。

□ 三分熟
□ 五分熟
□ 七分熟
□ 全熟

e·merge [ɪˈmɝdʒ]

動 浮現

英英 to become visible, apparent and known

例 The mermaid **emerges** from behind the rock.
美人魚從岩石後面浮現。

□ 三分熟
□ 五分熟
□ 七分熟
□ 全熟

e·mo·tion·al
[ɪˈmoʃənl̩]

形 情感的

英英 relating to the emotions

例 **Emotional** education is necessary.
情感教育是有必要的。

□ 三分熟
□ 五分熟
□ 七分熟
□ 全熟

em·pha·sis

[ˈɛmfəsɪs]

名 重點、強調

英英 special importance or value given to something by someone

例 The **emphasis** of the ad seems to be on the body shape of women.
廣告的重點似乎在女人的身形。

---

em·pire [ˈɛmpaɪr]

名 帝國

英英 an extensive group of countries ruled over by a single person or government

例 The British **Empire** colonized many countries.
大英帝國將很多國家設為殖民地。

---

en·close [ɪnˈkloz]

動 包圍

英英 to surround or close off something on all sides

例 The house was **enclosed** by a bamboo forest.
這間房子被竹林所包圍。

---

en·coun·ter

[ɪnˈkaʊntə]

名 遭遇
動 遭遇

英英 an unexpected or casual meeting someone

例 The mysterious **encounter** of the black cats is unforgettable.
遇到黑貓的神祕遭遇是無法忘懷的。

---

en·dan·ger

[ɪnˈdendʒə]

動 使陷入危險

英英 put something in danger

例 The polar bears are **endangered**.
北極熊陷入危險了。

---

en·dure [ɪnˈdjʊr]

動 忍受

英英 to suffer something painful or tolerate

例 **Endure** the pain for a while.
忍一下痛。

---

en·force [ɪnˈfors]

動 實施、強迫

英英 to compel someone with a law, rule, or obligation

例 The policeman **enforced** the law.
警察強迫實施法律。

---

en·force·ment

[ɪnˈforsmənt]

名 施行

英英 to make people obey a law or rule

例 The **enforcement** of law is strict in Singapore.
新加坡的法律施行很嚴格。

E

🎧 **Track 191**

en·gi·neer·ing [ˌɛndʒəˋnɪrɪŋ] 名 工程學	英英 the branch of study concerned with the design, building, and use of engines, machines, and structures 例 **Engineering** is about how to build bridges or buildings. 工程學是關於如何建橋樑或建築物。	☐ 三分熟 ☐ 五分熟 ☐ 七分熟 ☐ 全熟
en·large [ɪnˋlɑrdʒ] 動 擴大	英英 to make something or become bigger or larger 例 **Enlarge** the picture so as to see more details. 把圖片擴大才能看到更多細節。	☐ 三分熟 ☐ 五分熟 ☐ 七分熟 ☐ 全熟
en·large·ment [ɪnˋlɑrdʒmənt] 名 擴張	英英 the action of enlarging 例 The **enlargement** of the Edward's family was announced just now. 愛德華家族擴大的訊息剛才宣布了。	☐ 三分熟 ☐ 五分熟 ☐ 七分熟 ☐ 全熟
e·nor·mous [ɪˋnɔrməs] 形 巨大的 同 vast 巨大的	英英 very large 例 "The **Enormous** Turnip" is a quite popular story. 「拔蘿蔔」是個很受歡迎的故事。	☐ 三分熟 ☐ 五分熟 ☐ 七分熟 ☐ 全熟
en·ter·tain [ˌɛntɚˋten] 動 招待、娛樂	英英 to provide with enjoyment and entertainment 例 The magician **entertains** his audience with amazing magic tricks. 魔術師用令人吃驚的魔術招式娛樂他的觀眾。	☐ 三分熟 ☐ 五分熟 ☐ 七分熟 ☐ 全熟
en·ter·tain·ment [ˌɛntɚˋtenmənt] 名 款待、娛樂	英英 the action of entertaining or being entertained 例 The **entertainment** brought by Youtube films doesn't cost much. Youtube 影片所帶來的娛樂並不太花錢。	☐ 三分熟 ☐ 五分熟 ☐ 七分熟 ☐ 全熟
en·thu·si·asm [ɪnˋθjuzɪˌæzəm] 名 熱衷、熱情 同 zeal 熱心	英英 the feeling of intense enjoyment, interest, or approval 例 Ava's **enthusiasm** for stage performance was impressive. 艾娃對舞臺表演的熱情是令人印象深刻的。	☐ 三分熟 ☐ 五分熟 ☐ 七分熟 ☐ 全熟

en·vi·ous [ˋɛnvɪəs]

形 羨慕的、妒忌的
同 jealous 妒忌的

英英 feeling or showing envy

例 The beauty and the wealth are **envious** causes.
美麗和財富招致妒忌。

□三分熟
□五分熟
□七分熟
□全熟

---

e·qual·i·ty

[ɪˋkwɑlətɪ]

名 平等

英英 the state of being equal

例 The real **equality** between men and women has not achieved.
男人和女人之間的平等還未達成。

□三分熟
□五分熟
□七分熟
□全熟

---

e·quip [ɪˋkwɪp]

動 裝備

英英 to supply with the items or equipments needed for a purpose

例 **Equip** yourself with a good camera since you'll need it.
準備好的照相機因為你會需要它。

□三分熟
□五分熟
□七分熟
□全熟

---

e·quip·ment

[ɪˋkwɪpmənt]

名 裝備、設備

英英 the items needed for a particular purpose

例 This new medical **equipment** was donated by an unknown gentleman.
這個新的醫療設備是一位不具名的先生所捐獻的。

□三分熟
□五分熟
□七分熟
□全熟

---

e·ra [ˋɪrə]

名 時代

英英 a long period of history

例 The information **era** brought modern people a lot of anxiety.
資訊的時代，帶給現代人很多的焦慮感。

□三分熟
□五分熟
□七分熟
□全熟

---

er·rand [ˋɛrənd]

名 任務

英英 a short journey made to deliver a message or collect something

例 Could you run the **errand** for me?
你可以幫我跑腿嗎？

□三分熟
□五分熟
□七分熟
□全熟

---

es·ca·la·tor

[ˋɛskəˌletɚ]

名 手扶梯

英英 a moving staircase consisting of a circulating belt of steps driven by a motor

例 The **escalator** is there.
手扶梯就在那裡。

□三分熟
□五分熟
□七分熟
□全熟

---

es·say [ˋɛse]

名 短文、隨筆

英英 a short writing on a particular subject

例 The **essay** is written with clear logic.
這篇短文是用清楚的邏輯寫成的。

□三分熟
□五分熟
□七分熟
□全熟

🎧 **Track 193**

es·tab·lish

[əˋstæblɪʃ]

動 建立
同 found 建立

英英 to set up or build up on a firm or permanent basis

例 The national library of Poland was **established** in the 18th century.
波蘭的國家圖書館是在十八世紀建成的。

☐ 三分熟
☐ 五分熟
☐ 七分熟
☐ 全熟

es·tab·lish·ment

[əˋstæblɪʃmənt]

名 組織、建立

英英 the action of establishing or being established

例 Some government officials maintain good relationship with the military **establishment**.
有些政府官員跟軍方保持著良好的關係。

☐ 三分熟
☐ 五分熟
☐ 七分熟
☐ 全熟

es·sen·tial

[ɪˋsɛnʃəl]

名 基本要素
形 本質的、必要的、基本的
同 basic 基本的

英英 things or elements that are absolutely necessary; absolutely necessary

例 Your trust is **essential** to me.
你對我的信任是不可或缺的。

☐ 三分熟
☐ 五分熟
☐ 七分熟
☐ 全熟

es·ti·mate

[ˋɛstəˌmet]

名 評估
動 評估

英英 to guess the approximate calculation on the cost, size or value, etc.

例 The **estimate** of the air pollution in this report is accurate.
這份報告中空氣污染的評估是準確的。

☐ 三分熟
☐ 五分熟
☐ 七分熟
☐ 全熟

e·val·u·ate

[ɪˋvæljʊˌet]

動 估計、評價

英英 form an idea of the amount or value of something

例 The art treasure has been **evaluated** by an expert.
這份藝術珍品已經經過專家的估價了。

☐ 三分熟
☐ 五分熟
☐ 七分熟
☐ 全熟

e·val·u·a·tion

[ɪˌvæljʊˋeʃən]

名 評價

英英 judgment or calculation of the quality, importance, amount or value of something

例 The **evaluation** of our working performance will be carried out by Charles.
我們工作表現的評估會由查爾斯執行。

☐ 三分熟
☐ 五分熟
☐ 七分熟
☐ 全熟

e·ve [iv]

名 前夕

英英 the day before an event or occasion

例 On the **eve** of Christmas, Scrooge was visited by the ghosts.
在聖誕節前夕，鬼魂造訪史古基。

☐ 三分熟
☐ 五分熟
☐ 七分熟
☐ 全熟

e·ven·tu·al

[ɪ`vɛntʃʊəl]

形 最後的
同 final 最後的

英英 occurring or existing at a later time or at the end

例 The **eventual** decision is made.
最後的決定出來了。

☐ 三分熟
☐ 五分熟
☐ 七分熟
☐ 全熟

E

---

ev·i·dence

[`ɛvədəns]

名 證據
動 證明

英英 information or signs to tell what is true or valid

例 The **evidence** proves that Mark is guilty.
這份證據證明馬克是有罪的。

☐ 三分熟
☐ 五分熟
☐ 七分熟
☐ 全熟

---

ev·i·dent

[`ɛvədənt]

形 明顯的

英英 plain or obvious

例 It is **evident** that Miss Lin is not happy.
很明顯的，林老師不太開心。

☐ 三分熟
☐ 五分熟
☐ 七分熟
☐ 全熟

---

ex·ag·ger·ate

[ɪg`zædʒəˌret]

動 誇大

英英 to represent something as being greater than in reality

例 Mandy tends to **exaggerate** what happened.
曼蒂傾向誇大所發生的事。

☐ 三分熟
☐ 五分熟
☐ 七分熟
☐ 全熟

---

ex·am·i·nee

[ɪgˌzæməˋni]

名 應試者

英英 a person who takes part in an examination

例 The **examinees** are writing the test paper nervously.
應試者很緊張地在寫考卷。

☐ 三分熟
☐ 五分熟
☐ 七分熟
☐ 全熟

---

ex·am·in·er

[ɪg`zæmɪnɚ]

名 主考官、審查員

英英 a person whose job is to decide how well someone has done in an examination

例 The **examiner** walked around the classroom.
主考官巡視教室。

☐ 三分熟
☐ 五分熟
☐ 七分熟
☐ 全熟

---

ex·cep·tion

[ɪk`sɛpʃən]

名 反對、例外

英英 a person or thing that is not included in a rule

例 There is an **exception** to his preferences.
他的喜好中只有一個例外。

☐ 三分熟
☐ 五分熟
☐ 七分熟
☐ 全熟

---

ex·haust [ɪg`zɔst]

名 排氣管
動 耗盡

英英 a tube to waste gases or air from an engine or a car; to run out of something; to run out or empty something

例 Black smoke was emitted from the **exhaust** pipe.
黑煙從排氣管中排出。

☐ 三分熟
☐ 五分熟
☐ 七分熟
☐ 全熟

211

ex·hib·it [ɪgˋzɪbɪt]

名 展示品、展覽
動 展示

英英 an object or collection of objects shown in an art gallery or museum

例 The **exhibit** of the vase was broken.
花瓶的展示品破了。

☐三分熟 ☐五分熟 ☐七分熟 ☐全熟

---

ex·pand [ɪkˋspænd]

動 擴大、延長

英英 to make or become larger, longer

例 **Expanding** the territory was the emperor's dream.
擴大領土是皇帝的夢想。

☐三分熟 ☐五分熟 ☐七分熟 ☐全熟

---

ex·pan·sion
[ɪkˋspænʃən]

名 擴張

英英 the action or an instance of expanding

例 The software company made more profits by means of trade **expansion**.
這家軟體公司藉由貿易擴張賺取更多的利潤。

☐三分熟 ☐五分熟 ☐七分熟 ☐全熟

---

ex·per·i·men·tal
[ɪkͺspɛrəˋmɛntl̩]

形 實驗性的

英英 based on untested ideas or techniques and not yet established or finalized

例 This kind of **experimental** theater lacks audience.
這樣的實驗劇場缺少觀眾。

☐三分熟 ☐五分熟 ☐七分熟 ☐全熟

---

ex·pla·na·tion
[ͺɛkspləˋneʃən]

名 說明、解釋

英英 the details or reasons that someone gives to make something more clear or easier to understand

例 Give me a reasonable **explanation**.
給我一個合理的解釋。

☐三分熟 ☐五分熟 ☐七分熟 ☐全熟

---

ex·plore [ɪkˋsplor]

動 探查、探險

英英 to travel through an unfamiliar area for learning about

例 The researchers **explored** the forest ten years ago.
研究者十年前探查過這座森林。

☐三分熟 ☐五分熟 ☐七分熟 ☐全熟

---

ex·plo·sion
[ɪkˋsploʒən]

名 爆炸

英英 an act or instance of exploding

例 The **explosion** art show is held beside the river this year.
爆炸藝術秀今年在河邊舉行。

☐三分熟 ☐五分熟 ☐七分熟 ☐全熟

---

ex·plo·sive
[ɪkˋsplosɪv]

名 炸藥
形 爆炸的、（性情）暴躁的

英英 a substance which can be made to explode

例 **Explosives** are used to destroy the building.
炸藥是用以摧毀這棟大樓的。

☐三分熟 ☐五分熟 ☐七分熟 ☐全熟

F

ex·pose [ɪkˋspoz]

動 暴露、揭發

英英 to uncover and make visible or easy to be seen

例 The secret was **exposed**.
祕密被揭發了。

☐ 三分熟
☐ 五分熟
☐ 七分熟
☐ 全熟

ex·po·sure

[ɪkˋspoʒɚ]

名 顯露

英英 the state of being exposed to something dangerous

例 Too much **exposure** to the sun is harmful.
過度暴露在陽光下是有害的。

☐ 三分熟
☐ 五分熟
☐ 七分熟
☐ 全熟

ex·tend [ɪkˋstɛnd]

動 延長、擴大
片 extend the visa
延長簽證的日期

英英 to make larger in area

例 The old man planned to **extend** the collection of shells.
老人計畫擴大貝殼的收集範圍。

☐ 三分熟
☐ 五分熟
☐ 七分熟
☐ 全熟

ex·tent [ɪkˋstɛnt]

名 範圍
片 to some extent
有部分是……

英英 the area covered by something

例 To what **extent** would you like to discuss about the topic?
你想討論多少關於這個主題的範圍？

☐ 三分熟
☐ 五分熟
☐ 七分熟
☐ 全熟

Ff

fa·cial [ˋfeʃəl]

形 面部的、表面的

英英 of or affecting the surface

例 The **facial** expression of the monster is scary.
這個妖怪的面部表情是猙獰的。

☐ 三分熟
☐ 五分熟
☐ 七分熟
☐ 全熟

fa·cil·i·ty [fəˋsɪlətɪ]

名 容易、靈巧

英英 ease in moving, acting or doing something

例 James has **facility** in communication.
詹姆士是個擅於溝通的人。

☐ 三分熟
☐ 五分熟
☐ 七分熟
☐ 全熟

faith·ful [ˋfeθfəl]

形 忠實的、耿直的、可靠的
同 loyal 忠實的

英英 very loyal and steadfast

例 John is a **faithful** servant.
約翰是個老實的僕人。

☐ 三分熟
☐ 五分熟
☐ 七分熟
☐ 全熟

fame [fem]

名 名聲、聲譽

英英 when you are known by many people because of your achievement on a particular field

例 The **fame** of the stage actress has spreaded overseas.
這個舞臺劇女演員已名揚海外。

☐ 三分熟
☐ 五分熟
☐ 七分熟
☐ 全熟

213

🎧 **Track 197**

---

fan·tas·tic

[fæn`tæstɪk]

形 想像中的、奇異古怪的

英英 imaginative or fanciful, not reasonable

例 J. K. Rowling is good at creating **fantastic** beasts.
J. K. 羅琳擅於創造奇獸。

☐ 三分熟
☐ 五分熟
☐ 七分熟
☐ 全熟

---

fan·ta·sy [`fæntəsɪ]

名 空想、異想

英英 the imagining of impossible things

例 Dreaming without real action turned out to be a **fantasy**.
做夢卻無實際行動，最後只淪為空想。

☐ 三分熟
☐ 五分熟
☐ 七分熟
☐ 全熟

---

fare·well [fɛr`wɛl]

名 告別、歡送會

英英 an act of parting or an event of marking someone's departure

例 We should attend the **farewell** party of Mr. Smith today.
我們今天應該要參加史密斯先生的告別歡送會。

☐ 三分熟
☐ 五分熟
☐ 七分熟
☐ 全熟

---

fa·tal [`fetl]

形 致命的、決定性的
同 mortal 致命的

英英 causing death; leading to failure; having an important or crucial effect

例 The Death Cap mushroom is **fatal**.
毒鵝膏是致命的。

☐ 三分熟
☐ 五分熟
☐ 七分熟
☐ 全熟

---

fa·vor·a·ble

[`fevərəbl]

形 有利的、討人喜歡的

英英 expressing approval or consent

例 The wind direction is **favorable** for us.
風向對我們來講是有利的。

☐ 三分熟
☐ 五分熟
☐ 七分熟
☐ 全熟

---

feast [fist]

名 宴會、節日
動 宴請、使高興

英英 large meal or an annual religious celebration; to make pleasant

例 The **feast** contains a variety of night market food.
這個宴會包含很多的夜市食物。

☐ 三分熟
☐ 五分熟
☐ 七分熟
☐ 全熟

---

fer·ry [`fɛrɪ]

名 渡口、渡船
動 運輸

英英 a boat or ship for taking passengers and goods, especially as a regular service; to transport or carry in a boat

例 We took the car **ferry** in Kaohsiung.
我們在高雄搭汽車渡輪。

☐ 三分熟
☐ 五分熟
☐ 七分熟
☐ 全熟

---

fer·tile [`fɜtl]

形 肥沃的、豐富的

英英 producing or capable of producing a large number of good quality vegetation or crops

例 The land is **fertile**.
這塊地是肥沃的。

☐ 三分熟
☐ 五分熟
☐ 七分熟
☐ 全熟

F

fetch [fɛtʃ]
動 取得、接來

英英 to go for somewhere and bring something back
例 **Fetch** a piece of paper for me.
幫我拿一張紙來。

□ 三分熟
□ 五分熟
□ 七分熟
□ 全熟

fic·tion [ˈfɪkʃən]
名 小說、虛構
片 science fiction novel
科幻小說

英英 the story which describes about imaginary events and people
例 **Fiction** offers entertainment for readers.
小說為讀者提供了娛樂。

□ 三分熟
□ 五分熟
□ 七分熟
□ 全熟

fierce [fɪrs]
形 猛烈的、粗暴的、兇猛的
同 violent 猛烈的

英英 very violent and powerful
例 The dogs near the army camp are **fierce**.
軍營附近的狗是兇猛的。

□ 三分熟
□ 五分熟
□ 七分熟
□ 全熟

fi·nance [faɪˈnæns]
名 財務
動 融資

英英 the management of large amounts of money; to obtain or provide money for
例 What is your principle of personal **finance**?
你個人理財的原則是什麼？

□ 三分熟
□ 五分熟
□ 七分熟
□ 全熟

fi·nan·cial
[faɪˈnænʃəl]
形 金融的、財政的

英英 relating to finance
例 The company was facing a serious **financial** problem.
這家公司正面對一個非常嚴重的財政問題。

□ 三分熟
□ 五分熟
□ 七分熟
□ 全熟

fire·crack·er
[ˈfaɪrˌkrækɚ]
名 鞭炮

英英 a loud, explosive firework
例 The **firecracker** is dangerous.
鞭炮是危險的。

□ 三分熟
□ 五分熟
□ 七分熟
□ 全熟

fire·place
[ˈfaɪrˌples]
名 壁爐、火爐

英英 a space in the wall of a room for a domestic fire
例 Grandma enjoyed reading novels in front of the **fireplace**.
奶奶喜歡在壁爐前閱讀小說。

□ 三分熟
□ 五分熟
□ 七分熟
□ 全熟

flat·ter [ˈflætɚ]
動 諂媚、奉承

英英 to give praise or compliment insincerely
例 I'm **flattered**.
我感到受寵若驚。

□ 三分熟
□ 五分熟
□ 七分熟
□ 全熟

Track 199

flee [fli]

動 逃走、逃避

英英 to run away

例 Some organizations help the political criminals **flee** from their countries.
有些組織幫助政治犯逃離他們的國家。

☐三分熟
☐五分熟
☐七分熟
☐全熟

---

flex·i·ble

[ˈflɛksəbl̩]

形 有彈性的、易曲的

英英 capable of bending easily without breaking

例 You should remain **flexible** in order to handle the crisis this time.
你應該要保持彈性，才能應付這次的危機。

☐三分熟
☐五分熟
☐七分熟
☐全熟

---

flu·ent [ˈfluənt]

形 流暢的、流利的

英英 speaking or writing very fluently and smoothly

例 Tiffany is a **fluent** English speaker.
蒂芬妮說英語很流利。

☐三分熟
☐五分熟
☐七分熟
☐全熟

---

flunk [flʌŋk]

名 失敗、不及格
動 失敗、放棄
同 fail 失敗

英英 to fail to reach the required standard in a text

例 The lazy student **flunked** the math test.
這個懶惰的學生，數學考試不及格。

☐三分熟
☐五分熟
☐七分熟
☐全熟

---

flush [flʌʃ]

名 紅光、繁茂
動 水淹、使興奮、
用水沖洗

英英 a reddening of the face or skin; to flow and spread suddenly; to make excited

例 Remember to **flush** the toilet.
記得要沖廁所。

☐三分熟
☐五分熟
☐七分熟
☐全熟

---

foam [fom]

名 泡沫
動 起泡沫

英英 a mass of small bubbles formed in a liquid

例 The **foam** on the cup of coffee looks like a leaf.
這杯咖啡的泡沫看起來就像一片葉子。

☐三分熟
☐五分熟
☐七分熟
☐全熟

---

for·bid [fəˈbɪd]

動 禁止、禁止入內

英英 refuse to allow someone to do something

例 The website is **forbidden** of being accessed.
這個網站禁止進入。

☐三分熟
☐五分熟
☐七分熟
☐全熟

---

fore·cast

[forˈkæst]

動 預測、預報

英英 a prediction which is especially of the weather or a financial

例 The weather **forecast** is not accurate.
天氣預報不太準。

☐三分熟
☐五分熟
☐七分熟
☐全熟

for·ma·tion

[fɔr`meʃən]

名 形成、成立

英英 the action of forming or the process of being formed

例 The **formation** of good friendship takes time.
良好友誼的形成需要時間。

□ 三分熟
□ 五分熟
□ 七分熟
□ 全熟

F

---

for·mu·la

[`fɔrmjələ]

名 公式、法則

英英 a standard or accepted way of doing something; a mathematical rule used in a set of numbers and letters

例 This math **formula** was created to solve an engineering problem.
這個數學公式是發明來解決工程問題。

□ 三分熟
□ 五分熟
□ 七分熟
□ 全熟

---

fort [fort]

名 堡壘、炮臺

英英 a military building surrounded by a strong wall, where is for soldiers to live and is designed to be defended from attack

例 The **fort** in the building has historical value.
建築物裡的炮臺有歷史價值。

□ 三分熟
□ 五分熟
□ 七分熟
□ 全熟

---

for·tu·nate

[`fɔrtʃənɪt]

形 幸運的、僥倖的
同 lucky 幸運的

英英 lucky or involving good luck

例 The **fortunate** cookie contains a piece of note.
幸運餅裡包含一張紙條。

□ 三分熟
□ 五分熟
□ 七分熟
□ 全熟

---

fos·sil [`fɑsl]

名 化石、舊事物
形 陳腐的

英英 the remains or impression of a plant or animal embedded in rock and preserved for a very long time

例 The dinosaur **fossils** are found.
找到恐龍化石了。

□ 三分熟
□ 五分熟
□ 七分熟
□ 全熟

---

foun·da·tion

[faʊn`deʃən]

名 基礎、根基
同 base 基礎
片 solid foundation
　　穩固的基礎

英英 the lowest base of a building, usually below ground level

例 Will you tell me how you laid the **foundation** for your success?
你能告訴我，你是如何為你的成功打下基礎的嗎？

□ 三分熟
□ 五分熟
□ 七分熟
□ 全熟

---

found·er [`faʊndɚ]

名 創立者、捐出基金者

英英 a person who founds an institution

例 The **founder** of the fund was David Sharp.
這個基金會的創立者是大衛・夏普。

□ 三分熟
□ 五分熟
□ 七分熟
□ 全熟

🎧 Track 201

fra·grance

[ˈfregrəns]

名 芬香、芬芳

英英 a pleasant and sweet smell

例 The **fragrance** of flowers smells relaxing.
花的香味聞起來很放鬆。

☐ 三分熟
☐ 五分熟
☐ 七分熟
☐ 全熟

---

fra·grant

[ˈfregrənt]

形 芳香的、愉快的

英英 having a pleasant and sweet smell

例 The clothes **fragrant** bags are placed in your room.
衣服芳香袋放在你的房間。

☐ 三分熟
☐ 五分熟
☐ 七分熟
☐ 全熟

---

frame [frem]

名 骨架、體制
動 構築、框架

英英 a structure surrounding a picture or door

例 The **frame** of the blue whale is huge.
這條藍鯨的骨架很巨大。

☐ 三分熟
☐ 五分熟
☐ 七分熟
☐ 全熟

---

free·way [ˈfriˌwe]

名 高速公路

英英 a toll-free highway built for fast moving traffic travelling long distances

例 Take the **freeway** and you'll arrive at the farm in 30 minutes.
走這條高速公路，你就可以在 30 分鐘內抵達農場。

☐ 三分熟
☐ 五分熟
☐ 七分熟
☐ 全熟

---

fre·quen·cy

[ˈfrikwənsɪ]

名 時常發生、頻率

英英 something often occurs over a particular period

例 Do you know the **frequency** of car accidents on this freeway?
你知道這條高速公路上的車禍頻率嗎？

☐ 三分熟
☐ 五分熟
☐ 七分熟
☐ 全熟

---

fresh·man

[ˈfrɛʃmən]

名 新生、大一生

英英 a first-year student at university or at high school

例 Diane took a part-time job when she was a **freshman**.
黛安娜大一時打了一份工。

☐ 三分熟
☐ 五分熟
☐ 七分熟
☐ 全熟

---

frost [frɔst]

名 霜、冷淡
動 結霜

英英 the icy crystals that form directly on a freezing surface as moist air contacts it

例 I was asked to remove the **frost** on the road.
我被要求要移除馬路上的結霜。

☐ 三分熟
☐ 五分熟
☐ 七分熟
☐ 全熟

---

frown [fraʊn]

名 不悅之色
動 皺眉、表示不滿

英英 to bring your eyebrows together to show that you are worried or unhappy

例 His **frown** means dissatisfactions with what you said.
他的皺眉，意謂著他對你所説的話不滿。

☐ 三分熟
☐ 五分熟
☐ 七分熟
☐ 全熟

F

frus·tra·tion

[ˌfrʌs'treʃən]

名 挫折、失敗

英英 the act of frustrating or an instance of being frustrated

例 **Frustration** sometimes means a better opportunity.
挫折有時意謂著一個更好的機會。

☐ 三分熟
☐ 五分熟
☐ 七分熟
☐ 全熟

---

fu·el ['fjuəl]

名 燃料
動 燃料補給

英英 material such as coal, gas, or oil that is burned to produce power; to supply fuel; to take in fuel

例 Fill the truck with the **fuel**.
補充卡車的燃料。

☐ 三分熟
☐ 五分熟
☐ 七分熟
☐ 全熟

---

ful·fill [fʊl'fɪl]

動 實踐、實現、履行
同 finish 完成

英英 to achieve or realize something

例 My dream of being a good guitarist has not **fulfilled**.
我想要成為好的吉他手的夢想尚未實現。

☐ 三分熟
☐ 五分熟
☐ 七分熟
☐ 全熟

---

ful·fill·ment

[fʊl'fɪlmənt]

名 實現、符合條件

英英 the act of consummating something, suck as a desire or promise

例 The **fulfillment** of wishes makes people happy.
願望的實現讓人們快樂。

☐ 三分熟
☐ 五分熟
☐ 七分熟
☐ 全熟

---

func·tion·al

['fʌŋkʃənl̩]

形 作用的、機能的

英英 relating to a function

例 Is the system **functional**?
這個系統有作用嗎？

☐ 三分熟
☐ 五分熟
☐ 七分熟
☐ 全熟

---

fun·da·men·tal

[ˌfʌndə'mɛntl̩]

名 基礎、原則
形 基礎的、根本的

英英 a primary principle or rule

例 The web page includes the **fundamental** principles of making good tea.
這個網頁包含泡好茶的基本原則。

☐ 三分熟
☐ 五分熟
☐ 七分熟
☐ 全熟

---

fu·ner·al ['fjunərəl]

名 葬禮、告別式

英英 a ceremony in which a dead person is burnt or buried

例 Many people pay respect to the dead in the **funeral**.
在葬禮中很多人對亡者致敬。

☐ 三分熟
☐ 五分熟
☐ 七分熟
☐ 全熟

🎧 **Track 203**

---

fu·ri·ous [ˈfjʊrɪəs]

形 狂怒的、狂鬧的

同 angry 發怒的

英英 extremely angry

例 The teacher was **furious** yesterday as most students were not listening.

老師昨天發怒，因為大部分的學生都沒在聽課。

☐ 三分熟
☐ 五分熟
☐ 七分熟
☐ 全熟

---

fur·nish [ˈfɝnɪʃ]

動 供給、裝備

英英 to provide a building with furniture and fittings

例 They **furnished** the cafe with pink furniture.

他們用粉紅色的家具布置這間咖啡店。

☐ 三分熟
☐ 五分熟
☐ 七分熟
☐ 全熟

---

fur·ther·more

[ˈfɝðɚˌmor]

副 再者、而且

英英 in addition, besides

例 Taking a ship is cheap. **Furthermore**, we can enjoy the ocean view.

搭船很便宜，而且，我們可以享受海景。

☐ 三分熟
☐ 五分熟
☐ 七分熟
☐ 全熟

Gg

gal·ler·y [ˈgælərɪ]

名 畫廊、美術館

英英 a room or building which is used for displaying or selling of works of art

例 How about going to the art **gallery** this weekend?

這週末去美術館如何？

☐ 三分熟
☐ 五分熟
☐ 七分熟
☐ 全熟

---

gang·ster

[ˈgæŋstɚ]

名 歹徒、匪徒

英英 a member of an organized group of violent criminals

例 The **gangster** threatened the old lady with his knife.

這名歹徒用刀子威脅老太太。

☐ 三分熟
☐ 五分熟
☐ 七分熟
☐ 全熟

---

gaze [gez]

名 注視、凝視
動 注視、凝視

英英 to look steadily and intently

例 His **gaze** on the face of his wife seemed a bit sad.

他凝視著妻子的臉似乎有點悲傷。

☐ 三分熟
☐ 五分熟
☐ 七分熟
☐ 全熟

---

gear [gɪr]

名 齒輪、裝具
動 開動、使適應

英英 a toothed wheel that works with others to change the relation between the speed of an engine; to start or begin; to adapt toward some purposes

例 The **gear** is functioning properly.

齒輪運作正常。

☐ 三分熟
☐ 五分熟
☐ 七分熟
☐ 全熟

G

gene [dʒin]

名 基因、遺傳因子

英英 a distinct sequence of DNA forming part of a chromosome, which controls physical development or behavior

例 **Genes** were passed down from generation to generation.
基因世代遺傳。

☐ 三分熟
☐ 五分熟
☐ 七分熟
☐ 全熟

---

gen·er·a·tion

[ˌdʒɛnəˈreʃən]

名 世代

英英 all of the people born and living at about the same time

例 Protect the Earth for future **generations**.
為了未來的世代，我們要保護地球。

☐ 三分熟
☐ 五分熟
☐ 七分熟
☐ 全熟

---

gen·er·os·i·ty

[ˌdʒɛnəˈrɑsətɪ]

名 慷慨、寬宏大量
同 charity 寬容

英英 the quality of being generous

例 I appreciated your **generosity**.
我感謝你的寬宏大量。

☐ 三分熟
☐ 五分熟
☐ 七分熟
☐ 全熟

---

gen·ius [ˈdʒinjəs]

名 天才、英才

英英 very rare creative power or other natural ability

例 Mozart is a **genius** in the field of music.
莫札特在音樂的領域上是個天才。

☐ 三分熟
☐ 五分熟
☐ 七分熟
☐ 全熟

---

gen·u·ine

[ˈdʒɛnjʊɪn]

形 真正的、非假冒的
同 real 真的

英英 very true or what it said to be; sincere and honest

例 The leather bag is **genuine**.
這個皮製的袋子是真皮作的。

☐ 三分熟
☐ 五分熟
☐ 七分熟
☐ 全熟

---

germ [dʒɝm]

名 細菌、微生物、病菌

英英 a micro-organism that causes disease

例 There are **germs** on the doorknob.
門把上有細菌。

☐ 三分熟
☐ 五分熟
☐ 七分熟
☐ 全熟

---

gift·ed [ˈɡɪftɪd]

形 有天賦的、有才能的

英英 having special ability in a particular field

例 My brother is **gifted** in designing game script.
我弟在遊戲腳本的設計上很有天賦。

☐ 三分熟
☐ 五分熟
☐ 七分熟
☐ 全熟

---

gi·gan·tic

[dʒaɪˈɡæntɪk]

形 巨人般的

英英 very large

例 The **gigantic** peach is suitable to turn into a carriage.
巨大的桃子很適合轉變成馬車。

☐ 三分熟
☐ 五分熟
☐ 七分熟
☐ 全熟

🎧**Track 205**

---

gig·gle [ˈgɪg!]

名 咯咯笑
動 咯咯地笑

英英 a foolish laughter; to laugh in a quiet way at something silly

例 Those girls are **giggling**.
那些女孩在咯咯笑。

☐ 三分熟
☐ 五分熟
☐ 七分熟
☐ 全熟

---

gin·ger [ˈdʒɪndʒɚ]

名 薑
動 使有活力

英英 a hot, fragrant spice plant that is used in cooking; to make someone energetic

例 Drink some **ginger** tea and warm your body.
喝一些薑茶，讓你的身體暖和起來。

☐ 三分熟
☐ 五分熟
☐ 七分熟
☐ 全熟

---

glide [glaɪd]

名 滑動、滑走
動 滑行

英英 to move with a smooth and quiet way; to fly without power or in a glider

例 Nick's dream girl **glides** into the dancing room.
尼克的夢幻女孩腳步輕盈地走進舞蹈教室。

☐ 三分熟
☐ 五分熟
☐ 七分熟
☐ 全熟

---

glimpse [glɪmps]

名 瞥見、一瞥
動 瞥見、隱約看見
同 glance 瞥見

英英 to see someone or something for a very short time while passing

例 Take a **glimpse** of the picture.
看一眼這張照片。

☐ 三分熟
☐ 五分熟
☐ 七分熟
☐ 全熟

---

globe [glob]

名 地球、球

英英 the earth; the world

例 Traveling around the **globe** is fun.
環遊世界是有趣的。

☐ 三分熟
☐ 五分熟
☐ 七分熟
☐ 全熟

---

glo·ri·ous
[ˈglorɪəs]

形 著名的、榮耀的
片 a glorious victory
光榮的勝利

英英 having or bringing glory; very famous or impressive

例 The **glorious** building is open for visitors.
這個著名的建築物開放參觀。

☐ 三分熟
☐ 五分熟
☐ 七分熟
☐ 全熟

---

goods [gʊdz]

名 商品、貨物

英英 things for sale, or the things that you own; products

例 The batch of **goods** has been shipped to America.
那一批的貨物已經船運到美國。

☐ 三分熟
☐ 五分熟
☐ 七分熟
☐ 全熟

---

grace [gres]

名 優美、優雅

英英 elegance of movement or action

例 The **grace** of the princess cannot be copied.
公主的優雅是不可能複製的。

☐ 三分熟
☐ 五分熟
☐ 七分熟
☐ 全熟

---

grace·ful [ˋgresfəl]

形 優雅的、雅致的

英英 having or showing grace or elegance

例 Judy imagined herself as a **graceful** lady.
茱蒂想像自己是個優雅的女士。

☐ 三分熟
☐ 五分熟
☐ 七分熟
☐ 全熟

G

---

gra·cious [ˋgreʃəs]

形 親切的、溫和有禮的

英英 very kind, and pleasant, with a very good manner

例 A **gracious** smile delights the children.
親切的笑容讓孩子開心。

☐ 三分熟
☐ 五分熟
☐ 七分熟
☐ 全熟

---

grad·u·a·tion

[ˏgrædʒʊˋeʃən]

名 畢業

英英 when you receive your academic degree or diploma for finishing your education or a course of study

例 What would you do after **graduation** from school?
畢業後你想做什麼？

☐ 三分熟
☐ 五分熟
☐ 七分熟
☐ 全熟

---

gram·mar

[ˋgræmɚ]

名 文法

英英 the whole system and structure of a language or the rules about how words change their form and combine with other words to make sentences

例 The **grammar** is so difficult that many students have trouble understanding.
文法如此的困難，所以很多學生有理解上的困擾。

☐ 三分熟
☐ 五分熟
☐ 七分熟
☐ 全熟

---

gram·mat·i·cal

[grəˋmætɪkḷ]

形 文法上的

英英 relating to grammar

例 You'd better remember these **grammatical** rules.
你最好記住這些文法規則。

☐ 三分熟
☐ 五分熟
☐ 七分熟
☐ 全熟

---

grape·fruit

[ˋgrepˏfrut]

名 葡萄柚

英英 a large round fruit with yellow skin and an acid juicy pulp

例 These **grapefruits** are sour.
這些葡萄柚是酸的。

☐ 三分熟
☐ 五分熟
☐ 七分熟
☐ 全熟

---

grate·ful [ˋgretfəl]

形 感激的、感謝的

英英 feeling or showing gratitude

例 We feel **grateful** of your help.
我們感激你的幫忙。

☐ 三分熟
☐ 五分熟
☐ 七分熟
☐ 全熟

---

grat·i·tude

[ˋgrætəˏtjud]

名 感激、感謝

英英 thankfulness, appreciation of kindness

例 Is it hard for you to show **gratitude**?
對你來說，表達感激是有困難的嗎？

☐ 三分熟
☐ 五分熟
☐ 七分熟
☐ 全熟

🎧 **Track 207**

---

grave [grev]

形 嚴重的、重大的
名 墓穴、墳墓
片 a grave digger 挖墓者

英英 a hole dug in the ground where buried a person after they died; very bad

例 Stealing money is a **grave** matter.
偷錢是件嚴重的事。

☐ 三分熟
☐ 五分熟
☐ 七分熟
☐ 全熟

---

greas·y [ˋgrizɪ]

形 塗有油脂的、油膩的

英英 covered with fat or oil

例 These spoons are **greasy**.
這些湯匙很油膩。

☐ 三分熟
☐ 五分熟
☐ 七分熟
☐ 全熟

---

greet·ing(s)

[ˋgritɪŋ(z)]

名 問候、問候語

英英 a word or sign of welcome or a polite way to greet people

例 Write a **greeting** card to your friend some times.
有時候給你的朋友寫一張問候卡吧。

☐ 三分熟
☐ 五分熟
☐ 七分熟
☐ 全熟

---

grief [grif]

名 悲傷、感傷

英英 sorrow or great sadness

例 Mitch's **grief** at his mother's death is terrible.
喪母之痛使米奇肝腸寸斷。

☐ 三分熟
☐ 五分熟
☐ 七分熟
☐ 全熟

---

grieve [griv]

動 悲傷、使悲傷

英英 to feel sorrow or sad , especially caused by someone's death

例 **Grieving** for the one you love is normal.
為你所愛的人悲傷是正常的。

☐ 三分熟
☐ 五分熟
☐ 七分熟
☐ 全熟

---

grind [graɪnd]

動 研磨、碾
片 grind sb. down
長期欺壓某人

英英 to make something smaller or into powder by crushing

例 **Grind** some coffee beans.
研磨一些咖啡豆吧。

☐ 三分熟
☐ 五分熟
☐ 七分熟
☐ 全熟

---

guar·an·tee

[͵gærənˋti]

名 擔保品、保證人
動 擔保、作保
同 promise 保證

英英 a formal assurance that certain conditions will be done, especially that a product will be of a specified quality

例 How can you ever consider being a **guarantee** for Garry?
你怎麼會考慮成為蓋瑞的保證人？

☐ 三分熟
☐ 五分熟
☐ 七分熟
☐ 全熟

---

guilt [gɪlt]

名 罪、內疚

英英 the feeling of worry or unhappiness that you have because you've done something bad or wrong

例 She has certain feeling of **guilt**.
她有某種罪惡感。

☐ 三分熟
☐ 五分熟
☐ 七分熟
☐ 全熟

guilt·y [gɪltɪ]

形 有罪的、內疚的

英英 responsible for something bad or wrong you have done

例 If he is **guilty**, you should be as well.
如果他有罪,你也應該有罪。

☐ 三分熟
☐ 五分熟
☐ 七分熟
☐ 全熟

---

gulf [gʌlf]

名 灣、海灣

英英 a deep area of the sea almost surrounded by land, with a narrow mouth

例 You can see sunset near the **gulf**.
你可以在海灣附近看見日落。

☐ 三分熟
☐ 五分熟
☐ 七分熟
☐ 全熟

Hh

ha·bit·u·al
[həˋbɪtʃʊəl]

形 習慣性的

英英 done as a habit; regular

例 It is hard to change the **habitual** behavior.
改變習慣性的行為很難。

☐ 三分熟
☐ 五分熟
☐ 七分熟
☐ 全熟

---

halt [hɔlt]

名 休止
動 停止、使停止

英英 when something stops acting or moving

例 The policeman cried, "**Halt!**"
警方大叫,「站住!」。

☐ 三分熟
☐ 五分熟
☐ 七分熟
☐ 全熟

---

hand·writ·ing
[ˋhændˏraɪtɪŋ]

名 手寫

英英 writing with a pen or pencil

例 His **handwriting** is messy.
他的手寫字好潦草。

☐ 三分熟
☐ 五分熟
☐ 七分熟
☐ 全熟

---

hard·en [ˋhɑrdn̩]

動 使硬化

英英 to make something hard or harder

例 Don't let your heart be **hardened**.
不要讓你的心變硬。

☐ 三分熟
☐ 五分熟
☐ 七分熟
☐ 全熟

---

hard·ship
[ˋhɑrdʃɪp]

名 艱難、辛苦

英英 difficult or hard conditions of life

例 These **hardships** would disappear gradually.
這些辛苦逐漸消失。

☐ 三分熟
☐ 五分熟
☐ 七分熟
☐ 全熟

---

hard·ware
[ˋhɑrdˏwɛr]

名 五金用品

英英 metal tools or equipment, which is used in a house or garden, such as hammers and screws

例 Both nails and hammers belong to **hardware**.
這些釘子和鎚子屬於五金用品。

☐ 三分熟
☐ 五分熟
☐ 七分熟
☐ 全熟

Track 209

har·mon·i·ca

[harˋmɑnɪkə]

名 口琴

英英 a small rectangular wind instrument with a row of metal reeds which is played by blowing to make different notes

例 The **harmonica** is expensive.
這支口琴很貴。

☐三分熟
☐五分熟
☐七分熟
☐全熟

har·mo·ny

[ˋharmənɪ]

名 一致、和諧
同 accord 一致

英英 a pleasant music sound produced by different notes being played or sung at the same time

例 **Harmony** is a state of no conflict.
和諧是一種沒有衝突的狀態。

☐三分熟
☐五分熟
☐七分熟
☐全熟

harsh [harʃ]

形 粗魯的、令人不快的

英英 unpleasantly rough, very unhappy

例 A **Harsh** criticism offends people.
粗魯的評論得罪人。

☐三分熟
☐五分熟
☐七分熟
☐全熟

haste [hest]

名 急忙、急速

英英 in a hurry or urgency of action

例 Mike made **haste** to catch the bus.
麥克急著要趕巴士。

☐三分熟
☐五分熟
☐七分熟
☐全熟

has·ten [ˋhesn̩]

動 趕忙

英英 to do something quickly or to move quickly

例 My boss **hastened** to leave the party.
我的老闆趕忙離開派對。

☐三分熟
☐五分熟
☐七分熟
☐全熟

ha·tred [ˋhetrɪd]

名 怨恨、憎惡

英英 a strong feeling of hate or dislike

例 The murder case was caused by racial **hatred**.
這起謀殺案由種族仇恨所造成。

☐三分熟
☐五分熟
☐七分熟
☐全熟

head·phone(s)

[ˋhɛdˏfon(z)]

名 頭戴式耳機、聽筒

英英 a pair of earphones placed over the head for listening to music or radio

例 My daughter is fond of the **headphone**.
我女兒喜歡這個頭戴式耳機。

☐三分熟
☐五分熟
☐七分熟
☐全熟

health·ful [ˋhɛlθfəl]

形 有益健康的
片 healthful diet 健康飲食

英英 having or conducive to good health

例 Doing exercises is **healthful**.
做運動是有益健康的。

☐三分熟
☐五分熟
☐七分熟
☐全熟

hel·i·cop·ter

[ˋhɛlɪˏkɑptɚ]

名 直升機

英英 a type of aircraft without wings, which has large blades go round very fast on top

例 The child is excited about the chance of riding in the **helicopter**.
小孩對於能有乘坐直升機的機會感到興奮。

☐三分熟
☐五分熟
☐七分熟
☐全熟

H

herd [hɝd]

名 獸群、成群
動 放牧、使成群

英英 a large group of animals, such as hoofed mammals, that live together; to form or crowd into a flock or herd

例 The **herd** is rushing towards the river.
獸群往河邊衝。

☐ 三分熟
☐ 五分熟
☐ 七分熟
☐ 全熟

hes·i·ta·tion

[ˌhɛzəˈteʃən]

名 遲疑、躊躇
反 determination 決心

英英 the act of hesitating

例 My younger brother went to rescue the boy without **hesitation**.
我弟弟立刻趕去援救那個小男孩。

☐ 三分熟
☐ 五分熟
☐ 七分熟
☐ 全熟

high·ly [ˈhaɪlɪ]

副 大大地、高高地

英英 to a high or large degree or level

例 His heroic performance is **highly** praised.
他英雄式的表現，被大大的讚揚。

☐ 三分熟
☐ 五分熟
☐ 七分熟
☐ 全熟

home·land

[ˈhomˌlænd]

名 祖國、本國

英英 a person's native land or country

例 The poet's **homeland** serves as the poet's inspiration.
這個詩人的祖國是詩人靈感的來源。

☐ 三分熟
☐ 五分熟
☐ 七分熟
☐ 全熟

hon·ey·moon

[ˈhʌnɪˌmun]

名 蜜月
動 度蜜月

英英 a holiday taken by a couple who just married; to take a honeymoon holiday

例 Edward and Bella had an unforgettable **honeymoon**.
愛德華和貝拉有難忘的蜜月。

☐ 三分熟
☐ 五分熟
☐ 七分熟
☐ 全熟

hon·or·a·ble

[ˈɑnərəbl̩]

形 體面的、可敬的

英英 worthy of honor; honest and fair

例 Mr. Jefferson is an **honorable** gentleman.
傑佛森是個體面的紳士。

☐ 三分熟
☐ 五分熟
☐ 七分熟
☐ 全熟

hook [hʊk]

名 鉤、鉤子
動 鉤、用鉤子鉤住

英英 a piece of curved metal used for catching hold of things or hanging things on; to catch with a hook

例 The fish rod has a **hook**.
釣魚竿有鉤子。

☐ 三分熟
☐ 五分熟
☐ 七分熟
☐ 全熟

hope·ful [ˈhopfəl]

形 有希望的

英英 feeling or inspiring hope

例 We are **hopeful** of our country's future.
我們對國家的未來抱有希望。

☐ 三分熟
☐ 五分熟
☐ 七分熟
☐ 全熟

🎧 **Track 211**

---

ho·ri·zon [həˋraɪz]

名 地平線、水平線

英英 the line at which the earth's surface and the sky seems appear to meet

例 The ship has disappeared from the **horizon**.
那艘船從地平線消失。

- [ ] 三分熟
- [ ] 五分熟
- [ ] 七分熟
- [ ] 全熟

---

hor·ri·fy [ˋhɔrəˌfaɪ]

動 使害怕、使恐怖

英英 to fill with horror, make someone scared

例 The mud slide **horrified** many villagers.
土石流讓很多的村民感到害怕。

- [ ] 三分熟
- [ ] 五分熟
- [ ] 七分熟
- [ ] 全熟

---

hose [hoz]

名 水管
動 用水管澆洗

英英 a flexible tube which is used to direct water; to water something with a tube

例 You can use the **hose** to water the garden.
你可以用這條水管幫花園澆水。

- [ ] 三分熟
- [ ] 五分熟
- [ ] 七分熟
- [ ] 全熟

---

host [host]

動 主辦
名 主人、主持人、一大群
反 guest 客人

英英 a person who receives or entertains guests; to give entertainment to someone

例 It's your turn to **host** the party.
換你主持派對了。

- [ ] 三分熟
- [ ] 五分熟
- [ ] 七分熟
- [ ] 全熟

---

hos·tel [ˋhɑstl̩]

名 青年旅社

英英 a large house which provides cheap rooms, food and lodging for people to stay

例 Many backpackers like the **hostel**.
很多的背包客喜歡青年旅社。

- [ ] 三分熟
- [ ] 五分熟
- [ ] 七分熟
- [ ] 全熟

---

house·hold

[ˋhaʊsˌhold]

形 家庭
片 household furniture 家具

英英 a house and its occupants regarded as a unit

例 There is a **household** god in the Korean movie Along With the Gods.
在韓國電影《與神同行》裡有位家神。

- [ ] 三分熟
- [ ] 五分熟
- [ ] 七分熟
- [ ] 全熟

---

house·wife

[ˋhaʊsˌwaɪf]

名 家庭主婦

英英 a married woman whose work is caring for her family and doing the housework

例 The **housewife** has no pay.
家庭主婦沒有薪水。

- [ ] 三分熟
- [ ] 五分熟
- [ ] 七分熟
- [ ] 全熟

---

house·work

[ˋhaʊsˌwɝk]

名 家事

英英 regular work done in housekeeping, such as cleaning and cooking, etc

例 I have to do all the **housework** while my parents go traveling.
當我的父母去旅行時，我必須要做所有的家事。

- [ ] 三分熟
- [ ] 五分熟
- [ ] 七分熟
- [ ] 全熟

---

hu·man·i·ty
[hjuˈmænətɪ]

名 人類、人道

英英 the condition of being human

例 **Humanity** is born to be different.
人天生就是不一樣。

☐ 三分熟
☐ 五分熟
☐ 七分熟
☐ 全熟

---

hur·ri·cane
[ˈhɝɪˌken]

名 颶風

英英 a storm with a violent wind, especially found in particular a tropical cyclone in the Caribbean

例 The **hurricane** caused some destruction of the city.
颶風造成了這座城市的一些毀壞。

☐ 三分熟
☐ 五分熟
☐ 七分熟
☐ 全熟

---

hy·dro·gen
[ˈhaɪdrədʒən]

名 氫、氫氣

英英 a colorless, odorless, highly flammable gas which is the lightest of the chemical elements

例 When **hydrogen** combines with oxygen, water will be formed.
當氫氣和氧氣結合時，水就會生成了。

☐ 三分熟
☐ 五分熟
☐ 七分熟
☐ 全熟

Ii

ice·berg [ˈaɪsˌbɝg]

名 冰山

英英 a large mass of ice floating in the sea

例 The ship almost crashed onto the **iceberg**.
船幾乎要撞到冰山。

☐ 三分熟
☐ 五分熟
☐ 七分熟
☐ 全熟

---

i·den·ti·cal
[aɪˈdɛntɪkl̩]

形 相同的
同 same 相同的

英英 exactly alike or all the same

例 Emma's younger sister looks almost **identical** to her.
愛瑪的妹妹看起來跟她好像。

☐ 三分熟
☐ 五分熟
☐ 七分熟
☐ 全熟

---

i·den·ti·fi·ca·tion/
ID [aɪˌdɛntəfəˈkeʃən]

名 身分證

英英 an official document that shows who you are

例 Show me your **identification** card.
身分證拿給我看。

☐ 三分熟
☐ 五分熟
☐ 七分熟
☐ 全熟

---

i·den·ti·fy
[aɪˈdɛntəˌfaɪ]

動 認出、鑑定

英英 to recognize something or someone

例 The witness tried to **identify** the person who caused the accident.
目擊證人試著認出造成這場意外的人。

☐ 三分熟
☐ 五分熟
☐ 七分熟
☐ 全熟

I

229

Track 213

id·i·om [ˈɪdɪəm]

名 成語、慣用語

英英 a group of words whose meaning cannot be deduced from those of the individual words

例 "No pain, no gain" is one of the most common English **idioms**.
「不勞而獲」是最常用的英語成語之一。

☐ 三分熟
☐ 五分熟
☐ 七分熟
☐ 全熟

---

id·le [ˈaɪdl̩]

形 閒置的
動 閒混

英英 not working or in use; to waste time and don't know what to do

例 The old farm equipment is **idle**.
老舊的農具閒置在那裡。

☐ 三分熟
☐ 五分熟
☐ 七分熟
☐ 全熟

---

i·dol [ˈaɪdl̩]

名 偶像
片 a pop idol
流行音樂偶像

英英 a person how is admired by a group of people as fans

例 Leonardo DiCaprio is my sister's **idol**.
李奧納多・狄卡皮歐是我姊的偶像。

☐ 三分熟
☐ 五分熟
☐ 七分熟
☐ 全熟

---

ig·no·rant

[ˈɪgnərənt]

形 缺乏教育的、無知的

英英 lacking knowledge or education

例 How can you be so **ignorant**?
你怎麼能如此的無知？

☐ 三分熟
☐ 五分熟
☐ 七分熟
☐ 全熟

---

il·lus·trate

[ˈɪləstret]

動 舉例說明

英英 to explain something clearly with pictures, charts or by giving examples

例 You can consider **illustrating** a complex idea with simple charts.
你可以考慮用簡單的表格，舉例說明一個複雜的想法。

☐ 三分熟
☐ 五分熟
☐ 七分熟
☐ 全熟

---

il·lus·tra·tion

[ˌɪlʌsˈtreʃən]

名 說明、插圖

英英 the action or fact of illustrating

例 The **illustration** expressed what the writer didn't say.
這張插圖表現出作家沒有說出的事。

☐ 三分熟
☐ 五分熟
☐ 七分熟
☐ 全熟

---

i·mag·in·able

[ɪˈmædʒɪnəbl̩]

形 可想像的

英英 possible to be thought of or imaginable

例 The difficulty is **imaginable**.
困難是可以想像得到的。

☐ 三分熟
☐ 五分熟
☐ 七分熟
☐ 全熟

---

i·mag·i·nar·y

[ɪˈmædʒəˌnɛrɪ]

形 想像的、不實在的

英英 existing only in the imagination, not real

例 Blue Boy is Alice's **imaginary** friend.
藍色男孩是愛麗絲想像出來的朋友。

☐ 三分熟
☐ 五分熟
☐ 七分熟
☐ 全熟

i·mag·i·na·tive

[ɪˋmædʒənetɪv]

形 有想像力的

英英 good at creating something or produce ideas with imagination

例 Anne Shirley is an **imaginative** girl.
安·雪莉是個有想像力的女孩。

☐ 三分熟
☐ 五分熟
☐ 七分熟
☐ 全熟

im·i·tate [ˋɪmə͵tet]

動 仿效、效法

英英 to follow or copy as a model

例 Some performers can **imitate** the politician figures well.
有些表演者可以把政治人物模仿的唯妙唯肖。

☐ 三分熟
☐ 五分熟
☐ 七分熟
☐ 全熟

im·i·ta·tion

[͵ɪməˋteʃən]

名 模仿、仿造品

英英 an occasion when someone or something imitates another person or thing

例 His **imitation** impressed the audience.
他的模仿讓觀眾留下了深刻印象。

☐ 三分熟
☐ 五分熟
☐ 七分熟
☐ 全熟

im·mi·grant

[ˋɪməgrənt]

名 移民者

英英 a person who move to live in a foreign country

例 These illegal **immigrants** were sent back to their homeland.
這些非法的移民者被遣返回祖國。

☐ 三分熟
☐ 五分熟
☐ 七分熟
☐ 全熟

im·mi·grate

[ˋɪmə͵gret]

動 遷移、移入

英英 to come to live in a foreign country

例 One of my classmates **immigrated** to Canada with her parents.
我的一個同學跟著她的父母移民到加拿大。

☐ 三分熟
☐ 五分熟
☐ 七分熟
☐ 全熟

im·mi·gra·tion

[͵ɪməˋgreʃən]

名 （從外地）移居入境

英英 when someone comes to live in a different country

例 You need to fill out some forms for the **immigration**.
你需要填些移民入境的表格。

☐ 三分熟
☐ 五分熟
☐ 七分熟
☐ 全熟

im·pact

[ˋɪmpækt]/[ɪmˋpækt]

名 碰撞、撞擊
動 衝擊、影響

英英 the action of one thing coming forcibly into contact with another; to give influence to someone or something

例 The **impact** of the event is so strong that Kent didn't want to take MRT.
這件事的衝擊很強，以致於肯特不想搭捷運。

☐ 三分熟
☐ 五分熟
☐ 七分熟
☐ 全熟

im·ply [ɪmˋplaɪ]

動 暗示、含有
同 hint 暗示

英英 to say or communicate an idea without saying it directly

例 The message **implies** that he likes to be with you.
這則訊息暗示他想跟你在一起。

☐ 三分熟
☐ 五分熟
☐ 七分熟
☐ 全熟

Track 215

---

im·pres·sion

[ɪmˋprɛʃən]

名 印象

英英 an idea, feeling, or opinion on someone or something

例 Colin made a good first **impression** on his girlfriend's parents.
柯林讓女朋友的父母留下好的第一印象。

☐三分熟
☐五分熟
☐七分熟
☐全熟

---

in·ci·dent

[ˋɪnsədənt]

名 事件

英英 an event or occurrence

例 The killing **incident** occurred last week.
殺人事件上星期發生。

☐三分熟
☐五分熟
☐七分熟
☐全熟

---

in·clud·ing

[ɪnˋkludɪŋ]

介 包含、包括

英英 containing as part of something

例 The pet animals **including** tigers and crocodiles were raised by Andy.
安迪所飼養的寵物包括老虎和鱷魚。

☐三分熟
☐五分熟
☐七分熟
☐全熟

---

in·di·ca·tion

[ˏɪndəˋkeʃən]

名 指示、表示

英英 the act of indicating

例 Vehicles and passengers should follow the **indication** of the traffic lights.
車輛和行人應該要遵守紅綠燈的指示。

☐三分熟
☐五分熟
☐七分熟
☐全熟

---

in·dus·tri·al·ize

[ɪnˋdʌstrɪəˏlaɪz]

動 （使）工業、產業化

英英 to develop industries in a country

例 **Industrialized** countries develop quickly.
工業化的國家發展快速。

☐三分熟
☐五分熟
☐七分熟
☐全熟

---

in·fant [ˋɪnfənt]

名 嬰兒、未成年人

英英 a very young child or baby

例 Most **infants** seem to like to listen to their mothers' voice.
多數嬰兒似乎喜歡聽他們母親的聲音。

☐三分熟
☐五分熟
☐七分熟
☐全熟

---

in·fect [ɪnˋfɛkt]

動 使感染

英英 to pass a disease to somebody or something

例 The nurse was **infected** with SARS.
這個護士感染了嚴重急性呼吸道症候群。

☐三分熟
☐五分熟
☐七分熟
☐全熟

---

in·fec·tion

[ɪnˋfɛkʃən]

名 感染、傳染病

英英 the process of infecting; an infectious disease

例 It is hard to stop the **infection** of SARS in a certain period of time.
在某段期間內，要阻止嚴重急性呼吸道症候群的感染是有困難的。

☐三分熟
☐五分熟
☐七分熟
☐全熟

---

in·fla·tion

[ɪnˈfleʃən]

名 膨脹、脹大
片 the inflation rate
通貨膨脹率

英英 the action of an increase in prices

例 The control of **inflation** is related to the development of economy.
通貨膨脹與經濟的發展有關。

□ 三分熟
□ 五分熟
□ 七分熟
□ 全熟

---

in·flu·en·tial

[ˌɪnfluˈɛnʃəl]

形 有影響力的

英英 having great power or influence

例 This paper is **influential**.
這篇論文是有影響力的。

□ 三分熟
□ 五分熟
□ 七分熟
□ 全熟

---

in·for·ma·tion

[ˌɪnfɚˈmeʃən]

名 知識、見聞

英英 facts or knowledge about a person or event

例 The age of **information** causes great anxiety.
資訊時代造成很大的焦慮感。

□ 三分熟
□ 五分熟
□ 七分熟
□ 全熟

---

in·for·ma·tive

[ɪnˈfɔrmətɪv]

形 提供情報的

英英 giving useful information

例 Rita is very **informative**.
麗塔的情報豐富。

□ 三分熟
□ 五分熟
□ 七分熟
□ 全熟

---

in·gre·di·ent

[ɪnˈgridɪənt]

名 成份、原料

英英 any of the substances that are used to make a particular dish

例 The major **ingredients** in the corn soup include corns, ham, and onions.
這道玉米湯的主要成份包含玉米、火腿和洋蔥。

□ 三分熟
□ 五分熟
□ 七分熟
□ 全熟

---

in·i·tial [ɪˈnɪʃəl]

形 開始的
名 姓名的首字母

英英 occurring at the beginning; the first letter of someone's family's name

例 The **initial** letter of the surname Wang is "W".
王這個姓氏的首要字母是 "W"。

□ 三分熟
□ 五分熟
□ 七分熟
□ 全熟

---

in·no·cence

[ˈɪnəsn̩s]

名 清白、天真無邪

英英 the quality of being innocent

例 Do you have evidence to prove your **innocence**?
你有證據證明你的清白嗎？

□ 三分熟
□ 五分熟
□ 七分熟
□ 全熟

---

in·put [ˈɪnˌpʊt]

名 輸入
動 輸入

英英 something is put or operated by any process or system

例 Students learn to read by decoding the **input** message of the writer.
學生藉由解碼作者所輸入的文字訊息而學會閱讀。

□ 三分熟
□ 五分熟
□ 七分熟
□ 全熟

🎧 Track 217

---

in·sert [ˋɪnsɝt]/[ɪnˋsɝt]

名 插入物
動 插入

英英 to add something to something else; something which is made to go into something else

例 **Insert** your card quickly.
趕快插入你的卡片。

☐ 三分熟
☐ 五分熟
☐ 七分熟
☐ 全熟

---

in·spec·tion

[ɪnˋspɛkʃən]

名 檢查、調查

英英 the act or state of inspecting

例 Yearly health **inspection** is necessary.
每年一次的健康檢查是有必要的。

☐ 三分熟
☐ 五分熟
☐ 七分熟
☐ 全熟

---

in·spi·ra·tion

[ɪnspəˋreʃən]

名 鼓舞、激勵

英英 something or someone that gives you ideas for something

例 Jessie's **inspiration** is the key to her daughter's success.
傑西的鼓勵，是她的女兒之所以能成功的關鍵。

☐ 三分熟
☐ 五分熟
☐ 七分熟
☐ 全熟

---

in·spire [ɪnˋspaɪr]

動 啟發、鼓舞

英英 to make something feel they are able to do something when they think they can't

例 The landscape in the painting was **inspired** by Li Pai's poem.
這幅畫裡的景色是來自李白詩作的靈感。

☐ 三分熟
☐ 五分熟
☐ 七分熟
☐ 全熟

---

in·stall [ɪnˋstɔl]

動 安裝、裝置
同 establish 建立、安置

英英 place or fix equipment or machine in position ready for use

例 The engineer was **installing** a new computer system.
工程師正在安裝一套新的電腦系統。

☐ 三分熟
☐ 五分熟
☐ 七分熟
☐ 全熟

---

in·stinct [ˋɪnstɪŋkt]

名 本能、直覺
片 survival instinct
生存本能

英英 a natural ability or skill that

例 Animals' **instinct** helped them to survive in the jungle.
動物的本能幫助他們在叢林中存活下去。

☐ 三分熟
☐ 五分熟
☐ 七分熟
☐ 全熟

---

in·struct

[ɪnˋstrʌkt]

動 教導、指令

英英 direct or command

例 Ray was **instructed** by his boss to send a bunch of roses to Miss Su.
雷接受老闆的指令，送一束玫瑰給蘇小姐。

☐ 三分熟
☐ 五分熟
☐ 七分熟
☐ 全熟

---

in·struc·tor

[ɪnˋstrʌktɚ]

名 教師、指導者、教練

英英 a teacher of university ranking below assistant professor

例 The **instructor** asked the students to take the test quietly.
教師要求學生要安靜的考試。

☐ 三分熟
☐ 五分熟
☐ 七分熟
☐ 全熟

in·sult

[ɪnˋsʌlt]/[ˋɪnsʌlt]

動 侮辱
名 冒犯

英英 to speak something bad or unpleasant to abuse someone

例 The **insult** cannot be forgiven.
這樣的侮辱無法原諒。

---

in·sur·ance

[ɪnˋʃʊrəns]

名 保險
片 health insurance
健康保險

英英 the business of providing insurance

例 Does your sister have **insurance**?
你的姊姊有保險嗎？

---

in·tel·lec·tu·al

[ˌɪntḷˋɛktʃʊəl]

名 知識份子
形 智力的

英英 a person with a highly developed intellect and knowledge; describes someone is with high intelligence

例 The **intellectual** was arrested by the government.
這名知識份子被政府所逮捕。

---

in·tel·li·gence

[ɪnˋtɛlədʒəns]

名 智能

英英 the ability to learn and apply knowledge and skills

例 Everyone's **intelligence** is different.
每個人的智能是不一樣的。

---

in·tel·li·gent

[ɪnˋtɛlədʒəjnt]

形 有智慧（才智）的

英英 having intelligence, especially of a high level

例 Most people believe aliens are **intelligent** creatures.
多數人相信外星人是有智慧的生物。

---

in·tend [ɪnˋtɛnd]

動 計畫、打算

英英 to have the plan to do something

例 I didn't **intend** to move to Seattle.
我並沒有打算要搬到西雅圖。

---

in·tense [ɪnˋtɛns]

形 極度的、緊張的

英英 very nurvous and anxious

例 Most office workers are under **intense** pressure.
大部分的上班族處在極度緊張的狀態。

I

Track 219

in·ten·si·fy

[ɪnˈtɛnsəˌfaɪ]

動 加強、增強

英英 to become greater, stronger or powerful

例 Philip **intensified** the promotional activity for the new product.
菲力普加強新產品的宣傳活動。

☐ 三分熟
☐ 五分熟
☐ 七分熟
☐ 全熟

in·ten·si·ty

[ɪnˈtɛnsətɪ]

名 強度、強烈

英英 the state of being intense

例 The **intensity** of the earthquake reaches its climax for a while.
地震的強度在一段期間內達到最高點。

☐ 三分熟
☐ 五分熟
☐ 七分熟
☐ 全熟

in·ten·sive

[ɪnˈtɛnsɪv]

形 強烈的、密集的、特別護理的

英英 putting lots of effort in a show period of time

例 She needs **intensive** care for two weeks.
她需要兩個星期的特別護理。

☐ 三分熟
☐ 五分熟
☐ 七分熟
☐ 全熟

in·ten·tion

[ɪnˈtɛnʃən]

名 意向、意圖

英英 an aim or plan; the action of intending

例 His kind **intention** was misunderstood.
他的良善意圖被誤會了。

☐ 三分熟
☐ 五分熟
☐ 七分熟
☐ 全熟

in·ter·act

[ˌɪntəˈrækt]

動 交互作用、互動

英英 to react to; to act on each other

例 Betty has a talent to **interact** well with children.
貝蒂有與小孩良好互動的才能。

☐ 三分熟
☐ 五分熟
☐ 七分熟
☐ 全熟

in·ter·ac·tion

[ˌɪntəˈækʃən]

名 交互影響、互動

英英 when two or more people or things react to each other

例 Regular **interaction** between parents and children is necessary.
親子間有規律的互動是有必要的。

☐ 三分熟
☐ 五分熟
☐ 七分熟
☐ 全熟

in·ter·fere

[ˌɪntəˈfɪr]

動 妨礙
同 interrupt 打斷

英英 to put yourself involved in a particular thing when your involvement is not helpful

例 Don't **interfere** with his work.
不要妨礙他的工作。

☐ 三分熟
☐ 五分熟
☐ 七分熟
☐ 全熟

in·ter·me·di·ate

[ˌɪntəˈmidɪɪt]

名 調解
形 中間的

英英 coming between two related things in time, place, character, etc; to get involved in something

例 The series of grammar books have three levels—basic, **intermediate**, and advanced.
這套文法書有三個級數－基本的、中間的，和進階的。

☐ 三分熟
☐ 五分熟
☐ 七分熟
☐ 全熟

Internet [ˋɪntɚͺnɛt]

名 網際網路

英英 an international information network linking one computer to another

例 The are many traps of making friends on the **Internet**.
網際網路裡有很多交朋友陷阱。

☐ 三分熟
☐ 五分熟
☐ 七分熟
☐ 全熟

---

in·ter·pret

[ɪnˋtɝprɪt]

動 說明、解讀、翻譯

英英 to explain the meaning of; translate orally the words of a person speaking a different language

例 Can you **interpret** the concept for me?
你可否為我解釋一下這個概念？

☐ 三分熟
☐ 五分熟
☐ 七分熟
☐ 全熟

---

in·ter·rup·tion

[ͺɪntəˋrʌpʃən]

名 中斷、妨礙

英英 an interrupting or being interrupted

例 Your **interruption** of their conversation aroused some unpleasant feelings.
你打斷他們的對談，造成了一些不太愉悅的感覺。

☐ 三分熟
☐ 五分熟
☐ 七分熟
☐ 全熟

---

in·ti·mate

[ˋɪntəmɪt]

名 知己
形 親密的

英英 a very close friend; very close

例 I have **intimate** relationship with Joe.
我跟喬之間有親密的關係。

☐ 三分熟
☐ 五分熟
☐ 七分熟
☐ 全熟

---

in·to·na·tion

[ͺɪntoˋneʃən]

名 語調、吟詠

英英 the action of intoning

例 His son's **intonation** of reciting the poem is beautiful.
他兒子朗誦詩歌的語調很優美。

☐ 三分熟
☐ 五分熟
☐ 七分熟
☐ 全熟

---

in·vade [ɪnˋved]

動 侵略、入侵

英英 to enter a place, usually a country, as or with an army so as to subjugate or occupy it

例 Viruses have **invaded** into the body.
病毒入侵人體。

☐ 三分熟
☐ 五分熟
☐ 七分熟
☐ 全熟

---

in·va·sion

[ɪnˋveʒən]

名 侵犯、侵害

英英 an action of invading

例 An illness results from the **invasion** of the germs.
疾病導因於細菌的入侵。

☐ 三分熟
☐ 五分熟
☐ 七分熟
☐ 全熟

---

in·ven·tion

[ɪnˋvɛnʃən]

名 發明、創造

英英 the action of inventing something or creating something

例 The **invention** of TV was a miracle.
電視的發明是個奇蹟。

☐ 三分熟
☐ 五分熟
☐ 七分熟
☐ 全熟

Track 221

in·vest [ɪnˋvɛst]

動 投資

英英 to put money into financial schemes, shares with the expectation of achieving a profit

例 Did you **invest** in stock market?
你有投資股票市場嗎？

☐ 三分熟
☐ 五分熟
☐ 七分熟
☐ 全熟

---

in·vest·ment
[ɪnˋvɛstmənt]

名 投資額、投資

英英 the action or process of investing

例 You could also learn to make **investment** on artworks.
你也可以學著做藝術品投資。

☐ 三分熟
☐ 五分熟
☐ 七分熟
☐ 全熟

---

in·ves·ti·ga·tion
[ɪnˏvɛstəˋgeʃən]

名 調查

英英 the process of examining a crime or problem carefully, in order to discover the truth

例 Richard is in charge of the **investigation**.
理查負責這個調查案。

☐ 三分熟
☐ 五分熟
☐ 七分熟
☐ 全熟

---

in·volve [ɪnˋvɑlv]

動 牽涉、包括

英英 to include as a part or something

例 The case **involves** money, murder, and sex.
這個案子牽涉到金錢、謀殺和性。

☐ 三分熟
☐ 五分熟
☐ 七分熟
☐ 全熟

---

in·volve·ment
[ɪnˋvɑlvmənt]

名 捲入、連累

英英 the act or process of being a part of something

例 The **involvement** of government officials made the case tougher to crack.
政府官員的捲入，讓這個案子更難偵破。

☐ 三分熟
☐ 五分熟
☐ 七分熟
☐ 全熟

---

i·so·late [ˋaɪsˏlet]

動 孤立、隔離
同 separate 分開

英英 to keep something separate or place apart or alone

例 **Isolating** the witnesses is necessary.
隔離目擊證人是有必要的。

☐ 三分熟
☐ 五分熟
☐ 七分熟
☐ 全熟

---

i·so·la·tion
[ˏaɪsˋleʃən]

名 分離、孤獨

英英 the process or fact of isolating or being isolated

例 Robinson Crusoe was in **isolation** when he was on the island.
當魯賓遜・克魯索在島上時，他處於孤獨的狀態。

☐ 三分熟
☐ 五分熟
☐ 七分熟
☐ 全熟

---

itch [ɪtʃ]

名 癢
動 發癢

英英 an uncomfortable sensation that make you want to scratch the skin

例 My leg **itch** was caused by the mosquito bites.
我的腿發癢是蚊蟲咬造成的。

☐ 三分熟
☐ 五分熟
☐ 七分熟
☐ 全熟

Jj

jeal·ous·y

[ˋdʒɛləsɪ]

名 嫉妒

英英 a feeling of unhappiness or upset because someone has something that you don't have

例 **Jealousy** turned a beautiful queen into an ugly witch.
嫉妒讓一位漂亮的皇后變成醜陋的巫婆。

☐ 三分熟
☐ 五分熟
☐ 七分熟
☐ 全熟

ju·nior [ˋdʒunjɚ]

名 年少者
形 年少的

英英 of or connecting to young or younger people

例 **Juniors** are enthusiastic about online games.
年少者對線上遊戲很狂熱。

☐ 三分熟
☐ 五分熟
☐ 七分熟
☐ 全熟

Kk

keen [kin]

形 熱心的、敏鋭的、熱衷的

英英 very eager, enthusiastic, interested in something

例 Steven is **keen** in learning different languages.
史蒂芬對於學習不同的語言很熱衷。

☐ 三分熟
☐ 五分熟
☐ 七分熟
☐ 全熟

knuck·le [ˋnʌkḷ]

名 關節
動 將指關節觸地
片 near the knuckle
幾乎可説是下流

英英 a part of a finger at a joint where you can bend your fingers, hands or legs; to press or rub with the knuckles

例 Grandma's **knuckle** was painful.
奶奶的關節痛。

☐ 三分熟
☐ 五分熟
☐ 七分熟
☐ 全熟

Ll

la·bor [ˋlebɚ]

名 勞力
動 勞動

英英 workers who works with physical and mental effort; to work with physical and mental effort

例 **Labor** Day is a public holiday in America.
在美國的勞動節是國定假日。

☐ 三分熟
☐ 五分熟
☐ 七分熟
☐ 全熟

lab·o·ra·to·ry/

lab [ˋlæbrəˏtorɪ]/[læb]

名 實驗室

英英 a room or building for scientific experiments, research, or test

例 Scientists are working in the **laboratory**.
科學家在實驗室工作。

☐ 三分熟
☐ 五分熟
☐ 七分熟
☐ 全熟

J
K
L

🎧 **Track 223**

---

lag [læg]

名 落後
動 延緩

英英 a period of time behind or a delay; to make progress more slowly or to fall behind

例 The movie on the tour bus is always **lagging**.
遊覽車上的電影總是在延緩播放。

☐三分熟
☐五分熟
☐七分熟
☐全熟

---

land·mark

[ˈlændˌmɑrk]

名 路標

英英 a sign or feature of a place that is easily seen and recognized from a distance

例 The London Eye is one of the most famous **landmarks** of London.
倫敦之眼是倫敦最有名的路標之一。

☐三分熟
☐五分熟
☐七分熟
☐全熟

---

land·scape

[ˈlænskep]

名 風景
動 進行造景工程

英英 all the visible views of an area of land; improve the appearance of a garden, park, etc. by means of landscape gardening

例 The **landscape** of Ali Mountain is beautiful.
阿里山的風景好美。

☐三分熟
☐五分熟
☐七分熟
☐全熟

---

land·slide/ mud·slide

[ˈlændˌslaɪd]/[ˈmʌdˌslaɪd]

名 山崩

英英 a mass of rock and earth slides down from a mountain or cliff

例 The **landslide** happened so suddenly.
山崩發生的如此突然。

☐三分熟
☐五分熟
☐七分熟
☐全熟

---

large·ly [ˈlɑrdʒlɪ]

副 大部分地

英英 mostly, almost completely

例 The publishing house is **largely** female.
這家出版社大部分是女生。

☐三分熟
☐五分熟
☐七分熟
☐全熟

---

late·ly [ˈletlɪ]

副 最近

英英 recently, not long ago

例 **Lately**, Sam went hiking again.
最近山姆又去健行。

☐三分熟
☐五分熟
☐七分熟
☐全熟

---

launch [lɔntʃ]

名 開始
動 發射

英英 to start or begin; move a boat or ship from land into the water; to start the engine to do something

例 The rocket was **launched** into the space.
火箭被發射到外太空。

☐三分熟
☐五分熟
☐七分熟
☐全熟

---

law·ful [ˈlɔfəl]

形 合法的
同 legal 合法的

英英 permitted by, or recognized by law or rules, legal

例 **Lawful** marriages don't guarantee happiness.
合法的婚姻並不保證快樂。

☐三分熟
☐五分熟
☐七分熟
☐全熟

L

lead [lid]

名／動 領導

英英 to cause someone or something to follow with one

例 You need wisdom to **lead** your country.
你需要智慧來領導你的國家。

☐ 三分熟
☐ 五分熟
☐ 七分熟
☐ 全熟

---

lean [lin]

動 傾斜、倚靠

英英 to move the top of your body into a sloping position

例 **Lean** on the door.
倚靠在門邊。

☐ 三分熟
☐ 五分熟
☐ 七分熟
☐ 全熟

---

learn·ed [ˈlɝnd]

形 學術性的、博學的

英英 having much knowledge because of studying for a long

例 The **learned** scholar has ways to pursue what they want to know.
博學的學者有方法追到他們想知道的。

☐ 三分熟
☐ 五分熟
☐ 七分熟
☐ 全熟

---

learn·ing [ˈlɝnɪŋ]

名 學問

英英 studying to get knowledge or skills

例 **Learning** is not one-step work.
學問並不是一蹴而成的工作。

☐ 三分熟
☐ 五分熟
☐ 七分熟
☐ 全熟

---

lec·ture [ˈlɛktʃɚ]

名 演講
動 對……演講

英英 an educational talk to a group of people, especially one of students in a university

例 We are asked to attend 10 **lectures** in three years.
我們被要求在三年內參加 10 場演講。

☐ 三分熟
☐ 五分熟
☐ 七分熟
☐ 全熟

---

lec·tur·er
[ˈlɛktʃərɚ]

名 演講者

英英 a person who gives lectures or speeches, especially as a teacher in higher education

例 The **lecturer** is from National Taiwan Normal University.
演講者來自於臺灣師範大學。

☐ 三分熟
☐ 五分熟
☐ 七分熟
☐ 全熟

---

leg·end [ˈlɛdʒənd]

名 傳奇

英英 a traditional old story from ancient times, that people tell about a famous even

例 Have you heard of the **legend** of becoming werewolves?
你有聽過變狼人的傳奇嗎？

☐ 三分熟
☐ 五分熟
☐ 七分熟
☐ 全熟

---

lei·sure·ly [ˈliʒɚlɪ]

形 悠閒的
副 悠閒地
片 leisurely pace
悠閒的腳步

英英 very relaxed and unhurried

例 Take some **leisurely** activity while you're free.
當你有空時，做一些休閒活動吧。

☐ 三分熟
☐ 五分熟
☐ 七分熟
☐ 全熟

🎧 **Track 225**

li·cense/

li·cence [ˈlaɪsn̩s]

名 執照
動 許可

英英 a permission allows someone to do something officially or legally to permit or authorize by license; give a license to sb.

例 Have you got your driving **license**?
你拿到汽車駕照了嗎？

☐ 三分熟
☐ 五分熟
☐ 七分熟
☐ 全熟

---

light·en [ˈlaɪtn̩]

動 變亮、減輕

英英 make or become lighter in weight, or become brighter

例 The whole room is **lightened**.
整個房間變亮了。

☐ 三分熟
☐ 五分熟
☐ 七分熟
☐ 全熟

---

lim·i·ta·tion

[ˌlɪməˈteʃən]

名 限制

英英 a restriction or reducing something

例 The **limitation** of alcohol will be lifted if you are eighteen.
如果你滿十八歲了，酒精的限制就會取消。

☐ 三分熟
☐ 五分熟
☐ 七分熟
☐ 全熟

---

liq·uor [ˈlɪkɚ]

名 烈酒

英英 strong alcoholic drink

例 Drink a cup of the **liquor** and you'll be drunk right away.
喝一杯烈酒，你馬上就會醉。

☐ 三分熟
☐ 五分熟
☐ 七分熟
☐ 全熟

---

lit·er·ar·y

[ˈlɪtəˌrɛrɪ]

形 文學的

英英 related to the writing or content of literature

例 The **literary** atmosphere surrounds the café.
文學的氣氛圍繞著咖啡館。

☐ 三分熟
☐ 五分熟
☐ 七分熟
☐ 全熟

---

lit·er·a·ture

[ˈlɪtərətʃɚ]

名 文學

英英 written works which are regarded as having artistic merit

例 Children's **Literature** is fun.
兒童文學很有趣。

☐ 三分熟
☐ 五分熟
☐ 七分熟
☐ 全熟

---

loan [lon]

名 借貸
動 借、貸

英英 a thing or money that is borrowed, usually a sum of money that is expected to be paid back with interest

例 Could you **loan** me 10,000 dollars?
你能借我一萬美元嗎？

☐ 三分熟
☐ 五分熟
☐ 七分熟
☐ 全熟

---

lo·ca·tion

[loˈkeʃən]

名 位置

英英 a place or a position in a place

例 The **Location** of the treasure is still a mystery.
寶藏的位置仍然是個謎。

☐ 三分熟
☐ 五分熟
☐ 七分熟
☐ 全熟

lock·er [ˈlɑkɚ]

名 有鎖的收納櫃、
寄物櫃

片 locker room 更衣室

英英 a small lockable cupboard, sometimes in a row of several

例 The gold coins are in the **locker**.
金幣放在收納櫃裡。

☐ 三分熟
☐ 五分熟
☐ 七分熟
☐ 全熟

---

log·ic [ˈlɑdʒɪk]

名 邏輯

英英 a way of thinking which is reasonable

例 Your **logic** is a bit odd.
你的邏輯有點怪。

☐ 三分熟
☐ 五分熟
☐ 七分熟
☐ 全熟

---

log·i·cal [ˈlɑdʒɪkl̩]

形 邏輯上的

英英 of or according to the rules of logic or reasons

例 We find out the murderer because of **logical** inferences.
因為合理的推論，我們找到這個謀殺者。

☐ 三分熟
☐ 五分熟
☐ 七分熟
☐ 全熟

---

lo·tion [ˈloʃən]

名 洗潔劑、化妝水

英英 a thick liquid that you apply to the skin as a medicine or cosmetic

例 The **lotion** smells good.
這罐化妝水聞起來真好。

☐ 三分熟
☐ 五分熟
☐ 七分熟
☐ 全熟

---

lousy [ˈlaʊzɪ]

形 卑鄙的

英英 very mean or bad

例 Those people are **lousy** as they don't clean up the table.
那些人好卑鄙，因為他們不清理桌面。

☐ 三分熟
☐ 五分熟
☐ 七分熟
☐ 全熟

---

loy·al [ˈlɔɪəl]

形 忠實的

英英 showing firm and constant to a someone or something

例 I'm a **loyal** person.
我是忠誠的人。

☐ 三分熟
☐ 五分熟
☐ 七分熟
☐ 全熟

---

loy·al·ty [ˈlɔɪəltɪ]

名 忠誠

英英 the state of being loyal or supportive

例 His **loyalty** to the company is without doubt.
他對這家公司很忠誠。

☐ 三分熟
☐ 五分熟
☐ 七分熟
☐ 全熟

---

lu·nar [ˈlunɚ]

形 月亮的、陰曆的

英英 of or relating to the moon

例 The **lunar** calendar shows that tomorrow is the last day of the year.
陰曆顯示出，明天就是這一年中最好的一天。

☐ 三分熟
☐ 五分熟
☐ 七分熟
☐ 全熟

L

🎧 **Track 227**

lux·u·ri·ous

[lʌgˋʒʊrɪəs]

形 奢侈的

英英 characterized by luxury; giving great pleasure

例　To smoke three packs of cigarettes is not only harmful but also **luxurious**.
抽三包菸，不但對你的身體有害，而且也太奢侈。

☐ 三分熟
☐ 五分熟
☐ 七分熟
☐ 全熟

lux·u·ry [ˋlʌkʃərɪ]

名 奢侈品、奢侈
片 a luxury holiday
　　豪華假期

英英 great comfort and extravagant living

例　The **luxury** car looks fashionable.
這輛豪華房車看起來很時髦。

☐ 三分熟
☐ 五分熟
☐ 七分熟
☐ 全熟

Mm

ma·chin·er·y

[məˋʃinərɪ]

名 機械

英英 a group of machines or the components of a machine

例　The **machinery** is heavy and expensive.
這臺機械又重又貴。

☐ 三分熟
☐ 五分熟
☐ 七分熟
☐ 全熟

mad·am/ma'am

[ˋmædəm]/[mæm]

名 夫人、女士

英英 a polite way of beginning a formal letter to a woman

例　**Madam**, may I serve you?
夫人，我可否為您服務？

☐ 三分熟
☐ 五分熟
☐ 七分熟
☐ 全熟

mag·net·ic

[mægˋnɛtɪk]

形 磁性的

英英 very attractive or with power with a magnet

例　He has **magnetic** voice.
他有磁性的聲音。

☐ 三分熟
☐ 五分熟
☐ 七分熟
☐ 全熟

mag·nif·i·cent

[mægˋnɪfəsənt]

形 壯觀的、華麗的

英英 very good, excellent, impressively beautiful

例　Johnson's villa is **magnificent**.
強森的別墅很華麗。

☐ 三分熟
☐ 五分熟
☐ 七分熟
☐ 全熟

make·up [ˋmekˌʌp]

名 結構、化妝

英英 colored substances used on your face to improve or change your appearance

例　Have you finished **make-up**?
你化完妝了嗎？

☐ 三分熟
☐ 五分熟
☐ 七分熟
☐ 全熟

man·u·al [ˈmænjʊəl]

名 手冊
形 手工的

英英 a book giving instructions or information how to do something or use something; done or made by the hand

例 The **manual** is to guide you through the shelf composition work.
這個手冊會引導你完成書架組裝的工作。

☐ 三分熟
☐ 五分熟
☐ 七分熟
☐ 全熟

---

man·u·fac·ture
[ˌmænjəˈfæktʃɚ]

名 製造業
動 大量製造

英英 produce something, especially on a large scale using machinery in factory; the organized action of making products

例 **Manufacture** of plastic products should pay more tax because of waste handling.
塑膠產品的製造業應該要因為廢物處理繳更多稅。

☐ 三分熟
☐ 五分熟
☐ 七分熟
☐ 全熟

---

man·u·fac·turer
[ˌmænjəˈfæktʃərɚ]

名 製造者

英英 a company that makes products in large numbers

例 The **manufacturers** of dolls in Taishan County have long gone.
泰山鄉的娃娃製造商早就離開了。

☐ 三分熟
☐ 五分熟
☐ 七分熟
☐ 全熟

---

mar·a·thon
[ˈmærəθɑn]

名 馬拉松

英英 a long-distance running race, slightly over one of 26 miles, equal to 42.195 km

例 **Marathon** this time is to arouse the awareness of saving the ocean animals.
這次的馬拉松是要提升拯救海洋生物的意識。

☐ 三分熟
☐ 五分熟
☐ 七分熟
☐ 全熟

---

mar·gin [ˈmɑrdʒɪn]

名 邊緣
同 edge 邊

英英 an edge or border

例 The **margin** of the dress has ocean waves.
這件洋裝的邊緣有海洋波浪的格式。

☐ 三分熟
☐ 五分熟
☐ 七分熟
☐ 全熟

---

ma·tu·ri·ty
[məˈtjʊrətɪ]

名 成熟期

英英 the state or period of being mature

例 **Maturity** of a butterfly is in the last stage of its life cycle.
蝴蝶的成熟期，落在生命週期的最後階段。

☐ 三分熟
☐ 五分熟
☐ 七分熟
☐ 全熟

---

max·i·mum
[ˈmæksəməm]

名 最大量
形 最大的

英英 the greatest amount, size, or number

例 **Maximum** of people on the bridge is 15.
這座橋最多可容納 15 個人。

☐ 三分熟
☐ 五分熟
☐ 七分熟
☐ 全熟

M

Track 229

mea·sure(s) [ˋmɛʒ∂(z)] 動 度量單位、尺寸	英英 to find the exact size or amount of something 例 **Measure** the length of the pants. 量量這件褲子的長度。	□三分熟 □五分熟 □七分熟 □全熟
me·chan·ic [məˋkænɪk] 名 機械工	英英 a worker whose job is to repair and maintain machinery 例 **Mechanics** worked hard to fix Mr. Smith's car. 機械工認真工作，修理史密斯先生的車。	□三分熟 □五分熟 □七分熟 □全熟
me·chan·i·cal [məˋkænɪkl̩] 形 機械的 片 a mechanical device 一種機械裝置	英英 relating to or operated by a machine or machinery 例 **Mechanical** work is a kind of practical job. 機械工作是種實用的工作。	□三分熟 □五分熟 □七分熟 □全熟
mem·o·ra·ble [ˋmɛmərəbl̩] 形 值得紀念的	英英 worth remembering or easily remembered 例 The graduation trip was **memorable**. 畢業旅行是值得紀念的。	□三分熟 □五分熟 □七分熟 □全熟
me·mo·ri·al [məˋmorɪəl] 名 紀念品 形 紀念的	英英 an object stands for a particular person or event; serving to keep remembrance 例 The key chain can serve as a kind of **memorial.** 這個鑰匙圈可以當成一種紀念品。	□三分熟 □五分熟 □七分熟 □全熟
mer·cy [ˋmɝsɪ] 名 慈悲	英英 compassion or forgiveness shown towards somebody you have authority over 例 **Mercy** is a kind of virtue. 慈悲是種美德。	□三分熟 □五分熟 □七分熟 □全熟
mere [mɪr] 形 僅僅、不過	英英 something is not large or important 例 Your enthusiasm in reading is not just a **mere** seed in children's heart. 你對閱讀的熱愛，不僅僅只是孩子心中的種子 。	□三分熟 □五分熟 □七分熟 □全熟
mer·it [ˋmɛrɪt] 名 價值	英英 excellence, a good point or quality 例 The **merit** of the encyclopedia is beyond your imagination. 這本百科全書的價值超過你的想像。	□三分熟 □五分熟 □七分熟 □全熟

M

mes·sen·ger

[ˋmɛsn̩dʒɚ]

名 使者、信差

英英 a person who carries or delivers a message from a person to another

例 Hermes in Greek and Roman mythology is a **messenger** god.
在希臘和羅馬神話裡，赫密斯是信差神。

☐ 三分熟
☐ 五分熟
☐ 七分熟
☐ 全熟

---

mess·y [ˋmɛsɪ]

形 髒亂的
同 dirty 髒的

英英 untidy, dirty or not clean

例 Your room is **messy**.
你的房間好髒。

☐ 三分熟
☐ 五分熟
☐ 七分熟
☐ 全熟

---

mi·cro·scope

[ˋmaɪkrəˏskop]

名 顯微鏡

英英 an optical instrument to make small objects look larger in order to magnify them

例 When Robert was doing his scientific study, he liked to use **microscope**.
當羅伯特在做科學研究時，他喜歡用顯微鏡。

☐ 三分熟
☐ 五分熟
☐ 七分熟
☐ 全熟

---

mild [maɪld]

形 溫和的

英英 not violent, severe, or extreme

例 Her tone of talking to the kitty is **mild**.
她對貓咪講話的語調是溫和的。

☐ 三分熟
☐ 五分熟
☐ 七分熟
☐ 全熟

---

min·er·al

[ˋmɪnərəl]

名 礦物

英英 a solid inorganic substance of natural occurrence, which is formed naturally under ground

例 **Minerals** include calcium and iron.
礦物包含鈣和鐵。

☐ 三分熟
☐ 五分熟
☐ 七分熟
☐ 全熟

---

min·i·mum

[ˋmɪnəməm]

名 最小量
形 最小的

英英 the least or smallest amount or size

例 **Minimum** consumption per person is NT$150.
一個人的最低消費是臺幣 150 元。

☐ 三分熟
☐ 五分熟
☐ 七分熟
☐ 全熟

---

min·is·ter

[ˋmɪnɪstɚ]

名 神職者、部長
片 the prime minister
首相

英英 a head or leader in charge of a government department

例 The **minister** led the whole crowd to sing hymn.
神職人員領著全部的群眾唱聖歌。

☐ 三分熟
☐ 五分熟
☐ 七分熟
☐ 全熟

---

min·is·try

[ˋmɪnɪstrɪ]

名 牧師、部長、部

英英 a government department headed by a minister

例 The **ministry** is chatting with a small boy.
牧師正在和一個小男孩在聊天。

☐ 三分熟
☐ 五分熟
☐ 七分熟
☐ 全熟

🎧 **Track 231**

---

mis·chief

[ˈmɪstʃɪf]

名 胡鬧、危害

| 英英 harm or injury caused by someone's bad behavior
| 例 It is the one way to keep my nephew out of **mischief**.
這是唯一可以讓我姪子不再胡鬧的方法。

☐ 三分熟
☐ 五分熟
☐ 七分熟
☐ 全熟

---

mis·er·a·ble

[ˈmɪzərəbl̩]

形 不幸的

| 英英 very unhappy or depressed
| 例 Two children raised in the family are **miserable**.
在這個家庭裡所養大的兩個孩子很不幸。

☐ 三分熟
☐ 五分熟
☐ 七分熟
☐ 全熟

---

mis·for·tune

[mɪsˈfɔrtʃən]

名 不幸

| 英英 bad luck, an unfortunate thing
| 例 You should take him away so as to avoid **misfortune**.
你應該要把他帶走，才能避開不幸。

☐ 三分熟
☐ 五分熟
☐ 七分熟
☐ 全熟

---

mis·lead [mɪsˈlid]

動 誤導

| 英英 to give the wrong impression or direction to
| 例 Stop saying that kind **misleading** gossip.
不要再講那種有誤導性的八卦。

☐ 三分熟
☐ 五分熟
☐ 七分熟
☐ 全熟

---

mis·un·der·stand

[ˌmɪsʌndɚˈstænd]

動 誤解

| 英英 to fail to understand something correctly
| 例 We have **misunderstood** each other.
我們兩個曾經誤解過彼此。

☐ 三分熟
☐ 五分熟
☐ 七分熟
☐ 全熟

---

mod·er·ate

[ˈmɑdərɪt]

形 適度的、溫和的

| 英英 average in amount or degree
| 例 **Moderate** attitude is good for cooperation.
溫和的態度於合作上有益。

☐ 三分熟
☐ 五分熟
☐ 七分熟
☐ 全熟

---

mod·est [ˈmɑdɪst]

形 謙虛的

| 英英 not mentioning your own abilities or achievements all the time
| 例 Professor Liang is **modest**.
梁教授是謙虛的。

☐ 三分熟
☐ 五分熟
☐ 七分熟
☐ 全熟

---

mod·es·ty

[ˈmɑdəstɪ]

名 謙虛、有禮

| 英英 the manner of being modest
| 例 Her fake **modesty** bugs her classmates a lot.
她假裝謙虛的態度，讓她的同學們覺得有點煩。

☐ 三分熟
☐ 五分熟
☐ 七分熟
☐ 全熟

---

mon·i·tor

[`manətɚ]

名 監視器
動 監視

英英 a person or device that monitors a particular thing; to keep an eye on someone or something

例 The **monitor** is on top of your head.
監視器就在你頭上。

□三分熟
□五分熟
□七分熟
□全熟

M

---

month·ly [`mʌnθlɪ]

名 月刊
形 每月一次的

英英 a magazine published once a month; once a month

例 When can we get **monthly** pay?
我們什麼時侯可以拿到月薪？

□三分熟
□五分熟
□七分熟
□全熟

---

mon·u·ment

[`manjəmənt]

名 紀念碑

英英 a statue or structure built to commemorate a person or event

例 The **monument** is set to honor the heroes.
紀念碑是用以紀念英雄的。

□三分熟
□五分熟
□七分熟
□全熟

---

more·o·ver

[mor`ovɚ]

副 並且、此外

英英 also, besides

例 You can paint the stone. **Moreover**, you can't take it home.
你可以畫石頭。並且，你不能把它帶回家。

□三分熟
□五分熟
□七分熟
□全熟

---

most·ly [`mostlɪ]

副 多半、主要地

英英 on the whole, mainly or mostly

例 **Mostly** this is a strange situation.
這多半是一個奇怪的情況。

□三分熟
□五分熟
□七分熟
□全熟

---

mo·ti·vate

[`motə,vet]

動 刺激、激發

英英 to make someone to do something with a motive

例 You can **motivate** students to learn English by teaching them to sing.
你可以藉由教導學生唱歌來激發學生學英文。

□三分熟
□五分熟
□七分熟
□全熟

---

mo·ti·va·tion

[,motə`veʃən]

名 動機

英英 the enthusiasm behind one's actions or behavior

例 His **motivation** for learning English is strange.
他學英文的動機很奇怪。

□三分熟
□五分熟
□七分熟
□全熟

---

moun·tain·ous

[`maʊntən̩s]

形 多山的

英英 having many mountains

例 The town is **mountainous**.
這個城鎮多山。

□三分熟
□五分熟
□七分熟
□全熟

🎧 **Track 233**

mow [mo]
動 收割

英英 to cut down or trim plants with a machine or scythe
例 **Mow** the rice.
收割稻子。

□三分熟 □五分熟 □七分熟 □全熟

mu·sic tel·e·vi·sion /MTV
[ˈmjuzɪk ˈtɛləˌvɪʒən]
名 音樂電視頻道

英英 an organization that broadcasts popular music worldwide
例 The singer is playing the piano in this **MTV**.
歌手在音樂電視頻道彈鋼琴。

□三分熟 □五分熟 □七分熟 □全熟

mud·dy [ˈmʌdɪ]
形 泥濘的

英英 covered with mud
例 The road is **muddy**.
馬路是泥濘的。

□三分熟 □五分熟 □七分熟 □全熟

mul·ti·ple
[ˈmʌltəpl]
形 複數的、多數的

英英 having or involving several different parts or the same elements
例 **Multiple** intelligence were related to different kinds of talents.
多元智慧跟不同的才能有關。

□三分熟 □五分熟 □七分熟 □全熟

mur·der·er
[ˈmɝdərɚ]
名 兇手

英英 a person who commits a crime of killing someone
例 The real **murderer** is still not found.
真正的兇手還沒找到。

□三分熟 □五分熟 □七分熟 □全熟

mur·mur [ˈmɝmɚ]
名 低語
動 細語、抱怨

英英 to speak or say something very quietly
例 Grandpa **murmured** when he was looking for his socks.
當爺爺在找襪子時，他小聲地抱怨。

□三分熟 □五分熟 □七分熟 □全熟

mus·tache
[ˈmʌstæʃ]
名 髭、小鬍子

英英 hair which grows above a man's upper lip
例 His **mustache** makes him look more like a man.
他的髭鬚讓他看起來更像個男人。

□三分熟 □五分熟 □七分熟 □全熟

mu·tu·al [ˈmjutʃʊəl]
形 相互的、共同的

英英 doing the same thing to each other
例 **Mutual** help is necessary.
互助幫忙是應該的。

□三分熟 □五分熟 □七分熟 □全熟

mys·te·ri·ous
[mɪsˈtɪrɪəs]
形 神祕的

英英 very difficult or impossible to understand
例 **Mysterious** creature is hiding in this lake.
神祕生物藏在這座湖裡。

□三分熟 □五分熟 □七分熟 □全熟

Nn

name·ly [ˈnemlɪ]

副 即、就是

英英 that is to say

例 He is a manager; **namely**, a man who manages a department.
他是經理；也就是說他是一個管理一整個部門的人。

☐ 三分熟
☐ 五分熟
☐ 七分熟
☐ 全熟

---

na·tion·al·i·ty

[ˌnæʃənˈælətɪ]

名 國籍、國民

英英 status of belonging to a particular country

例 His **nationality** is America.
他的國籍是在美國。

☐ 三分熟
☐ 五分熟
☐ 七分熟
☐ 全熟

---

near·sight·ed

[ˈnɪrˈsaɪtɪd]

形 近視的

英英 someone who cannot see things clearly when they are far away

例 She is **near-sighted**.
她近視。

☐ 三分熟
☐ 五分熟
☐ 七分熟
☐ 全熟

---

need·y [ˈnidɪ]

形 貧窮的、貧困的
同 poor 貧窮的

英英 very poor, lacking of money

例 He is in a **needy** situation.
他在一個貧窮的狀況。

☐ 三分熟
☐ 五分熟
☐ 七分熟
☐ 全熟

---

ne·glect [nɪˈglɛkt]

名 不注意、不顧
動 疏忽

英英 fail to give care or pay attention to

例 The **neglect** of the keeping of the cellphone costs Victor a sum of money.
疏忽手機的保管，使維克托花了一筆錢。

☐ 三分熟
☐ 五分熟
☐ 七分熟
☐ 全熟

---

ne·go·ti·ate

[nɪˈgoʃɪet]

動 商議、談判

英英 to try to reach an agreement or deal by discussion

例 Grace refused to **negotiate** with her husband.
葛蕾絲拒絕去跟她丈夫商議。

☐ 三分熟
☐ 五分熟
☐ 七分熟
☐ 全熟

---

nev·er·the·less /none·the·less

[ˌnɛvəðəˈlɛs]/[ˌnʌnðəˈlɛs]

副 儘管如此、然而

英英 in spite of that

例 Tina wants to visit her aunt **nevertheless**.
儘管如此，蒂娜想要去拜訪她的阿姨。

☐ 三分熟
☐ 五分熟
☐ 七分熟
☐ 全熟

---

night·mare

[ˈnaɪtˌmɛr]

名 惡夢、夢魘

英英 a very frightening or unpleasant dream

例 My **nightmare** I dreamed of is lots of zombies approaching me.
我的惡夢是夢見很多的喪屍接近我。

☐ 三分熟
☐ 五分熟
☐ 七分熟
☐ 全熟

🎧 **Track 235**

---

non·sense

[ˈnɑnsɛns]

名 廢話、無意義的話

英英 words that make no sense at all

例 What my father said is **nonsense** to me.
我爸說的根本是廢話。

☐ 三分熟
☐ 五分熟
☐ 七分熟
☐ 全熟

---

noun [naʊn]

名 名詞

英英 a word that can serve as the subject or object of a verb

例 "Cats" and "hats" are **nouns**.
"Cats" 和 "hats" 都是名詞。

☐ 三分熟
☐ 五分熟
☐ 七分熟
☐ 全熟

---

now·a·days

[ˈnaʊəˌdez]

副 當今、現在

英英 at the present time

例 **Nowadays**, he becomes a psychologist.
現在他變成了心理醫師。

☐ 三分熟
☐ 五分熟
☐ 七分熟
☐ 全熟

---

nu·cle·ar [ˈnjuklɪɚ]

形 核子的

英英 using power released in the fission or fusion of atomic nuclei

例 **Nuclear** weapons should be forbidden.
核子武器應該要被禁止。

☐ 三分熟
☐ 五分熟
☐ 七分熟
☐ 全熟

---

nu·mer·ous

[ˈnjumərəs]

形 為數眾多的

英英 consisting of many members; many

例 There are **numerous** stars in the night sky.
在夜空中有為數眾多的星星。

☐ 三分熟
☐ 五分熟
☐ 七分熟
☐ 全熟

---

nurs·er·y [ˈnɝsərɪ]

名 托兒所

英英 a room in a house for the special care of young children; day care house or school

例 Pick up your son at the **nursery** at 5 o'clock.
5 點去托兒所接你的兒子。

☐ 三分熟
☐ 五分熟
☐ 七分熟
☐ 全熟

---

ny·lon [ˈnaɪlɑn]

名 尼龍

英英 a tough, lightweight substance with a protein-like chemical structure, usually used to make clothes

例 I used the **nylon** rope to tie the box.
我用尼龍繩去綁箱子。

☐ 三分熟
☐ 五分熟
☐ 七分熟
☐ 全熟

Oo

o·be·di·ence

[ə`bidjəns]

名 服從、遵從

英英 when people do what they are asked to do

例 **Obedience** is what you do.
你要做的就是服從。

□三分熟
□五分熟
□七分熟
□全熟

o·be·di·ent

[ə`bidɪənt]

形 服從的

英英 willing to obey an order from someone

例 The lad is **obedient**.
這個少年是服從的。

□三分熟
□五分熟
□七分熟
□全熟

ob·jec·tion

[əb`dʒɛkʃən]

名 反對

英英 an expression of disapproval or opposition

例 Joan's mother's **objection** to apply for the job troubled her.
喬安的母親反對她應徵這個工作，帶給她很大的困擾。

□三分熟
□五分熟
□七分熟
□全熟

ob·jec·tive

[əb`dʒɛktɪv]

形 實體的、客觀的
名 目標
同 neutral 中立的
　 goal 目標

英英 a goal that you plan to achieve; based on real facts and not influenced by someone's opinions or feelings

例 My father is not an **objective** person.
我爸不是客觀的人。

□三分熟
□五分熟
□七分熟
□全熟

ob·ser·va·tion

[ˌɑbzɝˈveʃən]

名 觀察力

英英 the action or process of carefully observing or monitoring

例 You should know when to exercise your **observation**.
你應該知道何時運用你的觀察力。

□三分熟
□五分熟
□七分熟
□全熟

ob·sta·cle

[`ɑbstəkl̩]

名 阻礙物、妨礙

英英 a thing that blocks in the middle of someone's way

例 The **obstacle** is just before you.
障礙物就放在你前方。

□三分熟
□五分熟
□七分熟
□全熟

ob·tain [əb`ten]

動 獲得

英英 to get something or come into possession of

例 To **obtain** the university diploma takes 1 year at least.
要取得大學文憑，至少需要一年。

□三分熟
□五分熟
□七分熟
□全熟

Track 237

oc·ca·sion·al

[əˋkeʒənl]

形 應景的、偶爾的

英英 occurring not often or irregularly

例 **Occasional** invitations are acceptable.
偶爾的邀請是合理的。

□ 三分熟
□ 五分熟
□ 七分熟
□ 全熟

---

oc·cu·pa·tion

[ˌɑkjəˋpeʃən]

名 職業

英英 a job or profession

例 An **occupation** is a job you choose to do.
職業是一份你選擇要做的工作。

□ 三分熟
□ 五分熟
□ 七分熟
□ 全熟

---

oc·cu·py

[ˋɑkjəˌpaɪ]

動 佔有、花費（時間）

英英 to have one's place or period of time

例 Excuse me, I'd like to **occupy** some of your time.
不好意思，我可以佔用一些你的時間嗎？

□ 三分熟
□ 五分熟
□ 七分熟
□ 全熟

---

of·fend [əˋfɛnd]

動 使不愉快、使憤怒、冒犯

英英 to cause to feel hurt or unpleasant

例 When you **offend** people, you need to say sorry.
當你冒犯人們時，你必須說抱歉。

□ 三分熟
□ 五分熟
□ 七分熟
□ 全熟

---

of·fense [əˋfɛns]

名 冒犯、進攻

英英 act or cause of upsetting or annoying sb.; insult

例 Tony's rude remarks are considered as an **offense**.
湯尼粗魯的言論被視為是種冒犯。

□ 三分熟
□ 五分熟
□ 七分熟
□ 全熟

---

of·fen·sive

[əˋfɛnsɪv]

形 令人不快的

英英 causing offence; involved in active attack

例 My cousin's remarks were **offensive**.
我表弟的言談是令人不快的。

□ 三分熟
□ 五分熟
□ 七分熟
□ 全熟

---

op·er·a [ˋɑpərə]

名 歌劇
片 opera glasses
觀劇鏡

英英 a dramatic play set to music for singers and instrumentalists

例 One of the most famous **operas** in the world is Puccini's Turandot.
世界最有名的歌劇之一是普契尼的《杜蘭朵公主》。

□ 三分熟
□ 五分熟
□ 七分熟
□ 全熟

---

op·er·a·tion

[ˌɑpəˋreʃən]

名 作用、操作

英英 the process of operating

例 This air conditioning system is in **operation**.
空調系統作用中。

□ 三分熟
□ 五分熟
□ 七分熟
□ 全熟

op·pose [əˋpoz]

動 和……起衝突、反對
反 agree 同意

英英 to disapprove of, resist; to fight against

例 Len **opposes** with his neighbor.
萊恩跟他的鄰居起衝突。

☐ 三分熟
☐ 五分熟
☐ 七分熟
☐ 全熟

o·ral [ˋorəl]

名 口試
形 口述的

英英 a spoken examination; using speech not writing

例 The **oral** test is in tomorrow morning.
口試在明天早上。

☐ 三分熟
☐ 五分熟
☐ 七分熟
☐ 全熟

orbit [ˋɔrbɪt]

名 軌道
動 把……放入軌道

英英 the path through which things in space move around a planet or star; to follow the path around a planet

例 The spaceship goes into **orbit** around Earth.
太空船進入環繞地球的軌道。

☐ 三分熟
☐ 五分熟
☐ 七分熟
☐ 全熟

or·ches·tra

[ˋɔrkɪstrə]

名 樂隊、樂團

英英 a group of musicians with string, woodwind, brass, and percussion sections

例 The **orchestra** is playing hard.
樂團很認真的在彈奏樂器。

☐ 三分熟
☐ 五分熟
☐ 七分熟
☐ 全熟

or·gan·ic

[ɔrˋgænɪk]

形 器官的、有機的

英英 relating to the living matter

例 The **organic** food is the food cultivated in specific ways.
有機食物是用特定方法所培養出來的食物。

☐ 三分熟
☐ 五分熟
☐ 七分熟
☐ 全熟

oth·er·wise

[ˋʌðɚˏwaɪz]

副 否則、要不然

英英 used to refer that result that you will get if you don't accept the advice or suggestion

例 You'd better leave now; **otherwise**, I'll call the guard.
你最好現在離開,要不然,我就會叫警衛。

☐ 三分熟
☐ 五分熟
☐ 七分熟
☐ 全熟

out·come

[ˋaʊtˏkʌm]

名 結果、成果
同 result 結果

英英 a consequence, a result

例 The **outcome** was that nobody won Jenny as a bride.
結果就是沒有人贏得珍妮做為新娘。

☐ 三分熟
☐ 五分熟
☐ 七分熟
☐ 全熟

out·stand·ing

[ˋaʊtˋstændɪŋ]

形 傲人的、傑出的

英英 excellent; clear noticeable

例 My elder brother's **outstanding** performance amazed my parents.
我大哥傑出的表現,使我的父母感到驚訝。

☐ 三分熟
☐ 五分熟
☐ 七分熟
☐ 全熟

O

Track 239

---

o·val [`ovl]

名 橢圓形
形 橢圓形的

英英 an oval thing or design

例 The **oval** cake looks like an egg.
這個橢圓形的蛋糕看起來就像一顆蛋。

☐ 三分熟
☐ 五分熟
☐ 七分熟
☐ 全熟

---

o·ver·come

[ˌovəˈkʌm]

動 擊敗、克服

英英 to defeat or succeed in dealing with a problem

例 **Overcome** the difficulty with all you can do.
盡你所能克服困難。

☐ 三分熟
☐ 五分熟
☐ 七分熟
☐ 全熟

---

o·ver·look

[ˌovəˈluk]

動 俯瞰、忽略

英英 fail to notice; to ignore something

例 The tower **overlooked** the snowy mountain.
這座塔俯瞰白雪覆蓋的山。

☐ 三分熟
☐ 五分熟
☐ 七分熟
☐ 全熟

---

o·ver·night

[`ovəˈnaɪt]

形 徹夜的、過夜的
副 整夜地
片 stay overnight 過夜

英英 for the duration of a night

例 The soldiers stand on the post **overnight**.
士兵徹夜站崗。

☐ 三分熟
☐ 五分熟
☐ 七分熟
☐ 全熟

---

o·ver·take

[ˌovəˈtek]

動 趕上、突擊

英英 to catch up with and pass while going or walking in the same direction

例 Remember to check the mirror before you **overtake**.
超車前記得要檢查一下鏡子。

☐ 三分熟
☐ 五分熟
☐ 七分熟
☐ 全熟

---

o·ver·throw

[ˌovəˈθro]

動 推翻、瓦解

英英 to remove forcibly from power or put an end to through force

例 The cruel emperor was **overthrown**.
那個殘酷的君王被推翻了。

☐ 三分熟
☐ 五分熟
☐ 七分熟
☐ 全熟

---

ox·y·gen

[`ɑksədʒən]

名 氧（氧氣）

英英 a colorless gaseous chemical element, forming large part of the earth's atmosphere and essential to life

例 People need **oxygen** to survive.
人們需要氧氣才能存活。

☐ 三分熟
☐ 五分熟
☐ 七分熟
☐ 全熟

Pp

pa·ce [pes]

名 一步、步調
動 踱步

英英 a single step taken by a person while walking or running; to walk with regular steps in the same direction and then back again

例 His **pace** is a bit slow.
他的步調有點慢。

☐ 三分熟
☐ 五分熟
☐ 七分熟
☐ 全熟

---

pan·el [ˋpænḷ]

名 方格、平板

英英 a distinct, usually rectangular section of a door, that fits into something larger

例 Look at the design of the glass **panels** of the door.
看看那扇門的玻璃方格設計吧。

☐ 三分熟
☐ 五分熟
☐ 七分熟
☐ 全熟

---

par·a·chute

[ˋpærəʃut]

名 降落傘
動 空投

英英 a piece of equipment made of a large piece of special cloth which allows a person or heavy object attached to it to descend slowly when dropped from a high position or in the sky; to drop something or someone from sky

例 Use the **parachute** when you're in danger.
在你有危險時，使用這個降落傘。

☐ 三分熟
☐ 五分熟
☐ 七分熟
☐ 全熟

---

par·a·graph

[ˋpærəˌgræf]

名 段落

英英 a distinct part of writing or text, beginning on a new line

例 Write three **paragraphs** at least for the essay.
為這篇作文寫至少三個段落。

☐ 三分熟
☐ 五分熟
☐ 七分熟
☐ 全熟

---

par·tial [ˋpɑrʃəl]

形 部分的

英英 existing only in part or incomplete, not whole

例 **Partial** food is wasted.
部分的食物浪費掉了。

☐ 三分熟
☐ 五分熟
☐ 七分熟
☐ 全熟

---

par·tic·i·pa·tion

[pɑrˌtɪsəˋpeʃən]

名 參加

英英 to take part or become involved in something

例 Your **participation** would be much appreciated.
我們將非常感謝您的加入。

☐ 三分熟
☐ 五分熟
☐ 七分熟
☐ 全熟

---

par·ti·ci·ple

[ˋpɑrtəsəpḷ]

名 分詞

英英 a word formed from a verb and used as an adjective or noun or used to make compound verb forms

例 The **participle** of "win" is "winning."
"win" 的分詞是 "winning"。

☐ 三分熟
☐ 五分熟
☐ 七分熟
☐ 全熟

🎧 **Track 241**

part·ner·ship

[`partnɚˌʃɪp]

名 合夥

英英 the state of being a partner or partners

例 My father had been in a **partnership** with my uncle for five years.
我父親跟我舅舅有五年的合夥關係。

□三分熟
□五分熟
□七分熟
□全熟

---

pas·sive [`pæsɪv]

形 被動的

英英 accepting or allowing what happens or what others do, without active response

例 Most students are **passive** learners in Mr. Lee's class.
在李老師的班上，多數學生都是被動的學習者。

□三分熟
□五分熟
□七分熟
□全熟

---

pas·ta [`pɑstə]

名 麵團、義大利麵

英英 dough made into various shapes, which cooked as part of a dish or in boiling water and served with a savory sauce

例 **Pasta** has many types.
義大利麵有很多種。

□三分熟
□五分熟
□七分熟
□全熟

---

peb·ble [`pɛbl̩]

名 小圓石

英英 a small stone made smooth and round by the action of water or sand

例 The road to the park is paved with **pebbles**.
通往公園的路是用小圓石鋪成的。

□三分熟
□五分熟
□七分熟
□全熟

---

pe·cu·liar [pɪ`kjuljɚ]

形 獨特的
同 special 特別的

英英 being exclusive

例 How **peculiar** the stinky tofu is!
臭豆腐是多麼的獨特啊！

□三分熟
□五分熟
□七分熟
□全熟

---

ped·al [`pɛdl̩]

名 踏板
動 踩踏板

英英 an object which is used for operating a machine or making a movement while pushing down with the food; to ride a bicycle

例 My childhood bicycle with **pedals** was no longer there.
我童年時代有踏板的腳踏車，已經不在那裡了。

□三分熟
□五分熟
□七分熟
□全熟

---

peer [pɪr]

名 同輩
動 凝視

英英 a person who is the same age or has the same social position in a group; to look intently

例 Most of the **peers** of my son were taller than him.
我兒子大部分的同輩都比他高。

□三分熟
□五分熟
□七分熟
□全熟

pen·al·ty [ˈpɛnl̩tɪ]

名 懲罰

片 maximum penalty
最高懲罰

英英 a punishment imposed for breaking a law, rule, or contract

例 The **penalty** for throwing the trash near the river is severe.
在河邊附近亂丟垃圾的懲罰是很嚴重的。

☐ 三分熟 ☐ 五分熟 ☐ 七分熟 ☐ 全熟

per·cent [pɚˈsɛnt]

名 百分比

英英 for or out of every 100, shown by the symbol %

例 20 **percent** of the travelers came from Taiwan.
有百分之二十的旅客來自臺灣。

☐ 三分熟 ☐ 五分熟 ☐ 七分熟 ☐ 全熟

per·cent·age
[pɚˈsɛntɪdʒ]

名 百分率

英英 an amount of something, often expressed as a number out of 100

例 Mark the pie chart with **percentages**.
用百分率來標示圓餅圖。

☐ 三分熟 ☐ 五分熟 ☐ 七分熟 ☐ 全熟

per·fec·tion
[pɚˈfɛkʃən]

名 完美

英英 the excellence or the process of perfecting

例 The design of the statue is near **perfection**.
這座雕像的設計近乎完美。

☐ 三分熟 ☐ 五分熟 ☐ 七分熟 ☐ 全熟

per·fume [ˈpɝfjum]

名 香水、賦予香味

英英 a fragrant liquid which is used to give a pleasant smell to one's body; to fill with a pleasant smell

例 The jasmine **perfume** is my mother's favorite.
這瓶茉莉香水是我媽媽的最愛。

☐ 三分熟 ☐ 五分熟 ☐ 七分熟 ☐ 全熟

per·ma·nent
[ˈpɝmənənt]

形 永久的

英英 lasting for long time; not temporary; forever

例 The painting left a **permanent** impression on me.
這幅畫作讓我留下永久的印象。

☐ 三分熟 ☐ 五分熟 ☐ 七分熟 ☐ 全熟

per·sua·sion
[pɚˈsweʒən]

名 說服

英英 the process of persuading someone to do something

例 The ad is not of much **persuasion**.
這則廣告不太有說服力。

☐ 三分熟 ☐ 五分熟 ☐ 七分熟 ☐ 全熟

per·sua·sive
[pɚˈswesɪv]

形 有說服力的

英英 good at persuading someone to do or believe something

例 **Persuasive** essay includes strong arguments.
有說服力的作文包含強而有力的論點。

☐ 三分熟 ☐ 五分熟 ☐ 七分熟 ☐ 全熟

🎧 **Track 243**

pes·si·mis·tic

[ˌpɛsəˈmɪstɪk]

形 悲觀的

反 optimistic 樂觀的

英英 thinking that bad things are more likely to happen always

例 If you're suffering, you have no right to be **pessimistic**.
如果你正在受苦，你沒有悲觀的權利。

☐ 三分熟
☐ 五分熟
☐ 七分熟
☐ 全熟

---

pet·al [ˈpɛtl̩]

名 花瓣

英英 the brightly colored parts of a flower

例 The **petals** of the orchid look like a butterfly.
蘭花的花瓣看起來像隻蝴蝶。

☐ 三分熟
☐ 五分熟
☐ 七分熟
☐ 全熟

---

phe·nom·e·non

[fəˈnaməˌnan]

名 現象

英英 a fact or situation that is existing and can be seen, felt or tasted, usually something unusual

例 Spiritual **phenomenon** occurred in this haunted house.
在這棟鬼屋裡發生過靈異現象。

☐ 三分熟
☐ 五分熟
☐ 七分熟
☐ 全熟

---

phi·los·o·pher

[fəˈlasəfɚ]

名 哲學家

英英 a person who studies about the meaning of life

例 Nietzsche is one of my favorite **philosophers**.
尼采是我最喜歡的哲學家之一。

☐ 三分熟
☐ 五分熟
☐ 七分熟
☐ 全熟

---

phil·o·soph·i·cal

[ˌfɪləˈsafɪkl̩]

形 哲學的

英英 relating to the study of philosophy

例 To be or not to be is a **philosophical** question.
生存還是毀滅，是哲學問題。

☐ 三分熟
☐ 五分熟
☐ 七分熟
☐ 全熟

---

phi·los·o·phy

[fəˈlasəfɪ]

名 哲學

英英 the study about the meaning of nature, university or life

例 Carpe diem is Frank's life **philosophy**.
及時行樂是法蘭克的人生哲學。

☐ 三分熟
☐ 五分熟
☐ 七分熟
☐ 全熟

---

pho·tog·ra·phy

[fəˈtagrəfɪ]

名 攝影學

英英 the study of photographs

例 I'm interested in **photography**.
我對攝影學有興趣。

☐ 三分熟
☐ 五分熟
☐ 七分熟
☐ 全熟

---

phys·i·cal [ˈfɪzɪkl̩]

形 身體的

英英 relating to the body

例 **Physical** education should be deemed as an important subject.
體育應被視為重要的科目。

☐ 三分熟
☐ 五分熟
☐ 七分熟
☐ 全熟

phy·si·cian/ doc·tor

[fə`zɪʃən]/[`dɑktɚ]

名 （內科）醫師

英英 a person qualified to practice medicine

例 The **physician** examined my heart.
醫師檢查我的心臟。

☐ 三分熟
☐ 五分熟
☐ 七分熟
☐ 全熟

---

phys·i·cist

[`fɪzɪsɪst]

名 物理學家

英英 a person who studies physics or work relating to physics

例 Stephen Hawking is one of the greatest English **physicists**.
史蒂芬・霍金是最偉大的英國物理學家之一。

☐ 三分熟
☐ 五分熟
☐ 七分熟
☐ 全熟

---

phys·ics [`fɪzɪks]

名 物理學

英英 the study concerned with the nature and properties of matter and energy

例 **Physics** is related to studying matter and energy.
物理學與研究物質和能量有關。

☐ 三分熟
☐ 五分熟
☐ 七分熟
☐ 全熟

---

pi·an·ist [pɪ`ænɪst]

名 鋼琴師

英英 someone who plays the piano

例 The **pianist** falls in love with a poet.
鋼琴師愛上了詩人。

☐ 三分熟
☐ 五分熟
☐ 七分熟
☐ 全熟

---

pick·poc·ket

[`pɪk‚pɑkɪt]

名 扒手

英英 a thief who steals from people's pockets

例 Poor children were trained to be **pickpockets**.
貧窮的孩子被訓練成扒手。

☐ 三分熟
☐ 五分熟
☐ 七分熟
☐ 全熟

---

pi·o·neer

[‚paɪə`nɪr]

名 先鋒、開拓者
動 開拓

英英 a person who explores or settles in a new region or place; to prepare a way

例 Frank Drake is one of the **pioneers** in the field of searching aliens.
法蘭克・德雷克在尋找外星人這個領域上是個先鋒。

☐ 三分熟
☐ 五分熟
☐ 七分熟
☐ 全熟

---

pi·rate [`paɪrət]

名 海盜
動 掠奪

英英 a person who attacks other people and robs ships at sea; to practice robbery while sailing in the sea

例 **Pirates** love treasures.
海盜喜愛寶藏。

☐ 三分熟
☐ 五分熟
☐ 七分熟
☐ 全熟

---

plen·ti·ful

[`plɛntɪfəl]

形 豐富的、充足的

英英 existing in or great quantities, sufficient

例 There is a **plentiful** supply of games to play with these children.
有足夠的遊戲可以跟這些孩子玩。

☐ 三分熟
☐ 五分熟
☐ 七分熟
☐ 全熟

P

🎧Track 245

plot [plɑt]

名 陰謀、情節
動 圖謀、分成小塊

英英 a secret plan to do something bad; to plan or scheme; to make something into small pieces

例 The **plot** of three trials is quite common in fairy tales.
在童話裡三次試驗的情節是很普遍的。

☐三分熟
☐五分熟
☐七分熟
☐全熟

---

plu·ral [ˋplʊrəl]

名 複數
形 複數的

英英 a word or form which expresses more than one

例 "Glasses" is the **plural** of "glass."
"Glasses" 是 "glass" 的複數形。

☐三分熟
☐五分熟
☐七分熟
☐全熟

---

p.m./P.M. [ˋpiˏɛm]

副 下午

英英 after noon

例 I'll meet you in Harry Potter café at 3 **p.m.**
下午 3 點哈利波特咖啡店見。

☐三分熟
☐五分熟
☐七分熟
☐全熟

---

poi·son·ous
[ˋpɔɪzəs]

形 有毒的

英英 harmful and able to cause illness or death

例 These mushrooms are **poisonous**.
這些香菇有毒。

☐三分熟
☐五分熟
☐七分熟
☐全熟

---

pol·ish [ˋpɑlɪʃ]

名 磨光
動 擦亮

英英 to rob something with brush or a piece of cloth to make it shine and become clean

例 These shoes are **polished**.
這些皮鞋擦得發亮。

☐三分熟
☐五分熟
☐七分熟
☐全熟

---

pol·lu·tion [ˋpɑlɪʃ]

名 污染

英英 damage caused to water or air by harmful substances or waste

例 Air **pollution** is getting more and more serious in Taipei.
臺北的空氣污染愈來愈嚴重。

☐三分熟
☐五分熟
☐七分熟
☐全熟

---

pop·u·lar·i·ty
[ˏpɑpjəˋlærətɪ]

名 名望、流行

英英 something is liked, enjoyed or supported by many people

例 **Popularity** is like a puff of smoke.
流行就像一陣煙。

☐三分熟
☐五分熟
☐七分熟
☐全熟

---

port·a·ble
[ˋpɔrtəbḷ]

形 可攜帶的

英英 able to be carried or moved easily

例 This website sells eco-friendly **portable** cup bag.
這個網站販賣對環境友善的可攜帶式杯袋。

☐三分熟
☐五分熟
☐七分熟
☐全熟

por·ter [`portə]

名 搬運工

英英 a person whose work is to carry luggage and other loads

例 The **porters** will come to move these boxes.
搬運工會來搬這些箱子。

□ 三分熟
□ 五分熟
□ 七分熟
□ 全熟

P

---

por·tray [por`tre]

動 描繪
同 depict 描繪

英英 to describe in a particular way

例 The lake is **portrayed** as beautiful as fairy's bathing pool.
這座湖被描繪美得就像仙女的浴池。

□ 三分熟
□ 五分熟
□ 七分熟
□ 全熟

---

pos·sess [pə`zɛs]

動 擁有

英英 to have as property; own something

例 The little boy **possesses** the ability to remember his past life.
這個小男孩擁有記得前世的能力。

□ 三分熟
□ 五分熟
□ 七分熟
□ 全熟

---

pos·ses·sion
[pə`zɛʃən]

名 擁有物

英英 the things or objects that you own

例 Love should not be **possession**, but admiration.
愛不應當成擁有物，而是當成仰幕。

□ 三分熟
□ 五分熟
□ 七分熟
□ 全熟

---

pre·cise [prɪ`saɪs]

形 明確的、準確的
同 exact 確切的

英英 very attentive to detail; very clear

例 At that **precise** moment of sinking, a hand grabbed me and pulled me up.
在往下沉的那一刻，有隻手抓住了我，把我往上拉。

□ 三分熟
□ 五分熟
□ 七分熟
□ 全熟

---

pre·dict [prɪ`dɪkt]

動 預測

英英 to state that something will happen in the future

例 My advisor's mood is hard to **predict**.
我的指導教授的心情難以預測。

□ 三分熟
□ 五分熟
□ 七分熟
□ 全熟

---

pref·er·a·ble
[`prɛfərəl]

形 較好的

英英 more suitable or better

例 Between juice and coffee, my **preferable** choice would be juice.
在果汁和咖啡之間，我比較喜愛的選擇會是果汁。

□ 三分熟
□ 五分熟
□ 七分熟
□ 全熟

---

preg·nan·cy
[`prɛgnənsɪ]

名 懷孕

英英 the condition of being pregnant

例 Don't ask her to carry heavy bags as she is in the stage of **pregnancy**.
不要叫她提很重的袋子，因為她懷孕了。

□ 三分熟
□ 五分熟
□ 七分熟
□ 全熟

🎧 Track 247

preg·nant

[`prɛgnənt]

形 懷孕的

英英 of a woman or female animal having a baby or young developing in the uterus

例 Being **pregnant** is a good news.
懷孕是件好消息。

☐ 三分熟
☐ 五分熟
☐ 七分熟
☐ 全熟

prep·o·si·tion

[ˌprɛpəˋzɪʃən]

名 介系詞

英英 a word that indicates the relationship between a noun or pronoun and other words in a sentence

例 "Of" is one of most commonly used **prepositions**.
"Of" 是最為常用的介系詞之一。

☐ 三分熟
☐ 五分熟
☐ 七分熟
☐ 全熟

pre·sen·ta·tion

[ˌprɛznˋteʃən]

名 贈送、呈現
片 oral presentation
　口語報告

英英 the action of showing something to someone

例 Lily's **presentation** of the book talk is wonderful.
莉莉介紹書的口語表現很精彩。

☐ 三分熟
☐ 五分熟
☐ 七分熟
☐ 全熟

pres·er·va·tion

[ˌprɛzɚˋveʃən]

名 保存

英英 the action of preserving; the state of being preserved, especially to a specified degree

例 Aunt Polly would love to handle fruit **preservation** for us.
波麗姑媽會很樂意幫我們處理水果保存的事。

☐ 三分熟
☐ 五分熟
☐ 七分熟
☐ 全熟

pre·serve

[prɪˋzɝv]

動 保存、維護

英英 to maintain its original state; keep safe from damage or injury

例 The body of an Egyptian is **preserved** well in the laboratory.
實驗室裡的那個埃及人的大體保存良好。

☐ 三分熟
☐ 五分熟
☐ 七分熟
☐ 全熟

pre·ven·tion

[prɪˋvɛnʃən]

名 預防

英英 keep from happening or stop someone from doing something bad

例 **Prevention** of crime is what we can do.
防止犯罪是我們所能做的。

☐ 三分熟
☐ 五分熟
☐ 七分熟
☐ 全熟

prime [praɪm]

名 初期
形 首要的
同 principal 首要的

英英 more important; the beginning

例 The **prime** task to do is to get the code.
首要要做的事是取得密碼。

☐ 三分熟
☐ 五分熟
☐ 七分熟
☐ 全熟

prim·i·tive

[ˈprɪmətɪv]

形 原始的
同 original 原始的

英英 connecting with the earliest times in history or stages in development

例 Drinking blood is pretty **primitive** behavior.
喝血是原始的行為。

☐ 三分熟
☐ 五分熟
☐ 七分熟
☐ 全熟

---

pri·va·cy

[ˈpraɪvəsɪ]

名 隱私

英英 something's right to keep their personal matters secret

例 Don't look at my diary; it's my **privacy**.
不要看我的日記；這是我的隱私。

☐ 三分熟
☐ 五分熟
☐ 七分熟
☐ 全熟

---

priv·i·lege

[ˈprɪvlɪdʒ]

名 特權
動 優待

英英 a special right or advantage for a particular person or group; to give an advantage to a particular person

例 Who gave you the **privilege** to be late to the classroom?
誰給你特權晚進教室的？

☐ 三分熟
☐ 五分熟
☐ 七分熟
☐ 全熟

---

pro·ce·dure

[prəˈsidʒɚ]

名 手續、程序

英英 an official way of doing something or managing something

例 To fill out the form is a part of the **procedure**.
填寫表格是手續的一部分。

☐ 三分熟
☐ 五分熟
☐ 七分熟
☐ 全熟

---

pro·ceed [prəˈsid]

動 進行

英英 to go on to do something, take an action to do something

例 You have my permission; you may **proceed**.
你有我的允許；可以去進行了。

☐ 三分熟
☐ 五分熟
☐ 七分熟
☐ 全熟

---

pro·duc·tion

[prəˈdʌkʃən]

名 製造

英英 the action of producing goods or the process of being produced

例 The over **production** of the computers resulted in the low price competition.
電腦的過度製造，造成了低價競爭。

☐ 三分熟
☐ 五分熟
☐ 七分熟
☐ 全熟

---

pro·duc·tive

[prəˈdʌktɪv]

形 生產的、多產的

英英 producing or able to produce large amounts of goods

例 Office workers are expected to be **productive**.
辦公室職員被期待要有生產力。

☐ 三分熟
☐ 五分熟
☐ 七分熟
☐ 全熟

P

🎧 Track 249

pro·fes·sion

[prəˈfɛʃən]

名 專業

英英 with special or particular skills, knowledge or experience

例 What's your **profession**?
你的專業是什麼？

☐ 三分熟
☐ 五分熟
☐ 七分熟
☐ 全熟

pro·fes·sion·al

[prəˈfɛʃən!]

名 專家
形 專業的

英英 a person having particular skills, knowledge or experience in a particular field; describe someone very knowledgeable and skilled in a certain field

例 If you can't fix my car, then you're not very **professional**.
如果你不能修好我的車，那麼你不能說是非常專業。

☐ 三分熟
☐ 五分熟
☐ 七分熟
☐ 全熟

pro·fes·sor

[prəˈfɛsɚ]

名 教授

英英 a teacher teaches in a university

例 **Professors** are usually busy with their researching work.
教授通常都在忙自己的研究工作。

☐ 三分熟
☐ 五分熟
☐ 七分熟
☐ 全熟

prof·it·a·ble

[ˈprɑfɪtəb!]

形 有利的
同 beneficial 有利的

英英 of a business or activity resulting in a profit or an advantage

例 Are you sure selling fruits is a **profitable** business?
你確定賣水果是有利可圖的生意？

☐ 三分熟
☐ 五分熟
☐ 七分熟
☐ 全熟

prom·i·nent

[ˈprɑmənənt]

形 突出的

英英 important, famous or particularly noticeable

例 The French male tennis player became a **prominent** tennis player.
法國男網球選手成為著名的網球選手。

☐ 三分熟
☐ 五分熟
☐ 七分熟
☐ 全熟

prom·is·ing

[ˈprɑmɪsɪŋ]

形 有可能的、有希望的

英英 having great potential or possibilities

例 To win the baseball game this year seems to be quite **promising**.
要贏得今年的棒球比賽似乎是有可能的。

☐ 三分熟
☐ 五分熟
☐ 七分熟
☐ 全熟

pro·mo·tion

[prəˈmoʃən]

名 增進、促銷、升遷

英英 action of raising someone to higher or more important position

例 Dorothy's **promotion** angered her co-worker, Susan.
桃樂絲的升遷激怒了她的同事，蘇珊。

☐ 三分熟
☐ 五分熟
☐ 七分熟
☐ 全熟

prompt [prɑmpt]

形 即時的
名 提詞

英英 acting very quickly or instantly; words which are spoken to an actor or an actress who has forgotten what he or she is going to say during a play

例 Your **prompt** reply will be much appreciated.
我們將會非常感激您快速的回覆。

☐ 三分熟
☐ 五分熟
☐ 七分熟
☐ 全熟

pro·noun

[ˋpronaʊn]

名 代名詞

英英 a word used instead of a noun to indicate someone or something mentioned before

例 "It" is a **pronoun**.
"It" 是代名詞。

☐三分熟
☐五分熟
☐七分熟
☐全熟

---

pro·nun·ci·a·tion

[prəˌnʌnsɪˋeʃən]

名 發音

英英 the way a word is pronounced

例 Jennifer's **pronunciation** is good.
珍妮佛的發音很好。

☐三分熟
☐五分熟
☐七分熟
☐全熟

---

pros·per [ˋprɑspɚ]

動 興盛

英英 someone or something becomes successful or flourishing

例 Wish your business **prosper**.
祝願您的生意興旺。

☐三分熟
☐五分熟
☐七分熟
☐全熟

---

pros·per·i·ty

[prɑsˋpɛrətɪ]

名 繁盛

英英 the state of being successful or flourishing

例 We wish you **prosperity** and success in the coming new year.
我們祝願您新的一年繁盛成功。

☐三分熟
☐五分熟
☐七分熟
☐全熟

---

pros·per·ous

[ˋprɑspərəs]

形 繁榮的

英英 very successful or flourishing

例 The ancient city in the desert was **prosperous** before.
沙漠中的古城以前曾是繁榮的。

☐三分熟
☐五分熟
☐七分熟
☐全熟

---

pro·tein [ˋprotiɪn]

名 蛋白質

英英 one of the many substances found in food such as meat, fish or eggs, that is necessary for the body to grow

例 If you don't like to eat meat, you could try to obtain **protein** from beans.
如果你不喜歡吃肉，可以試著從豆子裡得到蛋白質。

☐三分熟
☐五分熟
☐七分熟
☐全熟

---

pro·test [prəˋtɛst]

名 抗議
動 反對、抗議

英英 an action of expressing disapproval or an action of fighting against

例 People need courage and good strategies to **protest** against injustice.
人民需要勇氣和好的策略抗議不公不義。

☐三分熟
☐五分熟
☐七分熟
☐全熟

---

prov·erb [ˋprɑvɝb]

名 諺語

英英 a short old saying stating a general truth or piece of advice

例 A famous English **proverb** goes like this, "A picture is worth a thousand words."
有個著名的英國諺語是這樣說的：「一張照片勝千言。」

☐三分熟
☐五分熟
☐七分熟
☐全熟

P

🎧 **Track 251**

psy·cho·log·i·cal

[ˌsaɪkəˈlɑdʒɪkl̩]

形 心理學的

英英 relating to psychology

例 Playing tennis is like playing a **psychological** game.
打網球就像玩一場心理學遊戲。

□三分熟
□五分熟
□七分熟
□全熟

---

psy·chol·o·gist

[saɪˈkɑlədʒɪst]

名 心理學家

英英 a person who is an expert in the field of the scientific study of the human mind and its functions

例 Carl Jung is a well-known Swiss **psychologist**.
卡爾·榮格是有名的瑞士心理學家。

□三分熟
□五分熟
□七分熟
□全熟

---

psy·chol·o·gy

[saɪˈkɑlədʒɪ]

名 心理學

英英 the scientific study of the human mind and its functions

例 Carl Jung was the founder of analytic **psychology**.
卡爾·榮格是分析心理學的創辦者。

□三分熟
□五分熟
□七分熟
□全熟

---

pub·li·ca·tion

[ˌpʌblɪˈkeʃən]

名 發表、出版

英英 the process of publishing something, such as books or magazines

例 Is your picture book ready for **publication**?
你的繪本準備要出版了嗎？

□三分熟
□五分熟
□七分熟
□全熟

---

pub·lic·i·ty

[pʌbˈlɪsətɪ]

名 宣傳、出風頭

英英 an activity of attracting a lot of interest or attention from many people

例 Our **publicity** campaign for the new coffee maker will start from this weekend.
我們對新型咖啡機的宣傳活動會在這個週末開始。

□三分熟
□五分熟
□七分熟
□全熟

---

pub·lish [ˈpʌblɪʃ]

動 出版

英英 to prepare a book, newspaper, piece of music for public sale

例 The film novel about a cleaning lady falling in love with a merman was **published**.
一部關於清潔婦愛上人魚的電影小說已經出版了。

□三分熟
□五分熟
□七分熟
□全熟

---

pub·lish·er

[ˈpʌblɪʃɚ]

名 出版者、出版社

英英 a company or person that prepares a book, newspaper, piece of music for public sale

例 The **publisher** planned to promote fantasy novels series.
出版社計畫要推廣奇幻小說系列。

□三分熟
□五分熟
□七分熟
□全熟

---

pur·suit [pɚˈsut]

名 追求

英英 the action of pursuing

例 Is it worthy to spend your life in the **pursuit** of fame and money?
花一輩子的時間追求名聲與金錢值得嗎？

□三分熟
□五分熟
□七分熟
□全熟

Qq

Q
R

quake [kwek]

名 地震、震動
動 搖動、震動

英英 to shake or tremble or shudder with fear

例 Some scientists could predict the coming of **quakes** from animal behaviors.
有些科學家可以從動物的行為預測地震的來臨。

☐ 三分熟
☐ 五分熟
☐ 七分熟
☐ 全熟

quilt [kwɪlt]

名 棉被
動 把⋯⋯製成被褥

英英 a warm bed covering used to cover the body while sleeping; to make something into quilt

例 Emily loves the **quilt** weaver on the pattern of rainbow and garden.
愛蜜麗喜歡這條有彩虹和花園圖案的棉被。

☐ 三分熟
☐ 五分熟
☐ 七分熟
☐ 全熟

quo·ta·tion

[kwoˋteʃən]

名 引用

英英 a passage or phrase repeated by someone other than the originator

例 Proper **quotations** of famous people add certain flavor to your composition.
適當引用名人的話,會幫你的作文增添一些特色。

☐ 三分熟
☐ 五分熟
☐ 七分熟
☐ 全熟

Rr

rage [redʒ]

名 狂怒
動 暴怒
同 anger 憤怒
片 fly into a fit of rage
大發雷霆

英英 violent uncontrollable anger

例 The green giant was in a state of **rage**.
綠巨人在狂怒的狀態。

☐ 三分熟
☐ 五分熟
☐ 七分熟
☐ 全熟

rain·fall [ˋrenˏfɔl]

名 降雨量

英英 the quantity of rain falling in a area or in a period of time

例 The **rainfall** in the mountain area cooled the heat for a while.
山區的降雨量暫時冷卻了高溫。

☐ 三分熟
☐ 五分熟
☐ 七分熟
☐ 全熟

re·al·is·tic

[rɪəˋlɪstɪk]

形 現實的

英英 accepting things as they are real or in fact

例 It is not **realistic** to ask to be a millionaire without a good job or opportunity.
要成為百萬富翁而沒有一份好的工作或機會是不切實際的。

☐ 三分熟
☐ 五分熟
☐ 七分熟
☐ 全熟

🎧 **Track 253**

---

re·bel(1) [ˋrɛbl̩]

名 造反者、叛亂、謀反
同 revolt 叛亂

英英 a person who is doing something to resist to an established government or ruler
例 Joan of arc was considered as a **rebel** by many groups in the 15th century.
十五世紀時，聖女貞德被很多團體認為是個造反者。

☐ 三分熟
☐ 五分熟
☐ 七分熟
☐ 全熟

---

re·bel(2) [rɪˋbɛl]

動 叛亂、謀反

英英 to do something to resist an established government or ruler
例 Alice the little girl **rebelled** against unfair judging system in her dream.
愛麗絲這個小女孩在夢裡反叛不公平的審判系統。

☐ 三分熟
☐ 五分熟
☐ 七分熟
☐ 全熟

---

re·call

[ˋrɪkɔl]/[rɪˋkɔl]

名 取消、收回
動 回憶起、恢復

英英 the action of cancelling plans or taking back the orders; to recover or to call back to mind
例 Grandma **recalled** what it had been when she was a little girl.
奶奶回憶著當她還是小女孩時的情形。

☐ 三分熟
☐ 五分熟
☐ 七分熟
☐ 全熟

---

re·cep·tion

[rɪˋsɛpʃən]

名 接受、歡迎

英英 the action of receiving someone or something
例 *The Secret Garden* got good **reception** in the field of Children's Literature.
《祕密花園》在兒童文學的領域獲得好評。

☐ 三分熟
☐ 五分熟
☐ 七分熟
☐ 全熟

---

rec·i·pe [ˋrɛsəpɪ]

名 食譜、祕訣

英英 a list of ingredients and instructions for cooking a particular dish
例 Could you share your **recipe** of making a big pudding with me?
你可否跟我分享製作大布丁的食譜？

☐ 三分熟
☐ 五分熟
☐ 七分熟
☐ 全熟

---

re·cite [rɪˋsaɪt]

動 背誦

英英 to read out aloud from memory before an audience
例 My father asked me to **recite** Du Fu's poems when I was young.
當我小的時候，我父親要求我背杜甫的詩。

☐ 三分熟
☐ 五分熟
☐ 七分熟
☐ 全熟

---

rec·og·ni·tion

[ˏrɛkəgˋnɪʃən]

名 認知

英英 the action of recognizing or the process of being recognized
例 Letter **recognition** is usually in the first stage of language learning.
認字母通常是在語言學習的第一階段。

☐ 三分熟
☐ 五分熟
☐ 七分熟
☐ 全熟

R

re·cov·er·y

[rɪˋkʌvərɪ]

名 恢復

英英 the process of recovering

例 Don't worry about Amy; she's in the stage of **recovery**.
不要擔心艾咪，她在恢復的階段。

☐ 三分熟
☐ 五分熟
☐ 七分熟
☐ 全熟

rec·re·a·tion

[ˌrɛkrɪˋeʃən]

名 娛樂
片 recreation facilities
娛樂設施

英英 enjoyable leisure activity

例 People obtained **recreation** from visual and audial effects.
人們從視聽效果中得到娛樂。

☐ 三分熟
☐ 五分熟
☐ 七分熟
☐ 全熟

re·cy·cle [riˋsaɪkl̩]

動 循環利用

英英 to use again

例 These plastic bottles can be **recycled**.
這些塑膠瓶可以循環利用。

☐ 三分熟
☐ 五分熟
☐ 七分熟
☐ 全熟

re·duc·tion

[rɪˋdʌkʃən]

名 減少
同 decrease 減少

英英 the action of reducing something

例 **Reduction** of the amount of garbage is what we should do.
垃圾減量是我們應該做的。

☐ 三分熟
☐ 五分熟
☐ 七分熟
☐ 全熟

re·fer [rɪˋfɝ]

動 參考、提及

英英 to mention or refer to

例 My father often **referred** this place as his personal secret garden.
我的父親經常把這個地方稱作為他個人的祕密花園。

☐ 三分熟
☐ 五分熟
☐ 七分熟
☐ 全熟

ref·er·ence

[ˋrɛfərəns]

名 參考

英英 the action of referring to something

例 These books can serve as your **reference** books.
這些書可以當作你的參考書。

☐ 三分熟
☐ 五分熟
☐ 七分熟
☐ 全熟

re·flect [rɪˋflɛkt]

動 反射

英英 to make heat, light, or sound go return without absorbing it

例 The moonlights are **reflected** on the surface of the ocean.
月光反射在海洋的表面。

☐ 三分熟
☐ 五分熟
☐ 七分熟
☐ 全熟

re·flec·tion

[rɪˋflɛkʃən]

名 反射、反省

英英 careful and serious thought about something

例 **Reflection** of the sunshine hurt my eyes.
陽光的反射刺痛了我的眼。

☐ 三分熟
☐ 五分熟
☐ 七分熟
☐ 全熟

🎧 **Track 255**

re·form [rɪˋfɔrm]

動 改進

英英 to make changes in something in order to improve it

例 We need to **reform** this flawed testing system.
我們需要改進這個有弊端的考試系統。

☐三分熟 ☐五分熟 ☐七分熟 ☐全熟

---

re·fresh [rɪˋfrɛʃ]

動 使恢復精神

英英 to give new strength or energy to feel better

例 Drink some coffee and get **refreshed**.
喝些咖啡，恢復精神。

☐三分熟 ☐五分熟 ☐七分熟 ☐全熟

---

re·fresh·ment

[rɪˋfrɛʃmənt]

名 清爽、茶點

英英 the giving of fresh strength or energy

例 The honey cakes are prepared as the **refreshment** of afternoon tea.
蜂蜜蛋糕準備好當下午茶的茶點。

☐三分熟 ☐五分熟 ☐七分熟 ☐全熟

---

ref·u·gee

[ˌrɛfjʊˋdʒi]

名 難民

英英 a person who has been forced to leave their country in order to escape war or natural disaster

例 The picture of the **refugee** boy lying dead on the beach attracts the public's attention.
躺在沙灘上的死亡難民小男孩的照片，引起大眾的關注。

☐三分熟 ☐五分熟 ☐七分熟 ☐全熟

---

re·fus·al [rɪˋfjuzḷ]

名 拒絕
同 denial 拒絕、否認

英英 the act refusing someone to do or accept something

例 **Refusal** of Jim's proposal caused him to go to extremes.
吉姆的求婚被拒，造成他採用極端的手段。

☐三分熟 ☐五分熟 ☐七分熟 ☐全熟

---

re·gard·ing

[rɪˋgɑrdɪŋ]

介 關於

英英 about, concerning, regarding

例 **Regarding** the issue of same-sex marriage, my parents and I have different opinions.
關於同性婚姻的議題，我的父母和我有不同的意見。

☐三分熟 ☐五分熟 ☐七分熟 ☐全熟

---

reg·is·ter

[ˋrɛdʒɪstɚ]

名 名單、註冊
動 登記、註冊

英英 a record of attendance, usually in a class

例 The apartment is **registered** under my sister's name.
這棟公寓登記在我妹的名下。

☐三分熟 ☐五分熟 ☐七分熟 ☐全熟

---

reg·is·tra·tion

[ˌrɛdʒɪˋstreʃən]

名 註冊

英英 the action or process of registering or of being registered

例 You can fill out the form and take it to the **registration** section.
你可以填寫這張表格，把表格拿到註冊組。

☐三分熟 ☐五分熟 ☐七分熟 ☐全熟

R

reg·u·late

[ˈrɛɡjəˌlet]

動 調節、管理

英英 to take control on the rate or speed of a machine

例 You can use some coding systems to **regulate** the access to the website.
你可以使用一些密碼系統來管理該網站的入口。

☐ 三分熟
☐ 五分熟
☐ 七分熟
☐ 全熟

---

reg·u·la·tion

[ˌrɛɡjəˈleʃən]

名 調整、法規

英英 an official rule or the act of controlling

例 You should follow the safety **regulations**.
你應該要遵守安全法規。

☐ 三分熟
☐ 五分熟
☐ 七分熟
☐ 全熟

---

re·jec·tion

[rɪˈdʒɛkʃən]

名 廢棄、拒絕

英英 the act of abandoning or refusing something

例 No matter how polite a **rejection** email is, it is hurtful.
不管一封拒絕信如何的有禮貌，仍然會讓人受傷。

☐ 三分熟
☐ 五分熟
☐ 七分熟
☐ 全熟

---

rel·a·tive [ˈrɛlətɪv]

形 相對的、有關係的
名 親戚

英英 considered to something else; or related to something; a person who relates to you, such as your parents' brothers or sister or their children

例 On Chinese New Year, some **relatives** like to ask personal questions.
在中國新年，有些親戚喜歡問很私人的問題。

☐ 三分熟
☐ 五分熟
☐ 七分熟
☐ 全熟

---

re·lax·a·tion

[ˌrilæksˈeʃən]

名 放鬆

英英 the action of relaxing or the state of being relaxed

例 This ad of shower gel aims to emphasize the effect of **relaxation**.
這款沐浴乳的廣告旨在強調放鬆的效果。

☐ 三分熟
☐ 五分熟
☐ 七分熟
☐ 全熟

---

re·lieve [rɪˈliv]

動 減緩

英英 to remove your pain, distress, or difficulty

例 Watching soap drama can **relieve** working pressures.
看連續劇可以減緩工作壓力。

☐ 三分熟
☐ 五分熟
☐ 七分熟
☐ 全熟

---

re·luc·tant

[rɪˈlʌktənt]

形 不情願的

英英 unwilling and hesitant; not doing by your will

例 She's **reluctant** to tell us who she works for.
她不願意告訴我們她為誰工作。

☐ 三分熟
☐ 五分熟
☐ 七分熟
☐ 全熟

---

re·mark [rɪˈmɑrk]

名 注意
動 注意、評論

英英 the action of noticing or paying attention on something; to make a statement about something

例 The judge **remarked** that she was singing like she had used up all her life.
評審評論她唱歌的樣子就像她已用盡全部的生命。

☐ 三分熟
☐ 五分熟
☐ 七分熟
☐ 全熟

🎧**Track 257**

re·mark·a·ble

[rɪˋmɑrkəb!]

形 值得注意的

英英 extraordinary or needing noticed

例 Angie's ice-skating performance is **remarkable**.
安琪的溜冰表現是值得注意的。

☐三分熟
☐五分熟
☐七分熟
☐全熟

---

rem·e·dy [ˋrɛmədɪ]

名 醫療
動 治療、補救

英英 a medical treatment for a disease or injury

例 One possible **remedy** of treating cough is honey tea.
治療咳嗽的可能療法之一是蜂蜜茶。

☐三分熟
☐五分熟
☐七分熟
☐全熟

---

rep·e·ti·tion

[ˌrɛpɪˋtɪʃən]

名 重複、重做

英英 the act of doing or saying something again

例 **Repetition** is one way of remembering important things.
重複是記得重要事項的方法之一。

☐三分熟
☐五分熟
☐七分熟
☐全熟

---

rep·re·sen·ta·tion

[ˌrɛprɪzɛnˋteʃən]

名 代表、表示、表現

英英 the way that someone or something is shown or described

例 There are different artistic forms of the **representation** of sadness.
悲傷的表現，有許多不同的藝術形式。

☐三分熟
☐五分熟
☐七分熟
☐全熟

---

rep·u·ta·tion

[ˌrɛpjəˋteʃən]

名 名譽、聲望

英英 the beliefs or opinions that are generally held about someone or something

例 Doctor Hu has a good **reputation**.
胡醫生有好的名聲。

☐三分熟
☐五分熟
☐七分熟
☐全熟

---

res·cue [ˋrɛskju]

名 搭救
動 援救

英英 save from a dangerous or distressing situation

例 Will they succeed in the **rescue** of Leya's mother?
他們會成功救到莉雅的母親嗎？

☐三分熟
☐五分熟
☐七分熟
☐全熟

---

re·search [ˋrisɝtʃ]

名 研究
動 調查

英英 the detailed study of materials and sources in order to discover facts and reach new conclusions

例 His **research** on butterflies interest many people.
他對蝴蝶的研究讓很多人感興趣。

☐三分熟
☐五分熟
☐七分熟
☐全熟

---

re·search·er

[riˋsɝtʃɚ]

名 調查員

英英 someone who makes researches

例 The field **researcher** went to Ali Mountain to do further researches.
田野研究員到阿里山去做進一步的研究。

☐三分熟
☐五分熟
☐七分熟
☐全熟

re·sem·ble

[rɪˋzɛmb!]

動 類似

英英 to have a similar appearance to or have a common with

例 The watermelon **resembles** a rectangular box.
這顆西瓜長得很像一個四方形的盒子。

☐ 三分熟
☐ 五分熟
☐ 七分熟
☐ 全熟

res·er·va·tion

[ˏrɛzɚˋveʃən]

名 保留、預訂

英英 the action of reserving

例 Tina, have you made a **reservation** of a table?
蒂娜，妳訂位了嗎？

☐ 三分熟
☐ 五分熟
☐ 七分熟
☐ 全熟

re·sign [rɪˋzaɪn]

動 辭職、使順從

英英 to leave a job or position in a company or an organization

例 To be a full-time mother, Clara plans to **resign** from the company.
為了要當全職媽媽，克萊拉計畫要從這家公司辭職。

☐ 三分熟
☐ 五分熟
☐ 七分熟
☐ 全熟

res·ig·na·tion

[ˏrɛzɪgˋneʃən]

名 辭職、讓位

英英 an act of resigning

例 Peter's sudden **resignation** surprised all of his co-workers.
彼得的閃辭驚嚇到全部的同事。

☐ 三分熟
☐ 五分熟
☐ 七分熟
☐ 全熟

re·sis·tance

[rɪˋzɪstəns]

名 抵抗

英英 the action of resisting

例 This book teaches us how to breed crops with **resistance** to diseases.
這本書教導我們如何養出抵抗疾病的農作物。

☐ 三分熟
☐ 五分熟
☐ 七分熟
☐ 全熟

res·o·lu·tion

[ˏrɛzəˋluʃən]

名 果斷、決心
同 determination 決心

英英 a firm decision without hesitance

例 Jane is certainly a woman with **resolution**.
珍必然是有決心的女人。

☐ 三分熟
☐ 五分熟
☐ 七分熟
☐ 全熟

re·solve [rɪˋzɑlv]

名 決心
動 解決、分解

英英 firm determination; to solve a problem or something

例 The president's **resolve** to solve the tough problem is admirable.
總裁要解決棘手問題的決心令人佩服。

☐ 三分熟
☐ 五分熟
☐ 七分熟
☐ 全熟

🎧 **Track 259**

re·spect·a·ble
[rɪˋspɛktəbḷ]

形 可尊敬的

英英 considered to be socially acceptable

例 The staff of the organization, who saves homeless animals, is **respectable**.
這個組織拯救流浪動物的工作人員是令人尊敬的。

☐ 三分熟
☐ 五分熟
☐ 七分熟
☐ 全熟

re·spect·ful
[rɪˋspɛktfəl]

形 有禮的、恭敬的

英英 feeling or showing admiration and respect

例 In a **respectful** tone of voice, George's father stated why he came to visit Miss Tien.
喬治的父親以恭敬的口吻表達了他為什麼來拜訪田老師。

☐ 三分熟
☐ 五分熟
☐ 七分熟
☐ 全熟

re·store [rɪˋstor]

動 恢復

英英 to return something or someone to a former condition

例 It takes around five years to **restore** the house before its collapse.
要花五年時間，才能讓這棟房子恢復成倒塌之前的樣子。

☐ 三分熟
☐ 五分熟
☐ 七分熟
☐ 全熟

re·stric·tion
[rɪˋstrɪkʃən]

名 限制

英英 the action of restricting or the state of being restricted

例 Because of the **restriction** of noise, the concert is not allowed to be held in this area.
因為有噪音的限制，這場演唱會不允許在這個地區舉行。

☐ 三分熟
☐ 五分熟
☐ 七分熟
☐ 全熟

re·tain [rɪˋten]

動 保持、留住

英英 continue to keep or remain

例 My niece has a good memory to **retain** everything she studied.
我的姪女有好的記憶力，可以記住所有讀過的資訊。

☐ 三分熟
☐ 五分熟
☐ 七分熟
☐ 全熟

re·tire [rɪˋtaɪr]

動 隱退

英英 to leave one's job and stop working because one has reached a particular age

例 Catherine's mother is going to **retire** as a bank manager.
凱薩琳的母親即將從銀行經理的職位退休。

☐ 三分熟
☐ 五分熟
☐ 七分熟
☐ 全熟

re·tire·ment
[rɪˋtaɪrmənt]

名 退休

英英 the period of one's life after retiring from work

例 Ben's **retirement** party will be held next Monday.
班的退休派對下星期一舉辦。

☐ 三分熟
☐ 五分熟
☐ 七分熟
☐ 全熟

re·treat [rɪˋtrit]

名 撤退
動 撤退

英英 an army withdraw from confrontation with enemy forces

例 The general considered **retreating** from the battlefield.
將軍考量從戰場撤退。

☐ 三分熟
☐ 五分熟
☐ 七分熟
☐ 全熟

R

---

re·un·ion

[riˋjunjən]

名 重聚、團圓

英英 an event for a group of people how haven't seen each other for a long time to get together

例 Dominic's daughter expects him to appear at the **reunion** party of dumplings.
多明尼克的女兒期待他出現在餃子的團圓派對。

☐ 三分熟
☐ 五分熟
☐ 七分熟
☐ 全熟

---

re·venge [rɪˋvɛndʒ]

名 報復
動 報復
同 retaliate 報復

英英 harm or damage done on someone or something as a punishment

例 Hamlet took **revenge** for his father.
哈姆雷特為父親復仇。

☐ 三分熟
☐ 五分熟
☐ 七分熟
☐ 全熟

---

re·vise [rɪˋvaɪz]

動 修正、校訂

英英 to examine and improve text or writing

例 Are you sure you have **revised** this essay?
你確定你已經修正過這篇論文了？

☐ 三分熟
☐ 五分熟
☐ 七分熟
☐ 全熟

---

re·vi·sion

[rɪˋvɪʒən]

名 修訂

英英 a revised edition or form

例 I've made **revisions** on this paper.
我已經修訂了這篇論文。

☐ 三分熟
☐ 五分熟
☐ 七分熟
☐ 全熟

---

rev·o·lu·tion

[ˌrɛvəˋluʃən]

名 革命、改革

英英 an important change in a way to make a country or a place improve

例 During the cultural **revolution**, lots of temples were torn down.
在文化大革命時期，很多寺廟都被拆毀了。

☐ 三分熟
☐ 五分熟
☐ 七分熟
☐ 全熟

---

rev·o·lu·tion·ar·y

[ˌrɛvəˋluʃənˌɛrɪ]

形 革命的

英英 involving or causing dramatic change or innovation

例 Some people believed the Arab Spring was the first **revolutionary** wave.
有些人相信阿拉伯之春是第一波的革命浪潮。

☐ 三分熟
☐ 五分熟
☐ 七分熟
☐ 全熟

---

re·ward [rɪˋwɔrd]

名 報酬
動 酬賞

英英 a thing given in recognition of good effort

例 This chocolate cake is your **reward** for washing the dishes.
這塊巧克力蛋糕是給你的洗碗獎賞。

☐ 三分熟
☐ 五分熟
☐ 七分熟
☐ 全熟

🎧 Track 261

rhyme [raɪm]

名 韻、韻文
動 押韻

英英 words in a short poem, which have the same last sound to make reading easily; to make verses

例 **Rhyming** stories helps my cousins learn English better.
有韻文的故事幫我的表兄妹把英文學得更好。

☐ 三分熟
☐ 五分熟
☐ 七分熟
☐ 全熟

---

rhythm [ˈrɪðəm]

名 節奏、韻律

英英 a strong, regular repeated sound

例 The **rhythm** of the pop song is catchy.
這首流行歌的節奏是朗朗上口的。

☐ 三分熟
☐ 五分熟
☐ 七分熟
☐ 全熟

---

ro·mance [roˈmæns]

動 羅曼史

英英 relationship of love between two people; love affair

例 I'm not interested in your parents' **romance**.
我對你爸媽的羅曼史沒有興趣。

☐ 三分熟
☐ 五分熟
☐ 七分熟
☐ 全熟

---

rough·ly [ˈrʌflɪ]

副 粗暴地、粗略地

英英 in a rough or harsh way

例 Can you **roughly** describe what the dragon is like in your dream?
你可否大概地描述在你夢中的龍長得像什麼？

☐ 三分熟
☐ 五分熟
☐ 七分熟
☐ 全熟

---

route [rut]

名 路線
片 take a route
遵守某一路線

英英 a way or direction between two places

例 I've drawn the **route** to my new house for you.
我已經為你畫好到我新家的路線。

☐ 三分熟
☐ 五分熟
☐ 七分熟
☐ 全熟

---

ru·in [ˈrʊɪn]

名 破壞
動 毀滅
同 destroy 破壞

英英 to destroy completely

例 Scandals have totally **ruined** his political career.
醜聞已經徹底毀掉他的政治生涯。

☐ 三分熟
☐ 五分熟
☐ 七分熟
☐ 全熟

---

ru·ral [ˈrʊrəl]

形 農村的

英英 relating to the countryside

例 **Rural** life is beautiful in this poem.
在這首詩裡的農村生活是美麗的。

☐ 三分熟
☐ 五分熟
☐ 七分熟
☐ 全熟

Ss

sac·ri·fice

[ˈsækrəˌfaɪs]

名 獻祭
動 供奉、犧牲

英英 to give up something valuable to help someone

例 The **sacrifice** of animals is a part of the religious ritual.
動物的獻祭是宗教儀式的一部分。

☐ 三分熟
☐ 五分熟
☐ 七分熟
☐ 全熟

sal·a·ry [ˈsælərɪ]

名 薪水、薪俸、付薪水
同 wage 薪水

英英 a fixed regular payment paid for an employee, especially a professional or white-collar worker

例 Such a low **salary** cannot support a family with two children.
這樣低的薪水無法支持一個有兩個小孩的家庭。

☐ 三分熟
☐ 五分熟
☐ 七分熟
☐ 全熟

sales·per·son/ sales·man/ sales·wom·an

[ˈselzˌpɚs]/[ˈselzmən]/ [ˈselzˌwʊmən]

名 售貨員、推銷員

英英 a person whose job is selling goods or products

例 The **salesperson** always wears smiles on his face.
這個推銷員的臉上總是掛著微笑。

☐ 三分熟
☐ 五分熟
☐ 七分熟
☐ 全熟

sat·el·lite

[ˈsætḷˌaɪt]

名 衛星

英英 an artificial device placed to travel round the earth or another planet to get information or for communication

例 The **satellite** TV provides lots of channels.
衛星電視提供好多頻道。

☐ 三分熟
☐ 五分熟
☐ 七分熟
☐ 全熟

sat·is·fac·tion

[ˌsætɪsˈfækʃən]

名 滿足

英英 the state of being satisfied

例 You can drink different kinds of soda to your **satisfaction** in the pizza restaurant.
你可以在那家披薩餐廳喝不同的汽水，喝到滿足為止。

☐ 三分熟
☐ 五分熟
☐ 七分熟
☐ 全熟

scarce·ly

[ˈskɛrslɪ]

副 勉強地、幾乎不
同 hardly 幾乎不

英英 almost not; only just or only a very short time before

例 I could **scarcely** believe my ear when my father said I passed the GEPT test.
當我爸爸告訴我說我通過全民英檢考試時，我簡直不敢相信自己的耳朵。

☐ 三分熟
☐ 五分熟
☐ 七分熟
☐ 全熟

🎧 Track 263

scen·ery [ˈsinərɪ]

名 風景、景色

英英 the natural features of a landscape considered in terms of their appearance

例 The blogger said, "People is the best **scenery** in this trip."
這個部落客說，「人是這趟旅行中最好的風景。」

☐ 三分熟
☐ 五分熟
☐ 七分熟
☐ 全熟

---

scold [skold]

名 好罵人的人、潑婦
動 責罵

英英 a woman or a person who likes to tell off someone

例 I wonder why my sister-in-law could not stop **scolding** her children.
我在想，為什麼我的弟媳無法停止責罵她的小孩。

☐ 三分熟
☐ 五分熟
☐ 七分熟
☐ 全熟

---

scratch [skrætʃ]

動 抓

英英 a mark or wound made by scratching

例 My friend's cat **scratched** the sofa.
我朋友的貓抓壞了沙發。

☐ 三分熟
☐ 五分熟
☐ 七分熟
☐ 全熟

---

screw·driv·er
[ˈskruˌdraɪɚ]

名 螺絲刀

英英 a tool with a shaped tip and a handle, which is used to fit into the head of a screw to turn it

例 The **screwdriver** is a useful tool used to insert or remove screws.
螺絲刀是用來置入或移除螺絲的有用工具。

☐ 三分熟
☐ 五分熟
☐ 七分熟
☐ 全熟

---

sculp·ture
[ˈskʌlptʃɚ]

名 雕刻、雕塑
動 以雕刻裝飾

英英 the art of making three-dimensional figures and shapes by carving stone, wood, metal or clay

例 The **sculpture** of Cupid and Psyche symbolizes romantic love.
丘比特和賽姬的雕像象徵了愛情。

☐ 三分熟
☐ 五分熟
☐ 七分熟
☐ 全熟

---

sea·gull/gull
[ˈsigʌl]/[gʌl]

名 海鷗

英英 a gray and white bird with short legs and long wings, which lives near the sea

例 The **seagulls** fly around in a circle.
海鷗圍成一個圈飛行。

☐ 三分熟
☐ 五分熟
☐ 七分熟
☐ 全熟

---

sen·ior [ˈsinjɚ]

名 年長者
形 年長的
同 elder 年紀較大的

英英 a person who is older

例 Several **seniors** get on the MRT together happily.
幾個年長者一起開心得上了捷運。

☐ 三分熟
☐ 五分熟
☐ 七分熟
☐ 全熟

---

set·tler [ˈsɛtlɚ]

名 殖民者、居留者

英英 a person who settles in an area, especially one who is from another place or country

例 The **settler** in America worked hard to cultivate the land.
到美國居住的殖民者辛勤工作，耕種這塊土地。

☐ 三分熟
☐ 五分熟
☐ 七分熟
☐ 全熟

se·vere [sə`vɪr]

形 嚴厲的
片 severe toothache
　嚴重的牙痛

英英 causing very great, intense and serious

例 The math teacher is **severe**.
數學老師很嚴格。

☐ 三分熟
☐ 五分熟
☐ 七分熟
☐ 全熟

S

---

shame·ful
[`ʃemfəl]

形 恥辱的

英英 being a reason for feeling ashamed or causing shame

例 My mother has kept the **shameful** secret for a long time.
我的母親隱瞞這個可恥的祕密很久了。

☐ 三分熟
☐ 五分熟
☐ 七分熟
☐ 全熟

---

shav·er [`ʃevɚ]

名 理髮師

英英 a person whose job is to cut or style someone's hair

例 The **shaver** has good shaving skills.
這名理髮師有好的理髮技巧。

☐ 三分熟
☐ 五分熟
☐ 七分熟
☐ 全熟

---

shel·ter [`ʃɛltɚ]

名 避難所、庇護所
動 保護、掩護
同 protect 保護

英英 a place giving protection from danger for people

例 The **shelter** is built to house the refugees.
避難所是建來收容難民的。

☐ 三分熟
☐ 五分熟
☐ 七分熟
☐ 全熟

---

shift [ʃɪft]

名 變換
動 變換

英英 to change or to move to another position

例 The **shift** of working time improves his health.
工作時間的變換，改善了他的健康狀況。

☐ 三分熟
☐ 五分熟
☐ 七分熟
☐ 全熟

---

short·sight·ed
[`ʃɔrtˌsaɪtɪd]

形 近視的

英英 describing someone who can only clearly see objects or things that are close to them

例 Harry Potter is a **short-sighted** boy.
哈利波特是個有近視問題的男孩。

☐ 三分熟
☐ 五分熟
☐ 七分熟
☐ 全熟

---

shrug [ʃrʌg]

動 聳肩

英英 to raise one's shoulders slightly to express doubt or ignorance

例 Carla **shrugged** her shoulders and continued to eat lunch when she heard the news.
當卡拉聽到這則消息時，她聳了聳肩，繼續吃午飯。

☐ 三分熟
☐ 五分熟
☐ 七分熟
☐ 全熟

---

shut·tle [`ʃʌtl̩]

名 縫紉機的滑梭
動 往返

英英 transportation that travels regularly between two places

例 A bus **shuttled** between the department store and the City Hall MRT station.
公車在百貨公司和市政府捷運站往返。

☐ 三分熟
☐ 五分熟
☐ 七分熟
☐ 全熟

Track 265

sight·see·ing
[ˈsaɪtˌsiɪŋ]

名 觀光、遊覽

英英 the activity of visiting somewhere or of interest in a particular location

例 The **sightseeing** bus just arrived at the museum.
觀光巴士才剛抵達博物館。

☐ 三分熟
☐ 五分熟
☐ 七分熟
☐ 全熟

sig·na·ture
[ˈsɪɡnətʃɚ]

名 簽名

英英 a person's name written in a distinctive way on an official document or paper

例 Sign your **signature** in this blank.
在這個空格裡簽上你的名字。

☐ 三分熟
☐ 五分熟
☐ 七分熟
☐ 全熟

sig·nif·i·cance
[sɪɡˈnɪfəkəns]

名 重要性

英英 the importance

例 The **significance** of peace cannot be emphasized too much.
和平的重要性，再怎麼強調都不為過。

☐ 三分熟
☐ 五分熟
☐ 七分熟
☐ 全熟

sin·cer·i·ty
[sɪnˈsɛrətɪ]

名 誠懇、真摯

英英 honesty

例 The host of the TV program invites my father to dinner with great **sincerity**.
電視節目的主持人誠摯地邀請我父親去吃晚餐。

☐ 三分熟
☐ 五分熟
☐ 七分熟
☐ 全熟

sin·gu·lar
[ˈsɪŋɡjəlɚ]

名 單數
形 單一的、個別的

英英 single or unique

例 The word "child" is **singular**.
"child" 這個字是單數。

☐ 三分熟
☐ 五分熟
☐ 七分熟
☐ 全熟

site [saɪt]

名 地基、位置
動 設置
同 location 位置

英英 to locate something in an area or the base of a place on the ground

例 The monsters we'll fight with are at various **sites**.
我們要打的怪物在不同的位置。

☐ 三分熟
☐ 五分熟
☐ 七分熟
☐ 全熟

sketch [skɛtʃ]

名 素描、草圖
動 描述、素描

英英 a rough or unfinished drawing or painting; a draft of a drawing

例 The **sketch** of the beauty attracts the emperor.
美人的素描吸引了君王。

☐ 三分熟
☐ 五分熟
☐ 七分熟
☐ 全熟

S

sledge/sled
[slɛdʒ]/[slɛd]

名 雪橇
動 用雪橇搬運

英英 a vehicle used for travelling over snow or ice in either pushed or pulled way, or allowed to slide downhill

例 The **sledge** is drawn by two horses.
這部雪橇由兩匹馬拉著。

☐ 三分熟
☐ 五分熟
☐ 七分熟
☐ 全熟

sleigh [sle]

名 有座雪橇、雪橇、乘坐雪橇

英英 a sledge pulled by horses or reindeer

例 The Snow Queen pulled the boy onto her **sleigh**.
雪之女王把小男孩拉上她的雪橇。

☐ 三分熟
☐ 五分熟
☐ 七分熟
☐ 全熟

slight [slaɪt]

形 輕微的
動 輕視

英英 small in degree; very little or slight

例 Mr. Kaplan has a **slight** sore throat.
卡普藍先生有點輕微的喉嚨痛。

☐ 三分熟
☐ 五分熟
☐ 七分熟
☐ 全熟

slo·gan [ˈsloɡən]

名 標語、口號

英英 a short phrase which is easy to be remembered by people, and usually used in advertising

例 The advertising **slogan** was written creatively.
我們的廣告標語寫得很有創意。

☐ 三分熟
☐ 五分熟
☐ 七分熟
☐ 全熟

smog [smɑɡ]

名 煙霧、煙

英英 a mixture of smoke or gases which causes air pollution, especially in cities

例 Heavy **smog** hovered over London.
很濃的煙霧盤旋在倫敦上方。

☐ 三分熟
☐ 五分熟
☐ 七分熟
☐ 全熟

sneeze [sniz]

名 噴嚏
動 輕視、打噴嚏

英英 to make a sudden expulsion of air from the nose and mouth

例 Flowers make her **sneeze**.
花朵讓她打噴嚏。

☐ 三分熟
☐ 五分熟
☐ 七分熟
☐ 全熟

sob [sɑb]

名 啜泣
動 哭訴、啜泣
同 cry 哭

英英 cry loudly and takes in deep breaths

例 The woman's **sob** sounded terrifying at night.
這個女人的啜泣聲在晚上聽起來毛骨悚然。

☐ 三分熟
☐ 五分熟
☐ 七分熟
☐ 全熟

sock·et [ˈsɑkɪt]

名 凹處、插座

英英 a hollow of a piece of equipment which something fits

例 The **sockets** are beside the lamps.
插座在電燈旁邊。

☐ 三分熟
☐ 五分熟
☐ 七分熟
☐ 全熟

🎧 Track 267

soft·ware

[`sɔft͵wɛr]

名 軟體

英英 programs and other operating information used by a computer

例 Could you install the grammar checking **software** for me?
你可否幫我安裝這個文法檢查軟體？

☐ 三分熟
☐ 五分熟
☐ 七分熟
☐ 全熟

so·lar [`sola-]

形 太陽的
反 lunar 月球的

英英 relating to the sun or its rays

例 **Solar** energy can be converted into electrical energy.
太陽能可以轉換為電能。

☐ 三分熟
☐ 五分熟
☐ 七分熟
☐ 全熟

soph·o·more

[`safm͵or]

名 二年級學生

英英 a second-year university or high-school student

例 **Sophomores** are supposed to be more thoughtful than freshmen.
二年級學生應該要比一年級學生更有思考力。

☐ 三分熟
☐ 五分熟
☐ 七分熟
☐ 全熟

sor·row·ful

[`sarəfəl]

形 哀痛的、悲傷的

英英 feeling or showing sorrow

例 I felt **sorrowful** when I heard that my best friend had an accident.
當我聽見我最好的朋友出車禍時，我覺得很悲傷。

☐ 三分熟
☐ 五分熟
☐ 七分熟
☐ 全熟

sou·ve·nir

[͵suvə`nɪr]

名 紀念品、特產

英英 a thing that you buy in a particular place, that is kept as a reminder of a person or place

例 If you'd like to travel to Japan, bring me some **souvenirs**.
如果你想去日本旅遊，帶一些紀念品給我。

☐ 三分熟
☐ 五分熟
☐ 七分熟
☐ 全熟

spare [spɛr]

形 剩餘的
動 節省、騰出

英英 extra; available and not used

例 Do you have a **spare** safety hat to lend me?
你還有沒有備用的安全帽可以借我？

☐ 三分熟
☐ 五分熟
☐ 七分熟
☐ 全熟

spark [spark]

名 火花、火星
動 冒火花、鼓舞

英英 a small piece of fire which flies out from something that is burning or a flash of light made by electricity

例 The **sparks** flew out of the fireplace.
火花從火爐裡飛出來。

☐ 三分熟
☐ 五分熟
☐ 七分熟
☐ 全熟

spar·kle [`spark!]

名 閃爍
動 使閃耀

英英 to shine brightly and vividly

例 The diamond is **sparkling**.
鑽石在閃爍。

☐ 三分熟
☐ 五分熟
☐ 七分熟
☐ 全熟

spar·row [ˈspæro]

名 麻雀

英英 a small bird with brown and grey feather

例 The **sparrows** are chirping in the morning.
麻雀在早上吱吱喳喳叫。

☐ 三分熟
☐ 五分熟
☐ 七分熟
☐ 全熟

---

spear [spɪr]

名 矛、魚叉
動 用矛刺

英英 a weapon with a sharp metal tip, which is used for thrusting or throwing fish

例 Could you teach me how to catch fish with a **spear**?
您能教我如何利用魚叉來捕魚嗎？

☐ 三分熟
☐ 五分熟
☐ 七分熟
☐ 全熟

---

spe·cies [ˈspiʃɪz]

名 物種

英英 a set of animals or plants that have the same or similar characteristics to each other

例 The **species** on this list are endangered.
這個清單上的物種瀕危。

☐ 三分熟
☐ 五分熟
☐ 七分熟
☐ 全熟

---

spic·y [ˈspaɪsɪ]

形 辛辣的、加香料的

英英 strongly flavored with spice

例 Nina dislikes **spicy** food.
妮娜討厭辛辣食物。

☐ 三分熟
☐ 五分熟
☐ 七分熟
☐ 全熟

---

spir·i·tu·al

[ˈspɪrɪtʃʊəl]

形 精神的、崇高的
反 material 物質的

英英 relating to the human spirit and beliefs, as opposed to material or physical things

例 These novels are my **spiritual** food.
這些小說是我的精神糧食。

☐ 三分熟
☐ 五分熟
☐ 七分熟
☐ 全熟

---

splen·did

[ˈsplɛndɪd]

形 輝煌的、閃耀的

英英 magnificent or very impressive

例 Tang Bohu has **splendid** achievement in Shan shui painting.
唐伯虎在山水畫上有著輝煌的成就。

☐ 三分熟
☐ 五分熟
☐ 七分熟
☐ 全熟

---

split [splɪt]

名 裂口
動 劈開、分化

英英 a crack on something; to separate something

例 The **split** of the relationship cannot be restored.
這段關係的裂口無法修復。

☐ 三分熟
☐ 五分熟
☐ 七分熟
☐ 全熟

**sports·man/
sports·wom·an**

[ˈsportsmən]/
[ˈsportsˌwʊmən]

名 男運動員／女運動員

英英 a man or woman who plays sport well

例 The **sportsmen** and **sportswomen** stayed in the Athletes' Village.
男運動員和女運動員就待在選手村。

☐ 三分熟
☐ 五分熟
☐ 七分熟
☐ 全熟

🎧 **Track 269**

---

sports·man·ship

[ˈsportsmənˌʃɪp]

名 運動員精神

英英 when you behave in a fair and respectful way in the competition or race when playing sport

例 The **sportsmanship** includes some principles on fairness, ethics, and respect.
運動員精神包含公平、倫理學和尊敬等方面的原則。

☐ 三分熟
☐ 五分熟
☐ 七分熟
☐ 全熟

---

sta·tus [ˈstetəs]

名 地位、身分

英英 high rank or position; social standing

例 The difference of their social **status** separated the couple.
社會地位的不同造成了這對情侶的分離。

☐ 三分熟
☐ 五分熟
☐ 七分熟
☐ 全熟

---

stem [stɛm]

名 杆柄、莖幹
動 起源、阻止

英英 the main body or central part of a plant or shrub

例 A terrible storm broke the **stem** of the sunflower.
有個可怕的颱風破壞了向日葵的莖幹。

☐ 三分熟
☐ 五分熟
☐ 七分熟
☐ 全熟

---

sting·y [ˈstɪndʒɪ]

形 有刺的、會刺的

英英 with a thorn

例 The fish is **stingy**.
這條魚有刺。

☐ 三分熟
☐ 五分熟
☐ 七分熟
☐ 全熟

---

strength·en

[ˈstrɛŋθən]

動 加強、增強

英英 to make something stronger or more powerful

例 You need to **strengthen** your English grammar.
你需要加強你的英文文法。

☐ 三分熟
☐ 五分熟
☐ 七分熟
☐ 全熟

---

strive [straɪv]

動 苦幹、努力

英英 to make great efforts

例 We **strived** to win the basketball game.
我們努力贏得籃球比賽。

☐ 三分熟
☐ 五分熟
☐ 七分熟
☐ 全熟

---

stroke [strok]

名 打擊、一撞
動 撫摸

英英 an act of hitting with force

例 She avoided the fatal **stroke** of hammer.
她閃過了鐵鎚致命的一擊。

☐ 三分熟
☐ 五分熟
☐ 七分熟
☐ 全熟

---

sub·ma·rine

[ˈsʌbməˌrin]

名 潛水艇
形 海底的
動 以……潛水艇攻擊

英英 a streamlined warship designed to travel under the sea for long periods

例 The Russian **submarine** was armed with special weapons.
這艘俄國的潛水艇裝備了特殊的武器。

☐ 三分熟
☐ 五分熟
☐ 七分熟
☐ 全熟

---

sug·ges·tion

[səgˋdʒɛstʃən]

名 建議

英英 the action of suggesting something to someone

例 Gandolf's **suggestion** is wise.
甘道夫的建議是有智慧的。

☐ 三分熟
☐ 五分熟
☐ 七分熟
☐ 全熟

S

sum·ma·rize

[ˋsʌməˌraɪz]

動 總結、概述

英英 to sum up your expression in short words

例 Try to **summarize** the story in 100 words.
試著用 100 個字，摘要這則故事。

☐ 三分熟
☐ 五分熟
☐ 七分熟
☐ 全熟

surf [sɝf]

名 湧上來的浪
動 衝浪、乘浪

英英 to ride on a wave by the coast as it comes towards to land, usually with a surfboard

例 Let's go **surfing**.
讓我們去衝浪吧。

☐ 三分熟
☐ 五分熟
☐ 七分熟
☐ 全熟

sur·geon [ˋsɝdʒən]

名 外科醫生

英英 a doctor who is qualified to practice surgery

例 The **surgeon** looks professional.
這個外科醫生看起來是很專業的。

☐ 三分熟
☐ 五分熟
☐ 七分熟
☐ 全熟

sur·ger·y [ˋsɝdʒərɪ]

名 外科醫學、外科手術

英英 a medical operation which is practiced by a surgeon to remove or repair the damaged part of the body

例 Do the **surgery** right now.
現在就要動手術。

☐ 三分熟
☐ 五分熟
☐ 七分熟
☐ 全熟

sur·ren·der

[səˋrɛndə]

名 投降
動 屈服、投降

英英 the action or an act of surrendering; to give up something because you are not able to protect it

例 My son will never **surrender** under pressure.
我兒子絕不會在壓力之下屈服。

☐ 三分熟
☐ 五分熟
☐ 七分熟
☐ 全熟

sur·round·ings

[səˋraʊndɪnz]

名 環境、周圍

英英 the place where someone or something is around or in

例 Look at the **surroundings**; wolves might attack at any time.
看看周圍環境；狼群有可能隨時會攻擊。

☐ 三分熟
☐ 五分熟
☐ 七分熟
☐ 全熟

sus·pi·cious

[səˋspɪʃən]

形 可疑的

英英 doubtful about something or someone

例 The strange man looks **suspicious**.
這名奇怪的男子看起來很可疑。

☐ 三分熟
☐ 五分熟
☐ 七分熟
☐ 全熟

287

🎧 **Track 271**

---

sway [swe]

名 搖擺、支配
動 支配、搖擺

英英 to move slowly backwards and forwards or from side to side

例 The candle's flame was **swaying**.
蠟火搖晃。

☐ 三分熟
☐ 五分熟
☐ 七分熟
☐ 全熟

---

syl·la·ble [ˈsɪləbl̩]

名 音節

英英 a unit of pronunciation having one vowel and forming all or part of a word

例 In the word "goddess", there are two **syllables**.
在 "goddess" 這個字裡，有兩個音節。

☐ 三分熟
☐ 五分熟
☐ 七分熟
☐ 全熟

---

sym·pa·thet·ic
[ˌsɪmpəˈθɛtɪk]

形 表示同情的

英英 feeling or expressing sympathy

例 Sara was very **sympathetic** to the beggar.
莎拉對乞丐表示同情。

☐ 三分熟
☐ 五分熟
☐ 七分熟
☐ 全熟

---

sym·pa·thy
[ˈsɪmpəθɪ]

名 同情

英英 feelings of pity and sorrow for someone's misfortune

例 You should show **sympathy** to these poor children.
你應該要對這些可憐的孩子顯露同情心。

☐ 三分熟
☐ 五分熟
☐ 七分熟
☐ 全熟

---

sym·pho·ny
[ˈsɪmfənɪ]

名 交響樂、交響曲

英英 a musical composition for an orchestra, typically with four movements

例 The **symphony** is powerful.
這首交響曲很有震撼力。

☐ 三分熟
☐ 五分熟
☐ 七分熟
☐ 全熟

---

syr·up [ˈsɪrəp]

名 糖漿
片 cough syrup 止咳糖漿

英英 a thick sweet liquid made by dissolving sugar in water, usually used for preserving fruit

例 Children love **syrup**.
孩子們喜歡糖漿。

☐ 三分熟
☐ 五分熟
☐ 七分熟
☐ 全熟

---

sys·tem·at·ic
[ˌsɪstəˈmætɪk]

形 有系統的、有組織的

英英 done or acting according to a system or plan

例 Use a **systematic** way to finish this project.
用有系統的方法來完成這個案子。

☐ 三分熟
☐ 五分熟
☐ 七分熟
☐ 全熟

Tt

tap [tæp]

名 輕拍聲
動 輕打

英英 to hit someone lightly and gently; to hit slightly and gently

例 A bird is **tapping** on the window.
有隻鳥輕拍著窗戶。

☐ 三分熟
☐ 五分熟
☐ 七分熟
☐ 全熟

---

tech·ni·cian

[tɛkˋnɪʃən]

名 技師、技術員

英英 a person whose job is to look after technical equipment or do practical work in a laboratory

例 My friend was a laboratory **technician**.
我的朋友是實驗室技術員。

☐ 三分熟
☐ 五分熟
☐ 七分熟
☐ 全熟

---

tech·no·log·i·cal

[tɛknəˋlɑdʒɪkl̩]

形 工業技術的

英英 connecting with scientific knowledge or technology

例 One of the company's **technological** skills was stolen.
公司有項工業技術被偷了。

☐ 三分熟
☐ 五分熟
☐ 七分熟
☐ 全熟

---

tel·e·gram

[ˋtɛləˌgræm]

名 電報

英英 a message sent or delivered by telegraph

例 The **telegram** was sent from Beijing.
這封電報是由北京寄來的。

☐ 三分熟
☐ 五分熟
☐ 七分熟
☐ 全熟

---

tel·e·graph

[ˋtɛləˌgræf]

名 電報機
動 打電報

英英 a system or device for transmitting messages from a distance along a wire or radio signals; to transmit messages from a distance along a wire or radio signals

例 The **telegraph** was displayed in the museum.
電報機陳列在博物館內。

☐ 三分熟
☐ 五分熟
☐ 七分熟
☐ 全熟

---

tel·e·scope

[ˋtɛləˌskop]

名 望遠鏡

英英 an optical instrument designed to make distant objects look nearer or larger, containing an combination of lenses, or of curved mirrors and lenses

例 Use the **telescope** to observe the night sky.
用這臺望遠鏡來觀察夜空。

☐ 三分熟
☐ 五分熟
☐ 七分熟
☐ 全熟

---

ten·den·cy

[ˋtɛndənsɪ]

名 傾向、趨向

英英 a feeling towards a particular characteristic or type of behavior

例 Carrie has a **tendency** of lying.
卡麗有說謊的傾向。

☐ 三分熟
☐ 五分熟
☐ 七分熟
☐ 全熟

🎧 **Track 273**

tense [tɛns]

動 緊張
形 拉緊的

英英 to make tense; stretched very tight; showing anxiety and nervousness

例 You seemed to be **tense**.
你似乎滿緊張的。

☐ 三分熟
☐ 五分熟
☐ 七分熟
☐ 全熟

---

ten·sion [ˈtɛnʃən]

名 拉緊、緊張關係

英英 the state of being tense

例 Audience loves **tension** in the TV drama.
觀眾喜歡電視劇裡的張力。

☐ 三分熟
☐ 五分熟
☐ 七分熟
☐ 全熟

---

ter·ri·fy [ˈtɛrəˏfaɪ]

動 使恐懼、使驚嚇

英英 to cause to feel terror or scared

例 The horror film **terrifies** you?
這部恐佈電影嚇到你了嗎？

☐ 三分熟
☐ 五分熟
☐ 七分熟
☐ 全熟

---

ter·ror [ˈtɛrɚ]

名 駭懼、恐怖
同 fear 恐懼

英英 extreme fear; a cause of fear

例 The **terror** can be erased by providing sufficient security.
藉由提供足夠的安全感，恐懼會被抹去。

☐ 三分熟
☐ 五分熟
☐ 七分熟
☐ 全熟

---

theme [θim]

名 主題、題目
片 theme park 主題公園

英英 a subject or topic on speaking, writing, or thinking

例 The **theme** of the novel is about racial prejudice.
這本小說的主題是跟種族歧視有關。

☐ 三分熟
☐ 五分熟
☐ 七分熟
☐ 全熟

---

thor·ough [ˈθɝo]

形 徹底的

英英 complete with every detail; very great or much

例 Do a **thorough** check.
做徹底的調查。

☐ 三分熟
☐ 五分熟
☐ 七分熟
☐ 全熟

---

thought·ful [ˈθɔtfəl]

形 深思的、思考的

英英 thinking or consideration very carefully; paying attention to think

例 Grandpa is a **thoughtful** person.
爺爺是個喜歡深思的人。

☐ 三分熟
☐ 五分熟
☐ 七分熟
☐ 全熟

---

tim·id [ˈtɪmɪd]

形 羞怯的

英英 lacking in courage or confidence; very shy

例 The **timid** girl hides behind the door.
羞怯的女孩躲在門後。

☐ 三分熟
☐ 五分熟
☐ 七分熟
☐ 全熟

---

tire·some [ˈtaɪrsəm]

形 無聊的、可厭的

英英 very bored or impatient, having no particular things to do

例 Did you feel **tiresome** of the TV programs?
你覺得電視節目無聊嗎？

☐ 三分熟
☐ 五分熟
☐ 七分熟
☐ 全熟

T

tol·er·a·ble

[ˈtɑlərəbl]

形 可容忍的、可忍受的

英英 able to be tolerated

例 When the violence comes from your family, is it **tolerable**?
當暴力來自你的家人時，這是可以忍受的嗎？

□ 三分熟
□ 五分熟
□ 七分熟
□ 全熟

tol·er·ance

[ˈtɑlərəns]

名 包容力

英英 the ability of tolerating something or someone

例 Grandpa has high **tolerance** of naughty children.
爺爺對頑皮的孩子有高度的包容力。

□ 三分熟
□ 五分熟
□ 七分熟
□ 全熟

tol·er·ant

[ˈtɑlərənt]

形 忍耐的

英英 showing tolerance or able to endure specified conditions

例 It is not easy to be **tolerant** with people who are not like us.
要忍耐不太像我們的人，不是件容易的事。

□ 三分熟
□ 五分熟
□ 七分熟
□ 全熟

tol·er·ate

[ˈtɑləˌret]

動 寬容、容忍

英英 allow something that you dislike or something who you disagree with to exist or occur without interference

例 Do you think Mr. Lee will **tolerate** your being late to work again?
你認為李先生會再次寬容你晚來工作一事？

□ 三分熟
□ 五分熟
□ 七分熟
□ 全熟

tomb [tum]

名 墳墓、塚
同 grave 墳墓

英英 a large underground vault where a person is buried after they died

例 The vampire sleeps at his **tomb** during day time.
吸血鬼在白天時睡在自己的墳墓裡。

□ 三分熟
□ 五分熟
□ 七分熟
□ 全熟

tough [tʌf]

形 困難的

英英 very difficult to manage or deal with

例 The task is **tough**.
這個任務是困難的。

□ 三分熟
□ 五分熟
□ 七分熟
□ 全熟

trag·e·dy

[ˈtrædʒədɪ]

名 悲劇

英英 an event causing great suffering and distress

例 Romeo and Juliet is a famous **tragedy** written by Shakespeare.
《羅密歐和茱麗葉》是莎士比亞所寫的有名悲劇。

□ 三分熟
□ 五分熟
□ 七分熟
□ 全熟

trag·ic [ˈtrædʒɪk]

形 悲劇的

英英 suffering extreme distress or sadness

例 The general suffered from a **tragic** death.
將軍遭受悲劇性的死亡。

□ 三分熟
□ 五分熟
□ 七分熟
□ 全熟

🎧 Track 275

trans·fer
[træns`fɝ][`trænsfɝ]

名 遷移、調職
動 轉移

英英 move from one place to another or move to another occupation

例 Jack proposes to his boss that he should be **transferred** to another department.
傑克向老闆提議他應該要調到別的部門。

☐ 三分熟
☐ 五分熟
☐ 七分熟
☐ 全熟

trans·form
[træns`fɔrm]

動 改變

英英 to change something or someone completely to make them improve

例 The caterpillar was **transformed** into a butterfly.
毛毛蟲變成了蝴蝶。

☐ 三分熟
☐ 五分熟
☐ 七分熟
☐ 全熟

trans·late
[træns`let]

動 翻譯

英英 to express a text or an article in another language

例 Could you spare some time **translating** this paragraph for me?
你可不可以花些時間幫我翻譯這個段落？

☐ 三分熟
☐ 五分熟
☐ 七分熟
☐ 全熟

trans·la·tion
[træns`leʃən]

名 譯文

英英 the action or process of translating; an article or word that is translated

例 The **translation** of the novel is elegant.
這本小說的翻譯很優雅。

☐ 三分熟
☐ 五分熟
☐ 七分熟
☐ 全熟

trans·la·tor
[træns`letɚ]

名 翻譯者、翻譯家

英英 a person who does the translation work

例 Some **translators** are artists.
有些翻譯家就是藝術家。

☐ 三分熟
☐ 五分熟
☐ 七分熟
☐ 全熟

trans·por·ta·tion
[ˌtrænspɚ`teʃən]

名 輸送、運輸工具

英英 a system of transporting

例 What kind of **transportation** did you take to Kaohsiung?
你搭什麼樣的交運工具到高雄？

☐ 三分熟
☐ 五分熟
☐ 七分熟
☐ 全熟

tre·men·dous
[trɪ`mɛndəs]

形 非常、巨大的
同 enormous 巨大的

英英 very great in amount or size; extremely or very

例 He gained **tremendous** success in cooking art.
他在廚藝方面取得巨大的成功。

☐ 三分熟
☐ 五分熟
☐ 七分熟
☐ 全熟

trib·al [`traɪbl̩]

形 宗族的、部落的
片 tribal dress 部落服飾

英英 relating to characteristic of a tribe or tribes

例 The **tribal** weaving skill has passed down to the 17th generation.
部落的編織技巧已經傳到第十七代。

☐ 三分熟
☐ 五分熟
☐ 七分熟
☐ 全熟

tri·umph [ˈtraɪəmf]

名 勝利
動 獲得勝利

英英 a great victory or achievement, success; to win in a competition

例 Nick exclaimed "Thank God" when he learned about the news of **triumph**.
當尼克聽聞勝利的消息時，大喊出「感謝老天爺」。

☐ 三分熟
☐ 五分熟
☐ 七分熟
☐ 全熟

---

trou·ble·some

[ˈtrʌbl̩səm]

形 麻煩的、困難的

英英 causing difficulty or annoyance

例 Aunt Bella was in a **troublesome** situation.
貝拉阿姨陷入麻煩了。

☐ 三分熟
☐ 五分熟
☐ 七分熟
☐ 全熟

---

tug-of-war

[tʌg əv wɔr]

名 拔河

英英 a contest in which two teams pull at opposite ends of a rope until one drags the other over a central line

例 Try your best to win the contest of **tug-of-war**.
盡全力贏得拔河比賽吧。

☐ 三分熟
☐ 五分熟
☐ 七分熟
☐ 全熟

---

twin·kle [ˈtwɪŋkl̩]

名 閃爍
動 閃爍、發光

英英 a light or shiny stuff shine with a gleam that changes repeatedly from bright to faint

例 Stars in the night sky are **twinkling**.
夜空的星星閃爍著光芒。

☐ 三分熟
☐ 五分熟
☐ 七分熟
☐ 全熟

---

typ·ist [ˈtaɪpɪst]

名 打字員

英英 a person whose job is typing

例 The **typist** types really fast.
這名打字員打字很快。

☐ 三分熟
☐ 五分熟
☐ 七分熟
☐ 全熟

Uu

un·der·pass

[ˈʌndɚˌpæs]

名 地下道

英英 a road or path for people to pass under another road or a railway

例 The thief was hiding in the **underpass**.
小偷躲在地下道。

☐ 三分熟
☐ 五分熟
☐ 七分熟
☐ 全熟

---

u·nique [juˈnik]

形 唯一的、獨特的

英英 being the only one or unlike anything else

例 The design of the dragon pattern is **unique**.
這個龍的圖案設計是獨特的。

☐ 三分熟
☐ 五分熟
☐ 七分熟
☐ 全熟

🎧 Track 277

u·ni·ver·sal

[ˌjunəˈvɝsḷ]

形 普遍的、世界性的、宇宙的

英英 existing in any places worldwide or involving everyone

例 A **universal** problem we will ask is "What should I do when I grow up?"
普遍性的問題是「我長大後應該做什麼？」

☐ 三分熟
☐ 五分熟
☐ 七分熟
☐ 全熟

---

u·ni·ver·si·ty

[ˌjunəˈvɝsətɪ]

名 大學

英英 a high-level educational in a college at which students study for degrees and academic research is done

例 When I become a **university** student, I'd like to take a part-time job.
當我成為大學生後，我想要打工。

☐ 三分熟
☐ 五分熟
☐ 七分熟
☐ 全熟

---

up·load [ʌpˈlod]

動 上傳（檔案）

英英 to transfer data or file to a larger computer system

例 Miss Lee, can you **upload** the file I want immediately?
李小姐，你可否把我要的檔案立即上傳？

☐ 三分熟
☐ 五分熟
☐ 七分熟
☐ 全熟

---

ur·ban [ˈɝbən]

形 都市的

英英 characteristic of a town or city

例 Most **urban** legends seems to be quite mysterious.
多數的都市傳說似乎都是神祕的。

☐ 三分熟
☐ 五分熟
☐ 七分熟
☐ 全熟

---

urge [ɝdʒ]

動 驅策、勸告

英英 to encourage or advise someone to do something; strongly recommend

例 **Urge** your brother to give up the habit of taking drugs.
勸告你的兄弟，放棄嗑藥的習慣。

☐ 三分熟
☐ 五分熟
☐ 七分熟
☐ 全熟

---

ur·gent [ˈɝdʒənt]

形 急迫的、緊急的

英英 needing attention very soon, especially before any thing else, because important

例 Lisa is in **urgent** need of this amount of money.
麗莎對這筆錢有急迫的需求。

☐ 三分熟
☐ 五分熟
☐ 七分熟
☐ 全熟

---

us·age [ˈjusɪdʒ]

名 習慣、習俗、使用

英英 the action of using something or the way something is used

例 You'd better check the **usage** of this phrase.
你最好查一下這個片語的用法。

☐ 三分熟
☐ 五分熟
☐ 七分熟
☐ 全熟

Vv

vain [ven]
形 無意義的、徒然的

英英 something has no value at all; or something turns out to be useless

例 It is in **vain** to do so many things for a man who doesn't love you.
為一個不愛你的男人做那麼多的事，是沒有意義的。

☐ 三分熟
☐ 五分熟
☐ 七分熟
☐ 全熟

---

vast [væst]
形 巨大的、廣大的
同 enormous 巨大的

英英 very big or large, giant

例 A **vast** audience bought Jay Chou's concert tickets.
有大量的觀眾買了周杰倫的演唱會門票。

☐ 三分熟
☐ 五分熟
☐ 七分熟
☐ 全熟

---

veg·e·tar·ian [ˌvɛdʒəˈtɛrɪən]
名 素食主義者

英英 a person who does not eat meat but only vegetables

例 Most monks are **vegetarians**.
多數的和尚是素食主義者。

☐ 三分熟
☐ 五分熟
☐ 七分熟
☐ 全熟

---

verb [vɝb]
名 動詞

英英 a word used to describe an action, state, or occurrence, and forming the main part of the predicate of a sentence, such as hear, become, happen

例 "Run" is a **verb**.
"Run" 是個動詞。

☐ 三分熟
☐ 五分熟
☐ 七分熟
☐ 全熟

---

ver·y [ˈvɛrɪ]
副 很、完全地

英英 in a high degree; completely or absolutely

例 You are **very** beautiful.
你很漂亮。

☐ 三分熟
☐ 五分熟
☐ 七分熟
☐ 全熟

---

ves·sel [ˈvɛsl̩]
名 容器、碗

英英 a large boat or a hollow container

例 This set of silver **vessels** is expensive.
這組銀製的容器很貴。

☐ 三分熟
☐ 五分熟
☐ 七分熟
☐ 全熟

---

vin·eg·ar [ˈvɪnɪgɚ]
名 醋

英英 a sour-tasting liquid, usually made from sour wine, malt or cider, which is used to add flavor while cooking

例 Add a bit of **vinegar** into the iced tea.
加一點醋到冰茶裡。

☐ 三分熟
☐ 五分熟
☐ 七分熟
☐ 全熟

---

vi·o·late [ˈvaɪəˌlet]
動 妨害、違反

英英 to break or fail to comply with something, such as a rule or a law

例 Sir, you've **violated** the law.
先生，你違反了法律。

☐ 三分熟
☐ 五分熟
☐ 七分熟
☐ 全熟

🎧 **Track 279**

vi·o·la·tion
[ˌvaɪəˈleʃən]

名 違反、侵害

英英 an action of breaking or failing to comply with something, such as a rule or a law

例 **Violation** of law leads to punishment.
違反法律會帶來懲罰。

☐ 三分熟
☐ 五分熟
☐ 七分熟
☐ 全熟

vir·gin [ˈvɝdʒɪn]

名 處女
形 純淨的

英英 a person who has never had sexual experience; very pure and unmixed

例 Some people said **virgin** complex is a myth.
有些人說處女情結是一種迷思。

☐ 三分熟
☐ 五分熟
☐ 七分熟
☐ 全熟

vir·tue [ˈvɝtʃu]

名 貞操、美德

英英 good behavior showing high moral standards

例 Saving money is a **virtue**.
省錢是種美德。

☐ 三分熟
☐ 五分熟
☐ 七分熟
☐ 全熟

vir·us [ˈvaɪrəs]

名 病毒
片 a virus infection 病毒感染

英英 a submicroscopic infective particle which causes disease in human bodies or animals

例 **Virus** has been spread.
病毒已經擴散。

☐ 三分熟
☐ 五分熟
☐ 七分熟
☐ 全熟

vis·u·al [ˈvɪʒuəl]

形 視覺的

英英 connecting to seeing or sight

例 Black and white gave people a strong **visual** impression.
黑與白給與人們強烈的視覺印象。

☐ 三分熟
☐ 五分熟
☐ 七分熟
☐ 全熟

vi·tal [ˈvaɪtl̩]

形 生命的、不可或缺的

英英 absolutely necessary, essential

例 Fresh air is **vital** for human beings.
新鮮的空氣對人類來講是不可或缺的。

☐ 三分熟
☐ 五分熟
☐ 七分熟
☐ 全熟

vol·ca·no
[vɑlˈkeno]

名 火山

英英 a mountain or hill having a crater or vent through which lava, steam, dust, and gas are or have been erupted

例 The **volcano** is extinct.
這是座死火山。

☐ 三分熟
☐ 五分熟
☐ 七分熟
☐ 全熟

vol·un·tar·y
[ˈvɑlənˌtɛrɪ]

形 自願的、自發的

英英 done, given, or acting willingly

例 Why don't you do some **voluntary** work?
為什麼你不做些志願服務的工作？

☐ 三分熟
☐ 五分熟
☐ 七分熟
☐ 全熟

vol·un·teer

[ˌvɑlənˋtɪr]

名 自願者、義工
動 自願做……

英英 a person who willingly offers to do something

例 Does any of you want to be a **volunteer**?
你們有人想做義工嗎？

☐ 三分熟
☐ 五分熟
☐ 七分熟
☐ 全熟

---

vow·el [ˋvauəl]

名 母音
反 consonant 子音

英英 a speech sound in which the mouth is open and the tongue is not touching the top of the mouth, the teeth, or the lips

例 The **vowel** letter of "can" is "a."
"can" 這個字的母音字母是 "a"。

☐ 三分熟
☐ 五分熟
☐ 七分熟
☐ 全熟

---

voy·age [ˋvɔɪdʒ]

名 旅行、航海
動 航行

英英 a long journey which is traveling by sea or in space; to travel in the sea or in space

例 The **voyage** to a far away island is the boy's dream.
航海到遠方的島嶼是這個小男孩的夢想。

☐ 三分熟
☐ 五分熟
☐ 七分熟
☐ 全熟

Ww

wal·nut [ˋwɔlnət]

名 胡桃樹

英英 a nut with a hard round shell, tastes slightly bitter; the tree that produces these nuts

例 A squirrel was in this **walnut**.
有隻松鼠在胡桃樹上。

☐ 三分熟
☐ 五分熟
☐ 七分熟
☐ 全熟

---

web·site

[ˋwɛbˌsaɪt]

名 網站

英英 a location with some web pages, which provides information on the Internet

例 I have no access to this **website**.
我不知如何進入這個網站。

☐ 三分熟
☐ 五分熟
☐ 七分熟
☐ 全熟

---

week·ly [ˋwiklɪ]

名 週刊
形 每週的
副 每週地

英英 once a week or every week; a publication issued once a week

例 We have a **weekly** reading study group.
我們有每週一次的讀書會。

☐ 三分熟
☐ 五分熟
☐ 七分熟
☐ 全熟

---

wel·fare [ˋwɛlˌfɛr]

名 健康、幸福、福利
同 benefit 利益

英英 a person's or a group's the health, happiness, and fortunes

例 The **welfare** of my voters are my welfare.
我選民的福利就是我的福利。

☐ 三分熟
☐ 五分熟
☐ 七分熟
☐ 全熟

Track 281

wit [wɪt]

名 機智、賢人

英英 the capacity of thinking quickly or intelligence

例 Susan's **wit** is amazing.
蘇珊的機智是很驚人的。

□三分熟
□五分熟
□七分熟
□全熟

---

witch/wiz·ard

[wɪtʃ]/[ˈwɪzɚd]

名 女巫師／男巫師
片 witch doctor 巫醫

英英 a woman or man has special magic powers

例 The **witch** hunt lasted for a long time.
女巫獵捕行動持續了好長的一段時間。

□三分熟
□五分熟
□七分熟
□全熟

---

with·draw

[wɪðˋdrɔ]

動 收回、撤出

英英 to remove or take away; take money out of an account or take something back

例 He has decided to **withdraw** from the game.
他已經決定撤出這場比賽。

□三分熟
□五分熟
□七分熟
□全熟

---

wit·ness [ˈwɪtnɪs]

名 目擊者
動 目擊

英英 a person who sees an event happen; to see or know by personal presence

例 The **witness** of the accident was murdered.
這場意外的目擊者被殺了。

□三分熟
□五分熟
□七分熟
□全熟

---

wreck [rɛk]

名 （船隻）失事、殘骸
動 遇險、摧毀、毀壞

英英 a ship destroyed, disappeared or sank at sea; to destroy or cause, to smash or break forcefully

例 The **wreck** of the ship was still under the ocean.
失事的船隻殘骸仍然在海底。

□三分熟
□五分熟
□七分熟
□全熟

---

wrin·kle [ˈrɪŋk!]

名 皺紋
動 皺起

英英 a slight line appears on the skin of face, usually to show a person's aging; to make something rough or uneven in any way

例 Uncle Tom has **wrinkles**.
湯姆舅舅有皺紋。

□三分熟
□五分熟
□七分熟
□全熟

Yy

Y

year·ly [ˋjɪrlɪ]

形 每年的
副 每年、年年

英英 happening once a year or every year

例 The swallows pay us a **yearly** visit.
這些燕子每年造訪我們一次。

☐ 三分熟
☐ 五分熟
☐ 七分熟
☐ 全熟

yo·gurt [ˋjogət]

名 優酪乳

英英 a semi-solid slightly sour food made from milk fermented by added bacteria

例 Taste this bottle of strawberry **yogurt**.
嚐嚐這罐草莓優酪乳。

☐ 三分熟
☐ 五分熟
☐ 七分熟
☐ 全熟

youth·ful [ˋjuθfəl]

形 年輕的
片 youthful energy
年輕人的活力

英英 young or characteristic of young people

例 The solider is not **youthful** anymore.
士兵已不再年輕。

☐ 三分熟
☐ 五分熟
☐ 七分熟
☐ 全熟

語研力 E072

精準7000單字滿分版：
中級進階篇 Level 3 & Level 4

滿分六元素緊扣式架構，精準學習，無懈可擊！

作　　者	Michael Yang、Tong Weng ◎合著
顧　　問	曾文旭
出版總監	陳逸祺、耿文國
主　　編	陳蕙芳
執行編輯	翁芯俐
文字校對	莊詠翔
美術編輯	李依靜
法律顧問	北辰著作權事務所

印　　製	世和印製企業有限公司
初　　版	2022 年 10 月
出　　版	凱信企業集團 - 凱信企業管理顧問有限公司
電　　話	（02）2773-6566
傳　　真	（02）2778-1033
地　　址	106 台北市大安區忠孝東路四段 218 之 4 號 12 樓
信　　箱	kaihsinbooks@gmail.com

定　　價	新台幣 349 元 / 港幣 116 元
產品內容	1 書

總 經 銷	采舍國際有限公司
地　　址	235 新北市中和區中山路二段 366 巷 10 號 3 樓
電　　話	（02）8245-8786
傳　　真	（02）8245-8718

國家圖書館出版品預行編目資料

精準7000單字滿分版：中級進階篇Leve 3 & Level
4／Michael Yang & Tong Weng◎合著. – 初版. –
臺北市：凱信企業集團凱信企業管理顧問有限公
司, 2022.10
　　面；　公分
ISBN 978-626-7097-25-0(平裝)

1.CST: 英語 2.CST: 詞彙
805.12　　　　　　　　　　　111012528

凱信企管

用對的方法充實自己，
讓人生變得更美好！

凱信企管

用對的方法充實自己，
讓人生變得更美好！

凱信企管

用對的方法充實自己，
讓人生變得更美好！

凱信企管

用對的方法充實自己，
讓人生變得更美好！